Give Us This Day

Give Us This Day

A Brooke Burrell Novel

Tom Avitabile

This is a work of fiction. Names, characters, places, and incidents either are the product of the author's imagination or are used fictitiously. Any resemblance to actual events, locales, organizations, or persons living or dead is entirely coincidental and beyond the intent of either the author or the publisher.

Studio Digital CT, LLC
P.O. Box 4331
Stamford, CT 06907

Jacket design by Barbara Aronica Buck

Story Plant Hardcover ISBN-13: 978-1-61188-209-4
Fiction Studio Books E-book ISBN-13: 978-1-943486-74-8

Visit our website at www.TheStoryPlant.com
Visit the author's website at www.TomAvitabile.com

First Story Plant hardcover printing: October 2015
Printed in the United States of America

0 9 8 7 6 5 4 3 2 1

To my brave sister, Fran. Of all the heroes I write about, my own sister embodied the supreme character traits of courage, fortitude, and grace in facing an enemy that she knew would ultimately win. Not only this book, but a good part of who I am—the really good part—is dedicated to Fran and her husband and soul mate for sixty years, my other brother, Julius.

Chapter 1

Ominous Beginnings

15 DAYS UNTIL THE ATTACK

Will there ever come a morning when you wake up and just know that you are going to die that day?

Miles Wheaton tried to hit the pause button on the grim internal monologue that narrated his exodus along with hundreds of other cranky New Yorkers as they were forced off their train against the onrush of first responders.

Is there a sign? Or some dark omen that you might have overlooked?

Big, burly cops, EMTs, and firemen laden with emergency equipment squeezed down the narrow station steps as they funneled their way to the platform of the Twenty-Eighth Street IRT station. The concrete, recently redecorated by the poor unlucky bastard whose head had been separated from his body by the cold indifferent steel of the downtown number six train, was sprayed with blood.

Some form of harbinger, which in hindsight was heralding the moment when you should have hugged your loved ones and kissed them goodbye, one last time?

The guy had probably been sleeping or playing Candy Crunch on his phone and missed his stop, so he must have tried to leave the train by jumping out from between the cars, Miles reasoned to himself. He must have gotten snagged, so all that left the train was his head, which met a green-painted steel column on the platform. Miles shuddered, remembering the sound, like a pumpkin hitting the pavement from the fifth floor.

Thinking he might jump the line and not be late on this most important day, he instinctively reached behind him, but caught himself and the big mistake he was about to make, and then simply slid his ID wallet back into his pocket. He commanded himself to be patient now, content to fold in with the horde of rush hour, pre-caffeinated zombies lumbering and trudging their way up the subway stairs, the soles of their shoes scraping over the grimy steps as they slid sideways and snaked their way upwards.

Weaving through the throngs of descending emergency personnel, Miles ran a hand through his dirty blonde hair and tried to shake away the haunting, slow motion replay of the decapitation he'd witnessed a short distance down the platform from him. Try as he might to change the channel, he kept dwelling on the split-second gap between life, with all its distractions and concerns, and the serene, cold, calm of instant death.

Taking the last two steps onto Park Avenue South in one hop, the forty-two-year-old semi-pro racquetball player with an MBA and a minor in law escaped the subway, amid the wailing sirens and air-horns of still more arriving emergency services trucks.

.𝔊.

The folks on the fortieth floor of Prescott Capital Management were not aware of the underground drama and he tried to not let his face be the one-hundred-point headline type announcing it. He was good at concealing his thoughts and excellent at his craft. After three months of gaining trust and making alliances at Prescott, one of the top hedge funds in the nation, he would soon lower the boom. Somewhere around noon he'd have the last piece of the mosaic, and with it the end of all the probing, the seeking of connections by rotating the bits and seeing if they meshed. Soon, it would all bear fruit. He glanced down at the sixth grade math book in his hand. In a few minutes he would receive the final piece, albeit unwittingly, from Prescott's assistant comptroller, Joe Garrison. A picture of a money-laundering scheme would snap into crystal-clear focus. Revealing the conduits of funds, which ultimately contributed to blown apart bodies, and shattered lives. *Like decapitated men in trench coats soaked red with blood.*

"Morning, Mr. Wheaton."

"Hey, good morning, Nate. Is there any cinnamon raisin left?"

"Sorry, that new girl . . . she took the last one."

"Pumpernickel then . . . and a small tea." He had no stomach to eat anyway and ordering was purely perfunctory, as it was part of his established routine. Nate put the bagel and tea on a little round platter that hung off the edge of his coffee cart, like Starbucks on wheels. Miles put down the math book, fished out a five and waved his hand for Nate to forget the change. He headed down the office hall, seeing Patricia at her desk for what would be the last time. She had her hair up and wore glasses instead of her contacts, which usually meant some big shot was coming in. The happily married woman preferred the "librarian" look to offset her model-like features when powerful men were about. Miles was going to miss her.

At around 10:45, the day was progressing as planned, except Joe Garrison wasn't in yet. Mildly concerned, Miles was about to try his extension one more time when Morgan Prescott entered his office unannounced. The head honcho had someone in tow that Miles did not know.

"Mr. Prescott, what brings you down from forty-one?" Miles asked as he hung up the receiver and stood.

"Just checking on something, Miles," the impeccably dressed and coifed CEO said, as he stepped aside to let the other, lesser-dressed man enter the room. It was obvious that being dragged into whatever Prescott was up to further diminished the man's meek, shoulder-slumped demeanor. To Miles, he looked like an inmate being forced to perform in the Folsom Prison Shakespeare Festival.

"Who's this?" Miles asked, giving the captive fellow a welcoming grin.

"I'm surprised you don't know," Prescott said.

The hairs on Miles's neck went up. The timing of this little snap quiz set off alarm bells up and down his nervous system. He looked once again at the man that Prescott had ushered into his office. He truly didn't know him. He decided to stall; he reached out his right hand. "Miles Wheaton, nice to meet you."

The man in the off-the-rack suit reciprocated and firmly shook back. "John Delano."

The slight clicking from the grasp registered quickly in Miles's brain as the sound two heavy class rings would make in a clench. He glanced down as the man's hand went back to his side, and saw a college ring set with what looked like the same blood-red stone was set in the ring on his own hand.

Miles saw that Prescott, a keen observer of people, also caught Miles's recognition of the college rings.

Miles sat down behind his desk again and invited the men to sit in the two chairs in front of it.

"We're on a tight schedule; I just thought you two might know each other," Prescott said as he sat and picked up the elementary school math book from the edge of Miles's desk and gave it a curious look.

Miles nonchalantly glanced at his computer screen. On it an IM message appeared reading: *Working on it! Stall for time.*

Miles took a beat and feigned letting John's appearance sink in. "You know, you do look kind of familiar. But sorry, I can't place from where."

"No need to apologize. I don't seem to remember you at all, Mr. Wheaton."

Miles pointed his finger with a snap. "Wait a minute. Andover? Right?"

"Well, yes . . . but I still don't . . ."

Prescott wasn't looking happy. Obviously, if he suspected Miles was lying about knowing John, the clue from the ring was something he hadn't calculated.

The IM on the screen facing Miles read: *Andover Alumni—Got it!* Then it went away.

"So now, John, what was your major again?"

"I was in the economics pro . . ."

"Miles, we need to get along here." His strategy foiled, Prescott was now trying to short-circuit the next three or four minutes of drivel. "Maybe you and John can catch up later."

The screen then flashed: *John Delano, Economics grad '96, Summa Cum Laude. Fraternity: Phi Delta Epsilon.* Then a picture from the 1996 yearbook popped up and showed a young John with big, bushy mustache, sideburns, and big, thick-rimmed glasses.

"Sure, Mr. Prescott. John, let's catch up later. I am dying to find out how the laser is working out."

That caused John to ask, "The laser?"

"Laser eye surgery! C'mon, I remember now. You used to wear glasses as thick as coke bottles, and now not even contacts? Or was it just eye strain from cramming your way to Summa Cum."

John was caught; now he gave Miles a second look.

Miles then turned to Prescott, to deny John a really good look at his face. "And Mr. Prescott, I was thrown at first because this guy had the father of all mustaches, big handlebar job . . . with the side-burns . . . You look much better now."

"Thanks, Miles. I'm sorry; I still don't remember you but, yeah, I got Lasik about two years ago and the face hair was gone with my first interview . . ." John said.

Miles's computer screen now showed: *1996–2001 Citigroup Global Markets Inc.—VP European Diversified Financial Group* and the rest of John's resume.

"That's right, I heard you nailed a big job at Citigroup. International banking, wasn't it?"

"Well, I started as an associate," John admitted self-effacingly to Prescott, who was clearly their superior.

Miles laid it on thicker. "Yes, but if I remember correctly, you made MD in less than five years! Have I got that right, managing director in twenty quarters? Mr. Prescott, a lot of us wandered around aimlessly after Ando, but John here did well."

Then John hitched his head towards Prescott. "Mr. Prescott thought you were a frat brother of mine."

Prescott rolled with it but his shifting in his seat was a subtle tell that let Miles know he wished John hadn't pointed that out.

"But you weren't in PDE?" John added.

"No, but the typo in the version of my resume that Mr. Prescott got says that. Actually, I was Epsilon Omega Phi. For some reason the headhunters who reworked my res screwed it up and it came up, Phi Delta Epsilon. You guys were kind of the d.o.cees."

"What's a DEE OH CEE?" Prescott asked irritably.

Both John and Miles said in unison, "Dweebs on Campus." Then they both laughed and Prescott became almost brusque as he grabbed John by the arm. "Well, we've chatted long enough; we're due in Chandler's office."

Miles couldn't let the big sigh of relief out yet, but he was reeling in his satisfaction at dodging the bullet.

As they were leaving, John stopped, snapped his fingers and said, "So then you knew Benny J. He was Epsilon Phi like you, right? Whatever happened to him?"

Blood rushing from your face is no way to win at liar's poker so Miles gave it the "*Wait, that sounds familiar, let me see*" pose then turned his head towards the screen. On the screen, a list of names popped up under the heading: *Epsilon Omega Phi—1993–1996*. Miles needed to move closer to read it so he said, "Hold on a minute, just let me stop this alarm for my eleven o'clock meeting from going off . . ." As he feigned searching for the on screen "cancel" icon, he scrolled down the list. The fifteenth name down in alphabetical order was *Benjamin F. Jerold III—poli-sci—Minor Constitutional Law*. He then continued with his ruse. "That's it, damn annoying thing . . ."

Prescott walked around to Miles's side of the desk. "How do you stop that thing? I can never do it." Miles knew Prescott was lying and might have an inkling that somehow Miles was being coached or finding the answers online.

Miles double clicked on the clock icon and the dialog box showing his eleven o'clock meeting expanded on the screen, overlaying the IM box with its fraternity list, hiding it from Prescott's prying eyes. "Right here, sir." He clicked the cancel button as Prescott came around. "You just have to keep the panel open from the settings in the preference menu."

Miles then added his personal touch. "Anyway, old BJ 3? Last I heard he was going to run for something political. If his dad let him."

"Yeah, old man Jerold, he wanted him to come into the family firm. I liked Benny; do you still keep in touch?"

"No, we were never that close, which is why you and I never really hung out too much." Miles added a little wink to soften the still painful jab at the man's dismal college social life, which he just assumed from the pathetic picture in the yearbook.

"Well, nice catching up with you, Miles . . ."

"You too, John, see ya around sometime."

Prescott stridently marched off, his little test gone awry, and John stepped lively to catch up.

Once they were gone, Miles let out a well-heated sigh of relief. He turned to the knick-knack on his bookcase shelf that was behind and off to the right of his desk, and blew a kiss.

That could be considered sexual harassment, mister! appeared on the screen.

.𝕲.

In Brooklyn, on the third floor of a nondescript building, in a room with cubicles and monitors, Brooke Burrell-Morton sat in a gray pencil skirt and blue satin blouse, her suit jacket slung over the back of her chair. Her face was illuminated with the spill from the plasma display she sat behind. She smiled as she typed something else on her keyboard: *You handled that well, George.*"

.𝕲.

Miles bristled at the use of his real name but then the name "George" was deleted letter by letter and replaced with "M-I-L-E-S!" George Stover, US Treasury agent, aka Miles Wheaton, financial analyst/wizard, smiled and then tried to calculate whether the ambush test that Morgan Prescott had just pulled to trip him up was purely innocent, or something that could derail what was set to kick off in less than fifty-seven minutes now.

.𝕲.

Back at the Brooklyn HQ, Brooke then entered the event in her log with the notation that all future operations like this be armed with social as well as academic data on all possible connections that could blow a field agent's cover. Brooke typed in: *Mustering now. See you at zero hour*. She unconsciously looked at the video monitor to her right, which was showing her the surveillance video from George's bookshelf camera. With that, she removed the headset and got up as another agent took her place monitoring the office in which their star undercover agent had survived for the past three months. And more importantly, the last three minutes.

Brooke put on her Kevlar vest and checked her ID wallet to make sure she had her federal creds. She slid her Glock 23 into the Seven Tree quick-draw holster and slipped on her jacket. From the corner of her eye, she saw the young agent at the desk checking her out. "Keep your eyes on that monitor, Agent Wills . . . in case George needs more help." She pulled the elastic from her ponytail and let her blonde hair fall; she gave it a shake, then gathered it again and replaced the band so it was tighter as she headed for the elevator.

Chapter 2

The Raid

Harold Barnes, the director of FinCEN, who flew in from his Washington office at the US Treasury to be in on this takedown, greeted Brooke as she got on the same elevator from his temporary office one floor above. They were all leaving this building for the last time. "Three months of planning and operations and you'll have landed this fish in less than an hour. You designed and ran a good op, Burrell," the director said as he looked forward at the closing doors.

"You gave me a good team, sir, and George must have lived a charmed life."

Director Barnes nodded and grunted. He knew it was he who had gotten lucky, bringing Brooke in from civilian life to head up this major investigation. "I was amazed I could lure you back."

"You're timing was perfect, sir."

The director knew all too well that she had distinguished herself not only at the FBI, but working out of the White House on a super-secret operations cluster. "Can't be anywhere near as glamorous as working for the president's special ops group."

"Couldn't comment on that, sir." Brooke said, also looking straight ahead.

"Right, need to know only, sorry." The director had seen most of Brooke's file when the Secretary of the Treasury first suggested he try to get her to run this op. The unique thing about it was that it had been redacted but in opaque red, not the usual black. That indicated it was good stuff, top stuff, very secret stuff that she had distinguished herself doing. In fact, you had to be at the director level of a major agency, like him or above, just to even see her red-redacted file.

"How's married life been treating you?"

Brooke seemed a little thrown by the question. "Good, sir. Now that this assignment is wrapping up, I'll be heading back to Hawaii."

The President of the United States had agreed to let Brooke go and have a life with her navy commander husband. That was a good break for the director; her husband's sea duty took him away for months at a time, which had made her more amenable to his offer. "You're husband coming off patrol?"

"So they say, but you never know when."

The slight sigh in her voice hinted to the director that she was bored; after all, she was a woman of action, and the attempts at a family hadn't taken yet, so she was predisposed for this relatively easy assignment to stem the flow of corporate profits from finding their way to known terrorist organizations around the globe.

"The pay from this assignment has got to help if you're thinking about a family," he added as they blew through the glass doors and out onto the unseasonably warm Brooklyn midday.

.G.

For Brooke's part, this was a safe cakewalk of an assignment with a director's pay grade, which was a little win in the negotiation she was able to hold out for. Brooke didn't want to do this anymore, and that was her greatest strength in negotiating her temporary return to government service. "I'm happy with my contract, sir."

She had talked it over with her husband, Mush, a nickname he inherited from his Navy granddad along with the submariner's dolphins—and the 5.6 billion dollar missile boat that he commanded.

"Any thoughts about maybe staying on? We got a lot more easy cases like this."

Bingo! He's trying to recruit me. "The timing was good for this job, but I don't see that kind of opportunity ahead," Brooke said, but she was conflicted. Being a Navy wife was a noble role, but Brooke had two service stars on her record and had been involved in or led some of the biggest operations the United States government had ever conducted. Downshifting her life from the 120-mile-per-hour, on-the-edge, spine-tingling situational awareness with the existence of danger at every turn, to the quiet humility of 25 mph in a school zone didn't happen without the grinding of some gears.

She climbed into the backseat of the lead government Suburban next to Director Barnes for the fifteen-minute, siren announced, US motor pool convoy over the Brooklyn Bridge to Park Avenue South and Twenty-Eighth Street in Manhattan.

"You are telling me that volunteering as the Pearl Harbor High School girls' soccer coach compares to this?"

Brooke sighed and looked behind them to see that her troops were mounting up. Her mind flashed on the soccer field at PHHS, where the director had found Brooke when he personally flew to Pearl Harbor to recruit her. He had correctly surmised that the relative boredom of safe civilian life and the old kick of being back in the game would be tugging at her. The fact that, two months later, she was here in New York, running this op meant he was right . . . back then.

Right now she had to defuse the director's intention to secure her retention. She turned and said directly to the director's face, "Funny you should mention it. I was just wondering how the girls did against Maui Free School District High in the state semi-finals."

.6.

Inside of twenty minutes, the take down of what was suspected to be a multi-billion dollar money-laundering ring would be behind her, and the mountain of evidence they were about to capture would be on its way to the Justice Department. Sixteen hours after that, she was going to be on her way, jumping on Hawaiian Airlines number fifty-one, 10:00 a.m., non-stop, first-class cabin service to Honolulu, on Uncle Sam's tab.

As the web-like cables of the Brooklyn Bridge flickered by, she thought about how funny it was that of both her lives, one life always beckoned her away from the other. Why did she have this restlessness? Why was she attracted towards the action, only to be pulled back by the serenity of civilian life?

Chapter 3

Pop Quiz

Down on Twenty-Eighth Street, amid the chaotic aftermath of the subway death, the nine federal Suburbans crammed with heavily dressed agents and their weapons, and, more importantly, forensic accountants armed with hard drives and impounding tags, were hardly noticed by anyone. Anyone, that is, but the SUB cops trying to keep traffic minimally moving while allowing access to investigators and news folks.

.𝔊.

Forty floors above, George grabbed the sixth grade math book to give his unknowing chief informant, and someone he'd genuinely gotten attached to. The book was truly was a gift of sorts. Handing it to Joe was the last thing on George's to-do list before the take down. He had gotten the approval from Brooke a week earlier.

Down the hall, he breezed past Harriet's empty desk. She was Joe Garrison's assistant and probably on her coffee break. He entered the room. "Hey, Joe, I've got a favor to ask . . ."

He wasn't there. Miles turned around and went back outside. Harriet returned with a cup of coffee and a muffin. "Hi, Mr. Wheaton. What can I help you with?"

"I was looking for Joe."

"He's hasn't come in yet. Can I help you?"

"I was going to ask him to do me a special favor." He gestured with the book.

"You need help studying for the math test?" Harriet said with a twinkle in her eye that just pulled the strings at the corners of George's lips into a smile.

"Yeah, darn fractions. . . .Have Joe come see me when he gets in?"

"Sure thing. He should be along shortly. I heard the trains are all screwed up; somebody got run over. He's probably fuming, stuck in the tunnel, no cell service."

"Well, then make sure he has his coffee before he comes to see me." With that pleasantry he left to return to his office. *Damn, that plan got shot to hell,* George thought as he entered his office and threw the book down on one of the two green leather chairs across from his desk. His plan had been to ask Joe, who was his main source of information, to do him a favor and go downstairs at ten to twelve and wait for George's nanny to swing by in a cab and give her the textbook for his son. That way Joe, the only one in the company who he knew for a fact wasn't involved in the laundering, would escape the raid.

In actuality, the agents from the Treasury would be able to spot Joe holding George's imaginary son's math book down on the street and spirit him away from the bust. This way, if anyone in the company—or worse, the terrorists they were supporting—looked in Joe's direction, they'd think he was just luckily out of the building for an early lunch when it went down. But now, tardy Joe would have to take his chances, unless he got in within the next ten minutes. George started collecting his alter ego Miles's things. In fifteen minutes everyone would know he wasn't a financial manager but a fed, whose name wasn't Wheaton. George looked at his watch. *I'll give him five more minutes.*

Handing Joe the get-out-of-jail-free textbook wasn't the only reason to see Joe. Today, Joe was supposed to hand over the last piece of the puzzle that George needed to spring the trap on Prescott Capital Management and its illegal activities. Although Joe didn't know it, George had asked him to run a routine T&E report for the forty-first floor. George, acting as Miles, the project manager on Prescott's company wide, "trim the fat" initiative, asked Joe to quietly sort the travel and entertainment data in a way that made Miles's request seem like just a convenience. Joe was sure Miles had the printed expense reports anyway and thought nothing more of it than Miles just wanting them grouped by account number. Actually Miles/George, didn't have access to any reports, in any sort of order, so the whole thing was a bonanza.

With this final piece of information, Prescott executives could be traced and placed at key meetings and drop-off points around the globe as the money was handed off and washed from business to business. It would make the last three months of discovery iron clad in court, and leave no wiggle room for a cheesy defense lawyer to squirm his client out of prison time. In the end, it would be their signatures on receipts, which were the marks of petty greed, that would lead to their downfall. These were men who thought nothing of stealing and rerouting billions to the nefarious bad guys around the world without so much as a pang of guilt—but God forbid they didn't get their minibar bill reimbursed!

George looked at his watch. Time was up. He got up and went into Joe's office to print out the files he needed. It didn't matter now who saw him or what questions they asked. In six minutes it was all over for Prescott . . .

When Harriet entered Joe's office she was surprised to find Miles behind Joe's desk, "Mr. Wheaton?"

"Harriet . . ."

"What are you doing? Is there something you need?"

"Yes, Harriet. I am trying to print out a report that Joe was going to have ready for me at noon, and I can't wait any longer. But his computer is locked or something."

"Not usually. Here, let me take a look."

She sat behind Joe's desk as "Miles" moved over. She hit a few keys, then a few more, harder this time. "Oh, dear."

"What?"

"It looks like, like . . ."

"Like what?"

"Like his hard drive's been erased!"

It took a second, but George was already onto alternate plan B. "Is there a backup?"

"Only on the server, but I have to order whatever I want from archives. What were you looking for, Mr. Wheaton?"

"Expense report, last three years, forty-first floor, by account."

"Why would you . . . ?"

"Please, Harriet, never mind the why. Joe was running it. Any chance he did it last night and printed it or emailed it to you?"

"No, there was nothing . . ."

Marjorie came into the room. She was white as a ghost. "Harriet. Line two. It's Mrs. Garrison . . ."

Just then a bullhorn sounded as the same message was being broadcast on all seven top floors of the building. "Attention Prescott employees. This is the Financial Crimes Enforcement Division of the US Department of the Treasury. All employees are ordered to step away from their desks and head to the elevators. Do not touch anything and do not take anything. Anyone not complying will be arrested. Move now, people." Then it was repeated.

Both Marjorie and Harriet wore dumbfounded expressions but Marjorie was tearing up. "Harriet, line two."

Harriet picked up the phone, but it was dead. She gave it a screwy look then looked to Miles.

"Harriet, the feds have cut off the phones and the computers. We have to go to the elevator now," he said.

Marjorie was just short of hysterical. "But don't you understand? Joe . . . Mr. Garrison is dead! His wife just called to tell me. She was on line two . . ."

George felt like a bucket of cold water just got poured down his back. He left the office and ran up the steps to the forty-first floor. The agent at the door of the stairwell challenged him. "Sir, we are restricting access between floors. You'll have to wait here."

George pulled out his ID. "Treasury, I need to speak to Burrell."

The agent stepped aside.

On forty-one, Brooke was overseeing the operation as agents swept into every office, seizing anything that wasn't screwed to the walls. "George, your textbook man wasn't waiting outside."

"Brooke, he's dead, and I think you are going to find out everything's been erased. They were tipped off somehow. I'm afraid we'll have nothing but a big lawsuit by five o'clock."

As if on cue, Dalton Hornsby of Hornsby-Reynolds, the biggest, most expensive law firm in New York appeared and identified himself to Brooke. "They tell me you are in charge?"

"Yes, Director Brooke Burrell-Morton. Who are you?"

"I am counsel for Prescott Capital Management and I'd like to see your warrant to conduct this raid."

Brooke looked over her shoulder and said to the agent behind her, "Yuri, show the man the papers." She turned back to the lawyer. "Federal magistrate, six separate warrants covering all the LLC's holding companies and corporations that fall under Prescott, for all evidence and ancillary material in connection with our investigation."

"Which is what exactly?"

"Now *that* I don't have to tell you." She walked towards George. "Without your expense report, and if they scrubbed everything, we are dead."

"Dead . . . ?" That word forced a connection in George's brain, "Shit!" He jumped into the elevator and told the building manager, who was now pressed into being the operator of the only elevator running to the top floors, to take him to the lobby.

.𝕲.

Down on the subway platform, the train was still at the station, frozen in time from the moment the man had been decapitated. Yellow crime scene tape spanned the two-hundred-foot length of the south end of the platform, which was the distance the train had traveled after the conductor saw the gory event and pulled the emergency cord. It was also defined by the spray pattern of organic material and fluids that was the result of the violent separation of the head from the body.

For the fifth time George flashed his federal ID, this time to a burly transit cop inspector. "Treasury?"

"Yes, sir, have you identified the body yet?"

"Complicated. The head is beyond recognition and the rest of the body is entangled in the undercarriage between the fifth and sixth cars. The ME hasn't released the scene yet."

"Anything from the eyewitnesses?"

"Again, why is the Treasury interested?"

"I am hoping to eliminate the possibility that the body is someone who was part of a major investigation."

"You want to leave me your card, and I'll call you as soon as I know."

George didn't have a card. He was, after all, operating undercover. All he had was his federal ID, which was normally hidden behind his driver's license just in case somebody casually looked at his wallet. "If you don't mind, I'll wait a few minutes." George walked to the spot where the green column was splashed in red and pink. That was the point of impact. He was surprised when his cell phone rang. He looked up and saw that part of the station was under the street grating so the cell signal was able to penetrate for a few feet on either side of the airway.

"Where did you go, George? We are processing the physical evidence," Brooke said.

"Brooke, the subway death could be my source, Joe, the textbook guy."

"Sit tight. I am on my way down."

At the other end of the platform, uniformed transit cops were interviewing the hundreds of people that had been in the two cars on either side of the gap between the fifth and sixth cars as well as the forty or so people from the platform. They were about fifteen people in. Mostly they were taking names and numbers for future contact by detectives if the death was ruled suspicious. They did catch some utterances and write them down. But the usual fog of eyewitnesses was evident; one cop got a description of the man who "jumped" from between the cars as a white male, medium height, about fifty with a trench coat and laptop case. Another cop, thirty feet away, was getting a statement from someone in the car right ahead of the "jumper." The passenger described the man who went between the cars as a tall Hispanic man wearing a dark cloth coat, no case or even a newspaper.

Brooke found George on the platform. The news wasn't good. "You were right, someone tipped them off. As far as we can tell, all the data on the server and on the office computers was wiped clean."

"There is no way anyone inside knew what was going down," George said.

"Even textbook man?"

"His name was Joe, Joe Garrison. And no, he never showed the slightest hesitation or question about what I asked him to do. Mostly because everything I asked him to do was covered under my job description. This had to be a leak at another level."

Brooke was looking at the blood patterns. "This is odd."

"What is?"

She looked to the rear of the station. "The train was pulling out?"

"Yes, it happened as the train I just got off of was pulling out of the station. There were about a dozen probationary police officers present. The academy is a block or so away. They immediately locked down the station and didn't let anyone leave until the first responders arrived, ten minutes later."

"So, what? The victim jumped off a moving train?" Brooke said.

"Or was pushed from between the cars."

"And you think it's your Joe Garrison?"

"I don't know yet. The ME is trying to untangle the mess under the wheels."

"We should take over."

"What?" George said.

"We have to control the crime scene."

"If it's a crime!"

"I don't need any more than suspicion." She hit the button on her radio. "This is Burrell. I need a crime scene investigation team turnout to the southbound subway platform of Twenty-Eighth Street station on Park Avenue South. This is a level one priority. We need to preserve evidence of a possible crime scene. Authorization level, director, 07206."

"Wow. You can do that?"

"We'll find out. I used to be able to when I headed up the FBI's New York field office." Brooke then walked over to the inspector with all the gold braid on the visor of his hat and the golden eagles on his epaulets. "Inspector, I am Director Brooke Burrell-Morton on temporary assignment with the Treasury Department, Financial Crimes Investigations." She flashed her creds.

"Malcolm Johnson, transit. What can I do for you?"

"Sir, I need to take over direction of this investigation. We are on a national security mission and this death may be connected. Until that can be ascertained, I am going to ask that you treat this as a crime scene."

"You are what now?"

"You're kidding right?" Brooke said.

"Lady, you just can't—"

"I just did, and you better get on the horn to your immediate superior and see if he understands that I just took over your investigation and you are now working for the federal government in the gathering of evidence in a possible national security matter."

She waved him off as he radioed headquarters to check out her claim.

.𝕲.

Brooke walked over to the uniforms who were manning the staircase and showed her ID to the sergeant. "Sergeant, we need to lock down this entire station. Nobody leaves. This is now a potential crime scene in a federal case. Can you seal this place?"

He looked over to his commander, the inspector who was on his radio; he caught the man's eye and saw him reluctantly give the nod to follow this blonde's orders, whoever she was. "Sure thing, ma'am."

"Director Burrell-Morton, not ma'am."

He turned and barked orders to the five cops stationed on the stairs.

The inspector returned. "You have provisional authority to oversee the collection of evidence but I am told to inform you this is not a formal relinquishing of the crime scene at this time."

"Whatever, just preserve the evidence and separate and hold the eye witnesses." She turned to George. "Go push the ME nicely. If it's not Joe, then we'll give transit back their turf. I'm going back upstairs."

.𝕲.

As she walked through the lobby of the building now buzzing with what was happening on the thirty-fourth to forty-first floors, she saw a gaggle of well-dressed lawyers trying to get onto the one and only elevator now serving those top floors.

"Excuse me, excuse me . . ." Brooke said as she wove her way through the throng of suits. The agent holding them back allowed her to pass. That brought much indignation from the denied men. "Wait, who's she? How come she gets to go up?"

"She's the agent in charge, that's how come."

Brooke cringed when she heard the agent blurt that out. *Shit.* Now she was a target.

The team shouted out, "We are the counsel to the board of directors and as such have a right to represent our clients. We demand you grant us access to our legally bound duties."

Another shouted, "You cannot proceed without our clients' having legal counsel."

Against her better judgment, she engaged. "First off, your clients have the benefit of in-house counsel, who is also being detained as our investigation proceeds. Second, this is a federal investigation, involving serious issues of national security, so I am going to ask my man here to double check your credentials . . . very carefully . . . twice if he has to . . . to make sure they are in order." She nodded to the operator to close the doors and go. The last words she said as the door closed were, "You know . . . federal case!"

On forty-one, Brooke grabbed the lead agent of that floor. "Any sign of Morgan Prescott?"

"It looks like he left at 11:50. We're trying to find out where he went."

"Look, Bob, these guys are about to be lawyered up the wazoo by the dream team in the lobby. I just bought us maybe ten minutes. See how much you can get out of them before they clam up."

"Will do, boss."

Brooke found Harriet in the conference room; she was scared and slightly trembling. Brooke didn't know if it was the raid or the news that her boss was dead. "Harriet? Brooke Burrell-Morton. I am running this investigation."

"What's this all about? What do they . . . you, think we did?"

"Don't worry about all that right now. Tell me about Joe."

On cue, Harriet's waterworks flowed. "Joe . . . he's, he's gone."

"How do you know that?"

"Peggy . . . er, Mrs. Garrison called to tell us."

"Harriet, take my phone and call her, please."

She dialed and handed the phone back to Brooke.

"Hello, Mrs. Garrison, I am so sorry for your loss. I hate to ask you something at a time like this but if it wasn't important, believe me I wouldn't disturb you."

.𝔊.

Mrs. Garrison was looking out the window through red, teary eyes, down onto Broadway from the five-room apartment she had shared with her husband Joe for twenty years. "Who is this?"

"Director Brooke Burrell-Morton, Treasury Department."

"Thank God, you finally got back to me?"

Brooke was thrown, but went with it. "Mrs. Garrison, how do you know your husband is deceased?"

"Is this a joke? I called you people because you have to find him." She started to get hysterical.

Brooke heard another woman's voice on the other end of the phone consoling her in Spanglish. "Mrs. Garrison, please, I know it's hard, but please tell me what you know."

"Joe called me from the train. He was panicked. I heard him struggling, screaming. I heard the noise of the subway, then I heard him scream. Then screeching. Then I heard people screaming and saying he was dead. I screamed into the phone but no one heard me . . . Oh, where is he? I know he's dead." She began to hyperventilate as the Spanish-speaking woman who was with her tried to calm her down.

Brooke could not imagine the horror his wife had experienced hearing her husband die. "Mrs. Garrison, Mrs. Garrison, please try to hold on a little longer; I promise I'll call you back as soon as I learn anything." As she hung up the phone she momentarily flashed on her husband Mush, and the instantaneous image of her receiving a call like that from the Navy. Then in an unnecessary correction of procedure, she changed the mini-nightmare to a scene of two naval officers and a chaplain in full dress blues knocking at her door. She erased the momentary, sympathetic horror scene from her mind and focused on the matter at hand.

Brooke hung up. Harriet was crying and asked through her tears, "Where, where is Joe?"

"I'm afraid Joe could be the person who died in the subway."

Harriet gasped and wailed into her hanky, which muffled the cries.

Brooke dialed George. "It looks like your Joe may be the subway victim after all. I just spoke with his wife; she heard the whole thing over the phone. And from what she said, it sounds like he was pushed. I'm coming back down."

Chapter 4

Federal Case

The Secretary of the Treasury was not usually involved in day-to-day investigative procedures, but Warren Cass hailed from Wall Street. Many of his contemporaries, and a few fellow country club members, were connected to Prescott as well, so he asked to be updated hourly while this new enforcement phase was being executed. Up till now, FinCEN, the Financial Crimes Enforcement Network, was mostly that, a network. Essentially, it was a resource to local and national law enforcement agencies, supplying financial forensics and other services to help get convictions. Bringing a gunslinger like Brooke Burrell-Morton on board marked a change in the mission from support "bureau" to active enforcement "agency."

This being the first case for its new role, Cass asked to be kept informed minute by minute. That's how he knew there was trouble and why he canceled his afternoon appointments. Instead, he was now chewing-out his head of operations. "Did we make a mistake bringing in this woman, this Burrell?"

The undersecretary for operations, Moskowitz, answered, "Sir, you are assuming that the investigation was somehow compromised . . ."

"Wiped their hard drives and servers? Yeah, I'd say somebody hit the alarm," the Sec Tres said out of frustration.

Trying to keep the conversation calm, Moskowitz continued, ". . . somehow compromised, but I assure you if there was a leak it didn't come from our team."

"How can you be so sure, Steve?"

"Sir, as an agent, Burrell was one of, if not *the* best operative and planner in the business. Even you, sir, are not cleared for a full accounting of all the impossible four-cushion bank shots she has pulled off for this country and the president."

"Oh, right, I remember now. It was your cousin on the president's protective detail who recommended her."

"My cousin was assigned to her immediate superior, Dr. William Hiccock. He knew of Burrell because she was a member of Hiccock's team."

"After she was with the FBI. Yes I know."

"And after she saved all of New York and the tristate area from a gas attack that would have killed millions."

"Okay, I get it, she's James Bond, John Wayne, and Mother Teresa, all in one package. But I still got a busted play up in New York, and you haven't told me what I got for three months and one million seven hundred and eighty-seven thousand dollars' worth of manpower and overtime. Not to mention sneaking around and spying on people who are personal friends of mine . . . that I know and worked with!"

One of the agents who had accompanied Moskowitz was wearing an earpiece and turned his head as he pressed the bud deeper into his ear. "Sir, we are just getting word there was a death."

"One of those money managers shot at us?" Secretary Cass said.

"No, sir, a subway accident that could have impact on our investigation: apparently a key source to our deep mole in Prescott."

"Was it suicide, jumping in front of a train?"

"Or pushed . . ." Steve Moskowitz said.

"We don't know yet. Director Burrell has shifted her focus to the death and we should get some more information shortly," the agent reported, still monitoring his earpiece.

"This Burrell had better get some results soon."

.6.

By six o'clock that night, Brooke only knew two things for certain: her investigation was compromised and a murder had been committed. Three things: Hawaiian Airlines flight fifty-one, non-stop to Honolulu, would leave without her tomorrow morning. It was disastrous that Prescott Capital Management, LLC had somewho been tipped off.

Brooke knew she was now committed to initiating an investigation into the Treasury's internal procedures and personnel to find the leak. The murder, however, complicated everything by a factor of ten.

Brooke grabbed a yellow pad and pen from the CEO Prescott's desk that she had temporarily made her own and jotted notes, interrogating herself as a way of establishing where these fast-moving events had landed. The first question was why? Why kill someone who didn't knowingly aid our case? Who was it that ordered or felt threatened enough to improvise the death of Garrison? It had to have been an impromptu hit, she reasoned. Otherwise they would have hit him outside his house, or in an elevator. The subway during rush hour, being so public, was the least probable setting for a professional hit; too many witnesses and too little means of escape.

Brooke had the ability to see a crime like it was movie. To stop it and play it backward and forward. As she mentally reconstructed the decapitation scene from the movie of today, she had an insightful observation. Based on the fact that he died as the train was pulling out of a station, one that he used every day. That could mean that Garrison must have been detained. Someone had to have stopped him from getting off at his stop. And yet not cause a scene. Who could do that? Someone he knew? Maybe it wasn't a hit? Maybe he was escaping. Escaping? She circled the word then grabbed her phone and called George, who had taken over the COO's old office down the hall. "George, who didn't show up for work today and did anybody come in after the incident?"

"Good thought. I'll run it right now and get back to you," he said.

.G.

Seeing that the forensic accountants and the computer division had as good a handle on their tasks as they could, Brooke returned to her New York home. An apartment she had lived in and out of since she was first assigned to the FBI's New York field office. She'd flourished in the bureau, making investigations and arrests that, although she'd just been doing the job she was being paid for, had caught the notice of her superiors. Unknown to her, they'd scored each clean bust, each successful conviction she achieved, as a career-advancing step. She rose quickly through the ranks. And through it all, she'd come home to this apartment. Now, as a result of her time attached to the Quarterback Operations Group out of the White House, she had a place in DC as well, and she had the captain's quarters on base, now that she and Mush were living at Pearl Harbor.

She grabbed a coconut water from the fridge and plopped down in the well-worn leather recliner that was once her dad's. It was the odd duck in the room. Totally out of sync with the other furnishings, yet it was the safe-at-home cradle she longed to sink into on those nights when supersonic bullets snapped a few fractions of an inch over her head. Any closer and her time would have stopped, her lifeline abbreviated. She would have been given one doozy of a funeral, and then her body and the memory of her would start to erode. No one to miss her; no one to say her name.

But now the "memory of her" had an insurance policy, a shot of living on after her service and her life ended. The sole reason for this immortality was Brett "Mush" Morton. Not that he was a shaman or magician, but with him she had a chance at a family. He was the first male she had ever met who fit her puzzle of what kind of man she could create a family with. In the past, others had had some of the pieces, but when held up to the light of reality and stripped away of lust or any temporary emotional need, she'd seen holes. Small missing pieces that, although they were not needed at the moment to have a "relationship," were absent from the big picture. Mush was obviously different; she needed no similar critical analysis when it came to him. He was a perfect fit; no holes. They'd met when he saved her life. This had been a storybook way to meet someone who she could allow into her heart and then, together, find happily ever after.

.6.

From outside, on the Rue Saint Sulpice, it didn't look like anything was amiss at the Galerie Nouveau. Inside, the man with the gun spoke in clipped staccato speech. Four of the five gallery employees were huddled behind the large floor-to-ceiling canvas of "Dystopia Angénieux." It was a bawdy, bold work that contemporary critics hailed as "mass societal commentary in acrylic and mixed media," which blocked the view from the windows of what was happening within.

The two male employees were sweating and the two women were sobbing. Not knowing what was going on added to their terror. The staff didn't see these two men enter the rear of the gallery sometime during their early morning meeting.

.𝔊.

Two or one? If there was another man, he must be in the back office, Jacques, the assistant manager, thought and then finally asked with his hands up, "What do you want?"

"Nothing. Just be quiet. this will all be over soon."

"You are not Quebecois?"

The gunman, decidedly American, just remained mute.

A knock on the door caused Francine to jump and let out a little scream.

The gunman pointed at one of the men. "You, answer the door. Tell him through the glass that you are closed till ten, doing inventory. Sorry for the inconvenience. Don't say another thing. Don't try to signal or let on what's going on here. Otherwise . . ." He grabbed Francine, threw her down on the floor and forced the barrel of his AK-47 into her mouth; there was definitely the sound of a tooth breaking.

"Okay, okay, Messieurs, I will do as you say. Please . . ."

Francine moaned.

"Shut the hell up!" the gunman said as he kicked her without taking his eyes of the man. He then politely added, "And don't forget to smile . . ."

.𝔊.

In the back room, the other man had convinced the gallery's manager to use his password to gain access under the threat of killing the other four workers one by one. The man chose not to challenge the gun-wielding gas company man. As soon as he finished typing, he dutifully followed the instructions to breathe deeply as an ether-soaked rag was put over his nose until he was unconscious. Fareed rifled through the filing cabinets as the LED light on the hard drive, plugged into the gallery's computer, blinked. He quickly scanned the documents, shoving those that were not the ones he was looking for back into the drawer. Then he found the folder. He slid it inside his gas company overalls and closed the drawer. Then he took the opened end of a box wrench and disconnected the gas line from the heater. Soon the computer's light stopped flashing. He unhooked the drive and also slid it under his work garments. He then clicked on *Secure Erase* and then clicked to verify that he indeed wanted to erase the contents of the computer's drive. The progress bar said three minutes. Now that he had what he needed, he grabbed the bottle of ether from the desk and set the unconscious man's hands back on the keyboard. Fareed took one more look around to make sure he left no clues, then went out to the gallery to join Paul, the leader of this mission.

.𝔊.

First he bent down and doused the rag again, holding it over Francine's terrified face until her body went limp. Then he looked at the assistant manager and said, "Now you."

"Wait, what are you . . . ?"

"Look, it's only ether. It will put you to sleep while we leave, then you'll wake up and you can call the cops or your mother or your fucking wife. Just go sit behind your desk and breathe in, or I'll shoot you."

The rifle poking his chest made the point as Jacques sat at his desk.

"Just take a deep breath; you won't get a headache later if you do."

The other gunman had Patrice sit at her desk and repeated the same instructions. Then he turned to the last employee. "Over by the coffee machine . . ."

"Why? I sit over there . . ."

"Shut up or I'll kill you and everyone else."

Reluctantly, he walked over to the espresso machine and when he inhaled the fumes from the ether-soaked rag he collapsed right there, in front of it. His hand knocked the coffee tin, and it spilled the grounds to the floor.

Fareed looked at his partner.

"That's fine. I don't think it will matter . . ." Paul said.

Fareed shrugged and put on a gas mask he pulled from his gas company serviceman's bag then slid his rifle into it. He returned to the back room and, with his fingers, just barely screwed the gas line onto the fitting at the back of the heater. It was still leaking gas like a sieve, but looked like it was still hooked up.

When he returned to the gallery, his counterpart had his mask on, as the gas was now thick and choking. They grabbed Francine and propped her up at the little closing table.

They exited through the rear door of the gallery, the way they had come in. Once the door was shut, they proceeded to reconnect the old electric doorbell button.

That had been the key to the whole plan.

In the alley, they simply walked away. They were just two gas company service guys heading out to wherever, blending in with the rest of the early morning pedestrians and tourists in picturesque Old Montreal.

.6.

"Yes, and two orders of eggs with ham. No, no coffee, we have an espresso machine. And please, again, come around to the back door and just ring the rear bell. Oh, how much will that be? Could you bring change for twenty?" Fareed ended the call and, from the front seat of their car parked down the block from the gallery, they sat and waited for their order to arrive.

Chapter 5

The Englishman

14 DAYS UNTIL THE ATTACK

Her phone rang at 6:45; she rolled over and patted down the bed with closed eyes, feeling for the vibrating, ringing annoyance. She opened her eyes just enough to orient the phone so she was speaking into the right end. "Burrell."

"Director Burrell-Morton, my name is Smith. I am with the NSA. My challenge code is 'Gladiator.'"

Brooke opened both eyes and said, "Transistor," then she heard some gurgling sounds and Smith's voice now had a slight twangy echo to it. Brooke knew it was something called "phase shift," an artifact from the super encryption coding and decoding that the call was now being routed through.

"Hold for the director."

"Burrell, Walsh," the voice over the phone said.

That was a surprise. Brooke expected Barnes, the director of the FinCEN to be on the line, not Walsh, the director of the CIA. She swung off the bed, planted her feet on the ground, and put some strength in her voice, "Yes, sir."

"Our Middle Eastern desk has confirmed some big movements of funds in the last twelve hours. The fingerprints point to your op in New York. Be at 26 Federal Plaza at eight a.m. for a full briefing."

"Is this SWIFT intel?"

"In large part, but we also got a little lucky; you'll be filled in at eight."

Brooke killed the call. The Society for Worldwide Interbank Financial Telecommunication had been secretly cooperating with the US government since 9/11 when a few of their key stakeholders died in the World Trade Center—although that was not for publication.

Brooke cut her morning exercise routine down to only ten minutes, then jumped in the shower and was dressed and out the door by 7:20.

.𝔊.

At 26 Federal Plaza, she entered through the government employees' entrance and asked the uniformed FBI policeman at the desk to notify Mr. Yost. "Mr. Yost" was a code name used to call extension 7789. Every day there was a different name that would be directed to that number.

Even though the cop didn't recognized her at first, her tone, bearing, and demeanor told him she was a fed. It caused him to soften his request, which was usually more authoritarian. "Nothing personal, but I have to challenge you."

"Of course," Brooke said as she handed him her creds.

The guard saw the FBI retired banner on her badge and it immediately clicked. "Special Agent Burrell, sorry I didn't recognize you."

"It's okay. I've been gone awhile."

The professional courtesy continued. "Please wait for just a minute. Someone will be here shortly to escort you . . . Director." He smiled when he realized she'd been promoted.

Within one minute, a young man in a blue suit and yellow tie introduced himself by saying, "Gladiator."

Brooke responded, "Transistor." And he escorted her to the special elevators in the back. He flashed his ID to another guard and they got in. He slid his swipe card through a reader next to the button panel that included every floor. The doors closed and the elevator went down. The floor indicator atop the doors showed it was going up. Brooke figured that was for the benefit of everyone else in the building that wasn't cleared for Gladiator. The doors finally opened, and before them was a uniformed FBI officer wearing a sidearm seated behind a guard desk with an AR-15 assault rifle held in a locked bracket device by the edge of his desk. He scrutinized Brooke's creds and scanned the holographic imprint in the upper left corner.

Satisfied that he didn't have to kill her, he handed her ID wallet back and said, as if he were checking her into a Hilton, "Have a nice day, Madam Director."

They entered SEC CONF 2. Brooke mused to herself, *We are at least a hundred feet below Manhattan, carved into bedrock, with a single access point and machine guns at the door, and yet this twenty-by-thirty-foot conference room in the subterranean facility was where it was really, really secure?*

.6.

Four men were already seated as the digital clock on the flat screen at the end of the room flipped to 07:59:00.

CIA Director Walsh lifted his head and greeted Brooke. "Miss Burrell, thanks for coming in on such short notice. Or do you prefer, Mrs. Morton?"

"Mrs. Morton is a happy housewife and devoted high school soccer coach who lives in Hawaii and is madly in love with her husband. However, she does not hold a simulated rank in the Senior Executive Service of an SES-6.

"Director Burrell it is, then. Now I assume you know everyone here?"

"All but you, sir." Brooke addressed a white-haired fellow in a tan suit.

"I'm Otterson. I am Special Operations Directorate for MI6 in the Middle East."

"Director Burrell, Otterson is the stroke of luck I mentioned."

"Brooke, please," she said as she extended her hand.

Walsh started. "Otterson, or should I say, Nigel." Walsh nodded in deference to Brooke's call for informality at this level. "Please tell us what got you on the earliest plane out from London seven hours ago."

"It seems one of our analysts stumbled on a major art purchase through brokers operating out of Stockholm, Prague, and Denver."

"Which one of these three doesn't belong?" Brooke said out loud, then caught herself.

"Exactly, Brooke. That's why we dug deeper. Through cutouts and registered agents, we tracked the money to Shipsen-Deloitte, LLC, an art appraisal firm with offices in Stockholm and Grand Cayman, West Indies," Nigel said.

"Moving money around by buying and selling art to avoid international banking regulations?" she said.

"Yes, very astute of you," the Englishman said.

"I busted a ring out of SoHo when I was running the New York office."

"That would be FBI?"

"Yes it would, Nigel," she said.

"I knew your name was familiar."

"Caymans? They are still a British dependency, are they not?" Brooke said.

"Why yes. That is what piqued MI6's interest in these matters," Nigel said.

"Brooke, what are you thinking?" Director Walsh asked.

"Prescott's company has its second biggest office in London, and numerous accounts in the Caymans; and because activity between those offices would be Brit to Brit, so to speak, they are relatively 'under our radar.' Otterson . . . Nigel here, may have found a link that we could only surmised existed."

"Well, that's why you are at the table, Brooke. I have already talked to the head of MI6 and he's agreed to temporarily attach Nigel to us and, by extension, you. He is to be read in on all things Prescott."

"What is the command structure, sir?"

"Excuse me?"

"Does Nigel report to me?"

"Let's say you are co-equal."

"No can do, sir."

"What?"

"I run the show, or at nine tomorrow, Oahu time, I am on the field teaching control dribbling, and how to chip the ball, sir."

"Is that an ultimatum, Ms. Burrell?"

"That's the deal I have with US Treasury and approved by the president with his signature on my contract, sir. It's my investigation, and there has already been one death; things could get a lot more violent, sir, and with all due respect, I got the service stars and scars to prevail in that theater of operations . . . Sir."

Walsh was enough of a bureaucrat to recognize juice when he saw it. His male instinct was to dress Brooke down for speaking so brazenly to a superior officer, he being an SES-6 . . . *Oh, wait.* He hated the fact that the president had bestowed a rank equal to that of an agency director on Brooke. But the president's intent was clear: she got to do it her way. Even he at his grade wasn't cleared for all of her ops, leaving him to only imagine the kinds of things Brooke had done in service to her country that would be rewarded with that kind of confidence.

"Okay, it's your op . . . Director Burrell," the director of the CIA relented, and turned to Nigel. "Commander Otterson, thanks for making the trip over and for your report. Can I ask you to act as liaison between your agency in London and our Middle East desk? We'll forward any pertinent intelligence to Burrell's point person."

"Yes, sir. I shall."

"Good. Good. Well, I guess that concludes our business here this morning."

Everyone got up and collected their things. Walsh watched as Brooke reached across the table and shook Otterson's hand.

"You understand, it's no reflection on you, Nigel. I just had to be clear on who's running this op. It makes things less fuzzy when the bullets fly, you know."

"Quite," Nigel said.

Walsh stayed behind and was checking his secure Blackberry as Burrell and Otterson walked out together.

.Ꮾ.

In the elevator, Otterson broke the silence as he and Brooke watched the numbers descending as the elevator car was ascending. "One would almost expect to get the bends coming up like this."

"Do you dive much?"

"I used too, back in the day."

"So in which branch did you serve, Commander?"

"Royal Navy. Submarines."

"Ah, Silent Service. Good training for a spy."

"Actually, SAS was more germane."

Brooke broke out a smile and turned to him. "So you started as a Billy Badass?"

"Then the Royal Marines, but a .306 round shattered my tibia and that was my ticket to Vauxhall Cross."

"How long have you been with MI6?" Brooke knew the public location of the super-secret spy branch of the British government.

"Too long. I miss the life."

That thought resonated with Brooke. "It's crazy, right? How can we miss being all in, surfing the edge between life and death every second, while the only thing we fear more than death is failing at our mission? Yet, we can't stay away."

"That's because we are born warriors, which makes our sworn enemies the calm and quiet."

Brooke nodded, intrigued that she had never thought about it that way. "Submarines?"

"Oh, of course, your husband. He's a Morton!"

"I married a legacy."

"I don't know you well enough to ask this, but I'll risk the bullet: Any regrets?"

"No, no. Quite the contrary, I am in awe. He too was born a warrior. A loyal, committed, and brave person, almost right from the womb."

"So then, based on what little I know of your exploits, you are both soul mates," Nigel observed as the doors opened and he exited the "lift."

That made Brooke smile. This man that she'd known for less than twenty minutes nailed it. He answered a question that was always in the background chatter of her thoughts. A nagging inquiry buried deeper than the obvious "because I love him" mantra that occupied the front of her brain, but one which delved into the, "Why . . . why do you love him?"

It was a reflective mental exercise she performed from time to time to ensure there was more to her and Mush than the physical or the gratifying social benefits. The doors had almost closed when she realized she was still standing there motionless.

From outside the elevator, Nigel waved his hand in front of the sensor and the doors stopped closing and reopened.

"Thanks," Brooke said.

"Good luck with your investigation. I'll make sure any intel gets to the CIA in fast order. Pleasure to meet you. You are quite well known at Vauxhall . . . Ta-ta."

Brooke, who prided herself on situational awareness and clarity under fire, was lost in her thoughts. Even though it was a short, casual conversation, Nigel had drilled deep into her psyche, putting her off her game and into a mode of personal reflection. The last time she'd felt that way was when her dad had sat her down on the porch swing one warm summer evening and had the father-daughter talk that let her know it was okay that she was joining the Navy. That he was okay with her not following the path that the other girls in town were on. He'd wait for grandchildren; her sense of duty and desire to serve her country would certainly fill his heart with the same kind of pride as it would if she had given him a grandson to take hunting . . . adding, "for a few years . . . I think I'd like to take a kid out to the duck blind before I'm too feeble." Then he kissed her on the forehead. It was the last time she'd had a moment like that with him. That hug. Her reaching around him, his strong arms holding her close as she buried her cheek in his flannel shirt and sighed, "I love you, Dad."

Brooke suddenly snapped out of it and called out to this unexpected father figure, "Nigel, how long are you in town for?"

"Open ticket. I was expecting to be temporarily stationed here."

"My car's out front, and I have eggs and pretty decent coffee waiting for me uptown."

"Sounds delightful."

.6.

In the back of the inter-agency executive sedan, the privacy screen was up.

"What makes a man want to risk his life under the ocean, at crush depth for long, boring periods of time?" Brooke said in a tone of wonderment that was in marked contrast to the bold, professional demeanor she'd left outside the limo.

"Ah, you want to try and understand your husband. Well, all I can say is, there is a cocoon-like comfort, a warmness if you will. And it's exactly that contradiction to logic that makes the submariner a breed unto himself. There is no difference between an infantry officer, air force pilot, or surface skimmer when it comes to serving, but for the submariner, in my opinion, it's that camaraderie, that closeness as a well-trained, finely tuned team. All of us, the entire crew, operate like the arms of an octopus, doing multiple things in split-second timing to operate even the simplest maneuver aboard a sub. At its best it's like American jazz musicians, I suspect, all of one mind, performing a coherent piece of complicated music by each doing their job so well. It's an extra-sensory feeling when that connection happens—the rhythm and harmony of the crew is beyond most human experiences."

"Thank you. From what I know of my husband that fits better than anything I have ever heard."

"Your dossier mentions your own submarine adventure."

"I guess your agency MI6 would keep track of something like that."

"I know you are bound by secrecy, but from the tea leaves it seems you outsmarted the Russians and won the battle beneath the Indian Ocean."

"That's a pretty good analysis, considering the source is tea leaves."

"You know, British . . . tea . . . it all goes together . . ."

Brooke smiled again; Nigel seemed to bring that out in her. "So you think you have the money trail nailed through the art company?"

"Shipsen-Deloitte, yes. They have much activity that's far below the radar."

"More tea leaves?"

"A paid informant actually . . ."

"That beats a royal flush . . . hands down."

Brooke looked out the window as the morning sun was just hitting the Jersey side of the Hudson River. Her mind started making quick connections; she was making her list, a mental organization of pros and cons. She saw which side was the longest and made her decision. She opened her phone and turned to Nigel. "S'good you have an open ticket." Just then the call went through. "Director Walsh, Burrell here. I've decided to take your offer and have Otterson join my team." She turned to Nigel with her eyebrows up. "*If* he agrees to the chain of command." He nodded in assent. "No need to call him, he's right here. I'll put you on speaker."

"Commander, does that work for you?" Walsh said from the phone.

"As long as it doesn't preclude my reports to MI6."

"It won't," Brooke said.

"Then it works for me. Good hunting you two."

"Thanks, Director." She ended the call and extended her hand. "Welcome to the team, Nigel."

"Pleasure."

.𝔊.

They watched through the windscreen as the little Grenier á Pain classic Piaggio three-wheeled bread truck rumbled over the cobblestones and pulled up to the front of the gallery. The delivery girl opened the back of the van and took out a small shopping bag. She walked around to the side alley of the gallery and out of sight of the two men waiting in the car down the block.

.𝔊.

There was a whiff of something, something like rotten eggs; it caused her to make a face. She waved her hand in front of her nose to ward off the foul smell as she pressed the button on the frame of the backdoor.

.𝔊.

Paul looked over to his partner. They had both seen the man who stopped to look into the gallery's windows, but his partner shrugged. There was nothing they could do.

.𝔊.

The first ring of the bell didn't do the trick. But a few seconds later there was a longer, more deliberate ring as the delivery girl held down the button then emphatically pushed it three more times in a row. The third time, the contact that activated the bell's armature, that makes and breaks it's electrical contact thirty times per second, caused the most minuscule spark.

.𝔊.

They watched as the man turned to walk away from the front of the gallery when suddenly the windows blew out. In a blur, they saw the pedestrian get sliced to ribbons by the plate glass being blasted into the street, followed by a ball of flame and debris, along with Francine's body that flew out like a rag doll and flattened against a parked SUV, as the whole gallery exploded. The entire structure collapsed a split second later, as fire raged and dark black smoke billowed out onto the street and up into Old Montreal's morning sky.

Chapter 6

A Shocking Development

Out of Thin Air was a favorite Denver watering hole for bank employees, so naturally it was the best choice for Marsha Conklin's early retirement party. At forty-eight, her leaving the bank was uncharacteristically risky. But she had professed a desire to travel the world, and many in the bank suspected the new mystery man in her life was the reason.

Still, everyone was happy for her and wished her well with joke cards, gag gifts, and one really special present they all chipped in for: a gold Fendi watch. Marsha was truly moved, and she spoke with teary eyes as she stood up at the end of the table in the back room of the restaurant. "You have all been so kind to me over the years. Many of you have become like family. I am sad to leave, but I'm looking forward to great adventures and sharing them all with you from time to time on my Facebook page."

She was lying, but raising suspicions now was not wise. "So I just want to say, wherever my travels take me, each one of you will be there, right along with me."

There was applause and then the boss, Mr. Welsh, offered a toast. "To Marsha, may her journeys bring her joy and her joy bring more journeys." Not everyone took the toast in the way Mr. Welsh must have intended, but they all clinked their glasses and "here-here'd."

Doris, who was sitting next to Marsha, leaned over and said in a very conspiratorial tone, "So are you ever going to show us a picture of Mr. Wonderful?"

"Doris, there is no one. I don't know how that rumor got started."

"Marsha, in four weeks you went from frumpy transaction director to fashion plate, from Frowning Frannie to Happy Helen. You either have a new man in your life or a nuclear-powered vibrator. In which case, text me the name of that store, girl."

Marsha just smiled and suppressed the urge to scream out the name Paul.

Another employee asked, "So what's the first stop on your world tour, Marsha?"

She felt confident that she could reveal at least that much. "Tonight, I leave for the Cayman Islands!"

Everyone around the table oohed and aahed and she just lapped it all up.

.6.

On the winding road outside Stockholm, Detrick Panover was cranking up the volume on his Bluetooth as his MP3 player was synced to his car's twelve-speaker ultra-fidelity audio system. He was pushing it a little around the twisting turns that he navigated every day to and from his job at Shipsen-Deloitte, an art house whose blue chip reputation was second to none around the globe. Detrick's star had risen when he'd been the only appraiser on the planet to declare a recent find of Degas' sketches to be contemporary forgeries. Meaning the art pieces were of the time of Degas, but not by his hand. Other houses had lost millions on the deal, and although he'd saved his company from a major loss, he'd never felt adequately compensated. So when a certain party approached him with the offer of unbelievably good money just for enhancing a work's appraisal, he saw no immediate downside. After all, these were works far off any catalog or gallery listing. Not one of these uninspired scratchings would ever get to within a hundred kilometers of a serious museum or collector. No, the only victims here would be the insurance companies if these worthless pieces were ever lost or stolen. Of course, Detrick did not consider that his upward appraisal of these works—in many cases to one hundred thousand times their true insignificant value—was a crime. That was because his cut was five percent of whatever value he deemed they were worth. So if he felt like making €20,000 that day, he'd assess some detestable waste of canvas and oil to €400,000, with just the filing of a form. The

€400,000 wasn't real but the €20,000 was, and it would really be in his account that night. In three short months, he would lose the paperwork and erase the files and no one at Shipsen-Deloitte would ever be the wiser.

His take had been pretty healthy lately, as a batch of undeserving art had come across his desk by the same "investor/collectors" with whom he had made this very profitable deal. Enough to get a new flat and this €120,000 Tesla S-convertible with the P85 performance package. An all-electric masterpiece with the latest cutting edge tech and creature comforts that made saving the planet a pleasure.

.𝔊.

At the hairpin turn, ten kilometers down the road, a man threw a standby switch and the large generator in the back of his pickup truck started up. He then threw a second switch and the generator groaned as it fought against the load it was just connected to. The large capacitor, as big as a skid of bricks, buzzed. A voltmeter hooked to its terminals started rising, passing ten thousand volts. A wire from the generator was secured to an iron rod stuck four feet into the ground. He pulled on the wires connected to a large sport fisherman's reel to ensure the wire had slack. The large capacity reel was slot fitted into one of the holes in the bed of the truck. He pulled back the crossbow. It took a lot of strength to fight the two-hundred-pound pull. Once he latched the gut, he laid in the odd-looking arrow. Instead of a normal crossbow bolt, this one had a double-headed end made with two powerful, flat-ended magnets at the tips, each fifty millimeters around and set about one hundred millimeters apart. The thin wire led from the big fishing reel spool to the oddly fashioned bolt.

.𝔊.

Detrick had had enough of the music and decided to switch to the news channel. He hit the button on the steering wheel and said, "News." The car only took commands in English. But that would soon be fixed and he would be able to use his preferred German. He had paid €10,000 over the asking price to avoid the four-week delay in getting the car, but that meant accepting one that was already outfitted for an English lawyer.

.𝔊.

The principle problem of the man with the crossbow was that the Tesla ran silent, so he wouldn't know it was coming until he could see it when it entered the turn, and the driver instinctively slowed the vehicle approaching the two hundred ten degree hairpin turn on this side of the mountain. That only gave him about two seconds to aim and hit the target. It wasn't the best position but it was the only one across from the depression in the road that allowed for the full contents of the the two-hundred-liter drum of salt water to puddle across the roadway. He donned the big, heavy rubber gloves and made sure his knees and feet were totally on the thick rubber mat he had laid on the ground.

The voltage meter hit one hundred and fifteen thousand volts. The red S-type, came out from behind the bushes. He led the car through the sights on the crossbow. He pulled the trigger. Silently, except for the whirling of the reel of wire unspooling at a fast rate, the magnetic bolt slapped onto the side of the Tesla. Upon contact, the full jolt of one hundred and fifteen thousand volts discharged throughout the frame, chassis, and all the systems of the car, as the high energy current found a path to the ground through the salt water splashing up under the car from the roadway.

.𝔊.

As he approached the turn, Detrick heard the thump followed by a blinding flash as his digital dashboard flared up and burned out. Suddenly, his engine stopped and his brakes failed.

Inside the high-tech car, the electric sensors in the anti-lock circuit had fried with the impulse.

.𝔊.

The shooter watched as the car hit the guardrail at over seventy miles per hour. For its part, the rail held, but the light-weight car with the heavy batteries in the rear catapulted over the railing as it flipped and then tumbled down the side of the mountain some five thousand feet. The car disintegrated as it cart-wheeled and smashed against the rocky terrain, littering it with jagged parts, spewing corrosive battery acid, and flinging pieces of Detrick all the way down.

The man reeled in the magnetic bolt, which was dislodged as the car flipped. He shut down the generator, threw everything in the bed of the pickup and took off.

A few kilometers away, on a quiet country road, he stopped at the bridge over a deep river he had scouted two days earlier. He made sure there was no traffic in either direction. He went around back and opened the tailgate. He then drove across the road, positioning the truck to span the roadway. He then put it in reverse and floored it. The pickup lurched backwards and, just before it hit the low guardrail on the other side of the road, he slammed on the brakes. The huge seven-hundred-pound army surplus capacitor, the half-ton generator, the reel, the bolt, the empty drum, ground spike, and the rubber gloves and mat all went sliding off the high back of the truck, clearing the low railing, and plummeting into the deep river below with a gigantic splash. He turned and looked out the rear window into the truck bed to ensure that it was all gone. He then put the truck in drive and proceeded to drive normally over the bridge, albeit with his tailgate open. The driver of a passing Audi was none the wiser that all the evidence of a hybrid-car-killing "Taser" had just been eliminated.

As the man in the pickup drove, he reached into his pocket and pulled out a first-class ticket to the Cayman Islands in the name of Paul Grundig.

.𝔊.

Brooke was deep in a meeting with the US Attorney, Southern District and it wasn't going well.

"Director Burrell, without the last part of the puzzle, the T&E records, we'd just be making opposing counsel rich as they mount up billable hours while denying their clients were even in the places where the transactions and illegalities went down."

"Our techs are trying to recreate the files from the erasure event that took place. Our only lead witness is dead."

"Yes, that unfortunate business with the subway."

"It's looking more like he was murdered."

"You think he was silenced? Couldn't it be just a random murder?"

"It scores way too high on the coincidence scale for me."

.𝔊.

The flood protection gates of the Rokytka River in Prague are both an essential functional part of the city's infrastructure and a bit of a tourist attraction as well. All over the world, from Victoria Falls to the Colorado rapids, the force of rushing water instinctively draws human interest. So it was here as well, in this branch of the Vltava River where people often gathered to behold the power of nature as the big blue floodgates opened in balletic synchronicity and the surging waters burst out to the lower end of the river in Liben. The event's actual purpose was to control the flow in order to balance the river's moods.

So when the fourth gate from the east end was putting out considerably less volume than the others, the Water Authority engineers investigated. To their shock, they found the meter-and-a-half-wide gateway pipe clogged with the body of a 114-kilo man.

The Czech police were able to identify the poor fellow as Ebner Dubrovnik, a digital engineer who worked for a high tech company in Prague. The best they could figure was that, due to his blood-alcohol level, he fell off either a bridge or a boat on the river, and then floated downstream until his body got stuck in the floodgate.

.𝔊.

"A fleet boat of the Navy, a submarine with her fighting power still intact! And you'd take her back to Pearl? I don't believe . . ." Brooke hit the pause button. She thought she heard a knock at the door. She listened for a few more seconds then hit the remote again. "The best exec I could possibly get in the whole Navy. 'The backstop' I think you said, and the first command you give as a captain is to order a retreat!" the movie soundtrack continued.

Ever since she'd married a submariner she had developed an inordinate fascination with submarine movies. Also because she'd once played a dangerous game of cat and mouse between a secret

US submarine and a doomed Russian Akula-class boat. A situation in which she'd invoked her presidential authority as the mission's runner and taken over the control of the American submarine in the midst of a secret mission. A mission that was failing after an underwater collision fatally damaged the Russian sub that was on a similarly secret assignment. Her decisive leadership led to the detonation of a small Russian tactical nuke twenty thousand feet below the Indian Ocean. It was a brilliant gambit that she'd engineered, on the spot, to conveniently destroy any evidence of US involvement in the God Particle affair. So tight and well orchestrated was her improvised battle plan, that the Russians, to this day, have chalked up loss of their sub to a nuclear accident aboard one of their notoriously "leaky" boats. But that event, and all the other times she'd served her country as part of QUOG, the Quarterback Operations Group, a secret operations cluster run out of the White House by her old boss, Dr. William "Wild Bill" Hiccock, was highly classified.

For those reasons, her fascination with all things submarine had grown. This movie, *Run Silent, Run Deep*, hit very close to home. Clark Gable, the sub's skipper—or as she thought of it, the actor playing her husband, Mush—and his wife lived on base at Pearl. He was struggling with command and battling his exec officer, Burt Lancaster. Every one of these films brought her closer to her man, who was out there somewhere below the ocean on what was known as deterrent patrol. She didn't know if the deterrent was as effective in foreign policy as it was in deterring her domestic life, but she'd signed up for this duty when she signed the marriage certificate. The one good thing about being here in New York, on this now-extended case, was that it kept her mind off the emptiness she felt from time to time.

This time there was no mistaking the rapping at the door. She shut off the TV and walked over. "Who is it?"

"Nigel."

She unlocked the door and let him in. "What's got you knocking on my door at ten o'clock on a school night?"

"So sorry, but I just got this communiqué from our Middle East station." He headed to the kitchen table and flipped open his iPad. He pressed his thumb on the screen and a biometric scan identified him.

Brooke looked over at the screen as he held it upright on the table. It was a Skype-like picture of a man speaking in an English accent in some sort of control center with equipment behind him. "Highest confidence sources and incontrovertible surveillance videos indicate that a cell we have tracked from the ISIS camps in Somalia and through Yemen and found to be idle for the last twenty-seven days has just fallen off the grid. Our best guess is that they are now active. The cell has been classified as SOM37. A follow-up briefing paper as to methods and suspected capabilities is attached to this compression. The directorate considers this an imminent and present global threat. All resources are to be diverted to determining the SOM37's whereabouts, and potential target packages. All known methods and sources are to be pressed for any corroborating intelligence. Follow-up briefing via this channel as the situation dictates. This is a level A-one-A communication and should be considered a direct order from the directorate and superseding any and all previous orders to the intended recipient. Direct all inquiries and findings through normal secured channels to your immediate control and oversight officers. End of file, end of communiqué." Then there were three beeps and the screen went black.

"That's a very specific order, but are you reading me in on this because you think it relates to my—our—investigation? Or is this your way of telling me you've been reassigned?"

"Hardly. Look here at the briefing paper." He swiped his finger and the attachment opened up. He scrolled down. "Here, this little tidbit caught my eye."

Brooke scanned and read aloud. "Subject name unknown, likeness not available, physical description not available, alias: 'Sheik of Araby.' Referenced four times in decrypted messaging. Suspected theaters of operation: Austria, Sweden, Czech Republic, and Western United States." Brooke thought for a second. "Stockholm, Prague, and Denver!"

"And maybe something we haven't caught wind of yet in Vienna, Salzburg, or Innsbruck, Austria."

"I see. Okay, what kind of threat are we facing here?"

"I'll encapsulate the fourteen single-spaced pages of analysis."

"Thank you, you are very kind. Coffee? It seems like we are going to be up for a while."

"Tea, if it's no trouble?"

"Of course, I should have guessed."

She put on the kettle and set up a cup and a tea bag. She popped a K-cup in the coffee maker and pressed the button. She went back to the table. "All I have is Lipton. Is that okay?"

"Brilliant."

She sat and looked at the report as Nigel started in.

"The cell is thought to consist of muscle men, engineers, technicians, and intelligence types," he said.

"Engineers? Is that British intelligence for bomb makers?"

"No, it literally means engineers, but in groups like this, bomb makers are ubiquitous."

"So if it isn't a bang or a boom, then A, why are they active, and B, why were you watching them?"

"ISIS is gaining more and more footing in Africa. We believe they are following in the footsteps of Bin Laden and others who have used parts of Africa for staging and training for foreign attacks." He brushed his finger on the pad as he scrolled down the report, scrutinizing the paragraphs as they slipped by. "Where is it . . . ? Here, 'the capability of the engineers may lie in electromagnetics, induction, or generation.'"

The kettle went off and Brooke moved over to the kitchen counter. As she prepped the tea and sugared her coffee, she thought aloud. "Electromagnetics . . . electric power plants? Nuclear power plants? We don't have any mag-lev trains yet, so they can't attack those . . ."

She brought the cups to the table.

"Mag-lev trains? How do you know of things like that?" he said.

"I used to work for a science guy, Dr. Bill Hiccock. He was always war gaming technological attacks on America. Sounds like this one would fit his niche nicely."

"Hiccock. Is that the chap you were working for on the sub op?"

"Yes, the Quarterback Operations Group. It was a presidential action team."

"QUOG, I believe it was called."

"My compliments to MI6."

"Sorry to keep tabs, but I'm afraid it is necessary, because even a friendly ally can have rogue elements."

"I totally understand. Trust but verify."

"Exactly. Are you and the captain planning on a family?"

It was a little out of left field, but Brooke went with it. "That would be nice. Maybe once his tour is over. Why do you ask?"

"Apropos of our discussion in the elevator, could you do it, Brooke? Could you commit to family and close the door on all this?"

She reacted before she thought. "You don't think I can have both?"

"The question is, do you?"

Brooke sat, and all thoughts of the mission at hand cleared away from her brain as she was suddenly holding her pink, sweet-smelling daughter, little eyelashes, small, delicate fingers. In her mind, she held her close while rocking her in her arms. She heard gentle cooing as she focused on her baby's angelic face. Even that imagined scene raised an emotional need and desire for a child in her heart. Her reverie ended in a sigh, and she was back in the room with Nigel. "How about you. Do you have children?"

"Sadly, no."

"But Nigel, in today's world you can have your pick, a dashing man like you."

"Dashing is another word for old, I take it."

"No . . . not at all. I mean, there are lots of men your age having children."

"I might offer that there may be men having *another* baby. I've not had one, yet. It's a wholly different proposition to get on the horse at an advanced age rather than never forgetting how to ride in the first place."

"I cede your point, but I still think if you want something bad enough, you can make it happen."

"Excellent advice; make sure you remember that."

"Duly noted." She could see he was thrown by her terse, unemotional response to his genuine expression of concern. "Sorry, Nigel, that was a very nice thing to say. I'm just not comfortable having this conversation with someone I barely know."

"I quite understand, but one old warrior to a younger one, allow me a final word: Don't do what I did, Brooke. I risked much for Queen and country, faced danger and lived to have the nightmares, but the one thing that scared me to my bones, my greatest fear, was that all that could be taken away from me, not by a man with a gun or a bomb, but by a little baby armed with a rattle."

Brooke closed her eyes, letting his words sink in.

There was a knock on the door. Brooke opened her eyes. "Come in, George, it's open." She turned to Nigel. "I texted him to come over while I was making the tea. No reason not to get a jump on tomorrow."

They went back to the report from London and worked for another hour, then called it quits for the night.

George and Nigel shared a cab.

.G.

"We have our work cut out for us tomorrow," George said as he rolled down the window.

"With a little luck, my man on the inside will shed more light on how they are running this."

"So how do you like working with Brooke?"

"She's got what you American's call grit. If I had a daughter, I wouldn't be too disappointed if she were half the woman Brooke is."

"Grit . . . yeah, that's it."

.G.

"Damn hand." Dequa cursed under his breath. Every once in a while his hand involuntarily trembled. It was a result of the nerve damage he'd sustained in the early eighties from a piece of white-hot, razor-sharp Soviet shrapnel that had been embedded in his forearm. A souvenir he'd received while beating the elite Spetsnaz Brigade back into their mother Russia, north of Kondüz, in Afghanistan. The shaking made it hard for him to focus on the *Le Monde* newspaper he was trying to read in French. As he sat in the Starbucks on Sixth Avenue, no one would have guessed that he was a revered and famed mujahid. A fierce warrior and brilliant strategist, his victories earned him the equivalent of a general's rank . . . if the side he fought for wore uniforms and had ranks; but to his men and his cause he was proud of the title Commander Dequa Quraisha.

The headline of the *Montreal Gazette* and the subsequent story of the Galerie Nouveau's explosion was all the verification Dequa needed to know that the job he had ordered was done, and done well. No loose ends and no traces of their real intent. The authorities discovered the cause of the explosion just like the American, Paul, said they would—a loose gas main fitting. French police explained that everyone in the gallery had already been rendered unconscious from the gas at the time of the explosion. Then he read that the delivery girl, who also died in the blast, rang the old electric bell on the back door. Police theorized that that action, that ringing of the bell, created a small spark. And in the heavily contaminated air, it caused the gas built up in the entire gallery to explode.

Dequa was pleased to see no mention of any further suspicion, no discovery of tampered computers or missing files. So he knew that all traces of the eight hundred million dollars in bogus payments and the corroborating paper trail were gone. And with them another potential thread to expose their cell, their plot, and their mission, was cut. This mission and the ones he'd just completed in Prague and Stockholm was proof that the American convert, this former infidel, Paul, was good at his deadly craft. It eased Dequa's concerns about the next assignment he'd given him in the Caribbean.

He got up, collected his coffee cup and newspaper and placed them in the trash, then exited onto the avenue. He headed for Forty-Eighth Street to buy a guitar case from one of the few music stores that remained on that block.

Chapter 7

Natural Woman

13 DAYS UNTIL THE ATTACK

Marsha was so excited she could hardly eat a thing for breakfast at the Grand Cayman Marriott on Seven Mile Beach. Paul was due to arrive before noon. There'd been a package awaiting her when she checked in. It was from him and it was a very thoughtful and wonderful gift for their Caribbean getaway together. He had sent her tortoiseshell Gucci sunglasses, Louboutin lady's flat sandals, and an aqua-and-white Hermès Beverly Hills beach wrap. With a little note, "*For the sun and sands as we hold hands.*" The newly retired bank transaction officer actually clutched the card with the sweet sentiment to her chest.

So far this morning, enthused by his little present, Marsha got up really early and got the full salon treatment, a new hairstyle, a mani-pedi, and a facial. The song "Natural Woman" was playing on the spa's music system, and as her confidence in her attractiveness increased from all the attention she was getting, the refrain, *You make me feel, you make me feel, you make me feel like a natural woman.* kept rolling around in her head. Then she spent an hour in the hotel surf shop agonizing over a new bikini she'd dare to try. Although she was normally a one-piece wearer, Paul was really excited by her body. He had said he liked a woman with some meat on her bones, and since he was the only person she knew down here on the island, she thought she'd go a little wild. . . . *like a natural woman.* She'd also just endured a Brazilian wax to go with her new skimpier bikini; she wanted everything to be perfect for him.

She felt like she was sixteen again. Her body tingled just thinking of his arms around her and his touch. He was the most sexually skilled man she had ever been with; not that there'd been that many. Over the years she had gravitated away from men. Shunning the bar scene and focusing more on her work and Facebook.

Everything changed the day she met Paul. She couldn't believe that it was less than a month since she had met him. She remembered how surprised he'd been on their third date to learn she was in banking. He was a curator for a few smaller art museums around Europe. Places like Prague, Stockholm, and Vienna. *He has such innocent, childlike eyes*, she thought. She couldn't resist helping him. Especially after he told her how disreputable his former partners were, cheating him out of all those commissions. She had to admit it was all so exciting: having sex by night and setting up the electronic fund transactions by day. They'd spent almost two entire weeks together. Then he had to return to Prague, with a few other stops in between, before joining her here in the Caymans.

He was so sweet about it. Sharing his commissions with her. There was a lot of money in being a curator. Just one EFT alone was more than 750 million dollars, of which he munificently gave her ten percent of his ten percent. Tomorrow they'd go to the bank down here in the Caymans and withdraw their money. Thanks to him and his generosity, she'd be a millionaire. Seven and a half million would go a long way. She saw herself in the best spas in the world, a face-lift, maybe getting her breasts done . . . *Paul would like that.* And now that she was outside the jurisdiction of the US, any bank regulator's findings could not touch her. Part of her confidence was based on the fact that her little EFT for Paul was a needle in the trillion-dollar haystack of daily global transactions. She was sure his dirty former partners, those horrible cheats he'd told her about, weren't going to go to the authorities, lest they bring down prosecution on themselves.

The waiter came by and motioned with the teapot. She demurred, "Just the check, please."

Her phone rang and she dug it out of her purse. She didn't recognize the number. "Hello? Paul? Darling are you here, at the hotel?"

"At the airport. My plane was late. Listen, Marsha, I was originally intending to surprise you with this, but now time is very limited," he said.

"Surprise? I like the sound of that."

"Silly me, I rented a boat for us; a little picnic on a shoal out in the middle of the aqua-green sea. I saw it on a TV show."

She smiled as she held the phone close to her ear. "Sounds wonderful. We can't reschedule?"

"No, dear, they are booked solid; 11:30 is the cut off, then they'll rent the boat to someone else."

Marsha had planned a big welcome for Paul, in the room, mostly just champagne and strawberries, and her in a new negligee. But he was being cute, and spontaneous.

"I have the perfect new bathing suit to wear . . ." she whispered conspiratorially. "A bikini!"

"Now I'm surprised!"

"And beautiful new sunglasses and sandals and a silk wrap. You really shouldn't have."

"It was nothing, and I figured a woman never has enough sunglasses."

"Especially on a boat, you wonderful man."

"It is you who are wonderful. Thank you for going along with my crazy idea; it's just that it looked so romantic and it would just be the two of us."

"Mmmm, I like the sound of that." . . . *like a natural woman* . . .

.G.

Paul was on a public phone. He smiled. "Grab a cab from the hotel, and tell them to take you to the public pier in George Town. Look for me in a red thirty-foot Sea Ray, called *Sun Seeker Seven*. But darling, it's eleven now; could you possibly be there by eleven thirty?"

He pulled his cell phone from his pocket as it was vibrating. He refocused on the call with Marsha. "Great . . . I can't wait to see you too . . . marvelous Marsha." He then returned two blown kisses and hung up the pay phone. He immediately switched to the cell. "So sorry, I couldn't find my phone . . ." He continued the call as he walked away from the public phone and down the rocking slip of the Sun Seeker Boat Rentals' dock to the red motorboat.

.G.

At 11:25 a.m., Marsha got out of the cab with her beach bag, sun hat, new Gucci sunglasses, Louboutin sandals, and her Hermès beach wrap covering her new, shockingly revealing Carmen Marc Valvo bikini. There was a Sun Seeker Charters sign spanning the pier to her right. As she walked, she saw Paul checking the gas and waved.

He reached up and grabbed her by the waist and lifted her in his arms, swinging her into the boat, kissing her deeply and passionately. She melted into the embrace, her hat falling back off her head.

When they broke the embrace he once again apologized. "Dear, again so sorry not to have come and met you at the hotel, but I think you'll love this."

"It sounds lovely, and I adore the fact that you planned this . . . that you went through all this trouble."

"No trouble. Let's have a little toast before we head out." He gestured towards a champagne bucket sitting next to a tray of strawberries.

"Oh, Paul. Sometimes I really believe we are soul mates."

.G.

At 12:15 they had been running at quite a clip over the serene clear ocean. Paul checked his heading.

Marsha came up from the cabin after using the bathroom. "Paul, there's scuba equipment down there."

"It was the only way to get a boat. It was the last one they had for rent, so I had to buy the Scuba package because all the excursion boats were already booked. It was only a hundred dollars more. But we're almost there." He checked the chart. By his reckoning he was right in the middle of the spot they called the Maze. He throttled back the engine and took out his phone.

Marsha looked around. "Why are we stopping here?"

"Marsha, go sit up on the bow. Let me get a shot of you in that very sexy bikini."

"Paul . . ." She dismissed him, but then, "You really like me in this?"

"I wanted to make love to you the minute you got on the boat. I can't wait another second."

She kissed him and stepped onto the cushion and out onto the front of the boat. *Make love on the boat? Out here?* She looked around seeing nothing but horizon in all directions. *Why not?* She slid down one shoulder of her cover up, exposing her new underwire top. "How's this?"

From behind the wheel, Paul said, "Perfect."

.6.

At 1:30 p.m. exactly, he pulled up to the hotel's dock. She was smiling. She liked the way he was always prompt. She had flown all the way from England and left her suite twenty minutes early and walked down here just to be on time to meet him. It was crazy. Paul was always doing spontaneous things like this, wherever in the world she met him, but that's what she liked about these clandestine meet ups, as they called them.

When they spoke on the cell this morning, he'd told her to bring sunscreen. They were going to a small shoal where they'd have a very private lunch, then dinner tonight at Balla Qui. She hadn't seen him in a few weeks and he looked so good steering the red motorboat right to her at the dock.

He lifted her from her waist right onto the boat. They kissed and embraced as he swung her down to the deck.

"Oh, Paul. This is going to be magnificent. Thank you so much for the new sunglasses, this fabulous wrap, and these very sexy sandals. I was breathless when I opened your gift in the room. Oh and look, champagne and caviar. You are definitely a lady killer!" Her non-descript European accent was the mark of aristocracy.

An hour later they were spread out on a blanket with a picnic basket and cooler on the little isolated pink sand shoal that was a dot in the crystal-clear aqua water.

"I have to pee," Elanna said as she adjusted the elastic of her bottoms. She got up and walked over to the boat and climbed aboard.

Paul looked out over the waves and breathed in deeply. His mission was over. Tomorrow he'd fly back to New York, but for the rest of today and tonight he was celebrating in his unique style, with someone he actually wanted to have sex with. It was his reward for having to prostitute himself to get the cooperation of the less desirable people who were needed to accomplish the objectives. The fact that, in the end, they needed to be eliminated, didn't faze him; it was, after all, the cost of doing business. But with Elanna, it was pure pleasure. He saw her emerge from below as she sat on the edge of the boat and swung her legs over the side and hopped back down onto the sand.

She was topless, as was the way most European women enjoyed the beach. As she walked to him on the shifting fine-grain sand, she commented, "This is the perfect spot on the most perfect day."

"Yes, it is."

"You know, Paul, you don't have to send me expensive gifts just to fuck me."

"Nonsense, even a countess like you likes presents." He grabbed her and kissed her neck.

"True. But you, all by yourself, are present enough," She said smiling as she pulled back her long hair so he could nibble on her neck a bit more.

"But then how could I lure you away from the boys in Vienna?"

"It's easy, they're boys . . . they're fun . . . but you, you are a man and you know how to treat a . . ."—his hand found the spot and she caught her breath—"woman."

As she let a little moan escape she looked around. "Are we someplace called the Maze?"

"Oh yeah, you saw the chart on the boat?"

"Yes."

"No, that was the last renter, I guess. The Maze is where you go to see sharks."

"No, thank you. The only animal I want to be eaten by is right here." She turned and pushed him down onto the blanket then fell on him and kissed him.

.𝔊.

Right on time, at 5:00 p.m., Paul pulled alongside the dock at Sun Seeker Charters. He shut down the motors as the dockhand tied off the line. He helped Elanna off the boat and she went right to the ladies room in the rental office.

In the little dockside office, the clerk slid the clipboard with the rental agreement across the desk. Paul signed it. The man checked the signature and said, "Was everything in order, sir?"

"Yes. Everything was perfect. But unfortunately, I lost one set of diving weights. Slipped right out of my hands."

"No problem, sir. We can add it to your credit card."

"That will be fine. So sorry."

Elanna came out of the loo and stood beside him in her new glasses, sandals, and aqua-and-white beach wrap as he signed the new adjusted credit card slip at the desk.

Acknowledging her, the clerk inquired, "Did you both have a nice day?"

"Yes. We truly did," Paul said.

The clerk watched them leave, thinking that the lady must have lost the pretty hat she'd had on this morning, while they were out on the water.

At 7:00 p.m. that night they sat at the best table at the Balla Qui and spoke of plans to meet again. Elanna suggested that maybe they'd meet in New York in a few weeks. Paul suggested maybe a South Sea Island instead. "Ooooh, sounds lovely," Elanna said, then asked if they'd be sharing a cab to the airport in the morning.

Chapter 8

The Personal Touch

Based on the new intel delivered by Nigel, and the assessment that this was potentially an ISIS threat, Brooke's investigation got a shot in the arm, a ten million dollar injection. Overnight, she had a new command over one hundred more agents in New York, Washington, and London as well as researchers, forensic accountants, and translators. One of the ways to stop the attack would be to trace it from the point of finance through to the operating cell. "Follow the money" was not a new technique in the war on terror, just the least sexy. Nevertheless, her department heads were gathered around the table at 8:30 a.m. "Most of us know each other, but you may not know Nigel. He's MI6, assigned to this op, which as of oh seven hundred is officially now code named, *Operation Sweeper*."

She then went on to lay out clear lines of information flow and accountability. She reinforced the crucial timing aspect of imminent danger. She ended by challenging them to find these guys by financial forensics before all that was left was crime scene forensics. Then she opened up the floor to questions. "Jason?"

"Did you pick the name? Or was it computer generated?"

"I picked it. Wes?"

"Director Burrell, how does our number one POI, the Sheik of Arabia, play into this?"

"First off, at this level, first names only. It saves time. So it's Brooke. Second, our main person of interest is the Sheik of Araby, not

Arabia, and he's the only movement on the board right now. Everything else is static intel, right up until the Brits lost track of the entire cell."

"I understand that MI6 found multiple references to the Sheik of Araby in intercepts, but could there be something to that ID?" Jason said.

Nigel jumped in. "I queried that myself, turns out it's not an actual person or title, but a reference to a movie idol of the 1920s. The first superstar, if you will, a chap named Rudolf Valentino; he played the lead role in the silent film *The Sheik*, and women went by the millions to see this dashing, handsome man sweep ladies up in his arms and whisk them away to the Kasbah. It was so popular that a song called 'The Sheik of Araby' was written about him and the whole mystique the film created."

"So, is that a behavioral trait we should be scanning for?"

"Actually, at the risk of standing out as the only member of her majesty's secret service in the room, I'd have likened him more to James Bond. Even though we don't know his name, we can deduce from his movements which, as Director Burrell has noted, is the only thing in motion at this time, that he has a penchant for exotic places and using women as cover. His seduction seems more deliberate to a mission than romantic.

"So, Brooke, how do you want to go about this? Who can we bring in? Is there a cleared list?"

"We've got direct coordination with MI6 so their resources are at our disposal without jurisdictional barriers. Anything else, run it by me first. I got Homeland Security and DOJ looking over my shoulder, but to state it again, as clearly as I can: we are autonomous. Normally that's a one-way street, so if you want to go against traffic, flag me down first."

"Jeannine?"

"Any more word on SOM37's operational ability?"

"Nothing more than the initial reports, although right after this meeting I am going down to DC to tap an old friend for a favor and see if he can get some capability projections done. Any other questions? Bob?"

"Do we have our JDID number yet?"

"Good question, 'cause I am sure we all want to get paid. Actually, the accounting department out of treasury in DC opens at nine. You'll all have your charge back numbers by ten a.m. But hey, I only got ten mil and it's a big world out there. Let's not spend it all in one country. And don't forget to calculate overtime. It's all inside the ten! We'll meet again at five for a follow up. Any other questions? Jason?"

"Last I heard, you were retired. How did they get you back on the team?"

"I made them make me an offer I could refuse!"

"Wait, that's not the way that goes," Jason said.

"It is now," Brooke said as she closed her briefing book.

The meeting broke up and Jeannine was humming a tune as she collected her things. Brooke took note. "That's a jolly little tune, Jeannine."

"Yeah, it's been in my head for a few minutes now."

"Well, what is it?"

"I can't remember. My mom used to hum it. I never knew the words."

"Your mom still with us?"

"Yep, tearing up the shuffle board circuit, still taking cruises, trying to land a rich husband!"

"I like her spirit."

"Don't encourage her. At her age she should be tending to petunias, not gallivanting all over the place. But she is a hopeless romantic."

"Not a bad thing, Jeannine, not a bad thing."

Chapter 9

Brooke is in da House

Bill Hiccock had sent Brooke a Christmas card, one of those family portrait types. He, his wife Janice, and their son Richie looked like the kind of all-American family you used to see inside *Life* magazine, in a Campbell's soup or Chevrolet ad. Brooke owed her former boss much, but the one thing that stood out was the counsel he gave her when she expressed the desire to quit working for the president, for Bill, and for the intelligence apparatus of the United States. He'd had every right to pressure her to stay. He'd been in the middle of a major terrorist attack, and Brooke was his number one agent in the field. But after she won her second service star, the glamour had worn off. She'd wanted the other side of life. She'd wanted the rest of the having-it-all package. Instead of negotiating with her, he'd simply told her that her happiness was paramount, and if she wanted a life, she had certainly earned it, many times over. At that moment he'd gone from being a boss to being a big brother.

She felt guilty calling him from an active duty post only a year after leaving his Quarterback Operations Group. But she was in need of his special network, a resource of his own invention. As the Presidential Science Advisor, he had amassed an interconnected group, code named SCIAD or Scientific Community In America's Defense. It was a scientific and technological who's who of the biggest and brightest brains on the planet, all connected to him. He'd pose a "what if" question at noon and practically a whole new field of science would spring up overnight. Between the top-secret cleared core members and the redacted outer-ring participants, there were three hundred top minds working in parallel on any problem or threat facing America that Bill challenged them with. Her terrorist-engineer-based ISIS cell, SOM37, was a riddle he and his SCIAD network were uniquely capable of solving.

She sat in the back of the interagency motor pool car as her driver dealt with the guards outside the east gate of the White House. She reflected on her last day in "crown," or what the secret service called the executive mansion. On that day, she'd actually been invited up to the residence for a private breakfast with the president. The first lady had also given her a goodbye hug. It was quite a sendoff. Now, like any other visitor, she had to hand over her ID. Her A pass having long ago had the word "VOID" punched into it, was now just a memory in her desk drawer back home.

The car pulled up to the portico and Cheryl, Bill's former assistant and now deputy director of the QUOG group, greeted her. "Brooke! It's great to see you again." They hugged and Cheryl immediately pulled back. "I don't want to hurt your arm."

Brooke gave it a tap. "Healed as good as new, but thanks for the concern," Brooke hedged. The scar from the bullet, and the fact that she didn't need a weatherman to let her know when the weather was changing, was constantly with her. That was another souvenir from her last mission.

"So, Cheryl, I hear you are now deputy director of QUOG. Congratulations."

"The hardest part about running the Quarterback Operations Group is running the quarterback."

Brooke laughed. She knew her former boss, Dr. Bill Hiccock's type-A manic pace.

"I don't know how Janice deals with it. Bill is always going in ten different directions at once," Cheryl said.

"How is Bill's wife?"

"Janice? She has only six different directions, between their son, her post at the hospital, her charities, and somehow an eighty-mile-an-hour serve, tearing up the hard-true during what was supposed to be a friendly game of doubles tennis."

"They are made for each other, alright."

"Amen, Brooke."

Although the turnover at the White House was as regular as a timeshare condo in Boca Raton, Brooke was amazed at how many people engaged her, hugged her, and shook her hand all the way to Bill's office. Even as she waited in his outer office, folks dropped in. "I heard you were in the house . . ." "Welcome back . . ." "Welcome home . . ." "Good to see you . . ." was the constant refrain. But the best was the phone call she received as she was waiting.

In fact, when Cheryl announced, "The boss is on line one," Brooke didn't respond. It couldn't be for her. "Brooke, the president's on line one."

"For me?"

"Yes."

Brooke actually stood up. "Mr. President, what a surprise."

"Why didn't I know you were coming in, Brooke?"

"Well, sir. I . . . I . . . didn't know myself until last night."

"How are you, Brooke? How's my sub skipper treating you?"

"He's great, when he's around, sir."

"Just say the word, Brooke, and I'll promote him to rear admiral. Give him a nice, cushy desk job."

"Wow, I better be careful. I forgot who I was talking to. No, sir, he loves his job and is committed to serving his country; I can tough it out till his tour is over, sir."

"You know, Brooke, the real strength of our military is based on the courage of our military families."

"I couldn't agree more, sir. The more families I meet at Pearl, the more I see America's resolve."

"Amen, Brooke. Well, I have tied you up long enough. I'll put Bill on." Brooke was a little taken aback that Bill was with him. She thought Bill was "in the house."

"Good hunting with *Sweeper*."

Again, she was impressed; she had just decided on that name this morning, yet the president . . .

"Thank you, sir, for taking the time to say hello. I am truly honored."

She heard Bill grab the phone.

"Brooke, sorry; we had a last minute change of plans. I left you a voice mail."

"Yeah, about that. I'm not too good with voice mail. Where are you?"

"In the beast, on the way over to the Smith. Turns out that one of the president's old squadron buddies is being honored. He went from F-18 fighter pilot to the guy who invented the biofeedback flight control assist system. The boss grabbed me on his way out the door to the aerospace museum."

She heard the president say, "It's totally my fault, Brooke!" in the background as Bill continued.

"The secret service says we are back in the barn in eighteen minutes. The president's hopping the marine chopper to 'One.' Do you have time to wait?"

"Sure. Can I use your desk in the meantime?"

Brooke went into Bill's office and logged into Bill's computer using her old Quarterback ID. It worked! She was able to connect back to New York.

There was an email from Jeannine. She had called her mother and sang her the song that had been playing in her head, and it was called "The Sheik of Araby." Brooke laughed and went through scores of other emails and reports.

Twenty minutes later, Bill Hiccock walked into his office to find her at his desk. She got up and went to him. They hugged like NFL players after a game.

They were both all smiles and Brooke asked, "How's Janice?"

"She's got two research programs she's running while she's running me and little Richie. We do our best to let her know we couldn't get along without her, but she's forcing both of us to grow up anyway."

"Please tell her 'hi' for me and thank her . . . and you, for the lovely house warming present."

"Oh yeah, that thing . . . that . . ."

"Yeah, just thank her for me, okay? I'll give you back your desk." She leaned over to the keyboard and logged out. She then moved to the chair opposite his desk.

Bill sat in his chair. "So, Brooke, what can I do for you?"

"While I was on your machine, I downloaded and unzipped a secure compression with everything we know that relates to the op I am running, called *Sweeper*. I also redacted a briefing paper from it on the flight down and that's in the same folder under SWREDACT."

With the heavy thumping of Marine One's rotors in the background as the president's helicopter lifted off the helipad behind the

White House, Brooke briefed Bill. She needed him to put the redacted document out to the greatest minds on the planet to try to figure out what the bad guys could possibly be planning. In twenty-five minutes, all their business was concluded.

They got up and Bill walked her to his door. "You know, we could have handled this in a secure video conference. You didn't have to fly down here."

"Truth be told, I didn't know if you would have agreed. Especially to this next part."

"Oh-oh," was all Bill said.

.G.

"She did? The White House?" That got the Secretary of the Treasury's attention; he adjusted the phone to his "better" ear. "Did she meet with the boss? Oh right, he's on the way to Helsinki. No, that won't be necessary. I'll call over myself. Thanks for the heads up." He hung up the phone and didn't know what to make of the news he'd just received from his old friend Williams, the head of the secret service, namely that Brooke Burrell had visited the White House this morning. *Why? Is she working for the president in some direct way while also working for me? Is he using her to spy on me?* He hit the intercom. "Sally, get me Brooke Burrell."

"Why, she just walked in, sir. She is standing right in front of me," Sally said.

"Send her in, will you?"

.G.

The secretary got up from his desk and moved over to the couch by the small conference table as Sally escorted Brooke into his office.

"Can I get either of you anything?" Sally asked.

"Buttermilk would be great," the secretary said tapping his belly, a code between him and Sally. "Brooke?"

"Orange juice, if you have any."

"Sure thing," Sally said as she left, closing the door behind her.

"Brooke, what a surprise."

"Yes, well I needed to set up some things down here. And tap a few favors, so I figured rather than an impersonal email or the phone . . ."

"I understand. What kind of things are you setting up?"

"I have enlisted the help of Bill Hiccock. SOM37 is a new and different type of ISIS terror cell. More technical; 'engineery,' if that's a word?"

"I see, and how can Bill help you with that?"

"He's got a network of top minds . . . We are circulating a redacted description of the cell's supposed members and possible capabilities to his network. Maybe they can give me some inkling as to what they are up to, and what their targets might be."

"Brooke, this sounds like it is outside the scope of our investigation. I mean, ISIS . . . really?"

His statement sidelined Brooke. She hadn't anticipated that he would object. "Sir?"

"What I mean is, you're heading up this investigation for Treasury. Your mandate was to stem the flow of, and shut down the illegal transfer of funds from, US financial firms to various terror organizations around the world. This new line of investigation seems more appropriate for the FBI or CIA."

Brooke wondered if she had overstepped her authority. If she had opened up a simple forensic accounting investigation into a track, hunt, and kill operation on an ISIS terrorist cell.

While she paused, the secretary drilled down deeper. "I did not authorize or approve any type of clandestine or covert operation to root out active terrorist cells."

Brooke digested his position. Maybe she was too gung-ho. Maybe she just instinctively reacted and started chasing bad guys again; old habits die hard. She mentally checked off a list of decisions she had made that got her to this point.

There was a knock on the door.

"Come in, Sally."

Sally entered and placed the tray of milk and juice on the coffee table in front of the couch. "Will there be anything else?"

"No, thank you, Sally."

She smiled at Brooke, but Brooke was deep in thought and did not return the pleasantry, so she just left the room.

The secretary put Brooke's juice in front of her then took a sip of his buttermilk from his Department of Treasury mug. He waited for her to respond.

Brooke's face reset and she spoke. "Sir, our initial investigation in New York was compromised, somehow. It will be a small miracle if we can come up with enough evidence for a parking ticket, much less an indictment. The only lead we have is pointing us towards the end game of the financing, the actual operating cell. I see this extension of my investigation as totally consistent and the next logical step in tracking the money."

The secretary just took it all in, and then adjusted himself on the couch, crossing his legs and extending his arm over the back. "Can we speak candidly here, off the record?"

"I assume this is all off the record, sir."

"This town has buckets. The entire federal government is just a collection of buckets. My bucket is this department; Charles over at State has his bucket, and defense, transportation, and all the cabinet members have their buckets. What you are doing is messing with someone else's bucket. Maybe State's, maybe Homeland Security's. But to keep the money coming into this bucket, I need to make sure I am not dipping into someone else's. Do you follow me?"

"So you think I am creating a jurisdictional issue by crossing agencies?"

"Yes. Have you discussed any of this with the president?"

Brooke's radar beeped. *Of course, he's worried I have more pull with the president than he does.*

"Well, normally my conversations with the president are in a bucket of their own, sir, regulated and protected by about twenty federal statutes. However, I can assure you, my brief conversation with the president this morning was purely of a personal nature."

.𝔊.

It was now the secretary's turn to be thoughtful. *So she did speak with him this morning, even as he was headed to Finland. Personal nature? With Mitchell?* For a second he dallied in the tabloid-esque notion of gray-haired, grandfatherly, patrician, James Mitchell having an affair with this very good-looking blonde, former FBI agent. Then he quickly erased it from his mind.

The president, James Mitchell, had been an ally of his for thirty-five years. He was a good man, ex-fighter pilot and a reluctant winner of his first election six years ago. Maybe "reluctant" was too strong a word; "shocked" was probably more fitting. But soon it had been discovered that the first manipulation of a federal presidential election might have been responsible for his long-shot victory. Again, he did the right thing and went before congress when it was learned that he'd benefitted from the hacking of the system. But like the lucky fighter jock he was, he had been found to benefit "through no complicity on his part." So he'd evaded congressional flack and been given a hall pass back to the White House. Overall, he'd done well for America.

Cass didn't feel as lucky. The Prescott business up in New York and this Burrell woman's failure to finish the investigation would have its political consequences. *Personal nature?*

Was he being set up? Or worse, being used? Was the whole reason he was saddled with this Burrell woman, a quid pro quo by the president to Brooke in exchange for a little hanky-panky? His heartburn kicked in and his chest was on fire. She'd failed and now she was trying to cover her tracks by expanding the investigation and getting the president to cover for her. *Not in my department!*

.𝔊.

"Mr. Secretary?"

He snapped out of it and reached in his drawer and took out a pill case. He downed the pill dry, without water. He looked at Brooke.

"Are you okay, sir?"

Cass patted his chest. "Just a little indigestion, I'm afraid."

Chapter 10

Music and Movies

Paul could smell the marijuana as he exited the elevator and walked past the sign that read, "The Smoking of Any Substance on These Premises is Illegal under New York State Law." Ultra Sonic's rehearsal room number seven was to the left. He had his guitar case, as he'd been instructed to buy. The place was populated with musicians using the studios. Many of the men had long hair and various pieces of metal inserted into their ears, noses, and cheeks, which made him feel like he was in a strange land.

A young woman wearing black makeup and with tattoos covering her bare arms and midriff smiled at Paul. It was then he noticed her nose and cheek were pierced with insect jewelry. He was glad that his stock-in-trade good looks, the key to his success, still worked on this young . . . whatever she was, girl.

He entered rehearsal room number seven. Six men were already there. There was a piano, a corner stacked with many electronic keyboards, many microphones on stands, a wall lined with all kinds, sizes, and shapes of electric amplifiers, and a large set of drums. One wall was fully mirrored and the others, as well as the ceiling, were covered with dark gray foam panels in odd geometric shapes. Paul surmised it was to control the sound. He sat behind the drums; others had used the folding chairs that were stored against the wall in the room. He tapped his fingers on the head of the drum directly in front of him. It made a very resonant tone with the buzz of something under the drum. His curiosity piqued, he lifted it to see wires across the bottom. He snapped the wires and they made a sharp report.

The door to the room opened and Dequa entered. With him, the sound of the other rooms, whose bands had also changed on the hour, flooded in as they tuned up or started playing. When the outer and inner doors to the room were finally shut, all that could be heard was a low thumping and growl coming through the walls from the eight other music rehearsal rooms on the floor. Still, it was enough soundproofing that one could be heard while speaking in a normal voice.

Dequa was of average height with skin that could best be described as weathered leather, no doubt sun- and sand-blasted from the Afghan elements. His eyes moved like that of a commander of men, seeing strategically what others could not. His manner demanded respect even as he stood there surveying and counting the heads in attendance. He had entered with a guitar case and, once he sat, opened it and took out ten sets of large headphones. Each with a boom microphone attached. He then took out a standard iPod and plugged it into the powerful PA system that fed into the large speakers all over the room. Immediately the sounds of musicians talking, laughing, tuning up, and playing parts of songs filled the room. Eventually the band on the tape played and sang a song with many voices. It was very loud! As loud as if the band were playing right here in the room.

Dequa motioned for everyone to put on the headsets. Immediately the noise went away. Now the loud music in the room seemed as far away as that coming from the rooms next door. Dequa spoke and was remarkably clear in everyone's ears. He touched the headset with the word *Bose* on the ear cups and said, "Just like the ones they use in American football stadiums, these units cancel out all outside sound and the microphones only switch on when you speak."

The results were quite comfortable.

Then Dequa started the meeting. "Praise Allah, we are all here except for Ramal, who is finishing up in Bolivia. We will continue to meet in places like this until we separate for our assigned posts and targets. Ben-el Ram will distribute funds to you as we proceed."

Ben-el opened another guitar case that was stuffed with stacks of hundreds.

As he handed Paul a stack he said, "I congratulate you on Montreal."

"Yes, it went just like I planned it."

"Surely you mean it was the will of Allah."

"Well, yeah. I mean, it was he who guided my hands to do his bidding."

Ben-el nodded, but Paul could sense his questioning eyes tracking him as he walked away.

.𝔊.

Outside the room, Tyrone, one of the setup men at the Ultra Sonic Rehearsal facility opened the outer door and was about to open the inner door to room seven when he heard the band and singers. He decided to borrow a mic from another room that wasn't as full of as many musicians as he heard playing and singing through the door.

.𝔊.

They had rented the room for two hours, as always, with cash. Dequa had two hours of recording he'd made of a band in Los Angeles a month before. Tonight's meeting only lasted an hour and a half.

.𝔊.

As the "musicians" filed out of the room, Tyrone checked his watch. He liked that they were out early because it meant he could reset the room for the next booking at the top of the hour. He waited for them to leave then went into the empty room.

Wow, he thought, *these guys were really neat*. None of the amps were left on, like most musicians carelessly did. The drums must have been played exactly as they were because they were still in the studio's prescribed set up. Usually drummers moved and set up the drums and cymbal stands to their own height and style. Even the mics had been returned right where they were. With nothing to do but check the garbage pails, Tyrone took the few minutes he saved, went downstairs and smoked a j before the five o'clock turnover.

.𝔊.

Movie night on a fleet ballistic missile submarine was a little incongruous, but the constant war-ready alert status was a fatiguing existence.

This patrol by the gold crew of the USS *Nebraska* was thirty-eight days into a fifty-four day mission. Many men chose to jog around the missile bay as a way of burning off energy and breaking the monotonous routine of constantly listening for hunter-killer submarines that would kill you if they found you.

"What's on the bill tonight, COB?" Captain Bret "Mush" Morton asked the Chief of the Boat.

"*Run Silent, Run Deep*, sir."

Mush cringed a little. Submarine movies were always popular on subs, especially World War Two movies. Mostly because the men who served on today's wide-beam boats, who could jog around the boat and never had to duck pipes and conduits or hanging equipment, marveled at how small, cramped, and compact their former counterparts had had it. But he remembered this movie, especially the downer part, the fact that the captain dies at the end.

"Geez, COB, can't you run *Operation Petticoat* or *Destination Tokyo*? You know, something cheerful."

"Well, sir, I can see *Petticoat* being cheery, but *Destination Tokyo*?"

"Forget it, chief. I was just trying to avoid a funeral at sea."

"Sir???"

"Carry on, COB."

The Chief of the Boat aye-ayed and went aft.

Deciding to skip the flick, Mush returned to his quarters and found the printout of world threat assessments that was downloaded every night through the VLF system. It took a long time to receive the encrypted signal, but the text file was a situational report on all the hot spots in the world and any geopolitical nastiness that might result in him having to fire his missiles in offense or defense. Fleet decided long ago, having a sub skipper out of touch for up to six months at a time probably wasn't conducive to the decision-making process they relied on their commanders to engage in.

To avoid the blues that could result from reading exclusively about the conflict and unrest of what was essentially a redacted version of the president's daily briefing, Mush reminded himself that this wasn't a hometown paper he was reading. This dreary report was a culmination of all the bleak things happening all around a dangerous world, all neatly compressed down to three pages of negativity and depression. On the other hand, he trusted that this was the worst of it, and today it was par for the course. No sign of any little sparks that could erupt in a nuclear inferno.

He glanced over a blurb on a suspected terrorist cell that had fallen off the radar and was a concern to British Intelligence. Terrorist groups were hardly a threat to the national security that could be addressed by a submarine-launched Trident ICBM, but he was trained and his mission profile was to expect the unexpected. World War III, or the end of the world, however you chose to see it, could start in thirty minutes just as much under the wrong set of circumstances as the "proper" set.

He looked at the picture of his wife, Brooke, on his desk. Every time he looked at her he got the same hit. It was like an electric trickle enveloping him. He felt it as strong as the first time he'd seen her. It wasn't just her physical attractiveness, which was plain for all to be mesmerized by, but the subtlety in her eyes, her confidence and her achievements, the sacrifices and heroic acts she had performed for her country. The Navy made sure that he was the top one-tenth of the top one percent of warriors in the world. He was trusted with the autonomous power to destroy a billion or more lives. To that end, he'd been strenuously weeded out, selected, inspected, dissected, and analyzed to be beyond reproach and of a proper character and unquestioned integrity to hold the launch keys. Yet, she was his hero.

Chapter 11

The Beast with Two Backs

12 DAYS UNTIL THE ATTACK

"This woman is a nightmare, a goddamn opportunist, a concubine of the president! I tell you she's an albatross around my neck."

"That's a little dramatic wouldn't you say, Warren?" Julius Valente said as he shifted in his seat across from the man who held the Secretary of the Treasury position that he could have had.

"Dramatic my ass, Julie. She blew the Prescott raid. She has the ear and, for all I know, the cock of the president. I'm telling you, Mitchell is looking to get even with me for that pass I gave Selchow and his directors on that sub-prime violation."

"Mitchell doesn't seem like a backdoor kind of guy; I think if he wanted you to fry, he'd light the stove himself. Maybe his chief of staff or one of his advisors could hold a grudge . . . but you said she's in with him?"

"Look, Julie, I am not asking you for your opinion. I want you to get up to New York under the guise of being my appointed special investigator to help this woman find the leak. Then I want you to find out what I am dealing with here. If she and Mitchell are making the beast with two backs, I'll need that as leverage."

"Beast with two . . . ? Where do you get this stuff?"

"Julie, we go all the way back to Harvard. You are my oldest and most trusted friend in this town. I need you to do this for me. Your résumé is perfect for this post and no one will raise so much as a 'but' in objection."

Julius had done well out of Fordham University and after getting his masters at Harvard, the First Bank of Boston lured him away from an early life of government service, otherwise he'd have been a shoe-in for Sec Tres or to head up the Federal Reserve. Instead, he'd made his forays into government later in life, after he'd amassed his fortune in the private sector. He had been the Attorney General of the Commonwealth of Massachusetts, served as economic advisor to the last president and was currently a consultant for Global Strategies, a Washington think tank. Valente looked at his old friend. "You're really scared, aren't you?"

"I just don't like not knowing what I'm up against," Cass said.

"You might want to rephrase that double negative constructed sentence, Warren, or no one will believe you graduated in Harvard's top percentile. I accept the post. I get $3,000 a day plus expenses."

"Done!" Warren Cass waved his hand like a Roman emperor decreeing a new tax.

"Well, Cass, I'll leave you to your day. I've got a plane to catch," Julius said as he exited the secretary's office.

Warren Cass scribbled a note to the personnel department to set up a special account for "Julie" at "3K" per diem then fished through his drawer and found a prescription bottle and flicked out two capsules. His duodenal ulcers were really acting up because of this woman.

.G.

"Mallory, could you help me with something?" Dennis asked as he invaded her personal space behind her desk, causing her to scramble to close her Facebook page in the nick of time.

Mallory Edwards was the go-to girl in the office. She knew every procedure and could usually navigate the corporate obstacle course in record time. Many a VP or sales exec tapped her resourcefulness to fast track something that was bogged down in company procedure. "Sure thing, Dennis. What is it?"

"Do you have pump-out sheets for this quarter?"

"No, Mr. Deloitte hasn't released them yet."

"When is he due back?"

"Not until next week, I'm afraid."

"Not good. I need to prepare my report for Friday because I'm on holiday next week."

"I see." She let the moment hang, surmising what was coming next.

"Mallory, be a good egg and see if you can get me a copy of the report, will you?"

"Mr. Deloitte doesn't like it much when I go through his stuff."

"Truth be told, Mallory, I am in a bit of a jam here. What do say that you do me this favor and I'll bring you back that rare perfume you like from Paris?"

"Mitsouko, Eau de Toilette, by Guerlain . . . That's a very kind offer. You can't get that at Boots."

"So, what do you say?"

"I'll do it right during lunch. Shirley's going out today so I'll go into his office and get a copy."

Dennis kissed her on the top of her head. "You are an angel. Sorry to disturb your Facebook. Carry on."

Mallory closed her eyes. The threat was implicit. Dennis had just informed her that if she, for some reason, couldn't get him an advanced copy of the report, her dalliance in social media would come to the attention of either Mr. Shipsen or Mr. Deloitte. Both being old dinosaurs from the gallery and museum worlds and now the leading purveyors of art around the globe, they didn't know or care a wit about social media. One even called it "the devil's new plaything" . . . *the old coot.* She checked the upper right hand corner of her screen: *12:05.* The day had moved fast. It was already lunchtime. She got up and headed for Deloitte's office.

.ɞ.

Being a septuagenarian, Deloitte had manila folders lined up in double rows on both sides of his massive, gold-inlaid desk from the Medici Florentine period. The system was color-coded and clearly marked with labels as to the account or work of art or artist's catalog.

Shirley kept them neatly aligned in alphabetical order and up to date, which made it easy for Mallory to put her finger right on pump in/pump out. It was a monthly chairman's report that accounted for every deal and every prospect the huge art brokerage engaged in.

In three minutes, she returned the folder and aligned it as neatly as it was before. Her eyes fell upon the name *Normans* on one of the folder's labels. Suddenly she felt a pang of guilt. She needlessly looked up and around, listening for any inkling of being interrupted. More gingerly than she had just done when retrieving the records for Dennis, she peered into the Normans folder. Her eyes widened as a smile of satisfaction appeared on her freckled face. She gently closed and replaced the file, double-checking that it did not appear disturbed in the least.

She placed the Xerox copies of the Pump report in a yellow interoffice envelope and walked out of Deloitte's office with more spring in her step than when she entered. On her way back to her cubicle she placed the envelope in Dennis's in-box.

She could hardly contain herself at her desk. She picked up the phone and excitedly dialed the restaurant. "Russell Normans please . . ."

"He's waiting on six tables right now, love."

"I'm sorry but this is important."

.G.

"Mr. Deloitte, call for you on the house phone."

"Can you bring it here?"

"Sorry, sir. It is over by the front desk."

"Well, who is it . . . ? Nevermind." The seventy-year-old excused himself from his guests at the table and walked the forty feet to the gold, classic-styled boudoir phone in this Dubai hotel lobby. "Deloitte here. Who is this?"

"Mr. Deloitte, Russell Normans."

Deloitte pulled the phone away from his ear and looked at it incredulously. "Why on earth are you calling me?"

"I wanted to thank you for making that incredible deal on my piece."

The words stunned him. "How did you . . ." Then he caught himself. *Of course, Mallory.* "Normans, where are you now?"

"In my loft in Soho . . ."

"Well, I am flying in at 7:30 tomorrow night. What say we meet at 8:30? Oh, and bring Mallory. I'm sure she'll want to be there when I give you your check. Oh, and Normans, I am sure you understand how we do things. We control the publicity and release, so please, as a condition of your contract you are forbidden to discuss this with anyone. Including family! Do you understand? If you violate that agreement the deal is off and you get no check."

"I totally understand, sir."

"Good, Good. See you tonight." Deloitte hung up the antique phone then patted his pockets.

.G.

At the table, the Sultan of Brunei, Deloitte's guest and hopeful customer of rare eighteenth century Canaletto oils, tapped the British Ambassador to Dubai on the shoulder and said with a grin, "Look, Deloitte actually has a cell phone. Wonder of wonders."

"He does not look happy to use it, though," the ambassador undiplomatically added.

.G.

At 6:45, Mallory pulled up to the Soho address of Normans' studio. She was still mad at him for calling her employer and divulging what she had told him in confidence. But Deloitte's generous offer to celebrate the good news softened her ire. She'd gotten her hair done and a manicure because one does not have drinks with one's chairman of the board and her struggling artist boyfriend without looking tip top. All through her primping, she'd bitten her tongue as she conformed to the terms of the deal, not to disclose anything to anyone before it was made public. But it had killed her not to share this tastiest piece of gossip with her girl at the salon and all the other ladies who were endlessly bragging and gossiping.

Russell came out of the converted warehouse, which served as a commune for struggling artists in this famous part of London. She could see he was wearing his best t-shirt for the occasion. She was about to chastise him when she thought twice about it and reasoned, *he's charmingly esoteric* . . . a phrase someone had said of him and his work at her office. And now, thanks to her introducing him to her firm, one of his works just sold to a Middle Eastern collector for over twenty-five million pounds. That was incredible, more so because she never thought his work was really all that good; but he was cute and liked to paint portraits of her, including some of the more "intimate" studies of her as well. Tonight, though, he was a cute millionaire with a tight butt. Her smile dissolved as she noticed the man carrying a small tote who exited the building with Russell. She also saw the rather grim expression on his face.

The man opened the door and nodded his head for Russell to get in.

"Russ, who's your friend?"

"He's not my friend. You better do whatever he says . . ."

The man got in the backseat and brandished the .38 caliber gun in his pocket and said, "Drive."

.G.

Out on the country road he had directed them to, he tapped her on the shoulder. "Turn off the road here."

"What? Here?"

"Yes. Just do it!" He placed the gun at the back of her head for emphasis.

"Okay, okay."

The car rolled to a clearing amidst the trees. It was a moonless night, so once the headlamps were extinguished it was pitch dark.

The man turned on the car's dome light. "Now, you take your top off."

"What?" Mallory said.

"I am not going to ask you again. And you, take your pants down. Underwear too."

"What's this . . . ?" Normans said.

"Look, I told you no talking or I'll kill both of you right this instant."

Mallory opened her blouse and, using her arms as cover, got her top off without surrendering too much modesty.

"Off with the bra."

She shook as his request rattled her. She slid off her white lace bra. Covering her breasts with her hands. Tears welled up in her eyes.

Russell had his pants and boxers down around his knees.

"Now the panties . . ."

"You want me to take my knickers off? Why?"

"Are you too stupid to realize what I am going to do to both of you with this gun if you don't do to everything I am asking you to do . . . without talking?" He jutted the gun into the side of her breast this time.

She gasped at the sting of cold steel.

"Okay, now you, get on his lap facing him. Come on, you know how it's done."

"Why are you doing this?" Mallory cried as she fumbled to get her leg up and over Russell.

"I like to watch . . . Now get on with it."

Russell was shaking like a leaf and Mallory was crying so hard her nose was running. Her makeup ran down her face. She averted her gaze from the man with the gun and looked at Russell with fearful, questioning eyes.

"I can't . . . I can't do this," Russell said.

"I know. Here, both of you breath this in." He held up a rag he had just soaked with ether, opening a window as he did. "Breathe in fast; you won't have a headache later."

"What is this?"

"Don't worry, it will help you, like ecstasy."

Cautiously they both breathed in as the nozzle of the man's gun was between them. In ten seconds, Mallory fell back against the dashboard. Russell slumped in his seat. They were out cold.

The man in the backseat got out. He reached into his satchel and pulled out a rock, a jagged affair that came to a point at one end, then went under the chassis of the car.

.𝔊.

In two minutes, Paul had the hose from the exhaust coming around to the partially opened window of the driver's side. A towel from his satchel plugged the opening. The car was running. He looked at his watch. *Ten minutes should do it.*

He took the pointy rock and threw it far away from the car, into the woods.

Chapter 12

Lone Wolf Among The Flock

"It's a shame. She has such nice breasts," Constable Garret said as he processed the scene. It was indeed a sad sight; two young people, in the throes of lovemaking, taken off the planet by a hole in the car's exhaust.

"Probably caused by a rock they hit on the road that bounced up and perforated the pipe," the other investigator opined while clapping the dirt off his hands as he got up from under the car, "... based on the shape and mica residue around the pierced pipe."

Garret looked down at the woman's wallet. Her company ID said she worked at an art brokerage house on Savile Row and the man looked like a musician or some other microbe on the government dole, he wagered. The kind of patchouli oil smelling stray his own daughter might drag home to her flat. "They should have gone the hundred quid for a room," Garret said, writing their epitaph

.G.

At the same time as the discovery of the asphyxiated couple in the car, Deloitte was at his desk feeding the Normans folder into the shredder. The entire record of the temporarily inflated transaction, and his firm's 2.5 million pound commission, now harmlessly dropped into the waste bin in long, spaghetti-like strands. Looking down at the multi-colored tendrils, he mused to himself that the pile of trash had more of an artistic motif to it than this "artist's" best canvas. He then doubled checked that the catalog price of the late Russell Normans' dreaded piece had been reset to its initial hundred-pound price point.

.𝔊.

"Julius Valente to see Brooke Burrell-Morton," the trim man in the Burberry trench coat said as he handed his card to the receptionist at the Treasury headquarters in Lower Manhattan.

"Burrell-Morton . . . Burrell-Morton. Yes, she's here today in the temp offices. Just a second."

Julius looked around as the woman dialed the extension. He wasn't surprised the woman didn't immediately know who Brooke was as she was only on temporary assignment with Treasury and normally worked out of the offices that she had commandeered at Prescott Capital Management.

"Oh wait, here she comes now, I think . . . Ms. Burrell? Ms. Burrell, this is Mr. Valente, here to see you."

.𝔊.

Brooke hated being blindsided, especially in a lobby when she was running late. The man looked official enough. He was around five ten with well-coifed, more-salt-than-pepper hair, carrying a very expensive briefcase, and wearing Bruno Magli shoes. Still, it irked her to not know who he was before they met. She extended her hand. "Brooke Burrell-Morton. How can I help you?"

"I guess you're just coming in to work now?"

"I guess you have a reason for asking that?"

"I'm sorry, I just meant that Warren Cass said he would send you a heads up before my arrival."

"That's a name that gets you a backstage pass." She turned to the security guard at the desk in the lobby. "Sheila, is it?"

"Shelly, Director."

"Sorry, Shelly, could you give Mr. Valente here an 'A' visitor's pass?"

In the elevator Brooke asked, "Where are you out of, Mr. Valente?"

"Julius, please. And I am usually in DC, but as soon as we are in a secure place I'll explain what I thought Warren had already told you."

"Fair enough."

Brooke wrangled a secure conference room on the seventh floor. She closed the door and turned on the interlocking signal-jamming and shade-closing "Remo" switch. In three seconds, the room was isolated from prying eyes, ears, radios, the Internet, and satellites.

Valente handed her his gold-leafed card. "My card, Mrs. Burrell-Morton."

"Please, Julius, that's a mouthful. Just call me, Brooke."

"The secretary has asked me to join your investigation, now that it has been extended, and you'll be working more closely with the department. I have worked extensively with Treasury in the past and might be able to help you navigate some of the bureaucratic maze," Valente said.

Brooke sat silently; she took in the measure of Mr. Valente. She remained silent. It was becoming uncomfortable. Still, she held her silence.

Finally Valente broke the stillness. "I assure you, I am in no way here to intrude or monitor your investigation."

A small smile escaped Brooke's lips. "And yet that's exactly what I'm thinking." She hit the "Remo" switch and the green-lit "SECURE" indicator in the center console flashed "UNSECURED" in red, meaning the room was vulnerable to electronic eavesdropping and hacking. There was a clunking sound that connected the phone. It was a dead switch and an old mechanical relay, not digital. It physically broke the wire connection so that no one could hack it or use the wires to listen in. It was old-style "tech" blocking cutting-edge hacking and eavesdropping techniques. "Sweet" was how she remembered Peter Remo, the super geek and science whiz, describe it. He'd created them for the government after the Hammer of God affair, to take any system immediately off-grid.

Peter Remo lives in New York was the thought that momentarily flashed through her mind then was immediately replaced by the task at hand. She punched a phone number into the now-connected conference call phone in the middle of the table. As the speaker phone rang on the other end, she looked Valente in the eye. He never flinched. She respected that.

"Secretary's office. Mrs. Pretiger speaking."

"Sally, Brooke in New York. Is he in?"

"Hi, Brooke, sure. He's just finishing up a call. Can you hold a second?"

"Sure thing. How's your sister?"

"The cesarean knocked her out, but the baby's doing fine in the incubator."

"It must have been a tough call, but it sounds like she made the right choice."

"It was scary there for a minute, what with the car accident wracking her body like that."

"Still, saving the baby was a risk she'll be glad she took."

"I think so too, Brooke. Thanks for asking. By the way, you're coming in on the headquarters line; not uptown today?"

"I'm here just for the morning . . ."

Sally then put the call on hold.

Valente had a slight look of amazement on his face. Brooke just looked at him blankly.

"Why are you calling the Sec Tres?" Valente said.

Just then Mrs. Pretiger got back on the phone. "I'm connecting you now, Brooke."

"Brooke. What can I do for you this morning?" Cass was being very courteous.

"Mr. Secretary, you can start by telling me why you think you need to have me bird-dogged."

"What are you talking about?"

"Your old classmate you sent along to babysit me . . . judging from the Harvard '67 ring that he is now self-conscious of."

Valente caught himself turning his hand over to hide the ring.

Brooke opened up the throttle. "Warren, if I have lost your trust, then I am fine with packing it in and heading back to my life in Hawaii that was already in progress."

.𝔊.

In his office, Warren Cass shifted in his seat. Then he stopped as if Brooke could see him. "Brooke, I assure you, I asked Julius to assist you because now that your investigation has been derailed . . . a little . . . I thought you might need an extra hand, somebody I trust . . . to . . ."

"So you don't trust me?"

"No, Brooke, that's not what I meant . . ."

"Sir, you can't . . . you shouldn't be forced to work with anyone you don't trust. Why don't I just get on the next plane back to Pearl? I'll even rescind my contract at the end of the month. You'll be able to assign someone who has your confidence and the world will go on."

Cass began to sweat. He tapped his chest as the acid was rising in his esophagus. If she were indeed a direct line to the president, he'd know about this in five minutes. Mitchell would suspect he had flushed her to keep him in the blind. Although this investigation was serious, it was not the sole focus of the Treasury. He still needed his boss's, the president's, confidence on a host of initiatives to keep his signature on the new dollar bills they printed every day. He looked across the street, at the side of the White House his windows faced. He popped off the top of his pill bottle and popped another H2 blocker. He'd promised his wife Italy. More correctly, Ambassador to Rome when his cabinet post was up. James Mitchell had agreed to the deal. He couldn't risk that, certainly not for Julie. "Brooke, I am sorry you took this whole thing the wrong way, but you do have my confidence. Is Julius there now?"

"Yes, sir." She nodded to him.

"Warren . . ." He spoke up.

"Julius, thank you for your time. I can see your services will not be needed. Thank you for flying up today. Call me next week. The bass are still biting in Lake Wawasee!"

"Absolutely, Warren. No problem."

"Brooke, carry on. Keep me apprised of any new developments."

"Will do, sir."

.G.

She ended the call, looked at Valente and snapped her fingers. "Damn, I almost got out . . ."

"You don't want to do this?"

"Nothing personal, Valente, but this investigation was screwed from the inside. Somebody leaked to Prescott. Now I am scrambling to clean up internal Treasury crap while trying to uncover a terrorist money pipeline. That's got me looking in two directions at once. Not a good tactical situation to be in. You would have been a third distraction as I would have been forced to practice bureaucratic etiquette in your presence, and I don't have time for that shit."

"I understand completely."

"Good. Do you mind if I don't walk you out?"

"No, I can see you have a full plate. I'll let myself out."

"Thank you."

He got up and, at the doorway, turned and added, "Good luck and, for what it's worth, I think Warren has the right person heading this up." He turned and let the door close.

Brooke sighed. *Too bad.* She really liked this guy. She decided to keep his card.

.G.

Warren Cass sat there. A Cheshire grin was emerging on his face. His catspaw diversion worked. He hated to have used his old friend Julie like that, but the old boy played his part well, if unaware. His man on the inside of Brooke's team would have clear reign now that she'd found the "paw" he'd wanted her to find, satisfying her curiosity. His cell rang. He recognized the number and expected the call. "Julie, sorry to have made you come all that way."

"She's nobody's fool, that one."

"Never said she was, but I get your drift."

"She's really sharp, Warren, too sharp to cut herself on a scandal, if you ask me."

"Duly noted, but I will keep my guard up in any case."

"So about my contract?"

"Look, Julie, how about we call it a month and you take the next twenty-nine days off?"

"Works for me, Warren. See ya at the lake in Indiana?"

And with that little eighty-seven thousand dollar consolation prize, Cass said, "Talk soon," and hung up. Then he hit the intercom. "Okay, Sally, have my wife come in."

Cass got up and walked to the door. His wife Sharon entered and he hugged her. "Sorry, Honey, I was just finishing up an important call. How was your flight?"

"Fine, I slept for seven hours. Margie took a car straight from the airport so I came right here."

"You two have a good time?"

"Yes. I think she found a lot of good items for her little shop. Especially in Amsterdam. It was a very productive trip."

"Good, I'm glad it went well. Let's have a welcome home dinner tonight at Mario's."

"Ahh, you know I love that. Usual time?"

"Should be no problem; light day today."

"Good." She hugged him. "I'll let you get on with your day, dear." She turned to leave.

"Ah, ah."

"Oh, right." She reached in her purse. "I almost forgot."

She handed him a pill bottle with ninety of the H2 blockers that weren't available in the US. Lately, they were the only things that made his ulcer manageable. The eleven other bottles were packed away in her luggage.

.G.

Secretly meeting in a music rehearsal studio was very effective. Each cell member came from a different place and left separately. There were over two hundred rehearsal spaces like this in Manhattan alone, so they never had to frequent any establishment more than once. The early morning text that announced the location for that day to the nine members was innocuous enough: *351 w 130 f 105 r 106 @ 1600*. The cell member simply subtracted 100 from every number so the meet was at 251 West 30th Street Floor 5, Room 6, at 1500 hours, or 3:00 p.m.

When Paul arrived the eight other members were already there. After the noise was switched on, Shamal made his presentation on the elevations and topography of the area just above the Bronx. When the meeting was finished, earlier than the two hours booked, Dequa asked Paul to stay.

As the others filed out, the next band entered the room.

"I'm sorry, gentlemen, but we are still using the room," Dequa said in a tone that clearly wasn't a musician's timbre.

"Sorry, dude," was all the guitar player with the pierced eyebrow said as he backed out of the room and shut the door.

"Yes, Dequa, what is it?"

"First, if you are going to sit behind the drums, take these." He took a pair of drumsticks out of his case and handed them to Paul.

"Thank you."

"There is something else," he said as he meticulously coiled the wires from each set of headphones.

"What?"

"There is 7.5 million missing from the Denver transfer."

"That woman, the spinster from the bank . . ." Paul said.

"Do not," Dequa said dismissively. "Paul, I understand you are not born to the faith."

"But Dequa, I converted, freely of mind and spirit and . . ."

He raised his hand. "Enough. I do not judge you or your faith. That is for Allah to judge, praise be unto Him. Again, your belief may not be as strong as your lust for material things; this is of no consequence to me. But the money will be deposited within seventy-two hours or you will find your throat slit from ear to ear."

Paul attempted to protest.

"Enough."

The men left the room in silence.

Out on Eighth Avenue, Paul walked aimlessly. He was trying to decide what to do. He could kill everyone in the cell. Then kill off his own identity and surface in Australia, Bora Bora, or the Dominican Republic. He had safe houses in each of those countries. Dequa was right; he wasn't in this for the glory or the virgins at the end of the highway to heaven. *Stay or go?* To stay would cost him 7.5 mil, but he was in line for ten million for his part in the cell after the attack. Except, the chance of survival with the cell was ten percent; well maybe fifty percent with his own personal escape plan that he'd put in place. He weighed the numbers: *the 7.5 now or maybe live to get the full ten mil.* Either way it was far less than the 17.5 million he had planned on.

"Fuck it," the American-born jihadist uttered out loud as he crossed Forty-Second Street on the way to the Port Authority bus terminal. "I'll kill 'em all."

On the New Jersey transit bus to Hoboken, where he had a one-bedroom apartment in the lively college town that many considered the sixth borough of New York, he hatched a plan. His guitar case! He could hide an AK-47 in there and at the next meeting, shoot them all in the soundproof room. Leave early and have at least a two-hour head start before the bodies were even discovered. Forty-five minutes to JFK by cab, twenty minutes through security, 9:15 to Punta Cana . . . He could be in the DR three hours after the bodies were discovered. Perfect.

Chapter 13

Killer Rehearsal

The weight of the AK-47 made the guitar case heavier than usual. It made a thunk as he hoisted it up onto the overhead luggage rack of the NJT bus in Hoboken. None of the other passengers noticed the pronounced thud that wouldn't normally be associated with a lighter Fender bass guitar. As the bus entered the Lincoln Tunnel, he reached into his shirt pocket and double-checked the airline ticket: One-Way. Punta Cana. Departing JFK Terminal Five at 9:45 p.m. tonight. He had paid the fee for extra legroom that also gave him a breeze way through security and first boarding. The plane would be buttoned up and sealed before the rehearsal room door was knocked on as a five-minute warning preceding the next band that rented the room for ten o'clock sharp. They would find the eight bodies and never realize there was a ninth that had escaped. Especially since he had his strategy down pat. The .38 caliber snub nose, which was also in the case, being the key.

First, he'd ask one of the other men to sit behind the drums tonight. A band could have many guitar and keyboard players, but usually only one drummer, so he needed someone to die at the drums so as not to raise any suspicions. At 8:05 p.m., he would have to shoot fast. First he'd shoot Dequa in the head with the revolver then immediately spray the rest of the men in the room with the machine gun. He knew that the studio's soundproofing ensured that no one would hear the shots. After the shooting, he'd wipe down the rifle and put it in Dequa's hand, so his would be the only finger and palm prints on it. Then he would wrap Shamal's hand around the similarly cleaned snub nose. Orienting his body in the direction of Dequa. The police would deduce that Dequa went homicidal crazy and Shamal got a shot off, killing Dequa while he was dying. With everybody dead, he'd then don the hat and sunglasses Dequa always used when coming in and out of the rehearsal studio. Anyone who cared, which was a low probability, would just think the guy who'd booked the room for cash was leaving early. No one in the place knew or cared how many other musicians were in the room and so there was no record or head count of whom was in the studio in the first place. With the iPod running for two hours, all would seem and sound normal as people walked by.

Escaping to Punta Cana was a double precaution because there could be others, unknown to him, who were associated with the cell. And if his body weren't in the room, those others, if they existed, would look to find him and behead him.

The bus pulled into the Port Authority terminal. It was 7:40 p.m.

.𝔊.

"Anything else, Brooke?" George said, poking his head into her office.

Brooke looked up from her piles of printouts and glanced at her watch. "Wow, is it quarter to eight already?"

"Time flies when you are . . ."

"Not having fun . . ." She turned one of the large books of printouts around to face him. "Actually, George, can you look at this?"

George came in and placed his coat on the other chair in front of her desk and sat.

"Here's the PCM general ledger from last month. There are three figures here, each followed by a code number. That code number isn't in the index."

"Hmmm, 14TGG . . . Nope, that's a new one on me, too."

"It's out of format too; the codes are usually alpha numeric, two and two."

"This is two numerics, followed by three alphas. I never saw this kind of expenditure code while I was undercover here," George said.

"As far as I can tell, it adds up to 15.7 million. Anything on the T&E reports?"

"Yeah, at some point prior to our raid, somebody pulled the actual receipts from the forty-first floor stack. But we have been going through the American Express, MasterCard, and Diner's Club statements of all the executives down to the MD level to find corresponding expenses in those cities where we know transfers were made."

"If a managing director was the go-between how would he or she cover their tracks?"

"They are the work horses here. It's the higher ups that can lollygag on a golf course or Amazon River cruise and do the slow seductive dance to land a deal. But MDs are in the thick of it. Someone once suggested adult diapers for MDs because they calculated that pee breaks cost the company 1.1 million on average."

"Talk about pissing money away . . ." Brooke said.

"Nah, for my money, MDs don't figure into this; it's got to be a forty-first floor guy."

"Or gal!" Brooke said rifling through the Prescott roster of employees.

"Sorry, of course. I didn't mean to be chauvinistic . . ."

"No, not that. I mean, here, here she is. Cynthia Davidson, CCO," Brooke read the name at the tip of her finger on the needlessly small, ten-point-sized list of officers of the company.

"Oh right, sure. She's chief compliance officer. She'd certainly know."

"Find her, George."

"Tonight?"

"No, George. I'm beat. Let's call it for tonight."

He got up, grabbed his coat, and threw a casual, friendly salute and walked out. When he reached the street, he made a call he couldn't make in the office.

.𝔊.

Paul got on the elevator with a crush of musicians, many with guitar bags slung over their shoulders knocking into everyone else on the way in and as they settled in the elevator car. They were all trying to get to their various rehearsal rooms before eight. Paul got off on the sixth floor and found room 5, as the "*R105*" part of this morning's text indicated.

By one minute after eight, everyone was in the room including a face he had not seen before. He had asked Yusuf to sit behind the drums tonight and handed him the sticks. Dequa passed out the headsets and started the rehearsal tape playing loudly through the room's thunderous PA speaker system. Through the headsets, Dequa welcomed Ramal.

So this was the guy in Bolivia, Paul thought. *Too bad you picked tonight to show up.* He patted his guitar case and checked his watch. *Three minutes to go.* Paul hefted his case onto his lap and opened the latches.

One of the men spoke up, addressing the new face. "You are here to report on Bolivia?"

"No," Dequa jumped in. "Actually, Ramal has been in Elkhart, Indiana."

"Dunlap, actually, Dequa."

Paul's head pounded.

"Ramal is in charge of our internal security. After disposing of a loose end in Bolivia, he went to Indiana to ensure a certain package will get delivered." Dequa looked right into Paul's eyes.

Paul closed the latches on the case and nodded.

The meeting continued without incident.

.G.

The next day Paul was at the Merchant's Bank as the doors opened at 8:00 a.m. He went inside and in the name of Harry Wilson—his real name—of Dunlap, Indiana, transferred 7.5 million dollars from his private account into the same main account to which he and Marsha had transferred the other 67.5 million the week before. When it was done, he called his sister Eunice, who lived with his mom and her three kids back in Dunlap, just to see how they were doing.

Chapter 14

14TGG

11 DAYS UNTIL THE ATTACK

"There's a mister Peter Remo on line two," the voice on the intercom announced.

Brooke looked at the phone. Her eyes wandered. She was about to speak, but hesitated.

"Shall I put him through?"

"Actually, I am on a conference call on my cell. I can't take any calls right now," she lied. She immediately felt guilty, which caused her to pick up the receiver and hit 0. "Okay, I'll take the call . . ."

"He's already off the line. He left a number . . ."

"I'll get it later." She reflexively let out a sigh of relief. Then she caught herself. Why was she feeling guilty? It was a nonsensical emotion for her to experience. She'd done nothing wrong . . . yet.

"George would like a word."

Happy for the distraction, she overreacted. "By all means, send him on in."

George popped his head through the door smiling. "I got her!"

An hour later, Brooke and George were up in Westchester County, at the Bronxville home of Cynthia Davidson, who was the chief compliance officer at Prescott Capital Management. Her lawyer was also there.

Josh Wasserman was a crack attorney out of a big, white-shoe law firm. An office CCO at a hedge fund could bring in seven figures a year, so she could afford the best.

Brooke took out the small voice recorder, which she had planned to use to make sure she had an accurate record of the interview.

But before she started it, Josh put his hand over it and laid out the ground rules. "Nothing contained herein, no testimony that my client will give, is admissible in court and/or in any proceedings directed against her. Furthermore, in exchange for this cooperation, my client shall receive immunity from any and all crimes, misdemeanors or regulatory infractions, if any, are deemed to have occurred. Sign here please."

He slid two copies of the same statement that he just read over to Brooke, who scanned and signed both.

He then slid them over to George. "If you would sign as a witness in the space provided."

Wasserman collected the papers and, making sure it was all correct, placed one in his briefcase and handed the other one to Brooke. "For your records."

The interview started with the usual questions. "Is your name Cynthia Davidson . . . ? Do you reside . . . ? Did you work at . . . ? Did you know . . . ? Were you aware . . . ?"

Then Brooke took out a copy of the page from the ledger. "Cynthia, have you ever seen this accounting code before?"

Cynthia took one look at the three circled identical codes on the page, then brought her lawyer in close and whispered something in his ear.

"May we have a minute?"

"Sure." Brooke clicked off the recorder, collected her evidence book and she and George got up and left the room.

.G.

Out in the hallway, Brooke looked at some of the framed pictures on the wall.

"George, look at this."

"That's very interesting."

Brooke took out her phone and took a picture of the photo hanging on the wall. "Darn, the flash was on." She looked at what she had taken and it was just a big white spot in the glass of the picture frame. She swiped off the flash and reshot the photograph. Then popped a few more of all the photos on the wall for good measure. Josh stuck his head out and invited them back into the room.

Brooke pointed to the ledger sheet again. "Can you tell us what this code stands for?"

Cueing off the nod from her lawyer Cynthia explained, "One-four-tee-gee-gee stands for, 'one for the good guys.'"

"What does that mean?" Brooke was a little surprised at the informal denotation.

"Whenever there was an expenditure that, how can I put this, was recompense for someone whose time sheet didn't reflect the actual amount of time they invested in a deal, a board member and a few others we authorized released funds as a bonus or way of compensation for off-sheet devotion and/or saving a deal."

"Could it be entertainment?" George said.

"Well, yes."

"So for instance, if a deal was made over dinner and maybe clinched by a bottle of double malt, then the eighteen-year-old single malt would be a 14TGG charge?"

"Well, as an example, yes," Cynthia said.

"Fifteen point seven mil is a lot of booze," Brooke said.

"That's why I used the word *example*. No one except for the authorizer knew what the 14TGG was for. We never questioned it. It all happened above my level."

The questioning continued for another hour. When they were leaving, George asked one last question. "Cynthia, have you ever gotten any 14TGG money."

Brooke noticed that she must have felt a sudden chill, because she wrapped her sweater more tightly around her shoulders and looked to her counsel.

"We are still under immunity, correct?" the lawyer said.

"Of course," Brooke said.

"Well, this house," Cynthia answered.

For the second time in an hour, Brooke was surprised. She took her seat again and everyone followed suit as she turned the recorder back on.

Chapter 15

Setting the Mousetrap

Reviewing the transcripts from the recording she made of Cynthia's interrogation, Brooke confirmed her suspicions that an off-the-books slush fund of a major hedge house was somehow the conduit for funneling millions to terrorist front groups around the globe. But the nagging question was why? The stated goal of most terrorists was the disruption of capitalism with its forced democracy and blasphemous multicultural cooperation. That's why they hit London as soon as they were awarded the 2012 Olympics; it was a blow against multiculturalism. A hedge fund would be practicing suicide by inviting in a sworn enemy like ISIS and cozying up to radical fundamentalists. For the terrorist's part, they would certainly take Satan's money, but a hedge fund would have no reason to . . .

"A Mr. Remo on line two."

Brooke looked at the phone. She couldn't put this off any longer. She hit the blinking light. "Peter! How nice to hear from you . . . Everything's fine. Yes, he's doing quite well, thanks for asking . . . I'm here helping out Uncle Sam . . . For about three months now . . . Time does fly . . . Tonight? . . ."

She bit her bottom lip. She fluffed some papers on her desk a little too loudly. "Let's see, I can make drinks at 5:30 but I have a 7:30." She waited for him to decline. "Oh, okay then 5:30 at Harry's? See you then."

She hung up and felt a pang of guilt, but she couldn't live the rest of her whole life avoiding her past because she was married now. Her fling with Peter had been over well before she met Mush. However, she and Peter had worked together on a few really big and dangerous cases. So in her mind, she relegated her acceptance of Peter's invitation for drinks as just getting together with a workmate to swap old war stories, and that eased the case of the "guilts" she was having.

She dug back into the transcript but it only lasted a few seconds. She picked up her cell and swiped through her contacts. "Hello. This is Brooke Burrell . . . er . . . Brooke Morton," she said, correcting herself out of guilt. "Can Tina fit me in for a blowout at 4:30?"

.G.

A horse must have thrown a shoe, Warren Cass thought as he nudged the iron crescent with the tip of his riding boots, outside the paddock area of his ranch in the Maryland countryside. Here, away from his Federal Protective Service 24/7 security detail, he could speak freely on a private cell phone without concern of being overheard, except by Thunder, the beautiful, fifteen-hands-tall Arabian who was grazing to his right. He was listening to the New York lawyer, Josh Wasserman, recount the meeting between Cynthia and Brooke. Josh was being paid by him, "off budget," to represent Cynthia. More accurately, the taxpayer's hard-earned dollars were being put to good use protecting the Treasury secretary's reputation.

Warren had met Cynthia years back when she was the diligence officer of a small startup fund. They'd had some grand times together and it was she who'd introduced him to Morgan Prescott. Whatever Prescott was mixed up in, which he was duty bound as Secretary of the Treasury to uncover, he knew in his heart that Cindy, as he called her, would never be a party to it. His faith in her was in no way connected to the fact that he'd worn a wedding band all during his dalliances with the "madam of diligence." But that had been twenty years ago . . .

"So what do you think they believe they have discovered?" he said, patting the rare black coat and mane of the warm animal in the chilled air of dusk. He listened as Josh gave his take on what he thought they were after. When the call ended, he chided himself for not remembering that Cindy had reached out to him, her old fling, four years back when he'd been head of the Office of Management and Budget for the last president. She'd made a case for Prescott on some loosening of trade regulations with a few countries on the "no-trade" list. Warren was able to pull some high-level strings and Prescott's deal flew through. The hedge fund head had to have made a couple hundred million on the deal. He had forgotten, or didn't know at that time, that Cindy's bonus for reaching out to him had been a new house.

He made a mental note to check his archives and emails from that time to make sure there was nothing more than the normal governmental intervention to help a US commercial endeavor in foreign markets. Making those overtures for American business was something that was actually in the best interest of the government to do. It just couldn't be because his old girlfriend/mistress had asked him to do it. He was sure there was no record of communication between them that existed. The Prescott emails and letters and eventual regulatory findings were now all a matter of public record, and had passed the smell test during his Senate confirmation to head up the Treasury. Still, he'd double check.

His stomach was doing cartwheels and as he walked back to the house for his medication, a light rain fell. He turned up the collar of his ranch coat and wondered how he'd managed to forget that business about Cindy's house but, at seventy-two, sometimes it was a miracle he remembered to zip his fly.

.G.

Feeling like a piece of meat in a kennel was not a new experience to Brooke. In the testosterone-laced environs of the Navy, and later in the FBI, she constantly had to overcome the assumption that, since she was attractive, she therefore couldn't really be serious about her job. To counter this all-too-common bias, she'd developed a speech pattern and behavioral modes that effectively put any thoughts that she was merely there for window dressing to rest. But the men here at Harry's, and a few of the women, checked her out as she walked in. It made her feel like a prize steer being led to slaughter. She dismissed the turning heads as nothing more than the fact that she was fresh meat in this place of after-work regulars. She walked over to the bar and found two seats. She looked around as she climbed on the stool but didn't see Peter.

.𝔊.

A sandy-haired stockbroker in a pinstriped suit with a loosened tie and holding a longneck beer set his sights on Brooke the second she sat down.

.𝔊.

From the corner of her eye, she saw him circling in for the kill. The bartender placed down a coaster and asked, "What'll ya have?"

"I'd love a Pinot Grigio."

"Coming up!" the bartender said and turned to start a tab.

"There is no reason for you not to think this is a line, and even as I'm saying it, I know it sounds like one, but . . . Do I know you?" the arriving prospect proffered.

Brooke looked straight ahead and purposefully not at him. "Yes it is. You're right. And no."

"Huh?"

She finally turned to him. "Yes, I think it's a line, you are right, it sounds like a line, and no you don't know me."

"Okay, but . . . I really do. I've seen you before." He took the liberty to rest an elbow on the bar, squeezing into the space between her and the next stool.

"And I've heard that one before, too."

He snapped his fingers and blurted out, "Prescott!"

Brooke's voice went from casual conversation to police command. "Whoa. Stop right there. What is your connection to Prescott Capital Management?"

"I used to work there. You showed up on the last day. You were by the elevator. You're a fed or something."

"Yes, what did you do at PCM?"

"Was that a fed question or pretty-blonde-in-a-bar question?"

"Was that an evasive answer or a pretty-boy-behind-bars answer?"

"Look, I'm sorry to bother you. I didn't know how I knew you . . ."

"Well, now you know. What's your name?"

"Um, I really should get back to my buds over there."

"Are they ex-Prescott too?"

"I really got to go." He backed away and almost knocked over a poor waitress with a tray full of drinks.

Brooke was smiling when Peter came up beside her. "Well, you seem like you are in a great mood."

"Peter!" They hugged and he took the seat next to her.

"Well, Brooke, I have to say you look great. Married life seems to definitely agree with you."

"Thank you, Peter. It is pretty sweet."

"So is Mush here with you?"

"No, he's working."

"Oh."

Brooke was mildly shocked. "You seem disappointed?"

"Well, a little."

"Explain."

"I was hoping to have a chat with him."

Brooke let out a laugh that surprised Peter.

"What's so funny?" he said.

"Nothing . . . I'll tell you later . . . maybe." The bartender made his way back to their end of the bar with her wine. Brooke nodded to him and turned to Peter. "What are you drinking, Mr. Remo?"

Thirty-five minutes later, they were seated at a table. Peter was turning a glass by the stem between his fingers as he recounted his current project. "So I was hoping that your sub-driver husband would help me with some final details."

"I'm sure he'd love to help, as soon as he gets back. I'll ask him to call you." The time being two wines later than a half-hour ago, Brooke laughed again.

"Okay, lady, there's some kind of little funny thing bouncing around in your head. Are you going to let me in on it?"

"Oh, Peter . . . I was . . . I mean . . . Well, when you called, I thought, you know . . . You. Me. Our history."

"Okay, now I get it . . . Booty call?"

"Not as bad as that, but I definitely thought it was in that general direction." She began laughing again.

Peter feigned insult as he tried to control reflexively joining in the laugh. "Wait. What would be so funny about that?"

"Because you are so you!"

"What does that mean?"

"I'm almost feeling guilty coming to meet you, and all you want to talk about is IMF protection anagrams."

"EMP protection algorithms!"

"Whatever."

"So you are laughing to hide your female ego?"

Brooke stopped for a second. Considered his point. "I got to admit it's half relief and half a little disappointing that I didn't get to say no."

"See, it's exactly that kind of logic, or in this case lack of it, that makes Electro-Magnetic Pulse dynamics so much easier to understand than females."

Brooke glared at him, but couldn't hold it in and burst out laughing again.

Peter joined in and raised his glass. "To Impulse or EM-Pulse, whatever works. It's good to see you so happy, my friend!"

"To my friend. Thanks, Peter." They touched glasses and drank. "Wanna order something?"

Peter looked at his watch. "I thought you had a 7:30?"

"Well, that was another impulse, in case your impulse was the non-magnetic kind. Or wait . . . if there was a magnetic . . . attraction thing."

"Very good. Very funny, but hey, I'll always be attracted to you. But I'll always be your friend."

Brooke chewed on that statement. "Hold on, are you leaving a door open here?"

"No, I know you walked through a one-way door to get to the altar and, believe me, I am so happy for you. But I'll always have a special place for you and the sweet times."

"Paris."

"Yes, a few others."

"Wait, what others? We only spent one week together in France."

"Well, I got my own YouTube up here." He touched his temple. "Moments when I caught you being you. They are etched in my brain."

"I know I shouldn't ask, but like when?"

"Well, when we were working with Bill and I'd look over to you and you'd be taking in the crime scene, deconstructing it. The look on your face, the confidence, the way your eyes moved as if you could see it, watching the way it went down, like live TV in your mind. I fell for you more and more in moments like those."

"And all that time I thought you were just checking out my boobs."

"Didn't I mention all the while I was admiring you, it was happening right above the most ample . . ."

Brooke put her finger on his mouth. "Enough. My bad. I shouldn't have gone there." She pulled away her finger.

"AbleBodiedLawEnforcementOfficerIEverMet." He said it really fast to it get all in, in one word. Then smiled.

Brooke smiled, and raised her glass again.

He did likewise and added, "WithAGreatRack!" he sped through before he sipped.

"Peter!"

.G.

They were still telling stories and laughing when the waiter brought the dessert list.

"None for me."

Peter looked over the top of the menu. "Coffee?"

Brooke looked towards the waiter. "Better make it decaf." Then, to Peter, "Can't drink caffeine past three or I am walking the halls all night."

Peter turned from the menu to the waiter. "I see you have hot chocolate. I'll have one with extra whipped cream please."

"It's like I'm with a big kid. Cranberry and 7 Ups in wine glasses, hot chocolate, not even coffee . . ."

"I never got the drinking gene."

"I guess in the long run that's a blessing."

"And a curse. A lot of people don't trust someone who doesn't drink," Peter said.

"There are two sides to everything, I guess."

.G.

The sandy-haired broker, who had moved on to Shirley from accounting, glanced over and said under his breath, "Oh, she was meeting her dad!"

.G.

"So back to your job," Peter said as he found the raw sugar in the little silver holder that landed on the table.

"Temporary assignment," Brooke said, choosing not to acknowledge his sweeter-than-most sweet tooth.

"Noted."

"Again, what I can share with you is that at one level it doesn't make any sense. There's no greater sign of American capitalism than a hedge fund, yet why would one cooperate with those who are sworn to destroy the American economic system?"

"In the aftermath of 9/11, there were some very quickly silenced stories about a sudden movement of financial instruments. The shorting of airline stocks on 9/10, for instance."

"So you're saying ideology has nothing to do with it?"

"If I am a player, and I know something monumental is about to happen, I can make boatloads of income betting with or against it. Or being axed. You know, winning no matter which way it goes."

"No I don't know. Never heard of axe."

"I summer interned for my senior year at a trading house. That's when I thought my life was going to go that way. I soon found out they had a language all their own. The short-and-long game is classic. And you could make boat loads of cash . . . The key is knowing what's going to happen."

Brooke thought for a split second. "So if you knew two airlines were going to be used as weapons, and lose millions of dollars literally in one day . . ."

"Then shorting the stock makes you the genius of all time. Rich genius."

"Oh my god. So then funding an attack would give you that knowledge too," Brooke said.

"Yes. You would know when and where and make prudent market moves, or order 'put and call' contracts, accordingly, to trigger once the shit hits the fan."

"With that set up, a person could rake in a fortune without lifting a finger after the attack . . . At one level it's disgusting, but on another level it makes perfect sense."

"Business sense," Peter said.

.𝔊.

"Hey, Frank. Why don't you knock it off early? It is slow night, and there is no need for there to be the two of us to be working."

As usual, it took Frank a moment to untangle Yussie's mangled English, then he checked his watch: 11:20 p.m. Their shift ended at midnight. Since it was a temperate night, there would be no drains on the system and getting to the bar over in Woodside earlier meant a better chance to chat up some girl before the rest of the four-to-twelve shift invaded. And Yusuf was a pretty smart guy for an assistant substation technician. Frank suddenly had a stab of conscience. Yusuf was a scrawny kid who'd gotten a bad case of acne over in Egypt or Arabia or wherever the hell he was from, leaving his face scarred and pockmarked. That and the scrawny beard accounted for him and some of the guys at the plant calling him "the Terrorist" behind his back. But the kid was alright. "Thanks, Yusuf. I owe you one! You'll sign me out?"

"Sure, Frank, you go. You have good time."

"You're okay, Yussie!" Frank put on his jacket and put his blue Con-Ed hardhat on hook #37 where his coat was. Only Yussie's coat remained on the wall of hooks.

"See ya Monday!" Frank said as he swiped his FOB card to unlock the door.

.𝔊.

Yusuf had studied electrical engineering in Egypt then gotten his masters in France and went to work for the French. For a short time he'd worked at Électricité de France, then in 2006 he'd been transferred as Chief Engineer High Voltage Operations to their then new British subsidiary, EDF Energy, or as millions of Londoners knew it: the power company to which they paid their bills.

Yusuf took out his phone and texted a one-word message: *Clear*.

As soon as Yusuf landed in London he'd met a group of other immigrant workers that had a plan to strike a blow for the cause. Although the actual details were known only by a few and his part had been very small, he'd felt a surge of pride on July 7, 2005. Although all he'd done was deliver a package to an address on Kings Road. He'd always believed that package contained the detonators by which the bombs on the underground were set off. But he would never know. The cellular insulation that the support group had practiced could have meant his package was empty and five other men had delivered similar packages—one or more with the actual components. As an engineer, he well understood double redundancy and stress testing of systems. Whether he'd been the placebo or the actual deliverer was only an academic point, for all who were involved in the 7/7 attacks had served in the struggle against the Great Satan.

He was sure, however, his allegiance and loyalty had gotten him into this New York operations group of which he was now, definitely, a core member. Their meetings at the various music practice studios and the ingenuity of the plan meant certain glory for him and his cellmates.

His phone buzzed and the text message "*outside*" appeared.

.G.

"Peace be upon you, Dequa."

"His blessings on you, Yusuf. Show me the transfer switch."

They went into a large area, which hummed. There was a slight tickling sensation to the fine hairs on the skin, as the intense electrical field caused the iron in the hair and bloodstream to vibrate ever so slightly. Before them was something that at first looked like a great mousetrap. It was in fact a large relay. Its main function was to act as a circuit breaker to disconnect Manhattan and Queens from the national power grid in the event of a cataclysmic event . . . or so it was designed.

Next they went out into the transformer farm with the lights of Manhattan reflecting in the undulating waves of the East River just beyond its fence. At the side of the building lay many huge steel girders two feet wide and twenty feet long, for use in anchoring new or replacing old transformer footings.

"Will these be adequate?" Dequa said.

"Most assuredly."

Chapter 16

Offices and Meetings

10 DAYS UNTIL THE ATTACK

The following morning, after an evening of dinner and drinks with Peter Remo, Brooke knew two things for sure; one brought her relief the other raised her level of concern to new heights. First, that Peter Remo was not a threat to her marriage was a good thing, and that, to some extent, she wasn't tempted in any way to tease or test that fact gave her another notch on her self-esteem belt. However, the new thinking about Prescott's involvement in funding terrorists changed her day, investigation, and purpose. Now it was all about the question: Could Prescott actually have been hiring terrorists? That was a game changer.

And she learned one more thing: four glasses of white wine with a light dinner still gave her one bitch of a headache the next day. She'd forgotten what Mush had taught her to drink a glass of water with every glass of wine. It was how he avoided hangovers from clouding his command judgment the next day.

At 8:00 a.m. her team was assembled in the secure conference room. She started right in. "Good morning. Today I want to change the line of our investigation. Up to now we have been looking for some ideological sympathies by which to explain our suspicions that Prescott and his company's funds found their way to militant cells. Now I want us to invert the chart. Namely, did Prescott seek out terrorists, in effect engaging them to strike and using that information to buttress his positions in the market and take maximum profit from a man-made calamity?"

George was rolling the end of his pen around over his teeth as he rolled the new concept around in his head. "So in effect, look for active enlistment of bad guys to carry out Prescott's plan?"

"It may be the way to get what we know to line up better with a motive." Brooke had learned through her years with the FBI, and before that in the JAG corps, that you don't have the full story until all the parts line up. Sometimes looking at it another way, like walking around a pool table to see how the balls line up to a possible shot, suddenly lets you see the connections all the way to the pocket. She wanted her team to start looking at this from other angles.

"Jeannine, get me on the next plane out to DC and ask Secretary Cass for five minutes when I get there."

.G.

Looking out over the vast expanse of Central Park, Dequa felt a slight touch of vertigo from being sixty stories up. A police helicopter buffeted by, its rotor noise barely audible through the thick glass "walls" of this penthouse office. The copter was at the same level as his eyes. He turned away as a precaution, just in case they were taking photos or using long-range imaging to ID him. The butler appeared with his reflection shimmering in the black marble floors. He pointed up the semi-circular stairs that connected the first floor to the second level of the sixty-five million dollar duplex in the sky.

At the top, there was an office behind sliding glass doors that silently parted as he approached. Kadeem, a tall, serious man who had been Kitman's bodyguard forever, was on the other side and gestured for him to raise his arms. Knowing the drill, Dequa complied. After the security man patted him down, he stepped aside, allowing Dequa to enter the office.

There, in the large, sunlit, glass-walled office was the Desk. He thought of it often. It was a formidable piece, which hailed back to the Tsar Alexander. He wasn't sure if Kitman had purchased it or gotten it as a gift from a Russian oligarch. It surely weighed a thousand pounds, being crafted of rich, heavy ebony and mahogany wood with elaborate carvings and gold inlay. Yet, right in the middle of the surface, a flat, fifty-inch touch-screen computer was mounted into it, making a twenty-first century Windows desktop on the nineteenth century priceless desk's top. It was an atrocity to antiquity, yet its current owner, a "Tsar" of Wall Street, felt that since he owned it, he could desecrate it at will. Dequa sat in one of the chairs right in front of it and waited.

The wall to the right slid open and Mr. Kitman, or El-had Berani as he knew him in the mujahedeen, emerged from the small hidden room with the prayer rug on the floor. As he sat behind his desk, the wall silently closed without leaving a trace of an opening. "Chai?"

"Thank you for your kindness but I have had my tea for this morning."

"Then what do you have to report?"

"Our progress is right on schedule and much good fortune has come our way."

"So phase one is complete?"

"Yes and many elements of phase two are already in place, again, by His grace."

"Good, very good. So our date still holds?"

"Yes, phase three is still on track."

"What about the federal agents?"

"They have nothing. We were able to inflict the virus our Iranian friends didn't know they lent us."

"So you are confident that everything is erased and that destruction is total."

"In many ways, the Ayatollah would be proud, if he knew, that so far the best of the best of the American government's cyber experts can't retrieve what we have done. So they have no way to connect you or your company to Prescott."

"What about Prescott himself?"

"We still have our initial leverage."

"May this all indeed be a sign of our good fortune. Is there anything else?"

Dequa hesitated. "No . . . No, nothing else."

Kitman tried to figure out what was on his mind. "What is it, Dequa?"

Dequa looked around the office with all its capitalist trappings. He scrutinized the original artwork, sculptures, and busts that commanded small fortunes and in quantities that rivaled a museum's inventory.

Interspersed among the artwork on the walls were photographs of Kitman's yacht, private jet, and mansion in the Florida Keys.

Kitman followed his eyes. "Ah, you are concerned. Concerned that I have been seduced by all this," Kitman said, turning with his hands out.

"It is a far distance from the caves in Tora Bora."

"And I have shaved my beard and adopted western dress and speech, all in the name of the cause."

Dequa was well acquainted with the ways of taqiyya and kitman. That it was not deemed a sin to lie to one's enemies or to infidels. Then he looked at the wall behind which the prayer room was hidden and calmed himself. "I am not questioning your loyalty to the struggle, but are you sure you can give all this up when the time comes?"

"Last week, I was invited to Washington to attend an economic summit. I was twenty feet from the president. If the knives on the tables hadn't been plastic, I would have slit his throat before his guards could have shot me dead."

Dequa was immediately caught in a dilemma. Had Kitman actually assassinated President Mitchell on a whim—as strong a blow as that would have been—in order for it to have value, his ties to the cause would have needlessly been revealed. That would have compromised their current mission. And that mission would have a far more devastating and long-lasting impact than trading a replaceable president. For the attack they were on the verge of staging would ensure the fulfillment of scripture, of the caliphate itself. He chose his next words carefully. "It was the plastic that thwarted you? Not compromising our operational security?"

Kitman quickly amended, "Yes, of course, it was merely a momentary impulse, which I did not act upon exactly because it would jeopardize our grand event."

Dequa stood silent as he questioned himself. Had he pushed too far in questioning Kitman's resolve, causing him to recount that tale with more machismo and carelessness than one would demand of a leader? He decided not to press the issue but to make note of the impulse as a reminder that Kitman could, at some point if pressed, act out on impulse rather than follow the dictates of the supreme leader. "I understand the urge," Dequa said and he immediately witnessed a relaxing of tension from Kitman's face that he hadn't been aware of earlier.

"All of these trappings are the sheep's clothing in which I gain acceptance and rise above suspicion of the herd."

That analogy reminded Dequa that El-had was known as the Wolf. He had successfully decimated a Russian tank barracks by dressing the part of a Russian colonel and, once inside, killing thirty troops as they slept. Their seven T55 tanks had become useful tools against the very Russian invaders themselves, until the gas and artillery ammunition ran out. They'd used the last shell of each tank to disable the armored weapons when they'd finished with them.

"Is there any other damage from the Prescott matter?"

"A few loose ends, which will be trimmed by tomorrow, but nothing that could affect our ability to execute."

"Very well. Keep me informed."

.𝕲.

In her career, Brooke had taken the shuttle to DC a few hundred times. This time was different. This time she wasn't a subordinate, wasn't one of many working on a team; now she was the leader, heading up an op. At her new director-level status, the entire team worked for her.

This time she wasn't flying down to get guidance or approval, she was meeting with the Secretary of the Treasury to inform him of her change in investigative focus. As Brooke had found over and over again, nothing says total commitment and unassailable motives better than a face-to-face meeting. So even though it made a huge hole in her day, she deemed it worthwhile.

Somewhere between reading the reports from her field agents and the plane landing, she slipped off into a light nap. When the wheels hit the tarmac, she was jolted awake. A smile was on her face because in the REM phase of slumber she'd been on a beach in Hawaii with Mush.

.𝕲.

"Just a minute!" Cynthia called out, wondering why the doorbell had to ring right now. She wrapped her wet hair in a towel and threw on a robe. She looked for her slippers but couldn't find them, so she left wet footprints on the terracotta tile floor all the way to the stairs as she went down to the front door. She looked through the sidelight and saw it was a FedEx delivery person. "Sorry, I was in the bath." She signed for the package, and then realized she didn't have any money on her. "Hold on." She gently let the door remain ajar and went to the small telephone table by the door, opening the drawer she always kept tip money in. She counted out five bills and handed them to the deliveryman. "Thank you."

She rested the box on the secretary desk in the hall. She couldn't make out the sender's address. She used a letter opener and opened the small box. There was an envelope. She slit it open and read, "For the boat. A woman never has enough sunglasses." She was tickled to find Gucci sunglasses, Louboutin Flats sandals, and a lovely Hermès beach wrap carefully packed in pretty tissue paper. She sighed. "Oh, Paul. You are such a romantic." She actually danced her way upstairs to the bedroom with the box in her arms like it was Fred Astaire.

.G.

Since the Sec Tres' office didn't have a "Remo" switch, Brooke suggested that Cass meet her for a walk out on Fifteenth Street.

Five minutes later, Brooke and Cass were like tourists on the DC sidewalk.

"Okay, now why the spy novel tactic, Brooke?"

"There's a big leak, sir. At least out here we can speak freely."

"I don't like the insinuation that . . ."

"Sir, I have changed the course of my investigation. I no longer think Prescott was a part of the financing scheme. I believe now that they were actually the organizing element."

"You're saying Prescott deliberately financed terrorists?"

"Yes I am. I am no longer treating them as co-conspirators but as the initiator of the action."

"What would be the reason? Why would ISIS need the money? They are pulling in millions every day from captured oil fields. They could certainly fund any operation."

"Market manipulation."

The Sec Tres pondered the idea. "I see. If you can predict where, when, and how a major event inflicting damage on the country is going to occur you can use that knowledge to make prudent moves."

"Exactly. It fits the chatter and their own statements."

"How did you come to this?"

"The woman, Cynthia. She was a compliance officer but also kept the books. We stumbled over a code in the ledger. I believe that code was the slush fund. And furthermore, she knows it too. I want to offer her full immunity."

"You have that power. Why are you asking me?"

"Because I found this . . ." She held up her iPhone with the picture she had snapped of the framed photo hanging on Cynthia's wall that showed her, Cass, and Morgan Prescott on some kind of fishing trip.

Cass was stunned. Not so much in the revelation but in the deft way Brooke had, in one move, gotten what she wanted and pulled a power play over him. Yet, Brooke's move was shrewd in that it appealed to his survival instinct. With immunity, Cindy couldn't be pressured into revealing their relationship. "Sounds like the right move. But I assure you, Cynthia is in no way connected to me. As I remember, she was on that trip as a perk for some good work she had achieved."

"Well, all the same, sir. I wanted to give you the chance to tell me if there was anything more, before I proceed."

"No. No. There is nothing more." Cass looked out across Fifteenth, at the White House. He wondered if Brooke was going there next. He knew she was harboring a suspicion that he and Cindy were more than just casual acquaintances. *Damn, why do women hold onto emotional attachments like pictures* . . . That knowledge could be powerful if it was used against him. Of course, if he were able to get some dirt on her and her affair with the president, it could be a powerful bargaining chip, if it ever came to that. "Are you heading back to New York now?"

"Yes, sir."

"Well, keep me informed."

"Will do."

Cass walked back toward the Treasury building. He belched and it burned like fire. He took out his cell. "Sally, call the cafeteria and get me a glass of buttermilk. I'll be in, in five minutes." He then patted down his suit pocket for the H2 blocker pills he carried, just in case.

.𝕲.

Brooke took out her phone to get her driver to swing around and get her, when she noticed she had a text.

BROOKE YOUR OFFICE SAYS YOU ARE IN DC. GOT A MINUTE TO STOP BY? "A" PASS WAITING AT THE EAST WING PORTICO.

She called New York. "Move my flight to 4:30. I'll be at the White House with Bill Hiccock. Thanks . . . Okay, I'll deal with that when I get back to my office."

Chapter 17

Call Me Jim

Secretary of State Charles Pickering was sitting in Bill's office when Cheryl let Brooke in.

"Brooke! Perfect timing. You know Charles, right?"

"Of course, Mr. Secretary. How are you?"

"Jet lagged, but that goes with the job."

"Shame you can't rack up frequent flyer points."

"I'll mention it next time I testify before congress."

Bill smiled then drilled down to the reason for the impromptu meeting. "Brooke, Charles just passed along some disturbing news . . ." he said, extending his hand in an invitation for the secretary to take over and inform Brooke of his discovery.

"Well, it seems that some 'students' with FS-1 visas are missing. After 9/11 we tightened up our monitoring of foreign nationals involved in sensitive areas."

"What area are we talking about?"

"Electrical engineering. But these aren't students; they are actual engineers, in some cases doctors and PhDs in electrical and electronic systems."

"So they weren't here to work but to study?"

"Apparently, but they aren't at the institutions they are supposedly attending."

"And you think they've gone to ground?"

"Seems a definite possibility."

"Okay, so far it sounds like an INS problem; why are you reading me in on this, Bill?"

"My network. I ran the names and the specialties past my sources, and this is only preliminary, but something bad could be coming. The touch point of common connection between these men is Prescott. The case you are working right now."

The Sec State was surprised. "You are working with Cass, Agent Burrell?"

She decided not to correct him. She held an SES-6 and was now at a director's pay grade. "Yes, and his investigation into PCM."

He turned to Hiccock. "You are full of surprises, Bill."

"Sorry there wasn't time to fill you in on every detail. And just for the record . . ." Bill stopped talking because the president came through his door.

"Sorry to interrupt, Bill. Hi, Charles, Brooke . . . don't get up."

Everyone sat back down.

"I just wanted to ask Brooke to come see me when she's done here."

"Of course, sir," Brooke said, a little caught off guard by the unprecedented request.

"Good. Well, carry on." He closed the door as he left.

As they all looked at one another, Bill noted, "It's his house. If he wants to barge in, who in the free world is going to tell him he can't?"

"How did he know I was here?"

"You're kind of a rock star around here, Brooke. Last time you were in the house, the office buzz lasted for days. A lot of women and men here admire you. I am sure Shirley or Cheryl or Mrs. Gladstone were mentioning it and he overheard," Bill said.

"Wow. Okay, let's get back to bad things coming . . ." Brooke crossed her legs and placed her intertwined fingers on her knee as she listened.

When the meeting was over, she asked Bill if she could use his phone. She dialed her office. "Better move my flight to 6:30. And have that report in the car picking me up at LaGuardia . . . Will do." She hung up and turned to Bill. "Any idea why the boss wants to see me?"

"Haven't a clue. Did you screw up or something?"

"I'm sure if I did, I am going to hear about it."

"I'll have Cheryl tell Mrs. Gladstone you are ready to see him."

.G.

That afternoon at two different airports, JFK in New York and Heathrow in London, two women headed down to the Grand Cayman

Islands. One of them, Elanna, complete with another new set of sunglasses and sandals was all smiles, as she was again looking forward to another secret rendezvous with Paul or "Mr. Kiss-Kiss Hump-Hump Bye-Bye-Till-Next-Time," as she liked to think of him.

From JFK, Cynthia was all tingly with teenage expectations over her upcoming discreet tryst with the new man in her life.

.G.

Brooke had to wait until 5:15 to see the president. Because of the shift in time, the meeting was moved from the Oval to the residence. The president had a 7:00 p.m. speech so Mrs. Gladstone suggested he relax up in the residence. It was where he could literally loosen his tie and kick back before the evening's schedule. She knew out of deference to the office and the power concentrated within, the president always wore a tie and jacket and so did every other male in DC who entered the White House during his administration. His residence, however, was a work-free zone for the most part. She knew he could unwind and be casual up there.

Brooke was escorted to the East Wing elevator and noticed the first lady's staff was light today. "Is FLOTUS out of the house?"

"Yes, she's in Omaha with her staff."

Brooke was a little disappointed. Mrs. Mitchell was a delight and she and Brooke had a "girls" way of letting their hair down and talking about life and not politics.

Brooke was sitting on the divan in the residence when the president came in with Mr. Jeffries, the White House steward, in tow. "Brooke, want a drink?"

"Just a Perrier, maybe."

"Make that two, Mr. Jeffries." He turned back to Brooke. "Lime?"

"Perfect."

On cue, the president sat across from Brooke, loosened his tie, sighed, and accepted the drink from the steward after he served Brooke. The president gave Mr. Jeffries a look where his eyes swept towards the door, and the man excused himself and left.

"I was disappointed that Mrs. Mitchell isn't in."

"You two . . . You seem like you went to college together."

"She was very sweet to include me in many of her social functions when I was stationed here."

"Can I let you in on a little secret?"

Brooke felt the choice of words were funny coming from the commander in chief. "Sure."

"She looks up to you, Brooke."

"Noooo. The first lady is the one to look up to. She has achieved so much and addressed issues long ignored in America."

"Nevertheless, she admires you."

"I . . . I . . . don't know what to say, sir. I am humbled by that."

"You are a good woman, Brooke, an excellent agent and a fierce patriot. You have achieved much and saved this country, and my administration, more than a few times."

"I am part of a great team, sir. We all serve."

"Well you are a star on that team . . ."

"Thank you. Can we talk about anything else, sir?"

President Mitchell laughed. He took a swig of his drink. "Okay, let's talk about what I wanted to see you about. Now, I am going to start by saying this is in no way official and I want you to forget that I am the president. Just between us, man to woman, friends . . ."

Brooke's head was swelling; her ego had gotten quite a stroking in the last few minutes. "Sure, go ahead, sir."

"Up here, when it's just us, I think we can dispense with the formality."

"Ahhh, sure. What do I call you, sir? I mean . . ."

"How about Jim; that's what I used to be called."

"You've got to give me a minute here, sir . . . Jim. This is a little weird, you know."

"I think you are handling it pretty well . . ." He gave her the smile that won him the White House twice.

"Well, what's on your mind . . . Jim?" She was still rattled by the breach of protocol, but . . .

.G.

It was after midnight when she exited Butler Aviation, the private aviation side of LaGuardia Airport, in New York, and got into the interagency car that had been waiting since 7:45. Her briefing papers were on the backseat and she told the driver she had to stop by her office before heading home. She focused on the papers but found it hard as she kept replaying the evening with . . . Jim.

Chapter 18

Sweet Cheeks

9 DAYS UNTIL THE ATTACK

Secretary Cass read the morning report from Brooke. The new revelation that the State Department and, somehow, the president's man Dr. Hiccock may have linked Prescott Capital Management to student visa violations, and that there may be a darker reason for it all, prompted him to call his counterpart at State. "Charles, I am learning that some potential terrorists may have been flagged by your department."

"Yes, and literally by accident; Hiccock over at the White House found a possible connection to that investigation you have going on up in New York."

"That's uncanny. And do you think he's onto something?"

"Your gal, Brooke, did."

"Wait, you spoke to Brooke Morton?"

"Of course. She was in the room."

"When?"

"Yesterday."

"The White House?"

"Warren, where else?"

"Of course. I just thought she flew right back to New York after my meeting with her yesterday."

"I think that's when Hiccock got her to drop by. Good thing too. James stopped in and personally asked to meet with her after our meeting."

"Mitchell requested a meeting with her and Hiccock?"

"No, just her."

"Interesting. Well thanks for the heads up on these possible bad guys. You going to the reception for the Saudi Ambassador?"

"As head of State, it's unavoidable. Will I see you there?"

"Yes, I know his father."

"Good, then there'll be someone there to actually talk to."

"See you then, Charles."

"Look forward to it, Warren."

Although not quite paranoia, Warren had an unsettling feeling after he hung up. *Brooke went to the White House? She met with Mitchell? Right after she informed me about Cynthia? Inform or warn? Was the whole reason for her trip down here to threaten me?* He ruminated on those thoughts for a few seconds then hit the intercom. "Sally, get me Williams."

.G.

The presidential detail of the secret service occupied W16, a remarkably small office under the Oval in the White House. Many times, the head of the detail, Brent Williams, answered the phone himself. "PDS."

"Brent, it's Sally. He wants to speak with you. Hold on."

"Brent, I was wondering if you have a minute to come over. I need to discuss something with you."

"Yes, sir. The boss is in the house so it's a little quiet here. I'll be there in fifteen?"

"Fine."

.G.

By 10:00 a.m., Brooke had lines of probability on the whereabouts and activities of four of the eight suspects she'd learned about yesterday at the White House. She buzzed George on the intercom. "George, call Wasserman. I want Cynthia in here on the double; maybe she has a memory of these 'students.'"

Brooke's intercom beeped. "There's a Mr. DeMayo and a Mr. Remo to see you, Director Burrell."

Brooke smiled; Jeannine not calling her Brooke meant the men were standing in front of her. Brooke liked that level of respect that Jeannine showed for her position. "Please send them in."

Although Brooke had seen Peter Remo the other night, she had not seen DeMayo since last Memorial Day at the Hiccock's barbeque. Brooklyn born, Vincent DeMayo had been a hacker for the mob when Bill Hiccock got him sprung from prison to help unravel the Eighth Day affair a few years back. *Kronos* was his preferred handle. She'd have to remember that; Kronos bristled if anyone called him Vincent. She had convinced Dr. Hiccock to assign Kronos to her and her investigation at the meeting that occurred in his office just a few days earlier.

Together, both men were the top technical brain trust of America. They had figured out and intuitively applied their collective genius to scores of small and large issues that helped Bill's Quarterback Operations Group stop many threats and thwart more than a few plots to destroy America and its way of life.

Kronos was thinner than the last time she'd seen him. Peter had a warm smile.

"Guys, thanks for coming in on such short notice. Let's move over to the table; it'll be more comfortable."

"Yo, Brooke, I thought you were finished with all this cop stuff," Kronos said.

"So did I, but Mush is still deployed and I made them an offer I thought they'd refuse. So I guess the moral here is, be careful what you negotiate for."

"Still, this is a pretty sweet gig you got here— and director to boot! Whoohoo," Kronos said.

"Thanks."

"So what's on your mind, Brooke?" Peter asked.

"You have read the briefings; and Kronos, I think you spoke to Bill this morning?"

"Yeah, he filled me in."

"So you know what I'm looking for. I need a plausible scenario that could make the pieces fit."

"So you are expanding your investigation?"

"Actually, Peter, you opened it up. Your 'put and call' theory has rung a lot of bells."

Kronos snapped his fingers. "Brooke, before I forget, can I get a look-see at those fried machines over at Prescott?"

"Done. Maybe you can shed some light on how they did it."

"Kronos and I were talking downstairs; we think this might be an EMP-based plot."

"That's the thing you warned us about that time in the Indian Ocean." She turned to Kronos.

"Yup. Same kind of disruptive impulse."

Brooke remembered back to when she'd been on a top-secret mission and a tactical nuke was about to explode underwater. It was Kronos who'd deduced that the US Navy control ship, a fishing trawler from which Brooke had run the deep-sea recovery op, should shut off and disconnect all its electrical equipment rather than be fried when the small-yield nuclear bomb detonated.

"Are we talking a small-yield nuclear weapon, here?" she asked.

Peter and Kronos looked at each other. Peter spoke. "Not likely. You wouldn't need these eight guys, all seemingly specialists in electrical engineering and electronics. You would only need the nuke and maybe some muscle guys to plant it."

"The profiles of these dudes here on the watch list, they got a specialty you don't need if you are going to just fry electronics after a nuke det."

Brooke was cautiously relieved; she had been part of the team charged with stopping a suitcase nuke detonation on New York. Luckily, it was a dud and only the first stage lit off. The real yield never exploded. Still, there was a spot on Thirtieth Street, a radioactive hotspot, now encased in a concrete egg that no one was going to crack for fifty thousand years. "That's a relief. So how do you get an EMP without a nuclear device?"

Once again, the men looked at each other. Kronos spoke this time. "Beats the shit out of me."

Peter hitched his head sideways towards Kronos. "Yeah, like he said . . ."

.G.

Lost on most folks was the fact that the secret service was, at one time, actually part of the Treasury Department before it was reassigned to DHS. It was during that time the then Under Secretary of Treasury, Warren Cass, had helped a young secret service officer, Brent Williams, out of a jam that could have derailed his career. For that reason, the now head of the president's protective detail was reviewing the logs and internal "chessboard" showing where all the "pieces" were at any given moment in the White House.

This was meticulously done. In the event of a national security emergency or a threat to the executive mansion, where they would have to "crash the house," it was the secret service's responsibility to wrangle every top-level admin member and/or all members of the NCA. Those national command authority figures were appointed by the president to carry out war, fighting, or other contingency management issues in the event of an alert.

This morning, all Secretary Cass cared about was Brooke's movements. Williams was finishing the report he had assembled within fifteen minutes of Cass telling him what he was looking for. "POTUS was in the Beast at 18:42. Motorcade arrived without incident at Hilton 18:57. Egress through service entrance. POTUS was on the stage 19:05. At 19:55 he was secured back in the Beast. We arrived at the East Wing portico at 20:10. He then retired for the evening in the residence."

"Wait. Go back. What time did he meet with Brooke?"

"The first time was in Quarterback's office. Sorry that's SciAd's office, sir, at 15:30."

"No, the second time, in the residence."

Williams checked his sheet. "17:18."

"And when did she leave?"

He scanned down . . . checked it again. "21:45"

"She goes up to the residence at a quarter after five and doesn't leave until quarter to ten?"

"Apparently."

"And the president leaves and comes back from a speech and she is there?"

"White House mess delivered dinner for two at 20:20."

"They had dinner at 8:20!"

"And she waited for him to return. Will there be anything else, sir?"

"No thank you, Brent . . . and again this is close hold."

"I understand, sir."

Williams turned to leave and Cass had a second thought.

"Dinner for two? Had the first lady eaten beforehand?"

"No, sir. FLOTUS was in Omaha as part of a six-state western swing this weekend. She's wheels down, Andrews, at 13:00 Monday."

Cass just sat there. Williams, sensing he was dismissed, left.

His wife's away; he has dinner with her. Right after she learns of a major breakthrough in her case and about Cindy and me. Yet, I don't find out till today. Cass's thoughts were coming at a hundred miles an hour. He couldn't believe Mitchell still held a grudge, but maybe with this dalliance with squeaky-clean Mrs. Morton, the wife of one of his most trusted commanders, Cass held a playing card to trump even the president's considerable clout.

.𝔊.

"So you will let me know the minute you two figure out what we might be up against?"

"Sure thing, Brooke," Peter said.

"Tootles on your loo," Kronos said.

Brooke was momentarily stumped, and then she got what the human robot was saying.

"Toodle-oo to you, too!" She buzzed George. "How did it go with Wasserman? When will Cynthia be in?"

"Ahhh, that's the thing . . ."

Brooke didn't like the sound of that. "Better come in here, George."

Thirty seconds later, George was standing before Brooke who was fuming.

"He let her leave? Just like that? In the middle of our investigation?"

"He says we never demanded she stay in New York, we just asked," George said.

"Lawyers . . . When will she be back from the Caymans?"

"He didn't know, but he's going to call her and find out."

"Call him again, George. Let him know we are not happy. I'm not happy. And if he doesn't produce her, here in my office, by Monday morning nine a.m. sharp, I'll slap an injunction on him and her!"

.𝔊.

Martadi, the woman at the front desk of the Seven Mile Beach Marriot Hotel in the Grand Caymans was starting to get short with the lawyer from New York who kept calling every twenty minutes. "No sir, she does not answer the phone and I have already checked the gym, the pool, and I have two boys on the beach who say she isn't there. I already sent someone to her room. Okay, I will try it one more time." As she put him on hold she let out a deep breath. *This man was relentless*. After letting Cynthia's phone ring at least ten times, she switched back to the call from New York. "I'm sorry, sir, but still I get no answer . . . Sir . . . Sir, with all due respect, I have sent three bellmen to the room in the last few hours. She is not in the hotel or on the grounds. Yes . . . I have your number . . . I will. Thank you for calling the Marriot Seven Mile . . ." She pulled the receiver from her ear before she finished the standard goodbye sign off, because he had hung up. It did not improve her mood.

.𝔊.

In the rehearsal room that night Dequa saw the suntanned Paul. The nod Paul gave him indicated that the loose end he had told Kitman about had been clipped. Dequa wished that Paul had a more cost-effective way of eliminating possible threats instead of two pairs of round trip tickets and two suites in two different hotels in the Caribbean, but he had to admit, no trace of his victims would ever be found. Besides, it was, in the end, Kitman's and ISIS's money. He turned his attention to the matters at hand. He put on the headset, started the iPod with the sounds of band practice blaring over the large PA speakers in the room and began speaking to all the men in the room over their headsets. "Tonight is the last night we will all meet together. From this point on, you will break up into your individual assault teams. The packets before you are to be returned to me before you leave the room. For the rest of the hour, memorize their contents. Then I will speak to each one of you separately about your orders."

Bored out of his skull, Paul drummed his fingers on the snare drum in front of him. Finally, Dequa called him over. He took Paul's headphone plug and inserted it into a separate box so that just he and Paul could converse over the blaring noise of the rehearsal recording.

"I have another special task for you. I hesitate to assign you, though."

"Why. Have I not done what is required in the past?"

"This one is more sensitive, delicate, and not a lost soul to be preyed upon."

"This intrigues me."

"This may get you killed."

Paul didn't like that. But he was too involved to say no. "Maybe not. Who is the target?"

Dequa pulled out a stack of pictures. He laid them out inside the empty guitar case before them.

Paul moved them around as he studied them. "I see what you mean . . ."

"This one is no middle-aged hopeless romantic waiting for a white knight to save her . . ."

"Yes. I can see that," Paul, the man they called the Sheik of Araby, said.

"The desire is to have her eliminated within three days."

"May I ask?"

"She is a forensic accountant; she was seen at the Davidson woman's home. We believe she may have learned much from your last 'date.'"

"So why should I fear an accountant?"

"Although she works for FinCEN, we can't trace her back more than three months. And she looks capable."

Paul looked again at the blonde in the picture. She did have the look of confidence that having skills might bring. "I might have to take a different approach with this one."

"The 'how' is not my concern. Just make sure she is gone in three days," Dequa said.

.G.

Jeannine pushed the coin holder into the slot and heard the five quarters drop into the laundromat's dryer. As it turned, she sighed, having crossed one more item off her to-do list. Even though she was sworn to secrecy, Jeannine was glad her boss was able to sneak away for a short weekend trip, to Camp David where she hoped that, between whatever meetings she had, she'd find a moment to rest in the beautiful Maryland countryside. Brooke had been going twenty-four/seven for three months before this new phase of the investigation kicked in and, she thought, really needed to recharge and reset. Besides, having her boss out of town for a short window from Friday night to Sunday afternoon afforded her the chance to catch up on the things in her own life that she had put aside, like the laundry.

.G.

Inspector Dvorak was getting uncomfortable. He had traced the dead man in the floodgate to Prague's underworld of gay and transsexual haunts. Here in this dark club frequented by men, he was not just a policeman looking to solve a mystery, but also a target. Every inquiry into the picture of the dead man was almost surely followed up by some kind of proposition or lewd reference. If he were gay, he would be as happy as a dog in a butcher shop. But as it was, he was very happy with his wife and would not even consider cheating on her with a willing female, much less a member of the same sex. However, some of these boys were very good looking. He could see the attraction, but only as an observer of all things human, not as a participant.

After getting hit on with an umpteenth proposition to "party," he got a hit on the picture.

"Oh my God! Ebner!" Ruben, the man in the leather jacket with white piping exclaimed.

"You know of this man?"

"Oh yes. Ebner was very much liked by the butches looking for a fatty."

"Fatty?"

"You know, boys with a little meat on 'em. More cushion for the pushin'?"

"Were you pushin' Ebner?" Dvorak said.

"Me. Goodness no. I like 'em big and strong, like you."

Dvorak let that come on roll on. "Who was he dating?"

"Dating is such a limiting word . . . but I know he was all damp over some Westerner. Fellow came in and just blew him away. I mean, yes, although they probably did that first!"

"Maybe you didn't understand but I am a policeman investigating a murder. So let's knock off the happy talk. Got a name?"

"No, but wait. . . . Hey, Sweet Cheeks, get your cute little ass over here."

Dvorak moaned then turned and was mildly taken aback as a young man in chaps—CHAPS, with nothing else on, exposing his bare rear end—walked over. "Yes. Oh, hello . . ."

"Down, boy, he's straight."

Dvorak scowled at Ruben.

"Well, you couldn't be any more obvious!" Ruben said defending his statement. Then he turned to Sweet Cheeks. "Who was the stud that Ebner was all gaga over?"

"Oh, you mean, Paul?"

"That was it, Paul!"

"He was hot. Had that whole reluctant-straight-looking-to-explode thing going on. Delicious."

"This . . . delicious Paul got a last name . . . Sweet . . . Cheeks?" *When in Rome*, Dvorak thought.

"Oh well, let me think . . . No. No, I don't believe I ever caught his name, but I'd be his catcher any time!"

Dvorak could only guess by the context what that meant. "Please focus. Were they ever here?" he said, pointing down to the floor.

The two looked at each other. "Last Saturday night," they said in unison.

That fit with the fact that the body was found Sunday. "I'm going to have to ask both of you for your names in case I have more questions."

Dvorak took out his pad. When he was finished with Ruben and Sweet Cheeks, he went to the manager's office to review the surveillance tapes of last Saturday night.

Dvorak was frustrated. All the cameras in the club had good angles on Ebner, but there wasn't one good shot of his date, Paul. *Almost as if he was consciously avoiding the cameras*, he thought. That would mean Paul had a purpose beyond fatty love. He could have training. "Tradecraft" was a word that flashed through Dvorak's mind. If Paul was a professional, who and why would the target be a fat slob of a data analyst with bad taste in men? As he was leaving the club, he noticed a woman across the street. Actually, he noticed what she was doing.

He crossed the street. When she finished, he spun around and put his head approximately at the height of the camera on the ATM she had just used. The camera saw the whole club entrance on the right side of what its frame would be, if it were aligned like his head was now.

On his way home, Dvorak made two mental notes. One: review the bank's ATM security cam. Two: equality has come a long way. Apparently, there are now gay—hitmen—although he couldn't decide if that was a positive or negative development.

.G.

Dequa's packet of information on his new target had her living in an apartment in the west 50s. He was there, across the street, at 5:00 a.m. Monday morning. At around 7:20 a blonde, looking just like her picture, exited the brownstone and got into a waiting government vehicle. *Easy. Tomorrow I will kill the driver and sit in the driver's seat and kill her when she gets in.*

His plan dissolved when the driver got out to open the door and his jacket swung open and he saw the man's service weapon. As she got in, he also saw she was strapped. *This wasn't going to be easy.*

.𝔊.

One half-hour later, Paul walked up and down the street in front of the federal building where he had followed her by cab.

Wearing a hat one time, sunglasses the next, then both, then just a jacket then none he walked casually along with one eye on the building. He did this to avoid suspicion and be less obvious on any surveillance cameras. An inert person in the same spot waiting for someone to leave would be spotted in short order.

After all, this was the federal area. Huge, car-stopping mechanical barricades were cut into the streets. Guardhouses were everywhere and bomb-sniffing guard dogs inspected every vehicle that had the proper ID to enter. This four-block part of the city was essentially an armed federal fortress.

In the end, Paul concluded that since this was not a suicide mission, he would have to find another way to get to his target.

.𝔊.

Jeannine, holding the morning briefing book, greeted Brooke as she got off the elevator with a cup of coffee.

"Thanks, Jeannine."

Jeannine leaned in and, in a conspiratorial tone asked, "How was your weekend?"

Answering in the same manner, Brooke whispered, "Too short, but very good!" Then she took a sip and asked, "Did we hear from Cynthia Davidson or her lawyer?"

"No, but George wants five minutes first thing."

"Okay, but make it in an hour. I've got a lot to catch up on here."

"Sure thing."

Chapter 19

Bank On It

Dvorak's hunch that somebody may have been withdrawing money at the moment Paul left the club on Saturday paid off. He now had a clean image of Paul's face, although his body was obscured by the shoulder of the patron of the bank who took up most of the high-definition frame that the ATM snapped every three seconds while someone was using the machine.

Two hours later he had hits through Interpol's face recognition network.

Twenty minutes later he had "Paul Mumphries" at Havel Airport boarding a KLM flight to the Cayman Islands, traveling under a Dominican Republic passport. There, the trail went cold. He would have thought that Paul stayed on the Caymans' sandy beaches but there was no hotel, land record, or credit receipts in that name after he did a few criminal network searches. *That's a cold trail*, he thought, *professionally cold.*

However, going down to the island to check into his further whereabouts was out of the question. He could hear his chief now, laughing him out of the office when he asked for the expense voucher to go to the warm, sunny Caribbean.

So Dvorak did the next best thing. He sent out Paul's picture and a "wanted for questioning in a suspicious death" notation across Interpol's interconnects. Many countries all over the world including the US were on that network. The information was disseminated to the police agencies of those various nations on a regular basis. It was a painfully slow process but it was all he could do.

After a week immersed in the counterculture shenanigans of the men who love men, Inspector Dvorak booked a cabin on a lake outside of Prague for he and his wife to spend his few days off together. His intention was to make love to her till it hurt as a way to anchor his feet in his own sexuality, which had been challenged all week. He drove home smiling, happily thinking, *My poor wife.*

.G.

While Mrs. Dvorak was breathlessly loving the new amorous, pounding attention she was suddenly receiving, over and over again, from her husband, his little "All Points Bulletin" across the worldwide network was also getting a work out.

Officer Efrain Castro, a customs officer on night duty in the Grand Caymans ran the Czech Republic cop's photo file through their facial ID system as a matter of clerical routine, cleaning up the stacks of stuff that came in during the day. The photo file got many hits. It seemed Paul Mumphries, aka, Paul Grundig, aka Paul Ludwig had been in and out of Cayman three times in the recent past. No stay was longer than two days. This was not uncommon for an island nation where many people, and countries, kept their money in their notoriously uncurious banking system. Although most didn't travel under different assumed identities, especially since it would be a huge red flag. Another note was that "Paul of many last names" always returned to America.

The Cayman officer posted his findings back to the Czech Republic but also flagged the American TSA. Maybe they could pick up the trail.

.G.

McVickar Funeral Home in Chappaqua had been a family-owned business for one hundred and fifty years. Grandfathered in, it was originally a three-family house. But since they started offering cremation, local zoning laws and just the creepiness of it all, once the neighbors realized what was coming out of the chimney, forced them to move to the outskirts of town. That turned out to be bad for business. So the fourth generation funeral director, Ethan McVickar, was forced to move his his family's home from the high-priced end of Chappaqua to seek a more affordable abode in the modest clime of Yonkers. He was in his office when the knock on the door caused him to check his watch: 7:30 a.m. on the dot.

He went to the front door and unlocked it. "Good morning. Right on time. Come in; would you like a cup of coffee?"

"No, thank you."

"Well, let's step into my office; you can explain what you are here for. I didn't fully understand your proposition over the phone last night."

They sat at the small table in his office.

"Mr. McVickar, I represent a party that wants to buy the house on Hillview Lane in Yonkers."

"I see. Well as I told you last night, my wife and I have our hearts set on that house. We like the schools and it's on the end of the street so it has a minimum of neighbors."

"I understand; that's why I have asked to see you this morning. After we spoke, I talked to my client and I am prepared to hand you a cashier's check for five thousand dollars to walk away from the house and tear up your contract, no questions asked."

McVickar was impressed. "Wow, they really want it, don't they?"

"Yes they do. Do we have a deal?"

"Look, Mr . . . I never got your name?"

"Paul."

"Mr. Paul. We spent six months looking for a house that was just right. I am afraid I am going to have to say no to your generous offer."

"What if we raised . . ."

McVickar held up his hand. "I appreciate your position but I'm afraid we are not going to change our minds at any price."

"Very well. May I reserve the right to come back to you with a final offer? It may well be substantial enough to make your decision simple."

"Knock yourself out, but for now, we are set to move in two days from now."

Mr. Paul relaxed his posture in the chair and struck a different tone. "May I ask you something a little off topic?"

"Sure."

"I have always been fascinated with funeral homes and mortuaries. Truth be told, in my younger days I envisioned myself possibly becoming a mortician. But as so often happens, life has other plans."

"That is the truth; actually, I thought I'd be an engineer, but my older brother, who was into this business, died in Iraq, so it fell to me.

I'm afraid I made a small mess of things. We've had to downsize and cut some staff."

"Since it's early, would you mind showing me around?"

"No, not at all."

They walked through the home. Downstairs, he showed him the embalming room and the crematorium.

"Wow. So this is where you cremate the bodies?"

"Yes, we do it all here. The process is mechanized and the casket and all goes in this end and the ashes are sifted and ready for internment in the urn that we place on the other side of the wall."

"So it all works with just this switch?"

"Yes."

.𝔊.

By Monday afternoon, Brooke was seething. Cynthia Davidson had disappeared. She wanted her shyster lawyer, Wasserman's ass in a sling for letting her out of the country.

"The Caymans no less! What a schmuck," she vented to George. "Didn't he know that if you were ripping off a company or the government, the Caymans 'don't ask don't tell' banking laws were the perfect first stop on your way to living out your days in plush comfort in a country where they only know you as Mrs. Smith?"

As mad as she was at the attorney, it was also her screwup. She had given Cynthia a pass by not locking her up, or putting a bracelet on her, or hell, posting armed guards in her garden. Maybe because she'd seemed so innocent in all of this, or because she had been so forthcoming about her involvement in the "one for the good guys" slush fund . . . or was it something else? She hated her next thought, that somehow she'd cut Cynthia slack because she was connected to her boss in all this, Secretary of the Treasury, Warren Cass.

Brooke had a thought as she picked up the phone. "Nigel, what was the name of the art house out of the Caymans? Shipsen-Deloitte . . . right! Thanks.

"George, pack a bag and suntan lotion. Get down to the Caymans today and see if you can pick up Cynthia's trail. She's either there under another name or she's left under one. Find out which, ASAP.

And start at Shipsen-Deloitte. She may be hiding her assets as art purchases!"

"Right, boss." And he was out of her office like a shot.

His eagerness made her smile against her mood. She swiveled her chair around and looked out at Manhattan. The PCM executive corner office she had commandeered looked north, where the Empire State building loomed six blocks away.

She remembered as a little girl she and her brother Harley had gone to the top. She'd been nine, and her older brother had started doing his King Kong impersonation. She'd laughed so hard she nearly wet herself. He was her joy. He always made her laugh. Even after he died in Iraq, she would smile and sometimes laugh out loud remembering his antics and the things . . .

"Secretary Cass on line one."

"I'll take it." Brooke lifted the phone. "Good morning, sir."

"I was wondering if you got any further with your science guys."

"Sir, where are you today?"

"This morning I am in Detroit at the launch of a new car parts factory then heading into New York for a reception of the Saudi Ambassador. Why?

"Can you give me five minutes before the dinner?"

"I'm sorry, Brooke, schedule's tighter than a gnats . . ."

"Gnats ass. I had brothers, sir."

"Sorry. Can't we discuss this over a secure line?"

Brooke thought about it. "Are you staying over?"

"No, I am out of there at 10:30. Got a cabinet meeting at eight tomorrow in the big house."

"How are you getting to the airport, sir?"

"Nice try. I already have that ride filled by a reporter from the *Wall Street Journal* who's been hounding me for a story for two months."

"Well, sir, I will fly down tomorrow and catch you after your cabinet meeting." Then Brooke did something she immediately knew she might live to regret. "Safe travels, Mr. Secretary. Bye." She hung up without giving him a chance to say no.

She sat there for a second, her hand still on the phone. She reasoned that Cynthia's disappearance was not good for him in light of his past relationship with her. The woman was acting guilty, probably evading US law. She couldn't tell the man something so fundamental over a phone call. *I did the right thing*, she thought.

"Director, your one p.m. is waiting in the conference room," Jeannine said over the intercom.

Brooke got up and walked down the hall to the conference room. Her secretary met her midway.

"What do we got, Jeannine?"

"Inspector Johnson from New York transit, he was . . ."

"On scene commander in the subway; I remember him."

"You got Harrelson out of FBI, New York, and Damon Edwards from us. Here's your summary."

Brooke entered the room, shook hands all around and exchanged pleasantries, then sat at the head of the table. "Excuse me for minute while I catch up." She looked down and opened the file. The executive summary was on top and she made everyone in the room wait until she'd read it. Someone said something and she held up her hand while she neared the end.

Whoever it was stopped.

A few moments later, she closed the folder. "Sorry, I hadn't had the chance to read that before the meeting. Thank you for your patience. Now who was it that wanted to say something?"

"I was going to inform you that DNA and other factors confirmed that Joe Garrison was the subway victim. We didn't know that at the time that report you just read was printed last night."

"Thank you, Inspector Johnson. Okay, Harrelson, don't make my old office look bad here. Does the FBI have a lead on the Hispanic man last seen detaining or speaking with Mr. Garrison?"

"I'm afraid it's thin. Various cameras on the platform and on the street are sketchy. Though we now have reason to believe he may not be Hispanic but possibly dark-skinned Middle Eastern."

"On what are you basing that?" Brooke asked.

"Based on one ear witness who overheard them—definite Arab accent or at least regional."

"Damon, let's share the visa violations we got from State with these agencies and see if it clicks with our now Middle Eastern man."

"Why didn't we know of these violators before?" the inspector asked.

"These are all Middle Eastern men. Who may or may not be involved in any criminal or suspicious behavior. Until a second ago, we . . . you, were searching for a Hispanic."

"I see."

"Brooke, is there anything further on the means used to destroy all the data at Prescott?" Harrelson asked.

"Nothing yet, but my people are now leaning towards a fifth-generation computer virus; very cutting edge, possibly. Their initial thought of some kind of electrical impulse frying the memory didn't pan out because the damage would have not been limited to the data, but to the circuitry as well, and that all tested fine in the lab."

"Meaning?" Harrelson pushed.

"Meaning it wasn't a shotgun of electrical impulse that would have fried everything but, rather, a surgical strike. Using something they call a logic bomb. I expect we'll know something more shortly."

"Anything else you could tell us?" the inspector asked.

"We can possibly rule out a major attack by thermonuclear device from this particular group, based on what we believe to be their core competencies."

"Comforting notion." The inspector leaned back from the table.

"You asked. That's what I got. Anything else?" She looked around for someone to say something. "Okay then, we'll meet as the facts and situation warrant. Keep those daily briefs coming. I guess that's all." Brooke got up to leave. "Oh, one more thing. One of our key witnesses, Cynthia Davidson, disappeared down in the Cayman Islands. Kick the tires men; see if you can shake anything loose. Her sheet was in yesterday's file. And Inspector, if I thought it wouldn't result in me getting fired, I'd ask that you ticket and tow her attorney, Josh Wasserman's Mercedes, just to give the jerk a little taste of the grief he's put me through—letting her up and leave like that."

Brooke left.

"Harrelson, she's kidding, right?" the inspector said.

.G.

Jessica Goldstein had one more call to make tonight. She rifled through the files and came up with the form she was looking for. She dialed the number. As it rang she stapled a cancelation form to another form and placed it in her out basket. "Hello, Mr. Fareed? Jessica Goldstein from Yonkers Reality . . . How are you doing tonight? . . . That's good. Well, I am calling with some good news. The house you were interested in, the one at Hillview Lane in Yonkers, has come back on the market. Yes . . . I know . . . You are still interested I assume . . ." She let out a deep breath. "Excellent. Can you stop by our office tomorrow and bring a check for the 10% deposit and the filing fee? . . . That's super! . . . And I am really happy you got the house. I know how disappointed you were when it went into contract . . . Yes, well, not to tell tales out of school, but it looks like the previous buyers had a domestic falling out . . . Her husband—he was a mortician—just up and disappeared. He drove to work one morning and vanished without saying a word. She's devastated, the poor thing. But you know what they say, one person's loss . . . Okay then, see you tomorrow."

Chapter 20

Dressed to Kill

Brooke was curled up in her dad's old recliner, her feet up on the worn cushion. She was deeply ensconced in the latest John Lescroart thriller. It was the only guilty pleasure she allowed herself, especially now, in the middle of the expanded Prescott investigation. Although she lived a life of a character right out of one of the author's thrillers, most of the other books she'd read didn't capture the life as spot on as Lescroart.

At first she thought it was the neighbor's TV. Then a loud thump followed by yelling drew Brooke's attention to her apartment's front door. She put down the book, got up, and looked through the peephole. She couldn't believe what she thought she was seeing. She unlocked the deadbolt and opened the door. Brooke yelled, "Hey, break it up!"

Out in the hall, on the staircase, was a priest struggling with a young man. The startled kid stopped pummeling the priest, jumped up and fled down the stairs two at a time.

Brooke ran to the priest. "Are you okay?"

The priest turned and wiped blood away from his lip. His collar was torn and twisted. He gulped for air. "Yes. I'm okay."

"Good. I'll go chase down that son of a bitch." She started down the steps.

The priest's hand shot up and grabbed her arm. "No. Let him go."

"Why? He attacked you!"

"He's in enough trouble. He's really a good boy; it's just, there is this girl, see, and he is not welcome by her family. I am afraid he was here to borrow money from a friend so they could elope."

"So he attacked you?"

"I was trying to stop him. I guess it got a little heated."

Brooke got a good look. He was a handsome man. There was something captivating about his eyes. *Must have broke a lot of hearts when he went into the priesthood*, she thought.

"Would you like to come in and get some ice on that lip?"

"I couldn't impose."

"Nonsense. Here, let me help you up." She reached down to grab him by the waist but he waved her off and instead took her hand.

She led the injured priest into her apartment.

"You are so very kind. I didn't mean to interrupt your evening like this."

"Sit here, at the table. I'll get some ice from the fridge."

"I'd like to stand for a minute if you don't mind."

"Suit yourself," Brooke said as she turned her back on him to open the freezer door.

The priest reached under his jacket . . .

"Freeze!"

Brooke turned to the open doorway to see Nigel in a sideways crouch, with his service piece fully extended.

"It's okay, Nigel, the priest was attacked in the hall."

The priest adjusted his jacket covering the handle of the knife and held his side. "Yes, and the dear boy really had a solid punch to the ribs."

Nigel relaxed his stance and re-holstered his gun. "I saw the blood in the hallway and the woman downstairs said there was a scuffle. Sorry, Father."

"That is quite alright, my son."

"Nigel, this is father . . . ?"

"Paul. Father Paul." He smiled. "Well, Nigel, if you were a few minutes earlier"—he dabbed his bloody lip with the paper towel the ice was wrapped in—"you could have maybe helped me persuade Manuel to abandon his crazy notion of eloping with a very powerful man's daughter."

"Sounds like an urban drama set in the fifties. Like the old American black and whites we'd watch down on the West End."

"Nigel, what brings you here?" Brooke said.

"I have some late word from the office. You didn't respond to my voicemails, so I'd thought I'd drop by."

"Sorry, I'm not so much a voicemail person. Well, let's not talk shop in front of the father."

"Actually, I should be getting along," the priest said, taking his cue.

"Would you like me to call an ambulance?"

"No, that won't be necessary. I grew up around here. I've been in my share of fights. I'll be fine. Thanks for the ice, and for coming to my aid. God bless you." He got up and shook Brooke's hand, then Nigel's. "Well, I'll leave you two to talk your business. Have a good night."

"Good night," Brooke said as she closed her front door.

"Well, that was rather exciting," Nigel said.

"First time anything like that has ever happened in this building. It's usually so quiet."

"Something is bothering me."

"What is it, Nigel?"

"He never asked why I had a gun."

"You're right. That is odd. Maybe this is a rougher neighborhood than I thought."

"Still, don't you think a chap that just had a gun drawn down on him would be curious?"

"God works in strange ways . . ." was all Brooke could think to say with an apologetic shrug.

.𝔊.

8 DAYS UNTIL THE ATTACK

George was commiserating with Martadi, the front desk manager at the Marriot on Seven Mile Beach.

"He was very insistent, that New York lawyer," she said.

"Yes. He was very concerned for Ms. Davidson. So she never came back to the hotel?"

"No. She has the room for a week and she hasn't returned yet."

"Yet?"

"She is scheduled for checkout today."

"So she may be back to checkout?"

"I would hope so."

He turned to the local constable who was his Caymans police liaison. "Officer, I'd like to look in her room."

The local cop nodded to Martadi and she grabbed her passkey and led them to the elevators.

Up in Cynthia's room they found all her clothes and bags. There was an opened FedEx box and some tissue paper made neat by the stream of housekeepers who'd entered the room every day since she had gone missing. George took out his phone and snapped pics of the FedEx box, its address label and the brightly colored tissue paper. He also snapped the clothes in the closet, on the stand, and on the bed, and in her luggage. He shot the bathroom and her toiletries, hair products, and travel cases. He also found and snapped a card that read, "For the sun and sands as we hold hands, Paul." Then he tagged and bagged it.

"Officer, as soon as the one o'clock checkout passes, if she has not returned, I want you to have this room sealed and its contents impounded, then dusted for recent prints. Now I would like to see the hotel's security footage."

George was impressed; the hotel had just upgraded their system and was using high-definition cameras. The lighting in the lobby made for excellent clear, crisp pictures and an easy positive ID of Cynthia. "Please put all the footage of that woman, time stamped every time she comes and goes, on a thumb drive for me and send it to the US Consulate under my name."

He turned to his liaison officer. "I'd like to go to the customs house, now."

At the customs office, George met with Officer Efrain Castro. He was the local wiz with the video surveillance cams that were at all the island's ports of embarkation and transportation.

"Good day, Mr. Stover. How may I be of assistance to you?"

He held up his phone with a photo of Cynthia on it. "Officer Castro, can you search your airport and passenger ship tapes of the last seven days for this woman?"

"May I have your phone?" He took the phone from George and with fast thumbs sent the picture to his email.

He sat behind his two-screen computer and opened the email. He dragged the pic into a new program that read twenty-seven points or features of Cynthia's face. Then he put in a SIM card from a plastic box that was entitled GCM. "This chip was last updated at ten this morning and goes back eight days at Grand Cayman Airport."

The computer screen flickered as it sped through the thousands of images of deplaning passengers. It was a split screen being fed by two cameras; the right side of the screen showed the faces of arriving passengers while the left-hand side showed the backs of their heads. When departing passengers used the same gate, it was reversed, with their faces on the left. Every face had a generated box around it that would flutter for a few seconds then the image moved forward in time. Some of the boxes stayed for a while. George could see they had some resemblance to Cynthia, but apparently not all twenty-seven data points. Then the computer sounded a chime and the movement of the images stopped.

"Here she is, entering the country at 11:30 a.m. last Tuesday."

"Okay, your system works. Now can you tell me when she left?"

Two hours later, the machine had gone through the entire airport, cruise ship, and even bus station footage for the last eight days and Cynthia wasn't there. They even corrected for sunglasses but the list of probables that search generated really didn't fit her height and weight profile.

Then George had a thought. "Efrain, can you go back to her arrival?"

"Sure. What are we looking for this time?"

"There was a note in her room from a man named Paul. Let's see if she came here with anybody."

He zipped back to the second day of the disc's images to the time of her arrival. They watched the whole plane disembark. There were two unaccompanied men. Neither seemed the "hold hands in sand" type Just the same, their images were sent to the passport division to be viewed by the agents on duty to see if they remembered either of them with Cynthia.

"Well, Efrain, thanks for trying . . ."

"Sorry we couldn't find your woman. Could she have left the island on a private charter?"

"Maybe, but on the hotel lobby footage I saw, she isn't carrying anything overnight-like. You know, a bag or suitcase. I don't think she was planning on an extended tour."

"Sorry about not finding the other person named Paul."

George nodded as he turned to leave.

"Very popular American name it seems . . ."

George stopped in his tracks. "What do you mean by that?"

.Ꮆ.

"Nigel, I hope you are ready to tell me where Prescott is," Brooke said as she came back to her office with a cup of tea.

"My boys, back at the home office in Vauxhall, have him in Moscow."

"So he high-tailed it out of here and now he's un-extraditable in the arms of Mother Russia?"

"It would appear so."

"I'll get the Secretary of State to speak with the Russian foreign minister; maybe we can exchange ole Morgan Prescott for some low-level spy type."

"Good luck with that."

"Oh and Nigel, thank the chaps at MI6 for me, will you?"

"Of course. By the way, I still can't shake the idea that the priest wasn't rattled by someone aiming a pistol at his heart."

"You are like a dog with a bone."

"Bulldog or English fox hound?" he asked striking a pose.

"Otterhound, I think, Otterson."

"You certainly know your English breeds . . . Now, about the priest."

"Right . . ."

"What if we got it wrong?"

"Got what wrong?"

"No ambulance, no reaction to the gun . . . What if he was attacking the boy?"

"And the boy was defending himself . . ."

Nigel could see Brooke's mind grasp the alternative theory.

"He did stop me from chasing him . . . And he was looking to leave as soon as you got here," she said, piecing her way through it.

"Maybe he thought me a policeman? Last person he wanted to see."

"Nigel, it all fits. I think you cracked the case of the wayward priest!"

"Funny how things like that stay in one's mind . . . with all this Prescott business I mean."

"Speaking of the devil, if we make the deal with the Russians, can I ask you to go pick him up and bring him back to us here in the Capitalist Capital?"

"Sure, I really haven't much else to do."

"I'm sure something will come up soon. Meanwhile, why don't you take in the sights, see a show. Hey, the Circle Line is a hoot."

"Actually, I was thinking of a walking tour; you know, take in the neighborhoods, the churches, the different ethnicities . . ."

"Churches, huh?"

"Oh, I am a big fan . . ."

"And of course priests hang out in churches, so this sudden interest wouldn't have anything to do with . . ."

"'Parish' the thought," Nigel said with a proper English 'tisk-tisk'.

"Touché, Otterhound"

"Call if you need me." He headed for the door.

"Hey, you know, once I was in Switzerland . . ."

Nigel stopped and turned back to Brooke.

". . . and I did a little moonlighting while I was on another case and I have a 9-mm hole in my side as a reminder to NOT do that, too much, ever again."

"Duly noted, ta-ta . . ." He waved his open hand as he nodded his head and left.

Brooke just shook her head, smiled and said under her breath, to herself, "Not my ta tas, my side." Then she picked up the phone to call Secretary of State Charles Pickering to see if she had enough juice to convince him to get Morgan Prescott back in the USA.

.G.

George was in the US Consular Agency in the Caymans and was finishing his report to Brooke. They were using an encrypted form of Skype.

"So she didn't leave by any traditional or at least monitored means of conveyance," George said to the image of Brooke on the monitor in the consulate's conference room.

"And no idea of who this Paul on the card could be?"

"No one in the hotel saw her with any man and she booked single occupancy."

Brooke pondered all they had just discussed and then she had a thought. "George, can you have the techs put up that picture of Cynthia from the lobby of the hotel last time she left, and have them blow it up?"

George nodded to the tech who clicked on the image that was now buried on his desktop. The tech dragged it into the area that put it on the big monitor, then he zoomed into the high-def picture. On the little picture-in-picture box on the big screen, George could see Brooke analyzing the photo.

"Good, good. Okay, so here's what I think: George, that wrap she's wearing is a Hermès, it cost like four grand and it's the only one they make. Can't be too many wrapped around the rich and famous down there. Now, could you please let me see the other camera showing her leaving at the front door?"

The image on the screen shifted to the angle on the hotel's entrance from inside the lobby. The action of her walking jogged back and forth till the tech had a good, full-length, full-framed shot.

"Great, now please zoom in to her feet. That area right under her heel would be great."

Brooke leaned forward to scrutinize the shot. "Zoom more, please. Hold it. And, George, those shoes are killer sandals. See the red reflection in the dark marble floor under her lifted heel? Those are Lady Flats from Louboutin . . . like eight hundred for the pair. Cynthia's sense of style may get us a hit from those designers or high-end boutiques."

George looked up from the pad that he had scribbled the word "lewbatons" on but they just looked like a pair of silver sandals to him and the wrap was just like a thing a woman would cover herself with in a hotel lobby.

"Here's what I want you to do, George. Get that freeze frame of her leaving the hotel printed in color and then circulate it to every charter, fishing boat rental, and seaplane operator . . . and include their staff. Maybe somebody will recognize her from her outfit."

"Good thinking, boss."

"Female thinking, George!"

.G.

Mrs. Ratner in 1A was like the RA of 549 West Fiftieth Street. No one came in or out of her "dorm" without her notice. She was the one who told that man of the ruckus with the priest upstairs.

Mrs. Ratner approached the good-looking man on the stoop with her usual sunny disposition. "What do you want?"

"Frightfully sorry to bother you. But I was wondering if you knew a Ms. Brooke Burrell?"

"What if I do?"

"Well, I was hoping that you'd give her a message for me, if it wouldn't be too much trouble."

"What's the message?"

"Tell her Nigel came by and I found something. Meet me at . . . I'm sorry; can you write this down?"

"Don't got no pen."

"Allow me, madam," the English-accented man pulled a pen and pad out of his jacket pocket and handed it to her. "If you'd please, I have the most god-awful scrawl. You'd never be able to read it I'm afraid."

She took down the message, tore off the paper, and handed the pen and pad back to the gentlemen who nodded and bid her, "Adieu."

"Good looking man . . . Wonder if she's going to boff him." she said to herself as she closed the front door.

.G.

Brooke looked at her watch and decided she had to do something she might regret later, but it had to be done. She ran home to get dressed.

When she got to her brownstone, she heard the theme from the TV show *The Rockford Files* blaring out from old Mrs. Ratner's apartment. *Good, no third degree tonight,* she thought but still stepped up the stairs lightly, lest she get involved in a ten minute "how was your day, dear?" conversation.

In her apartment, she stripped, did a fast wash-up, and walked through a cloud of Chanel No. 5—she still liked the classics. She touched up her makeup and didn't want to take the time for eye shadow, so she went with a darker blush for night and put on her old faithful LBD, the little black cocktail dress that always fit the occasion. Then she grabbed the other accessory she wouldn't be caught dead without and strapped it high on her thigh. Then she slipped on her sweet, painful *peau de soie* pumps, grabbed her evening clutch, made sure she had her keys, and hit the lights.

On the way down, Jim Rockford was involved in some sort of shootout and so her exit was also not challenged.

.𝔊.

The Harvard Club was the perfect choice for the reception because the Saudi Prince had graduated from there back in 1992. Also most of the current lions of Wall Street and the government hailed from its legendary hallowed halls in Cambridge.

Brooke approached the reception desk.

"Welcome to the Harvard Club. May I have your name please?"

Brooke opened her ID wallet. She had jazzed it up a little with her FinCEN Creds on one side and her FBI badge (retired) on the other. She could see the confusion on the young girl's face whose only job was to cross names off lists.

Brooke decided to help her so she read her name off her tag. "Tiffany, can you get me the organizer of tonight's reception? Tell her it's official business."

The kid got up and backed away from Brooke like she was some kind of vampire. Brooke looked around. The hoi polloi were out in force. She was glad that she had gone home to change.

Tiffany returned with a harried woman in an Ann Klein A-line and earbud coil dangling from her ear. "May I help you?"

Brooke flashed her tin again. "Brooke Burrell, Treasury Department. I need to talk to the secretary."

"You mean Warren Cass?"

"Yes, Ms . . ."—she read her name tag—"Flaherty. I need to speak with him now."

"Let me call my security," she said.

"Listen, I outrank your security and I am only taking time with you as a courtesy. Now I am going to walk in there, see my boss, and be out of here in three minutes. Or I am going to slap you with a charge of interfering with an ongoing federal investigation, got it?"

Flaherty was dumbfounded. Brooke turned and went up to the metal detector. She put her leg up on a chair, raised her dress and un-Velcroed her leg holster, and handed her clutch and holster with her gun inside, to the guard. Then she flashed her ID at him. She walked uneventfully through the machine, reached around and took her bag and gun back from him.

Rather than giving another show to the male guards at the detector, she slid the holstered gun into her clutch.

She grabbed a flute of champagne off a passing waiter's tray and zeroed in on Cass on the other side of the room. He was talking to a man in an Armani suit and Arab Keffiyeh headdress.

The prince's head tracked her like a laser range finder. "Well, hello. Come join us."

Cass turned in the direction of the prince's megawatt smile and was surprised to see Brooke.

"These are my dear friends, Barry Kitman and Warren Cass, and I am . . ."

"Prince Abdula bin Rahman. Yes, I know of you, and I know Warren. We work together. But I don't know Mr. Kitman," she said extending her hand. "Brooke Burrell-Morton. Pleasure to meet you."

Brooke thought she saw a moment of hesitation on his face as if a mental connection had clicked in, but then Kitman just sheepishly smiled and nodded.

"Warren, you are a very lucky man," the prince said, interrupting her on-the-spot analysis.

Cass looked right at Brooke. "We'll see about that." Then he changed his tone. "Ms. Burrell, I didn't expect to see you here. I mean, I really didn't expect to see you . . . here." The last part as an aside through clenched teeth.

She turned to the prince. "A thousands pardons, Your Highness . . . Mr. Kitman. But may I borrow Warren for just a minute?"

The next-in-line to the House of Saud grabbed her hand and blew a kiss over it as he looked in her eyes. "If you promise to personally return him yourself."

"Has anyone ever refused such a dashing man?"

Cass rolled his eyes, and led Brooke out of earshot. "Now, what's got you interrupting my diplomatic duties?"

From the corner of her eye, she saw Flaherty parting the crowd, making her way to Brooke with two big private security guys in tow.

"Sir, I felt I owed you this—there's been an unfortunate development and it involves . . ."

Cass held up his hand and waved Flaherty and her men off.

Brooke deliberately didn't look at her. When Warren looked back to her she continued, "Cynthia has disappeared. She was last seen in the Cayman Islands. That was three days ago."

Cass, not a stupid man, immediately understood the position that put him in. "Thank you for coming to me with this first. Do you have anything incriminating on her?"

"No, sir. In fact if she hadn't run, I would have never have had anything at all."

Cass just looked out at the celebrants and the furrow on his brow told Brooke he was intensely considering his next words. Then he mumbled something.

Brooke could hardly make it out but it sounded like, "That's why George went to the Caymans."

Then he turned to her and said, "So, she is still listed as a friendly witness, right?"

"Until this."

"Would it be possible to not change her status for, say, seventy-two hours? You know, maybe this whole thing just spooked her. Maybe she just had to get away and think it out."

Brooke was about to inform him that it didn't look like that, but then she saw the genuine concern in his eyes. She decided to let him have . . . let Cynthia have, three more days. Besides, since she was missing, changing her status was a purely academic procedure. But it would stop a backlash from stinging Warren. Her job done, she said, "Please extend my sincere apologies to the prince." And she turned and walked out of the event.

Many heads turned.

He returned to his guest of honor, but the prince was quietly giving orders to his royal body man. He stood next to Kitman.

"She seems very capable," Kitman said.

"Brooke? Yes, she's a top asset. She's the one I told you about who was looking into PCM for me."

"That's right, I remember now," Kitman said as he took a sip of his Dewar's double malt.

As she walked through the lobby, an out-of-breath man with broad shoulders and an earpiece in his ear caught up to her. She didn't slow her stride.

"His Highness asked me to extend his heartfelt wish that you might join him later for dinner."

Brooke stopped. She laughed. "He did, did he?"

"Most assuredly."

"Look, that's very sweet, but I've seen this movie, and it doesn't end well." Brooke had solved the case of a murdered body man in Switzerland who'd performed the same service for his royal bad boy.

The bodyguard stood confused. "So what shall I tell the prince?"

Brooke held up her left hand and pointed. "Tell him he missed this when he kissed it."

The guard immediately understood the gold band and the diamond ring duet on her finger.

"I see . . . of course," he said with a bow.

She walked off but couldn't resist. She stopped and faced him once again. "Tell him I am flattered, though."

She turned and walked away with just the slightest spring to her step.

As she got out of the cab, she leaned on the bottom of the stoop of her brownstone and slid off the pumps. "Ahhh" She was glad to get those off her feet. Plus it would make her less audible as she ascended the stairs past Mrs. Ratner.

Using all her training she unlocked the front door as if she had picked the lock to the Royal Palace, then held the door until it silently closed, releasing the knob only once the door was fully closed and only then, slowly, with barely so much as a click as it passed the striker plate.

She turned and placed her bare foot on the first step and it creaked.

She winced and shut her eyes. Immediately heard the sound of the peephole of 1A snap shut, then the police lock clang, then the Medico lock clunk, then the deadbolt slide, then the door lock clink, the door chain rattle, and finally the doorknob squeak. "Good evening Miss-ses. Rat-ner," she said to the ceiling.

"Oh, I didn't know anyone was out here. Is that you, Brooke?"

Brooke turned and put on her Doris Day smile. "Why, yes it is Mrs. Ratner, and I was just looking forward to a hot bath and a good night's sleep."

"Went to a dance tonight? Ended early did it?"

"No, it was a little function after work, after a long day's work . . ."

"Well, it's good I bumped into you."

"Yes . . . bumped," Brooke said, a slight smile emerging on her face.

"Because I have a message from that nice British fellow that was here."

"Who was here?"

"A Mister Nigel?"

"Nigel? What did he want?"

She patted her housecoat. "Now where was it . . . He had me write it down . . . Oh, here it is . . . Please meet me at Tenth Avenue and Thirty-Seventh Street as soon as you get this. I found something about our friend, Prescott. But you have to see this, before anyone else . . ." She dropped her hands in a frustrated manner. "You know, now that I read it out loud, it isn't all that damn romantic, is it?"

"No, no, it wouldn't be . . . thank you." Brooke slipped on the dreaded pumps and went out to get a cab.

.G.

Mrs. Ratner watched her get into the cab through the sidelight. "Dressed like that, she'll definitely get to boff him." She turned to go into her apartment but not before putting her foot on the first step and pressing down to hear the creak. Smiling, she shut and locked, locked, locked, locked, and locked her door.

Chapter 21

A Little English on It

The northwest corner of Thirty-Seventh and Tenth was a construction site. The other corners were dark buildings with no lights burning past 6:00 p.m. The cabdriver looked out at the site and said, "This don't look like no party here, miss."

Brooke ignored him, threw down a twenty and got out.

"Geez, classy broad like dat, never woulda figured her for a hooka," the driver said out loud in the empty cab as he reset the meter and drove off.

.𝔊.

There was no sign of Nigel on the street. Brooke immediately assessed the situation. The chain link fence to the construction site was unlocked and open with no security guard in sight. She wobbled as she stepped off of the uneven plywood onto the tamped-down dirt in her totally-wrong-for-this-terrain pumps.

She only went in a little way. She strained to see into the shadows. She listened for any sounds . . . of anyone. She scanned the ground for recent footprints and then all the shadows and places someone might hide. The job site looked dead. She let out a relieved breath and turned to go. Then she thought she heard something . . . It sounded like a moan. She pulled her gun from her purse, shook off the leg holster and it hit the wheel-rutted dirt that her three-inch heels were now sinking into. Taking a chance, she called out in a loud whisper, "Nigel? Is that you? Where are you?"

There it was again . . . Definitely a moan or groan. Leading with her Glock, she moved her head trying to see if one of the shadows moved less than the background. At night, with no depth perception, things that were closer moved differently than things farther away when you moved your head from side to side.

At the end of a shanty was an open area. She would be exposed. She strained to see any sign of . . . There it was again. She slipped off her shoes, but looked down and saw in the dim light bent nails, screws, and shards of wood. She held her breath and held the shoes against the edge of the shanty and, with the butt of her gun, hit the heels until they snapped off. With a sigh a tragedy like that brings to a woman, she slipped the mutilated pumps back on. Brooke now walked funny but she had protection against tetanus. She swept the area through her gun site. Seeing no one, she went for it. Stepping like a gazelle, trying not to wrench her feet, she made it to the dark area across the open expanse. The moan was louder now. She took out her cell phone and, shielding the light from going anywhere else, scanned the ground before her. Feet, a man's feet. She panned the light up. Nigel. His face was beaten and a noose was around his neck. It was tied off just high enough so that every time he relaxed he choked himself. "Nigel!"

She got down on her knees and began to undo the noose until she could lift it off his head.

He was spitting blood as he choked on the words. "I found . . . the priest . . . Get out . . . Get out of here . . . He's not . . ."

She bent over a little lower to relieve the pressure on the knot. The timing saved her life; otherwise the first shot would have hit her in the head, but instead it got her on the top of her shoulder. She immediately rolled to her right in searing pain. The next shot smacked into Nigel's head with a wallop that banged his head back against the corrugated steel wall.

"Nigel! No . . ." she screamed.

Brooke's breathing was now rapid. Her shoulder was burning but she knew it wasn't a bad wound because it wasn't numb like the last time she'd gotten shot. She rolled behind a fifty-five-gallon steel drum. She glanced back over to Nigel with sorrow but the next shot hit the drum and made a contorted whine, snapping her out of it.

From the sound of the shot, she was able to locate the general direction that it came from. She lifted her gun over the edge of the barrel and fired. She then immediately looked over the ridge and saw a muzzle flash. She ducked as the bullet snapped over her head and pinged off the corrugated metal wall behind her. She blurted out, "I love you, Mush." Then took a deep breath and tried to steady herself and let her training and discipline take over.

The shooter was behind a dumpster. There were four or five of the containers in one spot. She looked back and saw Nigel slumped over. She dragged his body over behind the drum by his legs. She took out her cell phone and put the camera in video mode. She rested it on the rim of the steel barrel and pointed it in the general direction of the dumpsters. She said, "Sorry Nigel," and with her foot pushed his lifeless body to the other side of the drum.

Four shots rang out, three hitting their mark, dimpling Nigel's body with each perforation.

She stopped the video and replayed it. The shots came from behind the second dumpster, the one with two hinged tops, side by side—the flash came from the narrow space between the open lids and the top of the container. The shooter was crouching behind there and had a slot to shoot through, which afforded him maximum protection from her return fire.

She had to think of something. Then a strategy came to mind; maybe the shooter would think that Nigel's body was hers. In the dark, he might not be able to tell the difference. *Assuming he doesn't have night vision*, she thought. She listened to determine whether he was coming over to confirm the kill.

She waited but there was no sound, no movement. She looked at the video again. He was well protected; and then she saw a way.

With her shoulder screaming in pain, she lifted her clutch over the top of the barrel while she leaned over to the right side.

A shot rang out and the bullet went right through the bag. She aimed at the dumpster at a bit of an angle, right behind and to the left of the shooter. She fired three shots in rapid succession into the front of it, and heard the ping of the ricochets and then a moan. She was up and running, emptying her gun as she did. One of the last shots got the shooter right in his neck as he made one last attempt, in agony, to shoot at her.

She kicked away the gun as she grabbed her shoulder. She looked down at the shooter. In the dim light she saw the flow of blood gushing from his neck lessen with death. With her foot, she rolled him over to his side. There, puncturing the back of his shirt, was a small, bloody hole. Two . . . Three. She looked at the dumpster right behind and to the side of the shooter's position. There was a shiny dent where her hollow-point jacketed, 40-caliber bullet had hit and shattered into at least three fragments from the looks of it, puncturing his lung and possibly his kidney. "Thanks, Harley," she said, looking up to heaven and to her brother who'd died in the first Gulf War. He'd taught her to play eight ball and how to play the angles by putting a little "English" on the ball.

With her back against the other dumpster she slid down onto the muddy dirt, not caring about her dress. She shuddered and then lifted her head and closed her eyes. She thought of Hawaii, coaching the girls and making dinner for Mush out on the barbeque in the back of their captain's quarters by the palm trees. She had her hand on her shoulder; it was sticky wet with her blood. She looked over to where Nigel's body was sprawled out; it made her mouth curl into a frown as she dry weeped—crying without tears. She got a hold of her emotions long enough to take out her phone and dial the FBI New York field office—she knew the number. "This is former assistant director in charge of the New York office, Burrell, on temporary assignment to FinCEN, just involved in a shooting at Tenth and Thirty-Seventh . . . a construction site, two dead on the scene—down by gunshot and I, I need an ambulance. This is a national security level-one priority. Silent approach, no local response, federal jurisdiction only. Authorization, director level 07206. Be advised I am in plain clothes. Alert JTTF for NYPD protocols . . ." She stopped talking as she noticed something. She stood and rolled the shooter over onto his back again to get a better look at his face. It was the kid! The one who was fighting with the priest.

What did Nigel say? What did he say? She couldn't remember.

.G.

Harrelson met George at the emergency room. They could see Brooke sitting up in the bed. Owing to the superficial nature of her wound and the need for containment, the veterans hospital across town was decided on because the FBI could control the government staff and access.

Nigel's body and that of the dead shooter were also brought there for initial processing. In the morning, the locals would be brought in and the rules of containment followed.

"Is she crying?" George said.

"Hell, she just lost a member of her team, plus the emotions that must have built up during the shootout. I guess it all needs a way to escape."

"I guess here is as good a place as any," George said with a sigh. "Besides, from the looks of it, she got the drop on a guy who had the tactical advantage in an ambush."

"The legend continues . . ." Harrelson said of his former boss and Special Agent in Charge of the New York office of the FBI.

.𝔊.

Later, Brooke sat in the emergency room waiting for the mild painkiller to kick in. She turned her head to see the two butterfly stitches in her shoulder as the nurse checked on the seepage. "I hope the scar won't be too ugly for strapless gowns," she said to the nurse.

George and Harrelson approached, cutting off the nurse's response,

"You okay?" George said.

"I can't believe I lost Nigel. He was a very special man, George, with a lot to contribute. Gone too soon." The catch in her throat spoke volumes as to what a loss it was to her.

They waited a respectful amount of time before continuing. "Was he . . . was he on assignment for you?" Harrelson asked.

"No, he was following his own little crusade. Somehow, it got him killed." Brooke choked up. "They used him as bait to draw me out." She swallowed hard.

She steeled herself, grabbed a tissue and dabbed at her eyes and wiped her nose. "Anything on the shooter?"

"Not yet. His prints are not in the system; expanding to Interpol and ICC," Harrelson said.

"I saw him last night."

"Who? The shooter?" George asked.

"Yes, he was in a fight with a priest outside my apartment door."

George stayed silent as the pieces started to come together for Brooke.

"... and Nigel showed up. The priest knew his name." She continued reconstructing the events. "I remember now. Right before he died, Nigel said he'd found the priest. He was trying to tell me to run."

"So you think a priest is involved?" Harrelson handed over her service weapon and holster. Somebody had cleaned off the dirt from the construction site.

"Father... Father... Paul! Maybe the shooter got Nigel's name from him ... Oh God, Harrelson, check with NYPD. See if there's a dead priest on their sheets," Brooke said.

.𝔊.

Brooke was released from the hospital at 3:00 a.m. Harrelson drove her back to her apartment. "You sure you don't want to stay in a hotel tonight?"

"No, I'm good. Besides, all my stuff is here and I am supposed to be in court in the morning. Thanks for the lift. Get some sleep."

"Sure thing."

Brooke got out and walked up the steps in the hospital slippers she'd had to borrow.

.𝔊.

7 DAYS UNTIL THE ATTACK

She silenced her cell phone for the tenth time since she'd gotten to the office... late. The pain meds and the stress teamed up to make her sleep right through three alarms and a ringing cell.

Brooke had the pictures of the ten visa violators blown up and pinned to a wall in her office. A few days earlier, she had similar sets of photos disseminated to all law enforcement agencies, airports, rail and bus stations, as well as universities and sporting venues. If one of these engineers showed his face, she wanted to be able to swoop down and find out what he'd been up to. It was the universities that gave her the most flak. Tenured professors, who themselves were once on LBJ's list of radicals for opposing the Vietnam War, fomented a movement to stop the government from violating these foreign "guests'" rights. To that end, she was ordered to appear before Judge John J. Kelley as a defendant at 10:00 a.m. in federal court, part twelve.

"Director, it's 10:05; you are late for your court appearance," Jeannine said as she handed her the folder with the defense's case-in-chief prepared by the Treasury's lawyer, Fienberg.

On cue, her phone rang again. This time she took it. "Fienberg. Yeah, I know. I'm bad at voicemails. Stall. Look, I had a bad night . . . I broke a heel . . . Okay, I'm on my way."

It was a chunk out of her day that she could ill afford but judges had a way of getting your attention so Brooke grabbed her bag, and was walking out when she glanced at the pictures on the wall. She stopped dead in her tracks . . .

Chapter 22

Sweethearts

"Your Honor . . ."

"Mr. Fienberg, we have a huge backlog of cases and I've set aside ten o'clock for this case. I expect parties to be on time and ready to proceed when their case is called," Judge Kelley said from the bench.

"Your Honor, Director Burrell-Morton, as you know, is currently on a case . . ."

"There are no excuses. Either you're ready or you are in default, Mr. Fienberg."

"I beg the court's indulgence, she may be caught in traffic . . ."

"Nice try." He was handed a file from the court reporter. "Plaintiffs, are you prepared to move forward at this time?"

Brenda Nussbaum, the attorney for the professors who'd brought the suit against the government, stood up and said, "Yes, Your Honor, we are all here *on time* and ready to proceed. We move for a default judgment. Obviously, the government cannot defend its unfair profiling practices and apparently hasn't bothered to show up to this esteemed court."

"Save it, Miss Nussbaum. But I'll take that as a yes; the plaintiffs are ready." Judge Kelley looked at his watch. "Mr. Fienberg."

Even though he'd graduated Harvard Law twenty-two years ago, then clerked for a chief justice and had appeared before the Supreme Court five times as US Solicitor General, here, in this little court room, sweat was starting to bead on Jules Fienberg's head. He looked at the door anxiously then turned to the judge and smiled sheepishly.

The door to the courtroom opened and Brooke blasted in. She walked up to Fienberg.

Her attorney spoke in a louder than necessary whisper as she approached. "Ms. Burrell, it is inexcusable for you to be late to a federal court . . ."

"Stow it. I need to speak to the judge . . ."

"Mr. Fienberg, is this your client? Can we proceed?" Judge Kelley pressed.

Brooke and Fienberg didn't hear him as they were going at it.

"You can't."

"I have to."

"This is improper . . ."

"I don't care," Brooke said.

The judge interceded. "Mr. Fienberg, if it's not too much trouble might we proceed?"

"Yes, of course, Your Honor. Your Honor, my client, Ms. Burrell has a rather special request . . ."

"I'm sorry but tell your client I was doing special requests a half hour ago when this trial was supposed to begin. For now, please ask her to sit so that we can get going."

Brooke sat but continued arguing.

The judge hit the gavel. "The defendants are put on notice that if they do not display proper respect for these proceedings, they are flirting with a contempt charge!"

Brooke stood up. "Your Honor, permission to approach?"

The judge was thrown. "Ms. Burrell, only counsel may approach . . ."

Brooke reached down and with her good arm, pulled Fienberg up by his and pulled him towards the bench like a rag doll. "Fine, then he wants permission."

The judge looked to the court officer, then back to Brooke, then waved the officer off. Nussbaum quickly rose and headed for the bench as well.

"Your Honor, this whole case is about an improper profile of supposed guests in this country." She slammed down the picture of Shamal that she'd pulled off the wall in her office. "This man attempted to kill me last night and, as you can see, failed. However, he did succeed in the murder of a British government official. Here's his other picture." She placed down the ME's shot of the dead Shamal; blood caked around the hole in his neck.

"How did he die?"

"I shot the bastard."

The judge glared at Brooke.

Brooke opened the three top buttons of her blouse and pulled down the shoulder. "Not before he winged me. I was late because I was recuperating."

The judge made an expression as if he saw ants crawling on his dinner. He stared at the stitches and Brooke's still bright orange stained skin from the Betadine solution they'd used to disinfect the area. "You got shot?"

"Objection, Your Honor," Nussbaum said.

"You can't object in an approach!" the judge said still staring at Brooke's wounds.

"We have not been given proper discovery on this evidence much less its provenance. Plus, this sidebar testimony is prejudicial to my client's claims." Nussbaum was stressing her words, trying to break the judge's lock on the off-the-shoulder Brooke.

He turned with his hand up. "Hold your horses, counselor." He returned to Brooke. "You were wounded in a shootout last night and you are here now?"

"Your Honor, nine more of these sweethearts are out there right this minute. We have reason to believe they are planning a devastating attack on this city or this country; every second we waste is to their advantage. Also, by the way, these ten men were deemed by the US State Department to be in violation of their visas and that violation of immigration law is cited in plain language in the bulletins that accompanied the distributed pictures . . . That notation on the wanted posters negates any spurious claims as to profiling."

Nussbaum was shocked. "How come she gets to summate her whole case? You are bordering on reversible error, Your Honor."

Even Fienberg, her opposing attorney, winced at the landmine the woman lawyer just stepped on.

"Be very, very careful, Ms. Nussbaum." He continued his cold stare at her for a few seconds longer than was comfortable—just to make the point—then turned back to Brooke who was rubbing her shoulder. "Do you need a minute?"

"No, we may not have a minute, Judge."

"Okay, counselors step away . . . Go on, go back to your tables."

Fienberg was actually shaking; Nussbaum was blowing wind in indignation as she walked back.

Then the judge leaned toward Brooke, put his hand over the ever-present microphone, and said in a quiet voice that Nussbaum strained hard to hear but couldn't make out, "Director Burrell, I lost many dear friends in 9/11. Hurry up and get these sons-a-bitches. Nussbaum is a great lawyer. The plaintiffs may win this case—they have the law on their side: the government cannot profile. You have maybe two days, tops."

"He took his hand off the mic and said in a loud, punitive voice, "Ms. Burrell is excused from this trial today. Any necessary testimony can be taken at a mutually agreeable time for both parties."

He banged the gavel.

"Okay, Ms. Nussbaum, you may proceed with your opening statement. And I promise you nothing withstanding herein, or the events of the last ten minutes, will prejudice your case . . . nor will it support it."

.𝔊.

Brooke descended the majestic steps of the federal courthouse at Foley Square, unaware of the man watching her from the street. He was glad he was early because she wasn't supposed to be coming out for another forty-five minutes.

.𝔊.

All the way down the stairs her thoughts were replaying the way the judge excused her from this nuisance of a case. When she got to the bottom of the steps, she considered calling for a department car to come and get her. Her original driver had expected her to be in court for at least an hour, so he was gone. She looked up at the crystal blue sky and decided she'd call in, and if nothing were too urgent she'd walk a little bit and clear her mind. It was a hot day, but she could hardly remove her jacket to get cool and have her weapon exposed while walking down the street.

She suddenly realized she was starving. There was a nut vendor on the corner who was roasting peanuts and cashews in a sugary coating that made the street smell like the inside of a candy factory. Her regimen was at least an hour of workout three days a week, and intensive exercise on weekends. She knew it took thirty blocks of walking at a full clip to work off one Oreo. Yet, *that smell!* "Just give me a half bag."

"Lady, I no sell half. Only full."

"I'll pay for full, just fill it half way."

The vendor shrugged. "Okay, Lady. You da boss."

"Thank you," she said as she handed over four singles from her bag. Noticing the sudden shift in the vendor's eyes, she swung around like a top. Her jacket flared and as it did she pulled the gun from her waist clip and held it to the face of the large man who was now inches from her.

"Hiccock," was all the stranger said.

Brooke took a beat to process. She was still just as coiled and ready to strike, but that name bought him an extra second of life. "What about him?"

"He named his kid after me."

Brooke's stance imperceptibly loosened. "Then you're Ross."

"No, that's the kid's middle name and that was my partner. I'm Richard."

She holstered her weapon. "That's the right name."

"Thanks for not ruining my day."

"Well, Richard, you shouldn't get between a woman and her sweet tooth. "Nut?" She tilted the bag to him. The vendor, still shaking, slowly got up from the crouch he was in with his hands over his head.

"No, thanks."

She popped one in her mouth. "Mmm, warm." She poked around the bag and found another confection-coated nut. "I am going to risk a national security protocol breach and assume that you are Bridgestone."

"At your service . . ."

"So, Richard . . ."

"Please, Bridge. Richard was my dad."

"Okay, Bridge, why did you risk a full lead facial just now, and what are you doing here? Weren't you in the ghost business?" Brooke had remembered that Bridge and his partner were known only as the ghosts of the desert during the Hammer of God affair, but she also knew it was a double entendre, because they were very good at turning people into ghosts . . . before their time.

"Bill asked me to watch over you."

That stopped Brooke in her tracks.

Bridge continued, "He heard about Nigel and your brush with the hereafter, and since I was doing a little R&R over in Sandy Hook, he asked that I look in on you."

"Oh, he did, did he?" Brooke said, resting her hand on her hip.

"This isn't being received as he intended, is it?"

"You got that right, bucko."

"Bucko?"

"Bridge-o."

"Better . . ."

"He's doing that big daddy protective thing again, isn't he? Look, Bridge, I appreciate you blowing your down time on nursemaid duty but I don't need a big strong guy to protect me."

"Well, I . . ."

"Besides, that's what *I* do. We qualified on the same courses at Ranger school . . ." Then a thought entered her mind. "Is this because I got married? That's it isn't it? He thinks I lost my edge, got all soft, dreaming of my man and baking cookies . . ."

"Cookies are nice . . ."

"Well, I got some news for him . . . What?"

"Cookies are nice things to make . . ."

"Yes, okay, yes they are." She then laughed. "You're good! You got me right off my high horse there." She looked at her watch. Realizing she hadn't eaten since yesterday, she put the nuts in her bag as she checked her phone and saw the same ten messages from this morning.

"Mrs. Morton, I'd . . ."

"Brooke, Bridge."

"Brooke, I'd feel the same way if he did this to me."

"Hungry?"

"Not if candied nuts are on the menu."

.G.

"So he looks at me and says, 'And I thought I liked you,'" Bridge said, laughing.

"Well, you did just shoot his father," Brooke said, finishing her salad and taking a sip of her iced tea.

"It was a just little hole right through his arm before it went into the guy with the suicide plunger's heart," Bridge said with his thumb and forefinger spaced a quarter inch apart over his own wrist.

"You know, we had Thanksgiving at Bill's house and his father still ribs him about how Bill's friend shot 'em. So now I've met the legend," Brooke said feigning awe.

"How's Hank Hiccock these days?"

"As of last turkey day, still fishing, still driving Bill's mom crazy."

"That's good. So how are you and the sub driver doing?"

"Pretty good. When we see each other."

"Deployments can be tough . . ."

"Yes, but don't get me wrong. He's in a multi-billion-dollar machine, with enough room to go for a morning run around the boat, five hundred feet below the surface. It's not like he's forward deployed in some god-forsaken land where anyone at any minute can be the enemy. I mean, I worry, but he's pretty much in charge of his own fate."

"He going to kiss dirt anytime soon?"

"We've talked about it. But I would never hold him to an intention. We are both driven by our need to serve, I guess. I certainly can't judge him when I am sitting here in New York, being shot at and eating sweet nuts."

"How's the shoulder?"

"The son of a bitch winged me . . . but I think I can wrangle hazardous duty pay out of it."

He laughed. "If only we could, we'd be millionaires by now." The moment hung, then Bridge said, "Four."

"Twice," Brooke said pointing to her side then her shoulder.

"I win."

"You can have it. Being shot two times is twice too often."

"Double amen," Bridge said, looking around the sidewalk café they were sitting at on Spring Street. "The food here was pretty good."

Just then the waiter, as if on cue, came round to inquire about dessert. "And also, which is not on menu, is to be a nice crème brûlée. And is also a very nice tiramisu."

Bridge picked up on the waiter's accent. "*Net, nichego ne nado, tolko check.*"

"Siyu minutu," the waiter said, nodding as he collected the dessert menus.

"Russian, spoken like a true Moskvich. I'm impressed," Brooke said using the local term of endearment for a citizen of Moscow.

"My turn. Good ear," Bridge said.

"White Russian, the tsar's Russian, is a delicate nuance. My compliments," Brooke said as she took a sip of her chamomile.

"Spacibo."

Brooke looked across the street at the people going in and out of the SoHo shops. She needed to get back to her office. She took another sip of her iced tea, placed it down and looked at Bridge. "How much longer do you have left on your leave, Sergeant Major?"

Chapter 23

In The Crosshairs

"Excuse me, Director Burrell?"

"No, Charlene Logan. Director Burrell is on her way," Charlene said, turning around with a smile.

"Sorry, from the back . . ."

"Yes, that happens a lot."

"I'm Briggs from the Office of Emergency Management."

"Yes. Right there in the main conference room."

.Ɠ.

When Brooke got back to her office, there were thirty people waiting in the conference room. Last night's murder of Nigel and the attempt on her life had bumped this phase up to joint terrorism task force. In the room were members of the JTTF, the Office of Emergency Management, the Port Authority Police, NYPD and FDNY, and US Coast Guard. Also present were representatives of the governors of New York and New Jersey.

The ten photos were on the wall with a "DECEASED" swipe across Shamal's.

As she got to the front of the room the din quieted down. "Thank you all for coming. I was unavoidably detained in court. On the ride up, I finally looked at my phone. I had fourteen voicemails, most from the lawyer handling the government's case. But then I found this one." She touched the phone and turned up the speaker.

It was Nigel. "When is a priest not a priest? Brooke, I found the priest, but he's not a priest. He has been hanging 'round the street outside your flat for the half hour I've been watching him . . . Texted a photo to you and the boys back at 'six.' He's just . . ." Then there were the sounds of a scuffle, then the sound of a van door sliding open. Then someone was heard at a distance, "The phone . . ." and the last thing heard was a large crunching noise . . . then silence.

"What you just heard makes the events of last night conspiracy to commit murder. It also means the SOM37 is active and in New York. In addition, there may now be eleven of them." Brooke went to the wall and tacked up a blank page with only the words "The Priest" on it. Then Brooke put a clear plastic evidence bag onto the table; in it was a smashed and shattered phone. "NYPD just found this a half block from my home. The picture never got through; our techs tell us the contents of the phone are irretrievable. I am going to give my description of number eleven, the Priest, to a sketch artist right after this. We will circulate the likeness when it's done." She paused and looked around the room at the suits and uniforms. "This cell had the wherewithal to improvise a daylight snatch-n-grab inside of thirty minutes' notice. That tells me they are capable and thorough." She pointed to the destroyed mobile phone. "We are dealing with a trained cell, people."

She nodded at her assistant Jeannine, who distributed case folders to all present.

"We just updated these a few minutes ago; also first page. We have set up a JWICS page."

"A what?" the representative from the governor's office asked.

"That's Joint Worldwide Intelligence Communications System. Think of it like a very secure Google pages. We'll put everything that comes in up on this page. Username is the same as the codename for this operation, *Sweeper*; the password is, and don't write this down, memorize it . . ." She held up a piece of paper where she'd written in big red sharpie, *PenaltyKicK*. "One word, case sensitive, cap *P* and both capital *K*s. She panned the paper around the room without saying it out loud, and then tore it up as she spoke. "All of the operational details and profiles and evidence have been uploaded and are in these folders. I know I don't have to, but I'm going to remind all of you, this is a national security case of the highest order. Everything in this room, in these folders, or on the shared document online is need-to-know, top-secret, classified . . . Anybody didn't get that? I'll repeat it. Not even your spouses!

"I'm here all day to meet with each of you and drill down into what your agencies can bring to the table."

As she was leaving, Jeannine handed Brooke a message. "He called a minute ago."

"Get him back on the phone."

.G.

George was on the tarmac walking towards the twin-engine turbo prop puddle jumper to San Juan, where he'd connect with his plane back to New York, when his cell rang. He had to speak up over the noise of the runway. "Brooke, a cop out of Prague sent out a BOLO for a person of interest in the name of Paul Grundig. One of the LEO's down on the island here did some face recognition. This guy comes and goes. His last three points of embarkation, Prague, Stockholm, and . . ."

"Denver?" Brooke said over the phone.

"Yep. I really got to get on Trip Advisor. These towns are coming up a lot lately. I'm jumping on a 2:30 out of SJU; be back in the office by six. I sent you a full set of Paul Grundig's baby pictures. Oh and Brooke, the cop in Prague, an Inspector Dvorak, he was investigating an accidental death that might have been a hit. He got an ATM shot of this Paul guy exiting a nightclub with the victim." He cupped his hand over the phone as a plane took off over his head and spoke louder, "I said, it might have been a hit!"

.G.

Brooke hung up. "Jeannine, as soon as those pictures from George arrive I want to see them."

"Just did," she said handing the prints over to Brooke.

"Son of a bitch!" Brooke said as she was looking down at the Priest, albeit in a Hawaiian shirt in the Cayman airport.

.G.

Dequa was not pleased at the death of one of his team. "Although Shamal was muscle, his surveys of the secondary target up north were excellent; but he had completed that task. Losing him at this point in the mission is not a crippling blow. However, the fact that we are now exposed, is!"

"He was selected because he was trained in ambush," Paul said.

"He was selected because you selected him to do something that was your task."

"He had the better skill set. I gave him every advantage and intelligence."

"He was also more connected to us than you were," Dequa said.

"Are you saying you would rather it had been me who was killed?"

"You are less connected to us and also an American. You would have been a dead end. Killing the British agent was an error."

"Had the plan gone as we had intended, the authorities would have been led to believe this woman tortured and shot the man who managed to shoot and kill her before he died."

"I never thought that the police would believe that story, but that's all in the past now, and that is not where we are at present."

He handed Paul a folder.

"We are three days from our mission. You are now in charge of cell security. Keep the Americans away from us for three days."

Paul didn't know how exactly he would accomplish this, but this whole conversation could've ended with his throat sliced, so this reprimand was actually a reprieve of sorts.

.𝔊.

"Are you saying what I think you are saying?"

"You're the reporter. I'm just telling you what I heard."

Cass watched Diane Price roll the ice cube from her mojito around her mouth, confident that she was rolling the fantastic allegation that he had just revealed to her around in her mind.

She bit down on the cube and asked, "Why are you telling me this? He is your boss, you know."

"No, actually the American people are my boss. He and I both work for them. And they have a right to know."

"Know what? Where's the smoking gun? What is the ramification of this?" the TV reporter asked.

"C'mon, are you kidding me?" the Secretary of the Treasury said, then lowering his voice, aware that even the high-back booth they were sitting in wasn't soundproof.

"Look, I know it's a ratings grabber. I know it will be the story for months but, in the end, it's a personal failing, but does it go deeper?"

"Like you and your network wouldn't consider anything short of assassination to get Mitchell out of office."

"You are talking about assassinating his character."

"Maybe I misjudged you. Maybe you don't have the gravitas to bring this sordid story to the mainstream."

"Look, attacking me doesn't change the facts. I'm just saying, as sensational as it is, if I have something with criminality to it, then the story is bulletproof."

"Do your job and look into her. See how maybe she is getting certain perks and opportunities and, let's say, preferential promotions and sweetheart deals." He quickly checked off the list in his head and agreed with his own statement, what with the high salary she was getting and the SES-6 power she was given.

"Okay, okay, now you are giving me something Peabody Prize worthy. What's her name?"

.Ꮆ.

"Unless he's got Cynthia with him, tell him to pound sand." Brooke was too busy to deal with Josh Wasserman, the inept lawyer who'd let Cynthia slip out of New York's jurisdiction.

"There is a woman with him," Jeannine said over the intercom.

"Then send them in."

Brooke finished up the report she was editing and hit the save button as Jeannine knocked and entered.

"Who's this? Where's Cynthia Davidson?" Brooke said, referring to the twenty-something girl who entered with Josh.

"Director Burrell, this is Amanda Davidson, Cynthia's niece. She contacted me out of concern for her aunt. I think this is something you should hear."

"Sit down, Amanda, and tell me what you told Mr. Wasserman," Brooke said, gesturing to the chair with her hand.

"Yesterday was my twenty-first birthday. Aunt Cindy and I have been planning it for years. She was going to take me for a day at Elizabeth Arden then shopping for a new wardrobe at Bergdorf's; then we had tickets to see *Phantom* again. She took me to see it when I was Bat Mitzvahed. She said she wouldn't miss this for the world. She even planned her trip to see her boyfriend around it. She should have been back yester—"

"Hold it. You said, she went to visit her boyfriend?" Brooke said with her hand up.

"Yes, there was a new man in her life. She was so excited. She made me promise not to tell anyone."

"Did she mention his name?"

"Only once . . . Paul . . . I think. Oh, I just know something has happened to her. I called the hotel and they haven't seen her but then a policeman from the Cayman Islands left a message on my phone . . . I freaked and that's when I called Mr. Wasserman."

Brooke picked up her phone. "George, get in here."

"Ms. Davidson, I want you to go over everything one more time with the agent who is looking for your aunt as we speak. And don't leave out any detail, no matter how small or insignificant. You did a good thing coming here to tell us about this."

An hour after George debriefed Amanda, he'd reached the same conclusion Brooke had feared.

"So this Paul guy is our Sheik of Araby."

"According to Amanda, he's George Clooney, Clark Gable, and Hugh Jackman all rolled up into one killer package . . ."

"No pun intended, I'm sure. Okay, so this guy makes women swoon then kills them? Why? Who's he working for?" Brooke said.

"Got to be the same people who are behind Prescott."

Ten minutes later, Brooke was on the phone to the Secretary of Treasury. "Sir, we now believe that it's possible that your friend, Cynthia Davidson, may have come to a bad end. Intel shows a man with the alias Paul Grundig, who we now know was also the planner of my assassination and responsible for the murder of the MI6 agent, entered the Cayman Islands shortly before Cynthia went missing . . ."

Brooke examined the picture of Paul in her hand one more time as she listened to his question.

"No, sir. No sign of him yet. But a charter boat operator gave a positive ID of a photo of Grundig as having rented a few boats over these last months, and always with a woman. A woman dressed in the same manner as Cynthia was the last time we captured her on the hotel's surveillance . . .

"Yes sir, that's what I thought at first, but the woman always returned with him . . .

"No, sir, there is no body as yet. She has disappeared . . .

"Yes, sir. We are now backtracking everywhere this Paul Grundig has been . . .

"As it relates to the whereabouts of Prescott, sir, would you trust me if I said, if you don't ask, then I won't have to tell you something that might be better left unknown . . . in terms of congressional committees, sir? . . .

"Thank you, sir. Thank you for your faith in me. I will personally keep you informed of any developments . . . Thank you."

Brooke took a deep breath; not having to reveal her adding Bridgestone to the mix was a big hurdle she'd dreaded clearing all day.

.G.

Cass hung up with Brooke and sat thinking about Cindy. Specifically the way she'd made sex, "deliciously dirty." Even after he'd started to lose interest, she'd kept upping the ante. She'd gotten more seductive and more daring the more he pushed her away. That she went down to the Caribbean with another man didn't surprise him. To him, she was the most exciting combination: the meek, mousey administrator by day and a raunchy lioness at night. She just loved sex. Then he remembered the time in the back of the limo . . .

"Mr. Secretary, Diane Price."

Snapped out of his reverie, he sighed. "Put her through, Sally."

"No, sir, she is here. She wants to see you."

"Very well, hold my 3:30. Send her in."

Warren Cass got up, straightened his jacket, adjusted his tie, and stood in front of his desk.

Sally escorted Price into his office. "Would you like anything? Water, juice, coffee, or soda?"

"Nothing for me, thank you," the reporter said.

She looked over to Cass, but he waved her off.

When they were alone, the secretary said, "This is a surprise."

"It's a day for surprises all around . . . Why didn't you tell me she was working for you?"

"Is that relevant?"

"Duh . . . it goes to motive."

"Whose?"

"Yours!"

"It's irrelevant."

"I beg to differ. Look, if you have some personal beef with her, up to and including that she turned down your own advances to have an affair with the big dog, then you are just using me, my network, and the whole fourth estate to settle the question of your fragile male pride or pissing contest you're in with POTUS."

"I see your point. But there is no there there, Diane."

"Okay, if it's not sexual, maybe you hate the fact that she is working for you and knocking boots with your boss!"

"You are getting warmer." Cass sat back in his chair. He didn't expect and didn't like the allegation. He never considered that this would blow back on him as some kind of spurned lover or sexual revenge triangle. He decided to take an extraordinary step to eradicate even the hint of impropriety from this reporter's mind. "Can I ask for you to take an oath of secrecy?"

"I am a member of the press. I can't keep secrets from the American people."

"That's bull. We get cloaks of silence on most everything we do militarily."

"That's national security; that's different."

"This is also national security."

Diane let that sink in. "Wait . . . what? You really meant an oath of secrecy, as in Top Secret?"

"Yes. If you saw the whole picture then you'd know why this is so troubling."

Cass had seen the look on her face before. She could no sooner walk away from this story than a junkie from a needle.

"What happens now? Do you swear me in?"

He reached into his desk and fished through some papers and retrieved an Oath of Secrecy form and handed it to her.

She grabbed it and read it. "Serious enough. Does this cover everything or just what you want to tell me?"

"Once you sign that and take the oath, I'll clear you for what I have to share."

She signed it.

He reached around to his bookcase and pulled out his St. James Bible, a gift from Reverend Jesse Jackson, back in the day. "Okay, raise your right hand."

"You're serious?"

The look on his face was her answer. "I, state your name . . ."

Ten minutes later, Diane was in shock and not because of the alleged presidential affair. "I can't believe I am now sitting on the biggest story since 9/11 and I just signed away my first amendment right to tell it. A terror cell, operating here, having already attacked and planning to do more . . . It's hard to believe."

"What about the affair?" the secretary said.

"You are certainly focused, I'll give you that much. I will see what I can find out without revealing sources."

"It wouldn't be revealing sources now, Diane, it would be treason!"

"Wow. You really walked me right into this."

"You've been around Washington long enough. I didn't lead you anywhere you didn't want to go. But here's a little gift." He tossed a clipped booklet of twenty pages across his desk. "You can't copy or leave with this, but feel free to make all the notes you want."

"Wow. White House visitor logs . . . secret service White House visitor logs, at that!"

.G.

To Bridge, it was PFM, Pure Freakin' Magic, the way these Internet kids could dig up anything. In the old days it would have taken three weeks to pull together a tick-tock of a suspect. Today it took a little more than three hours. Hell, he even knew what the bastard had to eat in his limo on the way to Teterboro. He sat in the conference room alone reading the sheet on Prescott's activities.

Maybe it was because he was a sergeant or maybe he was just polite but Bridge stood when Brooke entered. Harrelson, the FBI agent, and FinCEN agent George Stover and a few others followed her.

Brooke waited for everyone to be seated. "We are very fortunate to have a new member of the team. For a whole lot of reasons we are all just going to call him Bridge. Bridge's MOS is need to know. Is that clear?"

Everyone around the room knew that if a person's Military Occupational Specialty was classified, he was one heavy asset. They all chimed in with nods and a few welcomes.

"I have asked Bridge to find Prescott. No one outside this room will be read in on his mission, or his real identity. He's most effective when he is invisible, and I intend to keep him that way."

George raised a question. "Bridge, will you be working alone?"

"Next question . . ."

"I'm good." George smiled; this guy was stone.

"Does he have a FEID number?" asked the operations manager, whose job it was to make sure everyone got paid.

Brooke jumped in. "Good you asked that. My salary will increase by his pay grade; I will hold his pay until he returns."

"Right. Need to know . . ." she said.

"You got it . . . Now are there any other questions?"

"Confirmation code?"

Bridge took this one. "In the unlikely event I need to contact the team, the all-clear challenge code is, 'Bling.' I start talking without that, just come in guns blazing."

.G.

Everyone around the room could see that the capable man at the end of the table was skilled and exuded situational toughness. Their minds wandered through the myriad of things he might have done for his country. Some just concluded that Prescott was as good as caught.

.G.

"Bridge, would you like to fill us in on Prescott's movements?" Brooke said.

"At 11:50 on the day of the raid, Prescott took the freight elevator down to the loading dock on the Twenty-Seventh Street side of the building. From the security camera on the dock, which was not erased because it was on its own system at the back end of the building, he is seen getting into a Maybach." Bridge pressed the remote in his hand.

The grainy video on the monitor rolled. "The E-Z pass registered to that plate was scanned on the New Jersey Turnpike western extension. Then the car was recorded pulling into the main terminal at Teterboro Airport. This is an airport right outside the city that serves business jets and private planes."

He hit the remote again and the airport flight log appeared. "Within an hour of that time, nine planes took off. Only one had filed an international flight plan; nonstop to the Czech Republic. It was a charter and the company and crew come up as just for hire. The payment leads to a dead end, but . . . Kronos and the boys are trying to crack that through other means."

"Thanks, Bridge," Brooke said. "Okay, people. We believe the Czech Republic is a jump off point for a below-the-radar hop into Moscow. I want all your best thoughts and contacts. Cash in any favors you may have to try and find Morgan Prescott in Russia. State already said they have no trail. And MI6 and the CIA are trying to get a line on him. But we are running out of time. Let's meet again at fourteen hundred and see what we have at that time."

She turned to Bridge. "Let's continue in my office."

.𝔊.

The ringing of an encrypted phone that was rarely used drew Kitman from his secret prayer room. He answered, "Yes, Sheik."

"I bring you fortunate news."

"That is good."

"We have just taken over the refineries in Syria. We will be able to send you an additional fifty million a day. Invest it wisely."

"This is an act of a great and merciful God, Sheik. It will make our endowment even grander and longer lasting."

"Blessings upon you," said the man known to the world, but not as the leader of ISIS.

"And upon you, Sheik."

.𝔊.

Julio Rodriquez and Darryl Gibson had washed the east facing windows down to Thirty-Second. They had started at 7:30 in the morning. Julio looked up at the hot sun baking him from both sides, with the reflection off the mirror-like Plexiglas of the building he was washing at Thirtieth and Lex. He looked down at the nearly empty buckets of water and turned to Darryl and said, "Time for lunch."

Darryl put down the squeegee and took a position at the end of the scaffold as Julio did the same on the other end. They released the safety straps and the window-washing scaffold swung a few inches away from the shear face of the sky scrapper. He steadied it with his hand on the mullion between the large windowpanes. Once it stopped swaying, Julio hit the lever and the winch at the top of the building started hoisting the rig up to the roof.

Six minutes later, they approached the edge of the roof. As the rig leveled off, they once again refit the safety hold straps and the rig was now flush with a platform from which they could step onto the roof and then take the elevator down to the street to get a sandwich. They'd take the buckets with them and fill them up and return to the roof in an hour or so.

As they entered the roof access door, Julio saw him first. A man stood there with a gun. The last thing Julio saw was the gun pointing at his head and a muzzle flash. Darryl didn't have a chance to react before he too was dead on the floor.

.𝔊.

Paul and Ali bin Ali stripped both dead men of their overalls and slipped them on. They walked back out onto the roof, lugging a large green case.

They hefted the heavy load onto the scaffold, stepped on, and then assumed their positions at each end. Paul hit the lever but the scaffold tilted, the far edge dropping lower. Ali dove for the case to stop it from sliding. He almost went over the side with it. Then Paul saw it: the safety strap. He tried to unhitch the seatbelt-like latch, but there was too much pressure on the buckle. He reversed the lever and the far edge of the scaffold rose. Once he saw the slack in the strap, he stopped the winch, and simply un-clicked the strap. He nodded to Ali and hit the lever down again.

The thirty-eighth floor on this side of the building was relegated to the machine room. There were no windows just louvers for air-conditioning ventilation. Free from eyes inside the building, they stopped the scaffold there. They opened their crate. Inside was a Javelin, FGM-148 shoulder-fired missile.

Chapter 24

On The Edge

Brooke and Bridge were in her office. "Do you foresee any issues with the extraction?"

"I got two good men inside the GUVD."

"The local Moscow cops?"

"Former minister of interior types who took a pay cut when the old regime went out of fashion. They know all the ins and outs of getting someone in and out."

"Fast work, Bridge."

"You know, a big part of what I do isn't all the bang-bang crap, it's keeping human contacts and assets warm."

"How'd 'ja warm up these two cuties?"

"Would you believe Yankees tickets?"

"This ought to be good."

"Vasily, he's the smart one, his son was visiting New York and he's a big Derek Jeter fan . . . Go figure. Anyway, I had done some work with the guy who is now the head of Yankee stadium security, back in the time before you need to know."

"Priceless."

"Two seats behind home plate later, we have our means of egress all set for me and Prescott."

"After you find him and after you break him out of whatever situation he is in," Brooke pointed out as a reminder that this wasn't going to be a day at the ballpark.

"Yeah, all that, too."

Brooke had a moment of contemplation. "Bridge, I am sorry you're going into this blind. I wish I had time to get you the proper intel. I don't like the idea of sending—"

Bridge interrupted. "Thanks, I appreciate the sentiment. But I've been in tougher scrapes. In the end, even the best laid plans of mice and men and control agents . . ."

"Oft times get all fucked up!" Brooke finished the bawdy homage to planning by bureaucrats.

"Zactly . . ." Bridge said.

.𝕲.

Charlene Logan had just finished copying the duty log for the next three days of the FinCEN investigation. The tall blonde distributed the reports to all relevant agents in the office. She stopped at Agent Worrel's desk. "Chet, how's your boy doing?"

"He's fine, just a little bump on his knee. But you know the schools these days . . . Every little thing . . ."

Charlene stopped listening as something outside the window caught her eye.

.𝕲.

From the scaffold on the side of the building two blocks to the east, Paul switched on the rangefinder. Through the sites of the launcher, he first aimed the laser finder in the middle of the top floor of the Prescott Capital offices. Then he saw a blonde near a window to the right. It certainly looked like the bitch that had killed Shamal, that "Brooke" agent. He smiled as he re-aimed the laser dot on her head through the window of the office she was standing in.

.𝕲.

There was a resounding thud, then the air in the room compressed and popped Brooke's and Bridge's ears. Then the horrendous sound of an explosion as the right wall of the office deflected and bulged as it was torn open. All the papers and books in the adjacent room, even the material of the chairs, instantly combusted from the flaming debris that blew through the ruptured wall. Bridge was in midair, diving over Brooke's desk. She was on her way down to the floor when the heat and flame scorched the entire office. It was as if the oxygen was sucked out of the room. They both gasped for air. Then the windows imploded. Showering them with glass.

Bridge looked at the door. The rug had now also caught fire and the flame was heading toward them, making escape that way impossible. He grabbed Brooke. "We have to use the window!"

Bridge picked up Brooke's desk chair and ran it around the broken shards of glass that remained in the frame. There was a strong rush of wind as the fire fed itself from the oxygen it drew in from outside. The new air abated her coughing, but at first Brooke didn't want to go out the window. Then she looked up and saw that Bridge already had one leg out.

"Come on, Brooke, there's a little ledge. It's our only chance!"

They both crawled out onto the lintel that jutted out and ran around the older building, right under the windowsills. They flattened against the wall. Bridge took off his belt and slipped the buckle end over a knob-like device that the window washer would use to fasten his safety harness to the window frame as he hung out to clean them. Brooke knew not to look down. Bridge then wrapped the belt around his hand and held Brooke back with the other. The flames blasted out of the window of the office they had just escaped. A secondary explosion rocked the building and Brooke almost lost her footing.

.G.

From the scaffold, Paul watched the devastation of the entire forty-first floor of the building two blocks away. He hit the lever and started the climb to the roof. Then he saw them through the black billowing smoke; two people out on the ledge. One of them was a blonde woman. Paul pulled out his gun. He took aim, but then his brain kicked in. The handgun would never make the shot.

.G.

Bridge knew it was bad. The smell of burning flesh told him there would be a great many casualties. The exterior wall they were flat against was heating up. The fire seemed to be a little farther to the left of where they were standing. "Brooke, do you think you could sidestep your way to the right?"

"Hold on. I mean, hold me." Brooke crouched low trying to keep her center of gravity back against the wall that was growing hotter and hotter by the moment. She used one foot to push off her high-heeled shoe then reversed the process. "Okay."

Now in bare feet, she inched to her right. Bridge followed. Sirens wailed. And Bridge could see flashing lights from the corner of his eye coming up and down Park Avenue. They both knew, however, that no NYFD ladder company could reach beyond the tenth floor. It would be a long time until some kind of rescue from the roof would come their way. And the walls of the forty-first floor were sure to crumble from the heat way before that. Twenty feet behind them, another window blasted out. And the distortion of the super-heated air bellowing out bent the view of downtown Manhattan into a funhouse mirror-like distortion.

.𝔊.

Brooke amazed herself by—at a time like this—running her fingers through her hair, and shaking loose pebbles. *No, not pebbles . . . little chunks of glass.* The windows were tempered. They didn't shard but instead just crumbled. That was why she and Bridge had not been sliced to death. Although she wondered if that had just forestalled the inevitable as she looked down at the fire engines, cop cars, and ambulances that didn't have a shot in hell of reaching them in time.

Bridge's leather shoes slipped on the pigeon shit that was layered thick on the narrow ledge. Brooke grabbed his arm and they both almost toppled over. It was her bad arm and she lost her breath from the pain in her shoulder that had been grazed by a bullet the night before.

"Thanks," Bridge said.

Brooke just nodded her head in short, abbreviated motion so as not to topple over.

"Look," Bridge said.

Brooke looked and saw a flagpole jutting out from the side of the building. She immediately knew what Bridge was thinking. "You think it will hold?"

"Maybe one of us at a time. You first; you're daintier."

Up against the wall, inching sideways, Brooke didn't risk turning back to him but she said, as she was sidestepping towards the pole, "Normally, I'd bristle at a crack like that, but right now I'll take it!"

She looked at the lines that ran to the pulley the flag was attached to. "They look a little skimpy."

"That's why you should go first. They might not hold me."

She watched as Bridge found another cleat to attach his belt to, and used his arm to hold her up against the building as she had to crouch a little to try to unthread the lines from the flagpole. She managed to unwrap the extra rope from the tie-off cleat and separated the two lines. At first she pulled on the top one, but quickly saw the flag moving out further, trying to get through the pulley out on the end. She grabbed the bottom line and pulled. The flag started coming to her. Then she saw the ring on the top line. It would surely get caught in the pulley out on the end. "It's a square knot. I have to untie it."

.G.

Bridge adjusted his grip on her, as she had to crouch a little more. He then went to check the belt hooked around the window washer's cleat and saw the wall ten feet from them starting to pull away from the building. He knew it was only a matter of time before the weakened structure might collapse across the whole floor. He decided not to tell Brooke to hurry.

.G.

She got the three-inch metal ring untied and was about to toss it when she thought better of it and slipped it inside her bra. She got all of the rope free of the pole and guessed she had twenty or so feet. Carefully, she pulled the length of rope to about half and doubled it.

"It's too short," she said to Bridge.

"Here, use this," he said, lifting the flag with his right foot. She grabbed it. She took the ring out of her bra and looped the rope through the ring and made a double knot. On the other end of the rope, she made a noose and ran the flag halfway through it. Doubled up like that, the flag added another three feet. Brooke slipped the ring over the tie-off cleat and tugged on it. It seemed solid. *What choice do we have anyway?* she thought.

She let the rope with the flag on the end drop. She held the top of the rope and steadied herself as she slowly sat down on the ledge. Bridge used his hand to keep her back on the ledge. She gripped the rope tightly with both hands and took a deep breath, and said softly under her breath, "I'm going to be home real soon, Mush."

.G.

Down on the street, a news crew was trained on the man and woman in a life-and-death struggle out on the ledge of the burning top floor of the building. Most folks on the street were also looking up. The crowd collectively let out a gasp, and scattered exclamations like, "Oh, my God. Oh, no. Oh, shit!" As they saw the woman slip and start to fall.

.G.

Brooke felt herself sliding off the edge and tried to stave off straining the rope, but wound up swinging out like Tarzan on the flimsy cord, only to crash back into the building with a pronounced thud that made Bridge wince. "You okay?"

"Yeah, I just hit my elbow." She looked at her hands, which were being strangled by the death grip she had on the thin rope. The thin lines making her fingers white from the lack of circulation. "God, give me the strength . . ." she said softly, reminding herself of her mother's favorite exclamation. Somehow that gave her a little burst of energy.

Bridge called down to her. "What did you say?"

"Talk about hazardous duty pay . . ."

Looking down at her, Bridge was emphatic. "Just pay attention to what you're doing. Can you make it to the window below?"

"I think so, but it's closed!"

"Shit!"

"How's the rope holding?" Brooke said, looking up to him.

Bridge grabbed the cleat the ring was attached to and gave it a tug. "Seems like it's holding."

"Let's hope so." Brooke oriented herself so that she was facing the façade of the building and gripped the rope; she lifted her legs and pushed herself off. She swung out about five feet as the ring in the cleat groaned from the added stress.

Holding her feet in front of her, stiffening her legs, she hit the window heels first and bounced off. "Whoa... Oh... Shit!" She banged back into the building, almost letting go again from the pain in her shoulder.

"You okay?" Bridge asked.

"Why does this shit always happen after a manicure?" she said, ignoring the pain by looking at her broken nail on the finger choked off by the rope.

She oriented herself to try again when suddenly they heard a noise. Bridge turned as the sound of the roof above the office next to the one they started in was beginning to collapse. He called down to her, "Make this one good, Brooke."

"Brooke took a deep breath and coiled up. She was about to push off when suddenly the window opened and a fireman stuck his head out and extended a pole. "Grab the pole, lady!"

Thirty seconds later, they tossed a new, thicker rappel rope with a belay device and carabiner at one end up to Bridge. They tied off the other end to a standpipe by the window and yelled up to Bridge. "Secure!"

He tied it around his waist as a safety line, and lowered himself onto the flagpole. Dangling with one hand, he snagged Brooke's rope with the other and let go of the pole. He lowered himself to the sill. The firemen pulled him in.

"Thanks," he said.

"Sir, miss, we have to get out of here. We came up the back freight elevator. But we'll have to take the stairs down..."

A huge crunching sound interrupted the firefighter as plaster fell in the room they were in. New York's bravest immediately took of his helmet and placed it on Brooke's head. "Let's go!"

They bolted out of the room as the ceiling collapsed and made it to the exit just as burning debris fell from the burning roof above. They double-timed it down the forty flights to the lobby.

The commander on the scene was surprised that Brooke was alive. "That was you hanging off the flag pole?"

"I need a casualty report. Who's the senior responder?" Brooke said out of breath, rubbing her hands to get the circulation back in them.

"First, you need to let us check you, over there, by the ambulance."

"No time. This was an attack on a federal office in the middle of a national security investigation. What I need is intel. If you can't give it to me, then who can?"

"Me. Inspector Rynes. Are you Burrell?"

"Yes."

He turned to his aide. "Notify the Secretary of the Treasury, we got her."

She addressed the same aide. "Better yet, let me speak to him."

The inspector ceded. "FDNY tells me most of the upper floor was fully involved. Right now, we have fourteen survivors, mostly from the offices towards the south side of the building, but the FDNY captain on the floor below has pulled his men, fearing imminent collapse, otherwise they'd still be trying to knock down the fire at the point of origin."

"Do we know the cause yet?"

"From the debris field down here on Park Avenue South, it looks like an explosive event. Followed by fire."

Brooke looked up at the black smoke billowing out. "We had metal detectors and package inspection. No one got a bomb up there."

Just then a female detective came over. "Sir, we have a multiple homicide two blocks away."

"Who are you?" Brooke asked.

"Detective second grade, Paige Greyson. Midtown South."

"Brooke Burrell, Treasury. So what makes you think we need to know about the homicides?"

"Two window cleaners and a freight elevator operator killed in the last hour."

"Window cleaners? What building, Paige?" the inspector said.

"Right over there, Thirtieth and Lex. See the scaffold on the roof right now?"

Brooke looked and saw a few cops' heads over the edge around the window-washing platform.

"And we found this on the rig." Greyson held up her iPhone with a picture of an army-green case. It was opened and inside had a cutout in the familiar shape of a Javelin shoulder-fired missile.

Just then the aide came over with a phone and handed it to Brooke. "Sec Tres for you, miss."

She took the phone. "Yes, I am fine, sir. We have lost a lot of good people this morning, sir. Still trying to get a survivors list now. Me? I got out with Bridgestone." Then she remembered he wasn't aware of Bridge. "Sorry, he's someone I was consulting with. I'll give you hourlies once I set up a temporary command post. Nothing definitive yet, but I got one sharp cookie of a detective here that thinks we may be talking a missile attack from a building a few blocks away."

Detective Paige Greyson smiled at the overheard complement.

Then Brooke saw the first stretchers emerging from the building. She ran over and walked with one on the way to the ambulance. Harrelson was burned and his arm deeply gashed. He was barely conscious. "Ben, hold on there, buddy."

"Brooke . . ."

"Who was with you?"

"Walters, Fred, and . . . and that new kid . . . What's his name . . . Oh, I can't remember the kid's name . . ."

"That's okay, just rest and get better. I'll come by and see you later," Brooke said as the stretcher's legs folded into the ambulance and the EMTs jumped in. She turned and saw George limping out the front door.

"Are you okay?"

"Yeah, I was in the bathroom when all hell broke loose. A woman collapsed in front of me on the stairs and I went to grab her and twisted my ankle. How many made it out?"

"Seventeen, you're eighteen," Brooke said as she resisted the impulse to grab his arm and help him walk.

George looked up at the smoldering top floor. The smoke trail had now expanded all the way uptown.

Brooke spent two hours aiding the injured and supervising the recovery.

Detective Greyson found her slumped on the side of a fire truck catching her breath. "Here."

Reaching for the coffee, Brooke thanked the female detective.

"We got a temporary command post set up across the street. There's a quiet place in there and a pretty clean bathroom."

"Yeah, it was getting to be that time."

On the way over to the bathroom she noticed something lodged in the windshield of a cab that was covered in bricks, dust, and debris from the building. Embedded right into the glass was a mangled cameo pin. With effort she removed it from the shattered windshield.

Brooke exited the bathroom and found a small office in the large blue and white motor home the NYPD had converted to a mobile command post. She shut the door and sat in the desk chair. She put her face in her hands and let out a deep breath. Then she felt something in her hair. She rolled out a glass pebble, another piece of the window they'd broken to get free. Then she pulled the broach out of her pocket. Charlene had a brooch just like it. She hadn't seen Charlene amongst the survivors. Then she thought of all the people she worked with, most of whom wouldn't be going home tonight, wouldn't be kissing their loved ones or hugging their kids, all because they worked for her in one way or another. Her bottom lip began to quiver and she had herself a good cry.

Five minutes later there was a knock at the door. She dabbed her eyes and said, "Come in."

"There you are," Bridge said.

"How are you doing, Bridge?"

"Fine. I've been to the roof."

"Any more survivors?"

"No, the roof on Lexington."

"Oh, sorry; I'm still a little shaken."

"You should be. That was quite a time up there," he said.

"Thank you for saving my life."

"Me? Thank you. I was going over when you grabbed me!"

"I don't remember that . . ."

"I'll never forget it."

"What about you? How are you?" Brooke asked.

"Hey, I do this job because I care. Losing twenty or so Americans to a terror attack in broad daylight, in Midtown . . . First that makes me sad. Then I get mad! You?"

"I had my little moment of damning the universe. Choking back the tears. Did you find anything over there?"

"They were definitely targeting us. From the roof, you can't see into the offices . . .

"But from a lower level of the scaffold you can see right in . . . about the thirty-eighth floor from the window-washing platform. I tried it. Damn, I don't know how those guys work in those things for hours on end."

"Wait. If they knew we were on the top floor, why the need to perch?"

"They were looking for something specific . . . or someone."

Brooke looked down at the twisted and bent broach that had been violently ejected from the office. Charlene's pin. The same Charlene who people often mistook for her. "The Priest!"

"Makes sense. He wants to finish the job."

"That means they are getting close to their attack or they wouldn't have risked this."

"Sure, and they either got really lucky or they knew we had half of New York's agencies in there."

.G.

"You have redeemed yourself, but do you know if the one you sought has been eliminated?" Dequa said.

"I placed the crosshairs right on her."

"Good. Now they will be distracted long enough for us to complete."

Dequa aimed his Canon SLR with the telephoto lens and took a few shoots of the power plant just north of them alongside the East River. He cupped his hand over the end of the lens to eliminate any unwanted reflections from the glass window of the Roosevelt Island tram car they were riding in. "The seawall appears to be at least five feet high at this time of day."

"I am not in favor of a water approach. Too many variables."

"As a secondary route?"

"Possibly, but I'd rather deploy at Twenty-First Street for a second wave."

"You may be correct." He lowered the camera and, as he was putting the lens cap on, casually said, "Before we are done here in New York, please eliminate the hostages."

"Even the children?"

"Yes. There must be no loose ends."

Paul let out a sigh. "Okay."

.G.

"Bridge, I am going to set up shop in my old office at FBI New York. I want you on the next flight out to Moscow. Morgan Prescott is our only lead. It's going to take at least a day to reestablish all the evidence and surveillance we lost this morning. *And the people,* she thought but did not say. "I have a SAM flight meeting you at Butler. You'll connect to Czech Air in Warsaw. I'll have everything we recover sent up to the Special Air Missions' plane. You should be in Moscow by ten tonight. Good hunting."

"All my stuff is over in Sandy Hook."

Brooke thought for a second. "Head to the Twenty-Third Street heliport. I'll arrange for an FBI chopper to ferry you over, wait, and then fly you over to LaGuardia."

"First class. I like your style, Brooke."

"Not a second to lose, Bridge. And be careful. I owe you my life from this morning."

"Just get these guys . . ." And he was off.

Chapter 25

To Russia with Haste

Sandy Hook was now a resort island at the mouth of New York Harbor. Back in the good old days of the cold war, it had been a coastal artillery proving ground and port defense installation, which housed anti-bomber missiles. From here, and bases like it up and down the eastern seaboard, a veritable curtain of Nike surface-to-air missiles kept *Leave it to Beaver* and all the Mousketeers safe and sound from the bad old Russian Bear. Bear Bombers that is, the USSR's long-range planes that could carry atomic bombs into the heartland. But they'd have to get through the Nikes first.

These days, in the age of space-based early warning satellites and mutually assured destruction by intercontinental ballistic missiles, bombers were the last things to worry about. So now the only three Nikes left on this sandy shoal were the two on Bridge's feet and the one he jogged around every morning, which was propped up on a skid launcher, its propellant and warhead removed long ago. It now stood as a statue in commemoration of its once-proud sentinel status.

A few of the officer's quarters on the old base were still maintained by the joint US Coast Guard and National Park Services as a kind of R&R for deserving service men and their families. If you did something really good or needed recuperation after a mission, you might find yourself designated by the Secretary of Defense as entitled to a few days or weeks at this first-class non-hotel, looking north across a sandy beach to the spectacular skyline of New York City.

Bridge grabbed his ready bag and three satchels of gear. He didn't know how far he'd get with much of it, but he was going to try to get it all into Russia. That gave him an idea. As he lugged his gear out to the waiting Humvee for the half-minute ride to the helipad, he called Brooke.

"Brooke? Look, I got some toys in some bags. Is there any way you can have some diplomatic puke meet me in Warsaw and maybe get these into Russia under diplo immunity?"

.𝔊.

"Got it. I'll call State and set it up. What's your ETA at the SAM?"

"Chopper pilot says fourteen minutes to the private aviation side of LaGuardia."

"I'll have ATC allow the chopper to land on the tarmac. That should save ten minutes."

"Good catch."

"Talk to me once you're settled in on the SAM."

"Will do."

Brooke ended the call. "George, call the home office. Get Sec Tres to get the FAA to allow Air Traffic Control LaGuardia to let Bridge's helo land on the apron next his Special Air Missions' flight."

"For when?"

"You got ten minutes."

"Tight, but we might just make it."

Brooke's phone rang. "Director Burrell? Hold for POTUS."

Brooke heard switching noises and then a familiar voice. "Brooke, Bill here. I am with the president."

"Hi, Brooke, are you okay?" the president said.

"Yes, sir, thank you for your concern. Sir, we lost a lot of good agents, civil servants, and staff today. Please keep them and their families in your prayers."

"Brooke, the president and I were wondering: Is there anything we should know before he speaks to the world?"

"Sir, we believe the attack was carried out with a shoulder-fired missile by a member of the SOM37 cell."

"Does the press have this?"

"Not so far. We've held it tight. Only a few here know."

"Brooke, are you sure there aren't any eyewitnesses talking to CNN right now, or somebody isn't selling the video of the missile streaking across the Manhattan skyline in broad daylight?" the president asked.

"Sir, in Midtown Manhattan, in broad daylight, everyone is looking down at their phones; no one looks up anymore. They tell me the missile travels at Mach 1.7, almost twice the speed of sound. It wasn't in the air for more than a split second between buildings that were three blocks apart. In fact, they tell me that by the time the sound of the second stage launch of the rocket hit the street thirty-eight floors below, the rocket had already slammed into my offices. So the sound would just bring people to the impact, not the launch. But we are canvassing the area for any security cameras and feeds that might have caught it. Also, every NYPD watch commander in the city has orders to send any and all people who thought they saw something to the FBI. We have a good chance of keeping a lid on this. Overall, we are using the FDNY investigation as cover, but to answer your question directly, sir, no we don't know if this is about to go to viral."

"Brooke, what is the FDNY saying?" Bill said.

"They are not ruling out a natural gas explosion. And I think we should stick to that."

"Why's that?" the president said.

"We won't be tipping our hand to the cell."

"I see. If they think they are still invisible then they might get sloppy?" The president followed her logic.

"It's the best I got right now, sir."

"I already have a press conference scheduled in twenty minutes. I will ask all Americans to pray in light of this unfortunate accident."

"Any leads, Brooke?" Bill said.

"We got a solid hit on one of their button men. He may be the one who orchestrated the missile attack this morning."

"How's Bridgestone?" Bill said.

Brooke was about to answer when the president jumped in. "Who? You mean that fellow I gave blanket immunity to once?"

"Yes, sir. He's up there in New York helping Brooke," Bill said.

"Helping? That's an understatement, Bill. He saved my life this morning."

"Where's he now?" the president wanted to know.

"Sir, if you don't mind, can Bill pick up and get me off speaker?"

"Hey, it's my phone. My office. My country, when you think about it, Brooke."

"When you put it that way, sir . . . Okay, but I was attempting to create a wall of plausible deniability, sir."

"Okay, now I'm nervous, but even more interested."

"Sergeant Bridgestone is on his way to Russia."

"Run that one by me again," POTUS said.

"Sir, we have good reason to believe Mr. Prescott is being protected in Russia."

"Protected by who? Don't get me in a diplomatic pissing contest with the politburo, Brooke."

"Sir, I don't know."

"What's his mission?" Bill said.

"Simple, find Morgan Prescott and bring him back here for questioning, hopefully in the next two days."

"Is Bridgestone going undercover?" the president asked.

"Bill?" Brooke said.

"Sir, Bridgestone is always undercover. He's a ghost."

"Anybody gets killed, and the feces are going to hit the air circulating device," the president said.

"Duly noted, sir," Brooke said.

"Brooke, why in the next two days?"

"Because, Mr. President, we believe we are in a forty-eight to seventy-two hour window before SOM37 launches their main attack."

"Based on what you just said, should we get the FBI or CIA into this? Hell, the Tenth Mountain Division?"

"I put my cards in Bridge's hand, Mr. President. He makes the smallest hole, first."

"Small and efficient rather than big and messy . . . I see your point," the president said.

"Still no idea what form the attack will take, Brooke?" Bill asked.

"No, we are trying to suss that out from the members we know of and what their core competencies are, but whatever it will be it doesn't look like it will be a minor affair, Bill."

"Brooke, no reflection on you, but I am going to order the Pentagon and Homeland to put some assets into place. Pre-position them, in case you need support on a multi-prong raid or, God forbid, recovery."

"Can't argue with that, sir."

Chapter 26

The Tsarina

Bridgestone entered the crisp Moscow night after a fourteen-hour trip that had him touching down in Casablanca for barely six minutes then continuing on via an old Royal Air Maroc L10-11 into Sheremetyevo International Airport. He was sure the ancient Lockheed plane had its last airworthiness inspection in the US when it was an Eastern Airlines jet, back in the 70s. Every time the old fuselage complained with a cranky rattle or disgruntled creak, he was reminded that the L10-11 held the distinction of the first wide-body airliner to ever crash.

Terminal D at Sheremetyevo Airport was all glass and steel. At first glance it looked like any other modern international airport. But the stony faces and ice-cold gaze of passport control officers immediately sobered you up with the kind of paralyzing "hospitality" only Soviet-weaned Russians were capable of.

The airport express train brought Bridgestone to the Belorussky train station. Its pompous gates opened to the bustling square revealing the typical Moscovian cityscape of glassy business centers crowding out the past, or in this case a small white church, as the heavy *Staline époque* buildings just across the road loomed forebodingly. He entered the Soviet-style metro building with his "ears," a piece of tradecraft he employed to tweak his own Russian speech pattern so he wouldn't call undo attention to himself by brandishing an "out of town" accent. Also, it helped him glean what the locals were talking about—the small talk that could slide him in or out of any situation without raising any suspicions.

He arrived near the Kitai Gorod Mini Hotel twenty minutes before his contact. He liked to be early so he could see if anyone had planned a little welcoming party. The neighborhood was what locals called the Old Moscow. Small, ramshackle mansions dotted her winding streets along with an uncountable number of churches. One was right next to the hotel. It was ornate, with white stucco and Wedgewood-blue trim. He looked up on the light pole and there it was, a camera. Russian authorities always liked to know who was going to church.

He sidled along, staying out of the range of the camera until he reached the hotel's entrance. This was a real cheapo hotel but clean. He got a room for forty-five dollars a night under the name Gennady Romanov. One of the windows had a spectacular view of the 1930s skyscraper on Kotelnicheskaya embankment. For a keen-eyed sniper it was a perfect position, he thought as he closed the drapes. He dropped his bag in the room and splashed some water on his face. There was a knock at the door.

Alisa Spirina was tall, thin, and erudite. The perpetual up angle of her celestial nose was part of her success as an operative in a class-conscious society where strains of nobility, even sixteen times and generations removed, could get you a tank of petrol while everyone else walked. Whether confronted by the old KGB or suspicious border guards, Alisa's "airs" were rarely challenged. The cold hard stare she could deliver on someone who thought they had authority over her got her access and egress to and from many tight squeezes. In the Russian parlance, most just assumed she was a *tzaritsa* or "tsarina" in English.

Bridge took in the sophisticated, poised, regal woman standing on the other side of his cheap hotel room door.

Then she spoke. "Well, fuck. Aren't you going to invite me in, you dick?" she said placing her hand on her hip.

"Nice to see you too, kid."

She walked in and gave him a peck on the cheek. "Long time."

"Alisa, you don't age. You look just the same as when I met you twenty years ago."

"No, I weighed less then."

"Baloney."

"No, I weighed less because you had just relieved me of my .45 automatic."

"The M1911A1 is too big a gun for such a dainty woman. You were better off."

"Screw you. But now I keep my weight down with a Mustang .380." She patted her inner thigh.

"Excellent choice, madam." He gestured towards the couch and they both sat. "Well, Alisa, what have you got for me?"

.𝔊.

An hour later they were standing on a road overlooking a large private compound of Vitaly Borishenko on the Nikoline Hill, the posh area outside of Moscow where all the members of the Russian elite lived.

Through binoculars, Bridge scoped out the defenses. "This isn't going to be easy. Perimeter patrols, three watchtowers, cameras, and what looks like infrared mirror beams. And probably some of the servants within are packing."

"If we were going in that way," Alisa said.

"You got another way?" he said with a sigh.

"You got a tux?"

.𝔊.

Alisa still had it. The poor schmuck at the limousine company office was turned inside out trying to make her happy. She must have said four times, "No, I am sorry, this just won't do," as the schlub kept bringing out bigger and bigger limos for her approval.

They were sitting in the backseat of the one that was "just right" for the Russian Goldilocks as they approached the compound. Alisa took out the gold-leafed invitation she had wangled from a society matron who was convinced she was secretly a Romamov incognito.

"Did you lift that?"

"Don't be absurd. Madam Bolotnikova thinks I will make the perfect accoutrement on the arm of her son, the unremarkable lieutenant."

"Whoa, so you've already got a date? Then that makes me chopped liver in this monkey suit," Bridge said pulling at the lapel of his hastily rented tux.

"Nonsense. This is the aristocracy, you Cossack. One doesn't just blind date their way to the matrimonial bed."

"Excuse me, *tzaritsa.*"

"You have my forgiveness." She held out her hand to be kissed.

"Nice nail polish . . ." was all she got from Bridge.

At the entrance to the compound, Alisa lowered the limousine's soundproof privacy divider and handed the invite to the driver to hand to the guards at the gate. The guard peered into the side window with a flashlight and, not seeing whatever he was looking for, waved them through.

The footman or whoever he was at the door scanned the invite with a barcode reader and when it beeped, stepped aside.

The ballroom was immense and impressive as it was a part of the grand mansion that this oil oligarch, Borishenko, lived in. From the rare Israeli marble on the floor to the Venetian glass chandelier, every element of the house broadcast the highest price as it always was with the Russian top dogs. Most folks were chatting and very few dancing, despite the noisy Euro pop coming from the band on the other side of the room.

"Alisa!"

Bridge did not turn, but Alisa did.

"Madam Bolotnikova, you look divine."

"Oh, I do alright for an old woman."

"Nonsense. You look positively regal in that dress and your hair . . . impeccable."

"Thank you, my dear, you are too kind," the older woman said as she finally looked at what Alisa was wearing. "And may I say, you are indeed the most stunning creature here tonight. I remember when I could wear seven-and-a-half-centimeter heels." Then she turned to Bridge. "And who is this dashing man?" Madam Bolotnikova said with just the slightest touch of disappointment discernable in her voice.

"Oh, this is Gennady Romanov."

Her eyes widened . . .

"My cousin."

Madam Bolotnikova had two simultaneous reactions that Bridge could read on her face. First, that as her cousin he was not a threat to her wimpy, no-account son who was looking to ruin some woman's life. And second, that she was correct in suspecting Alisa of secretly being a Romanov.

"Splendid, splendid. So glad to meet you."

Ten minutes later, Alisa returned from a trip to the loo. "Anatoly has invited me to his table."

"I thought we wanted Vitaly?"

"Close enough. It's his son."

"Could be even better. Where?" Bridge said, not looking at her.

"There is a garden walk, out the French doors on the right."

"How long will you need?"

"In this dress?" She adjusted the neckline to be a little lower. "Ten minutes."

Bridge watched as Alisa blasted through the phalanx of guests, security, and entourage that surrounded the young oligarch in waiting. The last few meters, urged on by Anatoly himself, who was waving aside his security at the sight of her.

Bridge turned and smiled as he headed to the bar. *So this whole shindig is for the twerp?* he thought. "Sparkling water with lime please," he said to the barman in Russian. A man stepped close to him. Bridge turned sideways to allow him to get to the crowded bar.

"*Spacibo.*"

"*Ne za chto,*" Bridgestone said.

The man ordered vodka and turned to look around the party, then continued in Russian, "Quite a gala."

Bridge just grunted.

"The woman you are with, is she someone of notoriety?"

Bridge's antenna was up. This guy could be State Security.

He agreed with the stranger. "She looks it, no?"

"Yes. She certainly does."

"I thought so too. But I found out she is a housewife from Rostov," he said as he took a long pull on the Perrier.

In genuine shock that he could have mistaken such a commoner from the Russian nowhere of Rostov as being an aristocrat, the man turned. "How do you know that?"

"Because I married her and made her one."

The man reacted with a sudden flush. He attempted to smooth over his faux pas by raising his glass "A toast to your good fortune in finding such a gem in a world of stones."

"*Spacibo,*" Bridge said as he returned the toast.

"*Ne za chto,*" the man said as he turned and walked off.

Only seven minutes! Bridge thought as he looked down at his watch upon seeing Alisa and the boy wonder walking towards the French doors.

Then he saw her. The one who could blow this whole op. She was moving like a shark, homing in on her prey. The people in her way were mere collateral damage as she single-mindedly advanced on Alisa. Bridge knew he had to intercept her, had to stop her. He stepped lively. He adjusted the gun tucked into the small of his back as he reached out to the woman. "Madam Bolotnikova. Madam Bolotnikova." His hand on her shoulder stopped her as she turned to him, "Yes . . . Gennady, isn't it?"

"You remembered. I was wondering if you were related to the great Bolotnikov?"

"Why yes, he was my great, great grandfather."

"I knew it."

"Well, good for you," she said as she turned to catch Alisa.

"It's just that I studied your ancestor. He was a great man, the son of an escaped bondman who changed the system and became the tsar's right hand!"

"Yes. Thank you. We all know about the rebellion." Her eyes were on Alisa now, disappearing through the doors with the man of the hour.

"Mother . . . she's leaving."

Bridge looked over and finally noticed the string bean standing next to the rotund woman. "You must be Sergei!"

A little taken aback, Sergei said, "I am . . . and you are?"

"This is Gennady Romanov, Alisa's cousin," his mother said, emphasizing the last name with a nod that seemed to confirm what she had suspected about Alisa's true lineage.

"Did you serve?" Bridge, the Special Forces sergeant, asked the kid who must have gotten through the Russian Army by looking at a picture of his mother every night.

"Yes. I was a lieutenant."

.𝔊.

Alisa and Anatoly found a secluded part of the vast gardens in the compound. Like all Russian oligarchs, the Borishenko family copied everything they saw in the West. This intimate garden corner was the exact replica of a Barcelona patio. Alisa was acutely aware of a security man keeping a watchful eye on his bratty charge. "This is a beautiful spot."

"You like it?" Anatoly said

"What's not to like? This is truly heaven."

He took out a small plastic bag. "We can make it a paradise," he said as he tapped the bag of white powder.

Alisa looked over her shoulder. "Won't somebody see?"

Anatoly sat on a stone bench and was now looking at Alisa's chest. "He's one of my bodyguards. He is used to me."

Alisa knew that wasn't good. She had to think of something fast. Then the frat boy, without benefit of college, gave her the opening.

"Of course, if you want something from me, what do I get from you?" He leaned back on his elbows as he asked the question.

Alisa smiled. She looked down at the bulge in his pants and said, "Like a trade?"

"Something like that," he said as he undid his belt buckle.

"You want me to make love to you with my mouth?"

"For starters."

"Hmmm. You sound like a man with a plan." She got on her knees. Drooped her shoulders, which purposefully exposed more of her bust line.

.G.

Bridge was now trying to get away from the mommy dearest and her spawn. "Perhaps we can chat later, but right now I am afraid nature calls. Madam, Sergei." He gave a slight bow and left.

"Come on, Sergei." She went out into the garden.

Bridge hung a left and went outside the building. He made a show of patting his hands on his jacket then asked the guard if he could bum a cigarette.

The guard said, "No smoking."

"What if I go over there by the cars?"

The guard looked around, and reached into his pocket and tapped out a cigarette then jutted his chin to the left as he said, "I go by the wall there."

"*Spacibo*," Bridge said as he walked off knowing that "over there" was probably out of camera range.

.G.

"But I can't do it if I am being watched. I have always been a shy, private person, especially when I am pleasuring a big . . ."—Alisa grabbed his bulge—"strong . . ."—she gave it a shake—"man . . ."—she leaned over and had her long hair brush his crotch—"like you. . . ." She pulled back, removed her hands and sat on her legs, and with the perfect amount of pout said, "I just can't while I'm being watched."

Anatoly was out of his mind with lust and called out, "Vlad. Go away, Vlad. Back in the house, please . . . and make sure no one comes out here." He looked over to make sure his protector had left.

Alisa followed his eyes and seeing that they were now unobserved, she got back into her seductive, spider-like mode as she caught his fly.

Anatoly watched as she slowly unzipped his pants.

She looked up. "Close your eyes. I told you I don't like being watched."

"What good is having a beautiful woman like you if I can't see you?"

"Please, just till I get started; then you can look." She let one strap from her gown fall off her shoulder. "Then I promise I will give you a lot to look at . . ." She cupped her hands over her dress and squeezed her breasts as she looked in his eyes.

"Yes. You do have a lot to look at." He obediently closed his eyes, his head tilted up towards the sky.

With her right hand, she massaged his crotch through his underwear while she reached into her bag with her left. "Ooooo, you got a lot to look at too, big boy."

She rolled her eyes because the line sounded corny, even to her, as she said it. Then she lunged forward and jabbed the syringe right into his neck.

"Ow . . . Ow . . ."

She held her hand over his mouth. "Shhhh shhhhh. It will all be over in three seconds." He wrestled to get out from under her hand and arm that she was now pinning him down with. But the weakness attacked his body and soon he was limp; all of him was limp. She re-buckled his belt and put her shoulder under his arm and got him up. She dragged him to the garden wall.

Bridge popped his head up as he was standing on the limo's trunk. He jumped onto the wall and then grabbed Anatoly and hoisted him up and over.

Alisa kicked off her heels, threw them over the wall, and climbed over as well.

They opened the trunk and put Anatoly next to the unconscious driver who was already bound and gagged.

"Perfect fit," Bridge said.

"See, it was just right!"

Bridge put on the chauffer's coat and hat then got behind the wheel.

Alisa got in the backseat.

Bridge was about to drive off when he suddenly stopped and put the car in park. "What if they are checking cars on the way out?"

.G.

The guard waved the big limo on then held up his hand for it to halt. The driver rolled down his window. "What's the problem?"

"We have to check the car?"

"The couple in the back, they are kind of in a hurry, if you know what I mean?"

The guard took out his flashlight and looked through the back window. He couldn't keep his eyes off the woman with her breast exposed as the man on top of her was humping away. He looked a little longer than he should until the woman opened her eyes, squinting from the light.

Suddenly self-conscious, he waved them through.

Bridge looked in the rearview mirror. When they were a hundred feet from the entrance he said, "You can stop now."

Alisa stopped lifting her leg, raising and lowering the unconscious driver's body she'd pulled on top of her. She rolled him off her and pulled up her dress and adjusted the straps. "I had a husband like him once."

Bridge laughed.

Chapter 27

Right Neighborly

"So you think it's going to be a technology attack?"

"Brooke, it looks that way . . . especially since there are no radiological or biological threats on the board right now. That doesn't rule it out, but it bodes for alternative methods," Remo said.

"So what do the alternatives include?"

"Kronos, you want to take that?"

"Well, there's high-fatality interruption or destruction and then there's denial of services, which could lead to deaths but not immediately."

"So give me a 'for instance.'"

"If you hack into air traffic control, you could do a lot of damage before they got wise and unplugged the system. Could crash one hundred to three hundred planes in a span of minutes . . . mostly on landing, when the pilots are the most vulnerable to controllers and glide path systems."

"Seems like a low estimate," Remo said.

"Well yeah, of the fourteen thousand airports in the US, only about five thousand are paved and fall under FAA control, but really there are only 376 that have regular service. So at any given minute some number less than that will have planes landing on them. And of course once a plane crashes at an airport nobody lands at that airport for hours. So at the most, you'd only get one per airport, if you are a bad guy."

"What else?" Brooke asked.

"Water supply."

"How could they manage that?"

"Obviously, there's the old throw-a-bucket-of-cyanide-into-the-reservoir, but the various water authorities would probably catch it before it got to an urban center, what with all the monitoring devices along the way. But if you could override the flow controls, then you could force floods, disintegrating streets, flooded subways and buildings, and a general stoppage of drinking water. Till they reboot the system. Anyone on a subway train would be dead from drowning before they got out from underground. Also there would be a diminishing of firefighting capability."

"There's only one problem with all these approaches, Brooke."

"What's that, Peter?"

"Most of the real broad hits that can do damage are hack based. And unfortunately you can do that from anywhere in the World Wide Web. Remember what the Norks did to Sony Pictures that time?"

"But we got a cell right here, not in North Korea. So the bad guys don't need to be here if they are only doing some kind of infrastructure cyber-attack?" Brooke said.

"Bingo," Remo said.

"Go back, boys. Find me some hands-on nightmare these yahoos could be up to. And don't stop to nap. Whatever they are going to do . . . it's close."

George entered and stopped them from leaving. "This is good, Brooke."

"I could use some good, George. Whatcha got?"

He laid down a copy of Shamal's picture in front of her. "Ten witnesses to Joe Garrison's death in the subway have ID'd Shamal, picked him right out from a stack of pics."

"So he was our Middle Eastern speaker?"

"It appears so, but here's the kicker." He placed down the picture of Paul from the ATM camera in Europe. "I threw this into the stack just for shits and giggles, and seven of the ten also identified him as being on the car at that moment."

"So this Paul character was an accomplice to Garrison's murder?" Kronos said.

"And one witness thinks he remembers better now; that it wasn't an argument but that the darker-skinned guy was trying to get Joe to go between the cars . . ."

"So, your buddy Joe was trying to escape when he got decapitated," Remo said.

"It could have gone down that way." George shrugged his shoulders.

Just then the phone rang. "Doctor Hiccock on line one."

"Guys, let me take this."

"Okay, we'll be down the hall. Tell Billy he sucks at sending me pictures of Richie," Peter Remo said.

"Will do." She waited for them to leave. "Bill, how did I know I'd hear from you again, today?"

"Brooke, tell me what you wouldn't tell the president."

"Bill, do you know we have tapes of everything that is in the air, 24/7 all around the world?"

"Yeah, we put that in after 9/11."

"Exactly. We did a three-day sweep after the raid here in New York and it seems we got a target hit on a small jet plane crossing into Russia."

"Let me remember. There are two types of return from an aircraft, skin and transponder."

"Right. And we got the skin, or target, track for that plane. Cross checking with the transponder tracks showed that it switched off its box over the Czech Republic."

"But then you could follow it on skin return?"

"Correct."

"Where did it land?"

"Moscow."

"Oops."

"Yeah, tell me about it."

"So you think it's the government?"

"Possibly, but we think we have a better working theory. The plane belongs to Vitaly Boreshenko."

"Who is he?"

"Aw, Bill, not keeping up with your Russian social registry these days, are you?"

"Changing diapers really cuts into my debutant life."

"He's one of the surviving Oligarchs."

"How or why would he play with bad guys?"

"Hopefully we'll ask him when Bridge gets him to tell us where Prescott went."

"So we could be talking about roughing up a key Russian businessman here?"

"Could get his Western capitalist Brooks Brothers suit mussed."

"Well, if anyone can pull this off without creating a second Cold War, it's Sergeant Major Bridgestone."

"My thoughts, and my operational model, exactly, Bill."

"Keep me in the loop."

"Will do boss, er . . . Bill." She hung up the phone and smiled. She was so used to calling Bill "Boss" from when she worked for him in the Quarterback Operations Group. Then she remembered. "Damn, I forgot to tell him to send Remo pictures of little Richie."

.G.

"What is our status?" Dequa asked as he flipped through some papers.

"We have 009, 101, 105, 205, and 314 all manned. Although there's a possible problem with 009." Yusuf reported using the official code numbers for the installations. The entire cell learned to adopt the protocol of their intended target. Besides most of them now held positions on the inside, so it was also natural workplace jargon.

"Really? That's disturbing," Dequa said.

"After hurricane Sandy they installed a new standard and it's just different than our intel."

"What is the yield?"

The question threw Yusuf; he and every member of his team had memorized every aspect of the attack. "Why, 317 million, of course." For Dequa to have not known this basic fact was unnerving to Yusuf.

Dequa saw the concern in his face. "The two 7FA CTG's are operating at 90%, otherwise it would be closer to 360. Is that also part of our bad intel?"

Relieved that his leader wasn't slipping, especially if he did those numbers that fast in his head, Yusuf said, "Possible; we'll know more soon."

"Can this new standard be overcome?"

"Ramal is working on it now."

"Good."

"How is the northern team's progress?"

"They report being on schedule and assets in place."

.Ϭ.

"Hey, Wally. Wally . . . right?"

"Wally" turned around. "Hello, my friend."

"Jim, Jim Aponte. I live across the street."

"Yes, nice lawn."

"Thanks, trick is lots of water. Good thing we're right by the reservoir . . . Anyway, you know I like working on my car whenever I can—"

"The Dodge Charger. Yes, I see it often."

"Labor of love, man. Anyway, I know what it's like to want to work on stuff, but I was wondering, would you mind maybe not doing all that hammering and drilling after eight at night? We got two babies over there and sometimes the racket . . . Well, would you mind toning it down at night?"

"I apologize. I had no idea anyone could hear me work."

"What are you guys working on over there. Doing a lot of metal work? Whatcha got, an old Caddy or '32 Deuce?"

"Soon you will see."

"Well, thanks. Sorry I had to mention it. If you guys ever want to come over for a barbeque or something, I got a smoker. I do a Puerto Rican mofongo with pulled pork that the pig's mother would love."

Waleed bristled. He forced a smile. "Sounds good."

"How many guys you got over there?"

"Why do you want to know that?"

"One pig or two?"

"It is just I and my three brothers."

"No women? Then you guys really need a good meal . . . This Saturday?"

"Next Saturday? We're busy this Saturday."

"Sure thing."

Jim turned to walk back across the sleepy suburban Yonkers street, back to his split colonial ranch with the large lawn that wrapped around the corner. "I'll have plenty of cold beers . . ."

Waleed's smile disappeared as he turned and walked back to his house with the extended three-car garage.

Inside the house, he joined the midday prayer. When it was over, he said to the other team members, "I am going to order six mattresses. We need to control the sound."

They walked into the garage from the kitchen and past the three U-Haul trailers that were side by side. They looked at the doors of the garage. Sunlight was coming through the sides. "Yes, six king-sized mattresses should do it. Plus we will dampen the metal with towels and pillows."

"Just two more days of shaping and we will be finished."

"Still, we can't afford to disturb the neighbors."

"They have said something?"

"Yes. We are invited to the devil's cookout. I don't want to repeat what he said to me."

"Should we kill him?"

"No, that would bring too much attention to this quiet block. We'll just keep the noise down."

.G.

Alisa adopted a Chechen accent and tone. "Anatoly is fine. Tell his father that if he ever wants to see him again, he can bring us Prescott. We trade and Anatoly gets to fuck all the girls he wants with Daddy's money, otherwise we fuck Anatoly then kill him. You have three hours to bring Prescott to Red Square and make sure he is only in his underwear. No clothes; just underwear or we will shoot him. Do you understand? Underwear only! Before you ask, here's proof of life." She handed the phone to Bridge in the backseat.

Bridge removed the gag.

"Help me. Help me. They're crazy. Get me out of here. Mmmph."

Bridge stuffed his mouth again and handed the phone back to her.

"Three hours or he's dead." Alisa threw the phone out the window of the limo as she turned around and reversed direction.

They took the Kievskoe highway, drove to a house right outside Moscow, which had a "For Sale" sign on the fence, and drove into the garage. Once inside they closed the garage door and brought Anatoly into the house, securing him in the basement and locking the door.

Then Alisa followed Bridge as he drove the limo to a secluded overlook. He opened the trunk and took out his knife. The driver lay there out for the count. Bridge considered silencing him for good; it would be in keeping with the national security priority of the mission. He grabbed his knife and slit the tape and zip cuffs. Then he lowered the trunk lid just short of it locking. They had put enough drugs in him that he would be out for six more hours, and this whole thing would be over in three, so there was no reason the man couldn't be spared.

.𝔊.

All the guests were unceremoniously ushered out of the great ballroom, many not even having a chance to retrieve their hats, coats, or stoles; all that could be heard was the whimpering of Mrs. Borishenkova in agony over the kidnapping of her son.

Dmitri, the head of security for the Borishenkos, walked across the empty marble dance floor, the clicking of his heels reverberating with every step. He made his way up to the dais, where his boss was furiously pounding the table.

"How the fuck could this happen? Right in my own house! Dmitri, you son of a bitch, how could you let this happen?"

"I will remedy that immediately." He turned. "Vlad come here."

Vlad stepped lively to his superior's command.

"Yes . . ."

Dmitri pulled out his gun and shot Vlad in the face at five feet. A pink flume exited the back of his head as his body crumpled to the floor.

The wife screamed then whimpered more loudly.

"That doesn't bring my son back you KGB clown," Borishenko said.

"No, but it makes everyone know"—he turned as he spoke to the staff—"that I will stop at nothing to retrieve your son and exterminate, very slowly, the rats responsible for this atrocity."

"Just get my son back."

"We will have him in three hours."

The oligarch looked up. "How can you be so sure?"

"The ransom call just came in."

"How much?"

"Nothing."

"What?"

"They want Prescott."

Borishenko sat back and considered the situation. "Who are they?"

"Probably Chechen rebels."

"Why would the Chechens want Prescott?"

"Does it matter, if you get your son back?"

"True. Tell our guest we can no longer offer him our hospitality."

"He is drugged downstairs. I will have the doctor revive him."

"Very well. Just get my Anatoly back, and if they have so much as harmed a hair on his head . . ."

"Not to worry. They will never escape once we get Anatoly."

"I don't want to know the details . . . just do it."

"I am afraid I must tap a favor at the ministry of defense."

"Another one? We already got Prescott here on my plane without an official flight plan."

"We will need troops to cordon off the area they have selected for the transfer."

"Where?"

"Red Square."

He held up his hands. "I don't want to know."

.G.

"You know I don't really want to blow up this house. It would be a shame. My sister wouldn't get her commission on the sale."

"I wasn't going to actually arm it. If we get killed there is no reason to kill the dopey kid. This is a bluff all the way . . . In fact, can you take a slap?"

.G.

Anatoly watched Alisa and Bridge come down to the basement. He was immobilized and gagged. There was an iPhone taped to a tripod in front of him. Bridge was carrying a brown paper bag.

Alisa removed the gag.

"Whatever you want, my father will pay. You don't have to do anything to me."

"Shut up and drink." She held a glass of water to his lips and he swallowed, some of the water running down his chin.

"Thank you. Whatever you want . . . mmmph."

She shoved the rag back in. Then she noticed Bridge pull out a brick of C4 with a cell phone wired to it. "What the fuck is that?"

"What do you think it is?"

"I thought we said we'd shoot him!"

Anatoly's eyes widened.

"His father's henchmen are planning how to kill us right now. We are both going to have be at the exchange to survive. So if they fuck with us, he gets splattered all over the neighborhood."

"No, there are children living next door . . . I won't let you kill them." She went for the bomb.

Bridge backhanded her and she landed on her side. "Shut up, bitch! This is my operation; the Muscovites didn't care when they murdered our children in Grozny! My sister, my mother, my brothers! Are you soft for this bourgeois elitist?"

Alisa got up, pulled out her gun and pointed it at Bridge.

"What are you going to do? You want to shoot me?" Bridge said with a smirk.

"No." She turned and aimed the gun at Anatoly. "No, I will kill him, now. And save the children."

Anatoly stiffened and moaned something monosyllabic through the rag stuffed in his mouth.

"No, you fool! With him dead you have sealed our fates! He must die at a time of our choosing. Trust me, if all goes as planned, he and everyone in this area will only be the first of hundreds of thousands of Russian dogs to die!"

Alisa made a conscious decision to listen to Bridge. Slowly, she lowered her weapon.

Bridge grabbed it. "Go upstairs. Prepare for our departure."

As Alisa went upstairs, he duct taped the bomb around the kid and the chair, right across his chest. There was a box with a red flashing light right next to the cell phone. Bridge inserted the metal end of the detonator's wire into the block of plastic explosives strapped to the kid.

Bridge went over to the iPhone on the tripod and called out, "Svetlana, call the phone!" The phone rang and Bridge touched the screen.

Since it was facing Anatoly, he could see "Svetlana" on the screen of the phone.

"It's FaceTime. We can see you, no matter where we are." When your father gets on the phone, you will see him and he will see you like you are seeing Svetlana." He removed the gag. "Now say hello!"

"Hello."

"How is the sound?"

"Good." He looked into the kid's eyes while he held up a red button on a cord that disappeared into his pocket. "You're a smart kid. See this button?"

The kid nervously nodded.

He brought his thumb right above the plunger. "Once I press it, it has to stay pressed or that bomb goes off. If your father does what we ask, I will hand him the button so you will live. If they shoot me or try to take it away." He lifted his finger away from the button. "Boom!"

The sweat on the kid's forehead told him he got the point. "Oh, and don't bother yelling. This old house is solid and there are no windows down here. Save your breath to speak with your father." He left the basement, locking the door.

Upstairs he put his hand on Alisa's chin and turned her head. "You okay? There's no mark."

"I'm fine. I had a husband like that once."

"How many have you had?"

"Enough now, I think."

He held up a red button on a cord connected to nothing, which disappeared into his pocket.

.𝕾.

"Is the northern unit ready?" The sheik asked over the encrypted phone call.

"Yes, they are testing one tomorrow morning," Dequa said.

"We will pray that they perform as designed."

"I will personally go and witness the test."

Chapter 28

Boom

6 DAYS UNTIL THE ATTACK

Dequa started out at 3:30 a.m. for the three-and-a-half-hour drive up to the old abandoned quarry in Seneca County. He arrived a half-hour late at 7:30, but immediately realized how it was the perfect spot and worth the drive. The quarry was like a bowl cut into the earth, surrounded on all sides by striated stone. The bottom was flat and had many long-abandoned rusting bulldozers and bucket loaders from when the company went out of business. The bowl shape meant that the sound would be directed up and not across the countryside.

Waleed and the rest of the team were already there, having towed the heavy U-Haul there before dawn. Waleed approached Dequa. "We were waiting."

"There was an accident on the Thruway."

"Well, let's get to cover."

There was a narrow slit cut into the side of the bowl. It was how the workers and equipment got in as the bottom got lower and lower over the years. Once on the other side, Waleed handed out ear protection. When everybody had the headsets on he gave the signal, and Fakhir dialed his cell phone. The call rang once and then there was a terrific explosion. They heard rocks and debris fall for a full ten seconds after the blast.

The smell of cordite and C4 was instantly everywhere as they walked back into the bowl. There was now a crater four hundred feet across and so deep they couldn't see the bottom until they were almost upon it. Fakhir brought a tripod right up to the hole and then pointed the laser range finder at the center, next to the mangled carcass of the barely recognizable U-Haul trailer. He noted the angle of the device then read off the distance to the bottom. Using simple trigonometry he made the depth to be fifty-five and one half feet.

"Perfect! Well beyond the forty we'll need. You crafted an excellently shaped charge, my brother."

"It was all in the hyperbolic hammering of the blast shield. It was noisy but I'm pleased with the results."

Dequa nodded to Fakhir then walked off through the slit to his car and back to the city.

Fakhir waved his hand and said, "Plant the charges." The other team members used a battery-operated drill with a four-foot-long auger bit on the end and made eight holes in the soft soil around the perimeter of the new crater. They dropped sticks of TNT with traditional PETN detcord in each hole. They wired it all to a timer, set it for one minute, and went back to the cover position. Thirty seconds later, there was another explosion. Fakhir and the team came out and saw that the sides of the crater were now blasted in and the bottom of the crater was filled in so much it was now merely a depression only ten feet deep, with all the evidence of the U-Haul and the half-ton steel downward blast reflector bomb buried deep. No plane passing overhead or curious person on foot would have a clue as to the spent weapon buried below.

.G.

Brooke had heard from her guy at the CIA that something had happened in Russia and that it involved a family member of the Borishenko clan. It was an odd feeling for her, being out of the action, being a spectator seven thousand miles away. Yet, she couldn't be everywhere, especially now since this was her operation. She needed to run it, not run around in it. With a deep breath she said to herself, "Keep your head down, Bridge." And then she tried to focus on the reports in front of her.

Something caught her eye, so she got up and went down to Remo and Kronos's office. "Hey, guys. There are fourteen 'students' who seem to have electrical degrees or work history."

Remo grabbed the report. "Hey, you're right, but this is real I squared R electrics."

"English por favor," Brooke said.

"Generation, transmission and power lines," Kronos said.

"But that's only 14 of 120 suspected H-1B visa violations and those are only what we suspect out of over 14,300 overstayers, as they are called, this year alone," Remo said.

"Brooke, we should look into it, but there are far more medical, chemical, and mechanical 'students' in the friggin' mix," Kronos said.

"That's because we went with a tech attack scenario as our sort routine key on the database," Brooke said.

"Also, Brooke, I know you've considered that our 120-person sample represents those who seem to have appeared since SOM37 went dark. But that doesn't preclude the possibility that others came earlier, or they have local support," Remo said. "You want to go back to the full list?"

"I've been offered the additional resources so I think we will. Meanwhile, I'll get the OEM and head of Con Ed security up here and give them the heads up." As she said it, Brooke had a pang of remorse that whoever came from OEM would be a replacement for the director of the New York City Office of Emergency Management, because the last one—she couldn't remember his name—had died yesterday in the rocket attack that almost killed her and Bridge. *God, was it only yesterday?*

Chapter 29

Taking Delivery

For the first time in years Red Square was empty. Not a soul was there. No Japanese crowds thronging round the Mausoleum, no rich Italians strolling by the glass windows of the Central Gum store. Even the beggars were absent from their favorite spots by the small red church in front of the State Historic Museum. It was obvious to Bridge that Borishenko had a lot of juice with the army. They must have swept through and ordered everyone out of the sixty-three-square-acre centerpiece of Moscow. Bridge could only imagine how many snipers, bazookas, and machine guns were pointed at him right now. He checked the rearview mirror of the small car he was driving: all clear. He pulled to the side of Saint Basil's Cathedral, parked and waited. An armored personnel carrier suddenly rumbled over the cobblestones and pulled right up to his car. A tall man in a full-length black leather coat got out.

Bridge rolled down the window and yelled in Russian, "Where's Vitaly Borishenko?"

"He's not here," the man in the coat said. "I am his head of security. We spoke on the phone. Where is the boy?"

"Borishenko, now, or I drive out of here and we'll do this all over again. Trust me, you will never find him in time. You know I didn't get this far without having a plan. Don't be stupid."

Bridge could see the veins popping in the neck of the man in the leather coat as he stood in the harsh headlights of his car. Bridge knew the man wanted to kill him right there for being so insolent. He saw the man turn and walk to the back of the carrier. A few seconds later, ten troops with heavy weapons came out of the back with Vitaly Borishenko in the center of their formation. Seeing this, Bridge got out of the car.

"Where is my son?"

"He's right here."

Borishenko squinted and tried to look into Bridge's car through the windshield.

"Not there, here!" Bridge held up the phone in his left hand and the plunger in his right.

Dmitri nodded his head in the direction of the phone to one of the soldiers. He lowered his weapon and cautiously approached Bridge. He carefully took the phone and double-timed it back to Borishenko.

"Anatoly!" Tears welled up in his eyes. "Are you okay?"

"Yes, Father. Do what he says. Do you see the bomb?"

"Yes. Yes. Don't worry, son, this will all be over in a few minutes."

"Those are good words, Vitaly. You've seen and talked to your son. You see he's alive but if I release the pressure on this plunger, he dies. So tell your boys, no shooting and no getting in my way or trying to jam the signal. It's fail-safed, so it's looking for a break in the signal to detonate. Now where's Prescott? My finger's getting tired."

Borishenko nodded to Dmitri, who waved to the rear of the armored vehicle.

From behind the carrier, Prescott was escorted by one of Dmitri's men. As he approached, Bridge saw that they had listened and he was only in a t-shirt and briefs. "Turn around," Bridge ordered and, not seeing anything like a gun or knife outlined in the man's skivvies, he gestured behind him. "In the car."

The guard put him in the backseat and rejoined his ranks.

"When do I get my son?"

"When I am safe and not followed. Keep the phone. I will call you when I am clear and tell you where he is. I have no interest in harming your boy. Unless you try something cute. Then he dies with me, wherever I am."

"Don't trust this Chechen," Dmitri said.

"I have no choice. He has won; all I want is my son back. Let him go."

"If you let him go you will never see your son. I am certain."

"Don't listen to him, Vitaly. if I release my hand, you will see him in pieces. Order him to comply."

"Dmitri, please!"

"You are making a mistake . . ."

"He's my son! Damn you. And this is how we are going to do it!"

Bridge got in the car, holding the button high so it could be seen through the windshield. He crossed himself with his left hand to put the car in gear while holding up the plunger. Without taking his eyes off the men in front he said, "Are you okay, Morgan?"

"They drugged me, but I am good." That statement made Bridge scrunch his eyebrows.

Dmitri's rage boiled over. "You fool, you are letting him go!" He reached for his gun and whipped around to shoot at Bridge when suddenly a dull *thwop* was heard as his skull exploded. Borishenko jumped back but was splattered with blood and bits of brain. The soldiers all hit the deck as Vitaly's security guys scrambled him back into the tracked vehicle.

As Bridge backed out of the square he said under his voice, "Nice shooting, Alisa."

Three hundred yards out, Alisa broke down the Paratus-16 sniper rifle and packed it in the case, then stood up and straightened her gown and left the roof of the Hotel Moscow. Once inside, she slid the collapsed rifle in the laundry chute and then pressed the elevator button.

The door opened to the lobby and a reception was in full swing. She grabbed a glass of champagne off a table and walked through like she was invited. At the doorway, she placed the glass on a waiter's tray and asked, "Ladies room?"

He pointed to the right; she went left, to the exit. As the Red Square was blocked, Okhotnyi Ryad was crowded with discontented tourists.

Outside, Bridge pulled up and she got in. She looked in the back. "Bridge, you didn't tell him about the clothes?"

"I was a little busy."

She handed him the folded slacks and shirt and socks. "Prescott, here put these on."

"We had to make sure you weren't the leader of this thing and that you wouldn't pull a weapon on us once you were in the car."

"Who are you people? Are you Americans?"

"Yes. We're here to take you back to America," Bridge said.

"No, you must take me back to Borishenko. Now!"

"What part of 'you are going back' didn't you get?"

"Do they know you are American?"

"Hey, pal, shut up," Bridge said.

"You are putting my family in danger!"

"What are you talking about?" Alisa said.

"If they think you are working for me, they will kill my wife and kids. They have them. They are holding them."

"All right, bullshit story time is over. We've seen your wife and kids and they are on your yacht in St. Thomas."

"No, that's not them. Those are imposters paid by someone to play my family. My wife Deidra and my three kids, Molly, Jennifer, and Chet are being held in my home on Grenada. They are under armed guard; if I didn't go along with them they were going to kill them. You've got to take me back, before they think you work for me."

"Who? Borishenko?"

"No, he's a just customer; the terrorists, they will kill them!"

Bridge looked at Alisa. She shrugged her shoulders. As they pulled into the American Embassy they hatched a plan.

.𝔊.

"You want me to what?" Brooke stood up from her desk, waved her hand at Agent Stover and motioned for him to listen in as she hit the speakerphone button. "Bridge, that could take hours to get approval, from State, Defense, and ultimately, I guess, the boss."

"That's why it's up to you, Brooke."

"Are you sure this is the only way he'll cooperate?"

"Prison time, fines, even the death penalty, if it comes to that, doesn't shake him. It's all about his family."

"Can't say I blame him," Brooke said.

"It's his only play," Alisa said.

"Who's that?" Brooke raised an eyebrow.

"That's Alisa. She's my local here and saved my life already tonight."

"Alisa, I owe you a drink sometime, girl," Brooke said in Russian.

"You got a deal," Alisa answered back in English.

.𝔊.

"George, get the chopper back and use the priority billing code to get a skeeter, wet and wild. File a flight plan for Grenada. Gear up for you and me. Pick someone else to be heavy with us," Brooke ordered.

"What's up, boss?"

"We are about to rescue Prescott's family."

"That's a little cowboy ain't it?"

"It turns out they had him in a wedge. We've got about a five-hour window before they find out it wasn't the Chechens and that Prescott is under our custody . . . and execute his entire family."

"Shit."

Two hours later the rescue team of three were at forty thousand feet in a government G5. George had just received a PDF of the layout of the Prescott Estate on the island of Grenada.

The State Department was applying a "full nelson" to the neck of the Grenadine government to allow the plane and its occupants to land unmolested and carryout the extraction with or without government troops in assistance. In the end, the negotiations came down to Brooke reading in the US Ambassador to Grenada in Barbados on the national security threat of which Morgan Prescott was the key. The ambassador sent the chargé d'affaires from the in-country US Embassy to personally meet with the president of the tiny island nation while Brooke and her team were in the air. Using his personal friendship and some diplomatic arm twisting, the ambassador secured the landing rights. The operational rights, for Brooke's team to actually do something in his nation, were sealed upon the promise of two new US Coast Guard cutters to be transferred to his small navy. The leader's caveat being that his troops would only play a support role and not take part in the extraction or any action connected to it.

Brooke was fine with that. She and George and Walker, all by themselves, had their shit wired tight enough, and even though they had never deployed as a team before, they had all been involved with extraction from hostile enemies. They would have to hit the ground running and make it up as they went along. "Adapt, innovate, and overcome," was all Brooke said to the two men she was about to go into battle with.

The odds leaned in their favor since they had the element of surprise, (Brooke hoped) plus night vision goggles, a JDI drone with high-definition infrared, and a whole goody bag of flash bangs, tear gas, and concussive grenades. The Heckler and Koch MP7 slung under her arm, the HK 416 with George, and the M4 carbine that Walker carried and made him center-mass deadly from twenty-five yards out was what she deemed adequate firepower for the job.

Brooke was hoping that the opposing force wasn't going to be the A team. After all, how badass did guards have to be to keep a forty-five-year-old socialite and three teenagers incarcerated?

Brooke was thinking about how smoothly things were going for a hastily organized extraction op that she would have preferred to have three weeks rather than three hours to prep for. Then, right on cue, Mr. Murphy and his law responded to her observation.

"South Com on the radio," the pilot informed her.

Brooke took the copilot's headset. "Burrell to South Com."

"Burrell, be advised, mechanical trouble delaying your asset from rendezvous oh-two-hundred hours local time."

"Crap!" Brooke hit the transmit switch. "Roger that, South Com. We'll make do. Burrell over and out."

"What's up, boss?" George said.

"The drone pilot from Southern Command won't be joining us. The transport plane he was flying out of McDill in is busted. We lost our drone operator."

"The thing is in the back. Do you think there's an instruction manual?" Walters said, hitching his thumb over his shoulder at the large anvil case that held the thirty-thousand-dollar toy.

"No, Walters, we are going to need all the guns we have going through the door. Can't spare you to be a drone jockey."

The pilot overheard the conversation. "Director Burrell, I can fly it, I think."

"It's not like a G5, Captain . . ."

"I know, but I bought a Radio Shack drone for my kids and I taught them how to fly it on the weekends, and I think I could handle it."

"Okay, why not. Captain, you've got the drone. I'll try and give you a few minutes to get acquainted before we go in."

The pilot smiled and the copilot looked over at him and just laughed and shook his head.

As they approached the estate, they did a final comms check. From the map George downloaded on the plane, they chose what looked like a blind spot in case anyone at all was watching the security system that Prescott had detailed to Bridge, who'd marked up the map and layout.

The moment came when Brooke had to make the call. Go or no go. She ran through the same mental checklist one more time. Her last check was to look up and ensure that the moon had not risen yet. "We ready?"

She got two clicks each over the comms. "Okay, we all get to go home tonight. Let's go."

That was what she always said, even back in her FBI days when she served with HRT. Only difference being, the hostage rescue team had ten times more assets and local LEOs with guns for support, not Grenadian troops waiting and watching to see who killed whom.

.G.

Five identical black GMC Yukons exited the box-shaped American Embassy onto Bolshoy Devyatinskiy Per. They passed the row of tightly spaced, large, beautiful concrete flower boxes that were in full bloom. Their true beauty being that they could stop a large truck from penetrating the perimeter. One by one the vehicles peeled off from the convoy at each cross-street.

Three of the Yukons headed to the Domodedovo Airport, one went to the Kazanski train station and the other headed out to the country. Each was driven by a State Department driver and had a Diplomatic Security officer in the shotgun seat, with an actual shotgun standing up, its barrel secured to the dashboard. In the back of each of the five vehicles were three people, two men and a woman. State Department employees all. The automotive shell game was to thwart any of Borishenko's men or their pals in the government from trying to disrupt the extradition of Prescott to the US.

A few minutes later, a cleaning van also pulled out of the driveway and rocked onto the same street, heading to the smaller Sheremetyevo Airport. Bridge, Alisa, Prescott, and one other man were sitting on overturned buckets in the back of the windowless van.

"Who's the driver? Can he be trusted?" Prescott said.

"Meet Vasily." Bridge gestured towards the driver's seat.

"Very nice to be meeting you," Vasily said in a heavy accent as he tipped his Moscow policeman's hat.

The other man in the van was the chargé d'affaires of the embassy, who would invoke diplomatic immunity for his three guests and get them onto an Air Canada flight with direct nonstop service to JFK.

The tickets were secured from the Canadian Embassy and the names John, Mary, and Jack Smith used as ID. The embassy staff quickly made up black diplomatic passports for the trio to ensure they would fly through the airport and onto the plane without being harassed.

Bridge took out a cell phone, dialed, and waited for the other end to pick up. "Vitaly. Your son is sleeping on the first bench from the main entrance to Sokolniki Park." He tossed the phone out the window.

The van pulled up to the service gate at the end of the runway. Vasily got out and spoke with the guard. A moment later he returned as the gate opened and he drove down the access road to the tarmac alongside the Air Canada jet at the terminal.

As they stepped up the service stairs outside the jet way, Prescott asked, "How did you get that Russian cop to help us like that?"

"Yankee ingenuity!"

In the gangway, a State Department employee met them and handed their tickets and passports to the chargé d'affaires. He, in turn, distributed them to Bridge and the rest. Then he showed his ID to the gate agent and asked to speak with the captain.

In short order, the captain had his official government form filled out, and within six minutes of their arrival through the back gate of Sheremetyevo Airport, they were in their first class seats aboard the Airbus 320 with the maple leaf on the tail.

Bridge and Prescott were sitting together and Alisa was in the same row, right across the aisle. The flight attendants were closing the cabin door when suddenly a shout from the jetway caused the stewardess to open it again. A man, out of breath and carrying a briefcase, stepped onto the plane. The door closed behind him.

The man nodded to the crewmember and she gestured for him to sit. He took the empty seat next to Alisa.

The plane pushed back from the gate and Bridge pulled an *Aeroflot* magazine out of the pocket on the bulkhead wall. Morgan Prescott crossed his arms and leaned his head against the window, closing his eyes.

Chapter 30

Rock Group

5 DAYS UNTIL THE ATTACK

Waterloo High School's geology club was ecstatic as Mr. Herns, the earth science teacher and his club of six future geologists, piled into the van. They were headed for an historic first this Monday morning. The "first" was the first true seismic event that had been recorded so close to their school. It was the also the first since they'd gotten the grant to buy a Guralp seismic monitor. Mr. Herns had lobbied the school board hard for the purchase because he saw it as an excellent opportunity to hone the skills of these students in monitoring and analyzing tectonic activity. The nearby event it recorded over the weekend had the added bonus of the epicenter being in an abandoned quarry. That meant the possibility of years of exposed, oxygenated rock being shaken off and a new peel of earth revealed. If that happened, it could be a treasure trove of geologic purity.

Susan Wackner, a sophomore in the group, got permission for her boyfriend, Brendon, the quarterback of the football team, to tag along, as they did everything together.

"So why are we going here again?" Brendon asked from the rear seat, his arm around Susan.

"We may have had a mini-earthquake in the old quarry early Sunday morning or it might be nothing more than a landslide . . ." Mr. Herns said to the rearview mirror.

"That would be bad?"

"On the contrary, Brendon, that would be awesome, because a new strata of rock may be revealed for us to investigate. We'll see."

Brendon stuck his finger in his mouth and feigned a quiet gag response. Susan slapped him playfully on his shoulder.

The van pulled through the weathered gates of the old quarry past the long-rusting machines and through the notch into the bottom of the man-made bowl.

Mr. Herns got out of the school van and immediately spun around, looking for where the landslide had occurred. "That's funny . . . Maybe it was a mini-quake after all. These walls don't look like they have been disturbed in years."

"A real mini of a quake; if it was only a point two-five on the Richter scale," Susan said.

Then Mr. Herns looked at the floor of the quarry. He walked about fifty yards in a circle. The he stopped and bent down. He gathered up a handful of the newly loosened dirt and smelled it.

"Look, Sue, he's eating the dirt. What a dipthoid," Brendon said.

"Don't be a child. I am sure he has a good reason." Then she yelled over, "Mr. Herns, what are you doing?"

"Come over here . . ."

The club came to where Herns was crouching. He held up his dirt-filled hand. "Smell that?"

"Oooo, eek, that's bad."

"Yeah, but that sweet smell mixed in there, that's glycerin."

"Like sugar?"

"No, it's what's left after you explode nitroglycerin."

"How do you know that?" Brendon said, trying to wrestle Susie's attention back from the rock geek.

"We used it in the search for oil."

"That's dumb, blowing up oil." Brendon grunted when he laughed.

"Brendon, we'd place dynamite at specific intervals and read the seismic wave the shock that the detonation produced. Knowing how kinetic energy travels through certain substances, we could determine what was under out feet."

"So it was like a sonic x-ray of the crust, Mr. Herns?"

"Exactly, Susan."

Brendon made a sour face and walked off.

"So that means they used dynamite here years ago?"

"They most certainly had to. It's how they cleaved the rim and brought down the rock to be excavated out by truck through the cut where we came in."

Brendon walked around the quarry, kicking the dirt and watching the wind take the plumes. He looked back and saw Susan enraptured with Mr. Herns. "Stupid rock lover," he said.

Then he hit something. He tapped it with his foot. It was tin or metal. First he scraped away the dirt with his foot. The he bent down and retrieved a license plate.

It was an Ohio plate. He smacked it on his open hand as he continued walking. Eventually he got bored and walked back over to the gaggle of nerds.

.𝔊.

"Are you guys done yet?"

"Brendon, whatcha got there?" Mr. Herns said.

"Some old license plate. From Ohio. I think it's a good sign; a scout from Ohio State gave me a good write up. I might get a scholarship to go there."

The thought that the term "scholar," even in the word scholarship, was used in relation to this particular teen bristled the educator within Michael Herns. This kid, Brendon, had as much academic drive as the dead pigskin of the football. His ability to throw the ball, however, ensured that his four-year college career would be paid for lock, stock, and barrel. Meanwhile, a true academic like Susan would probably wind up in a two-year community college for lack of funds. He repressed the urge to say something snotty to the kid and instead said, "Cool. Can I see it?"

Brendon handed it over.

"Ohio . . . trailer . . ." He flicked away some more dirt with his thumb. "This registration stamp is good till next year. Brendon, where did you find this?"

"Over there." He pointed to where he found it. "Just under the dirt."

"What is it, Mr. Herns?" Susan said.

"Odd. How would a current plate from Ohio get buried here?"

"Ah, who cares? I want it. I am going to put it over my locker." Brendon took back his new good luck charm.

Chapter 31

The Floater

"Well, well, only three fingers on the left hand! Given the apparent time the body was in the water, I would have said getting a positive ID was going to be difficult but the scarring here tells me these digits were surgically removed, or at least attended too some time ago, so there must be a record," the New York City Medical examiner opined as he assessed the waterlogged body before him.

"That's a break," Detective Rolland Harris said as he leaned over, looking at the body retrieved by NYPD divers that was now on the deck of the Harbor Unit, Launch #4.

The ME continued as he pulled back the pant legs a little more with blue rubber gloves on his hands. "And from the looks of this non-bloated part of the leg here—you see, just above the sever point—I'd say he was being held down at the bottom, probably by leg shackle tied to a great weight, which also created a weak spot here, just above the ankle. The abrasion around the cuff, brought on by the river currents, probably caused the leg to detach at this joint, freeing the body to rise to the surface."

"Okay, we'll search all missing persons for three fingers on the left hand. Anything else, Doc?" Harris asked while jotting down notes in his flipbook.

"Appears there was a tattoo on the upper forearm, but it is dilated by bloating and shedding skin. We might be able to shrink the skin and do a sub-dermatological penetration x-ray to read it under the exposed layer of skin."

"That'll help."

Back at the Midtown North precinct, an hour later, Harris answered the phone on the first ring. "Squad, Harris."

"Rolland, I got a hit on your floater," Joan McCabe, from the missing persons bureau, said over the phone.

"Great, Joan, who was he?"

"If it's him, he's Raleigh Dickson. Age fifty-three. Of 1334 Palmer Court, New Rochelle. He's got a wife and three grown kids. They reported him missing two weeks ago."

"Any mental condition or reason he'd just skip out on them?"

"No. He just never came home from work."

"What did he do?"

"He was in construction. Actually, demolition . . . Wait a minute; something else just came up in the search. He is a federal explosive licensee."

"Okay, that means ATF&E has got to have a file on him. Good work, Joan."

"Hey, don't you want to know about the fingers?"

"Let me guess, he lost them in a blast?"

"Yeah, that's what I thought. But no, he was hurt during the recovery operation at Ground Zero after 9/11."

"Ahhh hell, a guy like that winds up fish food. There is no justice in the world, Joan."

"At least he'll get a military funeral."

"Why?"

"He was a sergeant in the marines . . . explosive ordinance disposal."

"This gets worse and worse."

.𝔊.

In three hours, Harris had Dickson's ATF&E file and military record. The latter probably explained the tattoo on the man's arm. His wife and his kids didn't know of anybody who wanted to do harm to Dickson. And he wasn't a gambler or, as far as they knew, into any drugs or anything illegal. That clean profile made the hairs on Harris's neck stand up, because it could mean Dickson was dead because of what he did—explosives. So, he was now on the way to Empire City Demolition where Dickson worked.

At Empire, they were all concerned about Dickson. The news that he was dead shocked everyone. Harris asked that his desk be cordoned off until detectives could go through the contents to try and see if anything could shed light on his disappearance or, more importantly, why anyone would want to kill him.

"Is this the only place he worked?"

"Here and in the locker."

"What's the locker?"

"The ordinance locker, where we keep the charges."

"Can I see it?"

"Sure."

They went to a bunker out back. It was a solid steel building buried into the ground. Inside were wooden crates, lots of them.

"How much do you have here?"

"The feds limit us to thirty boxes of TNT shots."

"There are more than thirty boxes here."

"On the right, those are plastique."

"Why do you have plastic?"

"Plastique. We use it as cutting charges."

There was a pause and Harris finally said, "You're going to make me ask, aren't you?"

"Sorry, we make cutting charges when we are taking down a building. We shape the charge like a rope and adhere it to a main building girder at a forty-five-degree angle. When it detonates, it slices the girder, and the column slides apart down the slant." He swept his tilted flat hand from upper left to lower right to show the angle.

"So the plastique is like clay?"

"It's malleable, so we can make all kinds of different shaped charges for all kinds of different jobs. A shape or directed charge can be a hundred times more effective than just an omni-directional blast."

"You mean more than just an explosion?"

"Yes. Getting a detonation to do work, that's all in the shape and the timing of the shots. We don't so much blow up a building as we ring its bell and have the harmonics collapse the structure."

"Can I see this stuff?"

"What?"

"The moldable charges."

"Really?"

"Humor me."

The foreman went to the first box and was about to hump it over to a little table.

"Uh, no, from the back, please," Harris said.

"Why?"

"We're still humoring me, right?"

"Geez," he said as he slid between the crates. He got the last crate from the top of the ones by the back wall. He humped it over to the cop and placed it on the table. He took out a pair of wire snips and clipped the two nylon wire ties that sealed the box. He opened it without looking into it.

"So plastique is like sand?"

"What? Holy fuck!" the foreman said, looking down at the sand in the box that held no explosives.

An hour later, with the bomb squad observing, the men of Empire confirmed that of the fifty crates of C4-like plastique explosives, twenty had their contents missing.

The owner of Empire Demolition, Charles Manning, was waiting for his lawyer; Harris knew his whole business and everything he owned could be lost to federal, state, and city fines. He didn't even want to consider the prison term the man was facing.

"What made you think to look?" the borough commander who showed up at the scene asked Harris.

"Sir, I had the guy in charge of these explosives come up a floater in the Hudson. He was clean, but someone deep-sixed him. This was my nightmare hunch. And I figured, if I had taken some explosives it wouldn't be from the front of the stockpile where they'd be discovered sooner than those in the back.

"Are we sure the stuff disappeared from here?"

"Each case is unsealed, inspected, and resealed right here at the point of delivery. These boxes came into this locker full of explosives."

.G.

The afternoon bell rang at Waterloo High. Susan had history. Brendon had to continue his failing effort at algebra. Before they parted he said, "Friday night after practice we are going to Todd's house. His mom and dad are away. You wanna go?"

"I'll have to see if Judy can cover for me. I'll tell my mom we're going to go to the movies and get Chinese food. That usually gets me home at midnight."

"Sweet," Brendon said as he leaned over to give her a kiss before class.

"Brendon!"

He jumped as the principal called his name. He closed his eyes in annoyance. When he opened them, the principal, Mr. Herns, and a tough-looking, six-foot-four, two-hundred-plus-pound New York State Trooper were standing there.

Herns pointed up to the Ohio plate that Brendon had taped over his locker earlier in the morning. "That's it."

"The trooper reached up and, using a box cutter, sliced the tape and pulled the plate away from the locker's face. Then holding the plate only by the edges he slid it into a plastic evidence bag. He nodded to the principal who held out a clipboard. "Sign here, Brendon. The plate will be returned to you if it is not part of a crime."

"You eighteen, boy?" the trooper said.

"In two months, sir."

"Then your principal will have to co-sign as temporary guardian."

"What's this all about?" Brendon asked.

"Probably nothing," the trooper said as he tore off the top page of the duplicate form and handed it to Brendon.

.G.

Forty-five hundred miles east of Waterloo High, at Sheremetyevo Airport, the man in the tenth row aisle seat of the Air Canada plane opened his smart phone. He ignored the fact that he was in strict violation of the flight attendant's warning to shut off all electronic devices once the forward cabin door was closed. He cradled his hand around its screen. A photo of Bridge just taken with a long lens in Red Square came up. Then he swiped his finger and the next image was of Prescott. The last was a fuzzy surveillance shot of Alisa, taken at the event at Borishenko's house. He looked forward and deduced the likeness was close enough to the woman sitting across the aisle from the two men. He reached down into his carry-on and screwed the silencer into the barrel of the small .22 caliber pistol. The weapon that had been waiting for him in a water-tight plastic bag in the third stall's toilet tank in the airport's men's room. The one that was just beyond the security check point.

With one last twist, the muffler was in place. His plan was to shoot them before the plane took off. This way they'd be able to turn right around. He'd be handed over to the authorities and in an hour Borishenko's lawyers would have him out.

"Sir, sir you must sit down! We are on an active runway . . . Please get back to your seat," the cabin attendant yelled to the man who suddenly rose and headed to the front of the plane with his right hand under his *Pravda* magazine.

Bridge looked up in time to see the other man who was seated in their row, next to Alisa, get up and quickly intercept the man just as he got to the second row. The guy from their row simply shoved an ice pick into the man's shoulder. From under the magazine, a small-caliber gun fell to the floor as the would-be attacker cried out in agony, clutching his shoulder.

Passengers screamed. The man who came from their row then held up his ID. "I am GUVD. This man is my prisoner." He turned to the stunned cabin crew. "Tell the captain to turn this plane around." Then he turned back to the passengers in the main cabin as he handcuffed the guy. "I am sorry passengers, but we'll be off the plane fast and you'll be on your way." Then he bent down and picked up the little PSM "pistolet," a favorite of the old KGB. He turned and caught Bridge's eyes. He nodded with the smallest perceptible wink, and then escorted his prisoner to the back of the plane.

Alisa looked at Bridge and made a face like she was very impressed.

"I am amazed what two good seats at the ball park can get you these days," Bridge said as he continued reading his magazine.

Forty-five minutes later, the plane lifted off.

Chapter 32

Cowboys of the Night

The drone lifted off with a loud buzzing that sounded like a swarm of mosquitoes up close. Major Hanes, the Air Force pilot who'd flown Brooke's team down to Grenada, worked the controls. They were enough like the standard-looking R/C controller, although this had a good-sized screen and two red buttons. The major was quickly doing some maneuvers and rapidly learning how to fly the three-foot-wide aircraft and how it responded.

Brooke looked up as he made the drone go straight up. "The sound?"

"Let me get it to five hundred feet and see how much we hear."

Brooke looked down at the screen and watched as the image of herself and the major receded on the screen, getting smaller as the drone took its high-resolution night vision camera high up overhead.

"I can hardly hear it . . . good. You ready?" Brooke said.

"I think I got the hang of it."

They watched the screen as the drone angled and moved east over the Prescott estate. It was three o'clock in the morning so he switched to infrared. The only heat signatures were coming from the air-conditioning unit and a light fog of heat coming from what was designated on the floor plan map as the security system for the estate.

"So those glows must be from the heat of the TVs and surveillance equipment in the office. I don't see anyone on perimeter defense," Brooke said.

"I'll turn up the sensitivity and do one more pass to check."

Brooke hit her comm. "George, no sentries. All's quiet. Got four heat signs in one area. Looks like the middle of the house. We have two more, one each in the east and northeast bedrooms. Marked Jennifer and Chet on the map. I am going to assume they are the guards.

"Walters, you take Jennifer's bedroom; George you take Chet's. I'll secure the family. We go on signal as soon as we are positioned. The doors and windows are alarmed so we got three seconds max before they react, if they are sleeping. Major, you keep an eye out for any surprises. Two clicks when you are in position, then on my three clicks we go."

.𝕲.

George was about to ask how come she took the easy room, but then realized, she could just as easily be walking into four guards in the room and not the family.

.𝕲.

Since her run was the longest, Brooke checked the layout drawing they had been using as a map. She decided on the French doors off the main room as her point of entry. She got both George's and Walters' clicks within a few seconds of each other. She flipped down the night vision goggles and scanned the room through the glass, hoping to see the family sleeping on couches and chairs. No such luck. She tried the door handle but it was locked. She judged the door not to be dead bolted into the floor and ceiling because there was some play. That made kicking it in at the handle and lock the best way in. She took a deep breath, clicked her mic three times, grabbed her machine gun, and punch-kicked the door with a full Mae Tobi Geri style jumping front kick. The door flew open and a wailing alarm sounded.

.𝕲.

At that same instance, George had come through the porch door of the kid's room. The man in the bed shook and was startled at the alarm. He didn't immediately sense that George was in the room until he felt the barrel of the George's H&K. His eyes popped wide and George just uttered. "Uh, uh, uh."

.G.

Walters broke the glass in the window of the room he was assigned. The rousted guard scrambled for his gun on the nightstand. Walters laid down a burst onto the nightstand. The splintering wood and shattering lamp caused the man to recoil from his reach.

.G.

Brooke heard the shots but it didn't distract her from her main goal of securing the family. She looked up. The heat signatures she'd seen in the center of the house must have come from the room above; she took the stairs two at a time. At the top, she stopped and peered around the corner. Over the ear-piercing sound of the alarm she thought she heard screaming. She proceeded slowly down the hall, opening every door she encountered with a swift kick then going in low. Expecting to get shot is a good way to stay on your toes.

She kicked the third door in and the screams and whimpering were louder. She went in low and saw four people huddled in the corner of the room. She saw a huge ring bolted to the floor from which chains went to shackles on each of their legs.

Just then the major came over her comm. "Director Burrell, there's someone else in the house, maybe from the basement. I see you with the four. He's heading to you."

Brooke looked at the scared folks. "I'm here to rescue you. You'll be fine. I have got to go for a minute but I'll be back. This will all be over soon."

The older woman, the mom, said in a half-cry, half-whisper, "Thank you."

Out in the hall, Brooke looked left, the way she'd come. Her memory of the layout of the house was that the other way, down the hall behind her, lead to a dead end. There was a credenza along the wall of the hallway just beyond the door to the bedroom. She took cover behind it.

She trained her sights on the top of the steps. She saw the barrel first. Then both hands as the gun was pointed into the hall by the person behind the wall. The muzzle flashed as the person just fired blindly into the hallway. Brooke got smaller behind the furniture as it definitely took a few hits. After spraying what must have been a whole magazine. She saw the gun withdraw. *He's reloading*, she thought. Before she consciously told herself to do so, she was up and running to the stairs. The last few feet, she stretched out low and slid on her back across the polished wood floor with her gun pointing up.

The gunman was seating the mag, but had not yet pulled back the bolt to chamber the first round. He saw Brooke on the floor in full body armor, night vision goggles, a helmet, and with the H&K pointing at him. For a second it looked like he was going to try and pull the bolt back, aim, and shoot at Brooke. She jutted her gun further out from her body as if to say, *You really think you are going to do all that and get a shot off before this bullet goes from here into your chest?* The gunman had second thoughts and dropped his weapon.

"Turn around," she said.

With her leg, she kicked his rifle down the stairs. "Hands against the wall. Spread your legs."

At first he didn't comply, so she let out a three-shot burst just by his ear. "I ain't fucking around with you, asshole. Now hands on the wall."

That got his attention and he put his hands on the wall. Using her leg again, she nudged his feet out further so he was off balance. She got up on one knee, then the other. She got behind him and, with her hand on his collar, swept his feet from under him. Once on the floor, she put her knee on his neck. "Clear!" she called out. Then zip-tied his hands behind his back and hobbled his feet with another one.

She ran back to the room. She humped a mattress off one of the beds and dragged it in front of them. "Stay behind here." She then shot at the floor around the ring that was bolted down. As the bullets shattered the wood, she tugged on the chain and felt the mount give. One final tug and the ring was free. She then shot at the chains and two snapped free. The bolt of her gun locked open as she ran out of bullets. George came in and saw what she was trying to do. "I got this," he said as he shot the other two chains free. "Walters has the two others on the porch. The guy you got hogtied in the hall makes three."

"George, take the kids down and out of the house. Mrs. Prescott, is there anyone else we should know about?"

"No, there were only three." She started shaking. Brooke wrapped her arms around her and even through her body armor and gear, felt the woman relax. "Your family is safe and you will be back in America in a few hours."

Brooke led her out of the room. When they got to the stairs the gunman was still tied up on the floor. She noticed Mrs. Prescott's lip start to quiver. She shook again.

"What is it?"

"He's the one. The one. It's him."

"The one, what?"

"The one who raped me."

Brooke looked down.

Mrs. Prescott kicked him. "You son of a bitch. You filthy bastard."

Brooke let her get a few more shots in, and then gently nudged her back. "That's enough. He'll pay for what he did."

"It won't be enough. He raped us."

"Us?"

"Yes, this pig took my daughter! My sweet Polly. She's only nine!" She kicked him again as she sobbed.

Once again, Brooke stopped her from kicking. "Mrs. Prescott. Sometimes accidents happen."

The woman recoiled from Brooke's comment, speechless.

Brooke took out her knife and cut the zip tie that was around the man's ankles. She got the man to his feet and turned him towards the staircase. She put her leg out in front of him, and threw him down the stairs. He landed with a bone-shattering crunch at the bottom. Walters ran over to the moaning, groaning man and looked up to Brooke.

"He tripped."

Outside the house, medics were treating the family and soldiers were removing the shackles from their legs. The rapist was on a hardboard stretcher with his head immobilized. She overheard the paramedic say it looked like a spinal fracture and that he would be paralyzed from the waist down.

The chargé d'affaires was at the site. "What do you want to do with your three prisoners?"

"Get all you can out of them, then I don't care. Let the locals take them or send them back for prosecution. I got bigger fish to fry back in New York. She looked at the paralyzed man on the stretcher. "Besides, justice has already been served."

.G.

From one hundred yards out, Paul watched as the Grenadian authorities did a final sweep of the Prescott estate then sealed the main house and left. He chided himself for being an hour too late and knew Dequa was not going to like this development.

.G.

Four hours later, back in New York, the Prescotts were reunited and Brooke was sleeping in her own bed. Her last thoughts before slipping away were of her husband Mush and then she imagined him asking her how her day went. She laughed to herself in her reverie. It had been one hell of a day.

.G.

One of the horses in the stable kicked and brayed so loudly that Warren Cass jumped out of bed. He was in a cold sweat. He was scared and shaking. He reached into his drawer and pulled out a .38 revolver. He started for the stairs. His wife stirred. "Warren? What is it?"

"They're down there. I know it."

"Who? Who's down there?"

"Stay here."

.G.

Sharon Cass's blood immediately turned to ice as she shivered under the sheets, calling out in a loud, nervous whisper, "Warren, let the agents handle whatever it is. Get back in here."

He disappeared into the dark hallway.

She turned and hit the panic button by the bed. Immediately alarms rang. All the lights in the house and on the grounds went on and she heard men shouting.

Then a shot rang out from inside the house. She screamed.

An agent came through the door. "Are you all right, Mrs. Cass?"

"Yes. Where's my husband?"

"Please come with me," the agent said and then averted his eyes as the woman pulled off the covers and put on her robe and slippers. She hustled out of the room.

Sitting halfway down the staircase was her husband. He had his face between the newel posts of the stairs. He was breathing hard. An agent sitting next to him had Warren's gun in one hand and had his other hand on Warren's shoulder in a comforting gesture.

His wife slipped between them. "Warren, Warren, what's going on? What's the matter?"

Warren just kept looking through the posts.

The Federal Protective Service agent filled her in. "Mrs. Cass, he just fired a shot at one of my men. Luckily he missed. I came up from behind him and wrestled the gun out of his hand. Then he saw it was me and said, 'Oh, my God.' And now he's not answering me or you."

The woman's eyes filled with tears and she just put her arms around her husband.

Chapter 33

Hell Hath No Fury

Harris hated the feds. They always came in and screwed the pooch. Glory boys. Cops did the dirty work and then they came in and announced, "We'll take it from here," while keeping their hands clean and manicured. He hated feds. Therefore, being here at the security checkpoint in the New York headquarters of the FBI really burned his butt.

"I am on the job," he said showing his ID and gold detective's badge to the uniformed security man.

"Place your gun and cell phone in this metal box."

He did. The guard locked it and handed him the key with the tag number seventeen on it.

"You'll get it back upon leaving the building."

"Thanks. Now I feel all comfy." There wasn't a cop in the world comfortable with surrendering his weapon. But he knew the drill.

He didn't get two feet past the checkpoint when a skinny kid not more than a year out of college asked, "Who are you here to see this morning?"

"Director Burrell."

"Follow me." He walked towards an elevator apart from the rest. "ID please."

"But I already . . ." he sighed and handed it over.

The kid scanned it on a reader on the wall. The elevator opened and he pressed the floor button and got off before the doors closed.

Harris looked around the elevator, figuring this Burrell guy must be some real prissy fed.

When the doors opened, a blonde was standing in the hall. "Harris?" she said.

"Yes, I am here for Agent Burrell. Where is he?"

"Follow me."

The blonde was good looking and had nice legs from behind, and a nice behind from behind. She led him to an office at the end of the hall. They entered and Harris went to the man standing by the desk. "Special Agent Burrell? Detective first grade Rolland Harris, Midtown North Squad."

"I'm George Stover, US Treasury."

"Where's Burrell?"

"You walked in with her."

Harris closed his eyes momentarily. *Shit.* He turned and smiled. "Sorry, I didn't know you were you."

"I'm sorry to let it go on for so long but it's a long way between humorous interludes here."

"Nice to meet you, Agent Burrell."

"It's director."

"Okay, now I am oh-fer-two. Sorry."

"Look, let's get something straight right from jump street. I was head of New York FBI for three years. I am very aware that we feds are considered glory hounds; that you do all the hard work and we lap up the cream. Well, Harris, I run this little outfit and I am telling you that none of that shit happens here. In fact, if you haven't already, you should soon get a call from the chief of detectives informing you that you have been temporarily reassigned to my office."

"For how long?"

"We don't know how long we have, but you may or may not have stumbled across a part of a plot that could go down today, tomorrow, or the next day. That's why I am not going to get in your way. You need more help, you can take 'em from your squad or old friends or you might even learn to trust us here in the federales camp, but I ain't expecting any miracles. You got any problems with what I have told you so far?"

"As long as it's my collar when the shit clears."

"If we are all still here then, yeah, go ahead, knock yourself out. Until then, though, you run everything you learn, connect, or discover, by us. We are literally calling audibles here day and night until we ascertain the nature of the threat."

"How long you guys been on this?"

"It grew out of a routine money laundering case I was heading up when we stumbled on this terrorist plot. It had been in the background for months. George will read you in on where we are now, but we need to know fast where the explosives went and if they have anything to do with our trying to stop these skels before they hit us. Any questions?"

Harris liked this broad . . . woman, especially since she used NYPD lingo and was aware of the bad smell the feds left in most precincts. "Do I report here or to the squad?"

"Your cases have been off loaded to other dicks in your squad. You'll have a desk here, exclusively, 24/7 till either we stop 'em or we all get blown to hell. Whichever comes first." Brooke saw the look in his eye. "What?"

"When was the last time you were in the field?"

Brooke looked down at her watch. "In ten minutes, it'll be eight hours ago. Look, Harris, I am not a desk jockey. I've been in some tight shit and lived to lie about it."

"We all make our exploits grander than . . ."

"No, not exaggerate. I mean, non-disclosure, need to know only, the old, 'I'd tell you but then I'd have to kill you,' kinda stuff. So don't ever think I don't know what I am asking you to do or that I don't know how tough it is out there. I am one of you. If you got a different opinion and if there's time, I'll listen, but otherwise, never try to second guess me or ignore me and we'll get along fine."

Harris smiled. It was exactly what he would have said . . . if he had two days to think about it. "Sounds good."

"Welcome to the team. Don't spend more than a half hour with George. He's got a shit load to do too."

The men left and Brooke opened the report she'd started three times already this morning.

.G.

"Wow. She always like that?"

"Actually, no. It must be you. Your whole New York cop persona brought out a side of her I've never heard in the four months I've been on this case."

"What happened, two minutes and eight hours ago?"

"Not much. Director Burrell, Agent Walters, and myself just cowboyed in to an extraction mission, violated the sovereignty of a

Caribbean nation, shot it out with hostiles, then apprehended them and rescued four hostages and we were wheels down JFK at five a.m."

"I think I am going to like it here."

.𝕲.

"So it was for the whole weekend?" Diane Price chewed on the end of her pencil as her confidential source on the phone was confirming what had previously only been baseless rumors. "And the first lady was at the Vienna Women's Conference during all this?" She scribbled down *Vienna Women's Conference* right under a doodling of the name *Brooke*, where the *o*s were filled in to look like two eyes. Diane was playing by her source's rules. The person on the other end, a high-placed White House official agreed to only confirm or deny the statements Diane made. Offering up nothing, adding or subtracting nothing, just responding in the narrowest sense. "Did they leave together? Did they arrive together? Oh, that makes sense. Of course they wouldn't . . ." She let that conclusion-like statement hang without speaking, hoping the source would jump in and fill the silence, or object to the implication, but neither happened.

Ten minutes later, Diane had triangulated her story but she was still not satisfied. Although she had all the surrounding facts and the corroborating statements she felt she didn't have the actual story itself yet. Of course, the two people involved may be the only ones who knew those details. If her primary source making the allegation hadn't been the Secretary of the Treasury, she would have written it off as rumormongering. However, the secret service logs she was allowed to see, the confirmation that they were both at Camp David at the same time that the wife was in Vienna, certainly boded well for the claim that an affair was afoot. *Affair afoot,* she thought and immediately admonished herself for the cheesy tabloid headline. Then she thought again, *Is what I'm doing any nobler?* Still it was an astonishing accusation. She took a deep breath and decided she had enough to go to Eddy with and let him make the call.

.𝕲.

When Diane laid out what she had to Edward Knowles, the executive producer and senior editor of the network's nightly newscast, he was shocked. He had covered Mitchell's fledgling campaign as he made his dark horse, third-party run at the top job. Knowles always thought that maybe the former Air Force officer was a little off his rocker, making that kamikaze run at the oval office. Everyone in media wrote it off as the old fighter pilot trying to make a political point and to possibly garner enough votes at a second run four years hence.

No one was more shocked than James Mitchell himself, when he came out on top in the popular as well as the electoral vote on that election night six years ago. And even though there were allegations of voter fraud, which he himself brought forward in a rare move, the House and the Senate bestowed what amounted to a vote of confidence on him. He went on to win reelection for his second term with the indisputable margin of victory of fifty-eight to forty-two percent.

Knowles knew that anybody who spent ten seconds with the guy knew two things. He'd grab a gun and defend America in an instant and that he was the poster boy of a good family man. Which is what made this affair so outside the box. "Well, they say the job changes a man. Maybe Mitchell changed," he said after Diane filled him in on what she was ready to report to the country, if he gave her his editorial blessing.

"So you are giving me the green light?" Diane had the bristling energy of a teenager asking her dad for the car keys.

"Do you have two independently verifiable sources?"

"Two. Both high placed, but insisting on anonymity."

"Of course . . ."

"Well, can you blame them, Ed? Who's going to go on the record against a president with a fifty-seven percent approval rating?"

"That's exactly what's eating at me. Are you sure we aren't being used?"

"I've seen the secret service logs. I have confirmation of them being at Camp David . . . alone."

Eddy looked up at her. "No one's ever alone at David."

"Well, that's true." The moment hung as they both suddenly were frozen by the impact this story would have on the nation, its people, and history.

Diane assumed Eddy was thinking the same thing . . . "You want me to spike the story?"

"Are you crazy? As long as you are dead certain. Otherwise we are both dead—period."

"Thanks, boss."

"I wanna see your script before you go on the air, and I want a full package pre-recorded, family shots, times of tension, that time in New York with the suitcase bomb and that thing with the crazy computers. Not a slam piece, just a plain statement of the guy we all thought we knew . . . until tonight!"

"Got it."

.G.

Morgan Prescott was in a room with his family. The tears were drying up but they were all still misty eyed. He must have said to his wife Deidra a thousand times how sorry he was and she, just as many, saying that it wasn't his fault; *THEY* did this to him and to their family.

Prescott held his little girl, Polly, on his lap. She had been violated, as his wife had been. As a man, he felt so impotent, so useless. He'd failed at the primary responsibility of a male with a family, to protect them and keep them safe. He vowed that no matter what it took, therapy, counseling, support groups . . . whatever, even if he had to quit his job, he would do it to help them deal with the horror they had undergone. Every time his little girl shifted in his arms, he thought of how her innocence had been shattered by those monsters on the island. The thought of her lost childhood made him well up, his chest flutter. Even though the woman, Burrell, had made sure the bastard would never be able to commit rape again on anybody else's little girl or wife, for him it wasn't enough. He wanted to filet the guy, torture him for every minute that his daughter and his wife would suffer because of the violation of their bodies.

Agent Stover poked his head in. Prescott still thought of him as Miles Wheaton, the man he'd been instructed to check out for the kidnappers.

"Mr. Prescott, may I have a moment?"

"Of course." He handed his daughter to his wife. "Deidra, would you take her?"

Out in the hall, George found an empty room. "In here, please."

"So your name is George?" Prescott said a little shocked.

"Yes, George Stover, attached to FinCEN at Treasury."

"And you saved my family?"

"Well, me, Brooke, and Walters."

"I owe you a debt I can never repay. I feel horrible that I put them in jeopardy."

"Mr. Prescott . . ."

"Please, Morgan."

"Morgan, it's clear you had no choice in the matter."

"Still, I am in your debt."

"Morgan, there is something I need to know."

"Anything . . ."

"Why did Joe Garrison have to die?"

"Joe . . . ? Joe's dead?"

George was surprised. "Sorry, I thought you knew. I didn't mean to break it to you so coldly."

He sat stunned for a second. "Joe was one of my first hires. He came over from Bear-Sterns, back in the day. Joe was the best comptroller . . . Oh god, his wife, Peggy, I should call her."

"Do you know why he would have been killed on the morning of the raid?"

"How did he die? Was he in the office?"

"No, he never made it to work; he was killed in the subway."

"Dear God . . ."

George waited for the man to collect himself. "Did the people who asked you to check me out ever mention him?"

"Yes, once. They asked who you worked with. I told them Joe, Patricia, Jenny, Morris. Dear God, are they okay?"

"Yes, as far as I know they are fine."

"Well, wait, Agent Wheaton, er, Stover, were you, in fact, working with Joe?"

"That's the thing. He didn't know who I was, and the report I was getting from him that morning was innocent enough, just routine T&E reports mostly. As far as he knew, I was reconciling accounts for a possible tax audit. I actually kind of tricked him into it by saying my system was down."

"Look, for what it's worth, Joe had no idea about me being blackmailed or any of Kitman's put and calls. Those shorts and longs were all under Kevlar."

George wrote down the names Kitman and Kevlar. "Yes, I discovered that Joe was clean early on and, just so you know, Joe was getting a pass. I was getting him out of the building prior to the raid. I also wanted his alibi preserved in case I needed him to corroborate State's evidence."

"Based on what you just said, they, Kitman or whoever else, must have found out about your plans."

"Do you know if your handlers ever bugged your office or tapped your phones?"

Prescott had to think. "No. Maybe. They did seem to know a lot about my movements and where I was going."

George had his answer, or so it seemed. "Well, thank you, Morgan. I'll let you get back to your family."

"Agent, how long will we be here?"

"Brooke and Bridge still want to debrief you. After that it's hard to say . . . For your own safety this is the best, most secure place for all of you right now. I'll see what I can do about getting the US Marshalls to arrange for a safe house."

"I have a chalet in Vermont."

"I'll see if that's good with them. It shouldn't be too much longer."

.G.

"Cut it right there, after he turns to his right."

In the TV station's editing bay, Diane was feeling her oats, calling for shots and juxtaposing the Hallmark-type images of the Mitchell family from the early days of his presidency, before the terror attacks, and then more recent shots of an older-looking, grayer James Mitchell. The conclusion she was trying to draw was that not only did those attacks change him, in that they had surely taken their toll on America's father figure, but also changed his behavior.

"No, zoom in on his face instead then slow dissolve to the helicopter crashing into the building; then dissolve to the concrete nuclear containment egg they put around it, then back to Mitchell at the window of the oval office." She directed from the edge of her seat.

"Miss Price?" The editorial assistant came in.

"Yes," she responded without taking her eyes off the large screen that showed the edit.

"We only found one clip of Agent Burrell-Morton and graphics found the Navy ID photo of Commander Morton."

"Josh, can you put that up?"

The editor hit a few buttons and Brooke's pictures filled all the monitors in the edit control room.

"Wow, she's a good-looking gal. This may just click after all." Diane found the rationale to the affair, the oldest in the world: this Burrell woman was very attractive. Case closed! "Oh, I know . . . I want to do a slow dissolve between this shot of her and the one of the first lady, the one where she was caught frowning. Long, slow dissolve from the wife to the younger, prettier girlfriend."

Josh the editor looked up. "Yeah, she's a doll all right . . . Hey, wait. I've seen her before . . . When was it?" He thought about it for a second. "Phil, rack up that clip of the fire in New York two days ago."

It took a few seconds then Josh fast forwarded through raw footage of an office building fire touched off by a gas leak up in New York. "Here . . ." he said as he rewound the footage. It stopped on a close up of a woman hanging off a building on a flagpole. "Damn, it's her . . . Hold on, later I think there's a shot of her by the ambulance."

Diane's mouth was open and her head locked. She couldn't believe what she was seeing. "Damn . . ."

"She's a fucking hero?" Josh said.

"Worse . . . a victim." Stunned and deflated, Diane got up and left the edit bay. She walked out onto a fire exit that had a little landing most folks used to catch a cigarette. She stared at the back of the Capitol as she lit up a Parliament and took that first drag. Her nerves settled. She took one more puff and ground it under her feet as it fell through the metal lattice and onto the back alley. She walked briskly back to her office. She now knew what she had to do.

"Diane Price, MSNBC for Agent Brooke Burrell-Morton." She tapped her pencil and waited.

"Okay then, may I speak to Director Burrell-Morton?" She wrote down the word *director* and the word *promotion?* and circled it. "I know she's busy. I need to confirm a story before we go to air . . . I'll hold." Diane's computer on her desk was in sleep mode and the screen was dark. Her reflection looked back at her as she waited. A small pang of guilt arose from her and she hit the space bar. The screen came on and the reflection was gone. "No, I don't need to speak with the press spokesmen for the Treasury. I need Director Burrell-Morton . . . Very well, can I at least leave a message?"

Diane did something she hadn't done since she was thirteen. She bit her nail. Nervously pinching it between her teeth then tearing back a good chunk of the tip. The taste of her nail polish jogged her into dropping her hand and chiding herself. She heard the beep. "Director Burrell-Morton, my name is Diane Price, senior correspondent MSNBC. I am calling to see if you would like to comment on a story we are about to run which alleges . . . which alleges . . . that you are having an affair with James Mitchell the President of the United States. My number is 202-999-0100. If you'd like to comment in time for air, please return this call by six forty-five p.m. today." She hung up.

Diane relaxed her shoulders, but didn't remove her hand from the phone headset. She set her jaw and picked up again and dialed a number she knew well.

"White House Press Office . . ."

"Lynn, it's Diane Price. Can I get a minute with Connie? It's important and I am on a deadline."

Connie Cochran was a former Washington editor for *Time* magazine who'd gotten the press secretary job in Mitchell's second term. She and Diane had an understanding and were members of the news sisterhood clique. She owed it to her and to the practice of journalism to reach the parties in the story for comment. "Connie, thanks for taking the call. This is a big one. We are about to move a story that alleges Mitchell had an affair . . ."

Diane waited to gauge the reaction. And waited. She continued, "We have logs and eye witnesses that put the president and one Brooke Burrell-Morton, a former special agent, now assigned to Treasury, alone many times."

There was more silence. Then in a calm, flat voice Connie said, "Diane, are you sure all your logs and witnesses were legally attained?"

"Connie, this is tight. We put them together on three separate occasions. One for a weekend at Camp David while the FLOTUS was in Europe."

"This is the first I am hearing about this, Diane. Can I get a courtesy delay until I have a chance to see if there is any merit to these charges?"

"Sorry, Connie. But Eddy's all over this. The package is ready to go and it rolls at seven p.m. eastern."

"You are not giving me much time, Diane."

"I am so sorry, Connie, but that's where we are. If the administration would like to comment you have until 6:45 to call back."

"*If* I call you back. Till then, I have to go on record as no comment."

"I understand. Again, Connie, I am sorry for the short notice."

"Diane, don't play semantics with me. This is an ambush. And I won't forget this 'courtesy call.'" Then she hung up with ear-splitting punctuation.

It made Diane wince and actually freeze. She didn't mean to blindside her colleague, but this . . . this was a career maker. She could land the NBC anchor chair with a scoop like this. Connie would eventually get over it. She got up and headed to makeup.

.G.

Brooke saw the caller ID from MSNBC on the readout of her office phone but she made it a policy never to talk to the media. Besides, she was busy. She, Bridge, and George were finally debriefing Prescott after he'd been allowed a few hours with his family. That Brooke now considered him a reluctant co-conspirator was a sea change in the investigation. Having rescued his family, Prescott was very amenable to telling all.

"As I said to George earlier, I owe you all a debt I can never repay."

"Yes you can, Mr. Prescott. You can tell us everything you know. Every little detail no matter how small can be the key that unlocks the riddle of who this group is."

"I don't know of any group."

"Okay, then who do you think kidnapped your family?"

"I have no idea. I only got an email. It had a picture of my family and two men with guns pointed at them. They told me that I was to do whatever they wanted. That no one would know my family was captured. They had replaced my family on my boat and that in four weeks it would all be over."

"When was this?" Brooke said.

"Almost four weeks ago." Brooke looked to Bridge.

"So what did you do?" Bridge said.

"We set up put and calls for various municipal and governmental bonds, insurance industry, medical and energy and power sectors," Prescott said.

"Did securing those contracts to buy or sell set off any alarm bells with you?"

"Not at first, but then again I wasn't thinking clearly. They had my family..."

"I understand, but why did you suspect George?"

"I didn't. I got an email telling me to check on my people; that someone from the SEC may be in my company posing as an analyst. Miles ... er ... George was the last hired. I went through company HR records and found someone who matched his educational history. It was the only way I could think of to try and see if he was who he said he was when we hired him."

"How did all your files disappear on the day we raided your offices?" Brooke said.

"I don't know. I was out of the building ten minutes before the raid in a car to Teterboro."

"Did you arrange that?"

"No, again an email said be downstairs at 11:50."

"How did they know about the raid?" George said.

"Barry Kitman."

"Who?" Bridge said.

"Barry Kitman. His firm was big into the areas we were transacting. He also had the Secretary of the Treasury, Cass's ear," Prescott said.

Brooke was too good at liar's poker to react to Prescott's invocation of the secretary's name. But now she understood the instinctive bad feeling she'd had when she met Kitman at the Harvard Club, that she could sense he was guilty of something. "So, how would Kitman have known of our raid?"

"Well, it's obvious now. I mean, since you weren't with the Securities and Exchange Commission then the tip must have come from someone at FinCEN or Treasury."

"And you think Kitman was behind the leak?"

"Maybe his family was also kidnapped?"

Brooke nodded to an assistant. She knew it meant "get me everything on Barry Kitman immediately."

"In fact, we set up every contract for Kitman, not for us," Prescott said.

"Was that the 14TGG code?" Brooke said.

"Yes, we already had it set up and since it was a blind account, it made sense for me to use it for what I was forced to do for Kitman. I mean, they made it clear, if anybody found out, they'd kill my family."

Brooke looked at George. "Did you know about this, about Kitman?"

"I never saw any 14TGG proceeds. Never saw any documents or contracts with Kitman Global on them."

"Mr. Prescott, do you see the problem I am having here? Why should I believe you? You say you weren't set to make a killing on the put and calls, and yet George, who went through your company with a fine-tooth comb, never heard of KGI. How do you explain that?"

"Paper safe, securitized collateral issues under a lock and key of sorts."

"So, George wouldn't have had access?"

"Once set up, even I couldn't reach them. Only Kitman Global Investments. Probably just Barry himself."

"So Kitman plays big in all this?"

"Kev . . ." Prescott was about to answer when George interrupted.

"Brooke, can I have a minute?"

"Now?" Brooke said a little taken aback.

"Yes."

"Okay, let's take a quick break. Give us the room please?"

Everyone left and Brooke looked at George. "What is it?"

"This is hard for me, Brooke, but I was under orders from Secretary Cass to keep him updated regularly on the progress of our investigation."

"Hold it. You mean spy on me, us?!"

"I guess those words work. But I was under orders. You were an outsider. He wanted to make sure you weren't . . . weren't . . ."

"Going all cowboy on this?"

"You do have a reputation in high circles."

Brooke was seeing red, but she tempered her anger. "George, right now I want to throw you out that goddamn window, but there's been enough death around here, so you now have one minute to tell me everything."

"Not much to tell . . . He was really only interested in where you were going."

"As in what?"

"Well, the whole reason why I am telling you this is that he mentioned Kitman more than once."

"Whoa. Warren was worried about me digging into Kitman? Why?" Suddenly, Brooke knew the answer but didn't want to believe it. Her meeting Kitman and the prince with Cass at the Harvard Club the night she got shot. She also remembered the words that Cass had muttered that sounded like, "That's why George went to the Caymans." She chided herself for not picking up on his slipup of his knowledge of her operations. That tidbit could only have come from George.

"I don't know, but I think Kitman Global Investments and Secretary Cass are connected in some way."

Brooke was steaming; disloyalty was a good reason for summary execution in her book. She weighed the impact of firing George on the spot against the disruption a move like that would cause at this late stage in the investigation.

"George, where is your loyalty now?"

"Brooke, except for my orders to report in, it was always with the mission and you."

Brooke considered his choice of words. She had put her life in his hands on the extraction in Grenada; he'd performed, as she would have expected, what with him being the best agent at Treasury that she'd personally picked for her team.

"George, Cass is a crafty character. Did you know he sent an old college buddy to bird-dog me. Of course I rejected the idea, but now I see it was to cover your role as his eyes and ears. Crafty."

"Am I still on your team, Brooke?"

"How much did you tell him?"

"Not much . . . You kept it pretty straight and narrow. There was of course interest when you went after Cynthia Davidson . . ."

"For now obvious reasons. Did you know about her?" Brooke said.

"No, I just included it in my bi-weekly report. He came back asking to be informed of every move as it related to Cynthia. If it matters,

I never made judgments on your procedure or management style. In fact, personally I think you are brilliant at all this."

"Don't suck up, George, you're still in my shithouse."

"My reports were based only on facts. I never editorialized, never critiqued."

"George, I think a light just went on in my head. Did you ever mention Joe Garrison in your . . . report to the secretary?" Brooke edited out the words "in your spying on me" before she spoke.

Brooke could see the blood drain from George's face. "Holy shit."

The muted chopping of a helicopter flying somewhere over Manhattan was the only sound for at least a minute. Brooke tapped her finger on the desk. "Look, George, if Cass dropped the dime on Joe in his pal-around discussions with Kitman, that's on him, not you. There's no way you could have known any of this."

"Thanks, but it doesn't make me feel any less guilty."

"Believe me, it'll get so you can live with it."

"I don't know if that would be better."

Brooke looked at him. Her jaw set as it always did once she made up her mind. "George, you are on probation. We go on, but I don't want to worry about you behind my back."

"Brooke, I am still an agent of the US. If Cass did indeed tip off Kitman or the terrorists, then he broke the law, and I might have to arrest him. So I consider myself free of his directive, and no longer obligated to report to him. I'd like to stay on the team and see this through."

"Who said I wanted you to stop?"

A broad grin emerged on George's face.

.𝔊.

"Connie Cochran, White House," the floor director said running into the makeup room, pressing the production earphone in his ear.

Diane looked at her watch. It read six-fifty. "Tell her she called too late. We're past deadline."

"Er . . . she's not on the phone . . ." he said.

"She's here." Connie herself was standing in the doorway. "People, give us the room for a minute," she said in her former executive editor's voice.

Diane nodded to the hair and makeup people and, with curlers in her hair and a half-powdered face, gestured for Connie to take a seat.

"No, this will be quick. Here." She unceremoniously tossed a manila envelope into Diane's lap.

"What's this, a statement? It's too late . . ."

"Read it!"

Diane grabbed the hair scissors from the tray and slit the manila envelope open. "Secret service logs, yes, I have seen these."

"Then you are either very bad at reading or you were being set up. I highlighted the relevant part."

Diane scanned the document and her eyes widened. She looked up at Connie just as Connie's cell phone rang.

She answered it without saying a word into it and held it up to Diane. "It's for you."

"Diane, this is Delores Mitchell. As you see before you, you'll see the name Clarice Mitchell all three times you allege my husband was having an affair. For the record, Clarice is our niece. For reasons of protecting her privacy I am not going to get into the specifics except to say that both my husband and myself asked Mrs. Morton to counsel our niece. You see, and this is not for publication, she needed a mentor, and she and I never could get along. Both my husband and I not only think the world of Brooke, but she is a person of unquestionable loyalty and a patriot with rock-solid ethics. Truth be told, James and I consider her more of a daughter than a government employee . . . almost as much as our daughter, Marie. Brooke was kind enough to spend time and help guide a young girl struggling through some basic life issues. One night, while I was away, she had dinner with my husband in the residence. It was then—as the phone log in the package shows—that I called at 8:30 p.m., during that dinner, and both James and myself asked her to intercede on our niece's behalf. You also see phone logs for the weekend at Camp David, and a phone call from me, in which Brooke eased my concerns that Clarice was receptive to her help that day. There is no truth, not one scintilla of truth, to the disgusting allegations you are making. I trust that you, your network, and your network's president, Bob and his wife Leah, will agree that you don't want to fuck with the White House on this one. Thank you, Diane."

Connie could see the blood drain from Diane's face. She took back her phone from Diane's motionless hand and looked at the clock on the wall. "Well, eight minutes to air. We'll be watching to see what you decide to do."

Connie left.

Chapter 34

Phone Calls

4 DAYS UNTIL THE ATTACK

"Have you seen the news?" Remo said as he entered Brooke's office.

"No. What happened?"

"CNN has a video of something happening in Grenada."

"Good quality?"

"Nah, dark and you can hardly make out the faces."

"How hardly?" Brooke said.

"Not at all."

"I feel better now."

"Did you hear the other news?"

"Peter! I am kind of busy here."

"Sorry, Sec Tres is resigning."

"You buried the lead there, Peter."

Brooke picked up the phone and called her buddy Sally to see if their boss had actually resigned.

"Secretary's office."

"Sally, it's Brooke."

"You heard?"

"Is it true?"

"You tell me?"

"Huh?" That threw Brooke.

"Oh, Brooke, I didn't believe it. I mean, I know you, you would never . . ."

"Sally, slow down . . . What are you talking about?"

"The rumors . . ."

"Sally . . ."

"You are going to make me say it, aren't you?"

"Say what? Sally, I'm lost here."

"You really don't know?"

"Sally, everyone is playing twenty-one questions today. What?"

"Your affair."

"My . . . what?"

"You affair with Mitchell."

Brooke's breath left her body. Her head spun. The room rotated in slow motion, as if she were heading towards an accident. She tried to speak but just a gurgle came out.

"Brooke, Brooke? Oh God, are you okay?"

She caught her breath. She looked at Mush's picture on her desk. He would never believe such a thing. She knew he trusted her as totally and unconditionally as she trusted him. Still, what if he found out? *Found out what?* She immediately challenged herself. *Would Mush lob a three-megaton nuclear-tipped Trident missile into the White House out of jealousy?* That thought made her laugh.

"Well, at least you are laughing," a relieved special assistant to the Secretary of the Treasury said.

"Sally, how did this ridiculous rumor get started?"

"Warren . . . Well, Warren may have started an inquiry."

"Warren? Why would Warren do something as dumb as that?"

"I don't know, but he had the secret service in here a few days ago, and I know he met with that woman reporter from TV."

"And now he's resigning?" Brooke stood up.

"Effective at noon today."

"Wow. I'm stunned. But why would he do such a thing? I work for him."

.𝔊.

Sally bit her bottom lip and pulled the phone away for a second. The incident with the gun at Warren's house last night was not publicized. He was at Walter-Reade hospital ostensibly to treat an over-active ulcer, or so the cover story she was told to support said. She had heard that the psychiatrists in attendance were sworn to secrecy because of

Warren's sensitive cabinet post and the fact that an unbalanced head of the Treasury could erode confidence in America's economy worldwide. She felt bad about not sharing that with Brooke but . . . "He's been under a lot of stress lately, and I guess when he heard you were spending time at the White House . . ."

"Is that what this is about? Why that insecure son of a bitch." Brooke's tone immediately changed. "Sorry, Sally, I know you worked for the man and liked him."

"Oh, please, look what he tried to insinuate about you! You have a right to be angry."

"Sally, will your job be okay?"

"Me? Yeah, I've been here through five administrations and eight secretaries. They wouldn't know where the paper clips were without me. Federal employee here, Brooke; we never leave."

"Sally, do I have anything to worry about? You mentioned a reporter. Is this on the news?"

"No, and from what I heard, the first lady is going to make sure it stays that way."

"Oh my God, Delores! I should call her."

"Good idea."

"Love to your sister; tell her I was asking about her."

"Thanks, and Brooke, I didn't believe it when I heard it. I know you. I know what a good woman you are."

"Thanks, Sally, that means a lot to me. Let me know if you hear anything else. Talk soon."

.G.

She hung up and sat for a few seconds. It was fantastic . . . her having an affair with the president. Then she remembered he did ask her to call him Jim. *Nah, that was just nothing.* Then she rattled back through her brain. *Did I ever come on to him? Did I ever do or say or suggest anything inappropriate*? As she played back the handful of times she had met the president, nothing stuck out as untoward or suggestive.

She was feeling pretty clean in all this by her own mental checklist. Then her subconscious brought up the name, *Lyle*, and she was suddenly shifting in her seat. He'd been married when they worked together out of the Dallas field office of the FBI. He'd always been the perfect gentleman, maybe even more so, in that she noticed he never partook of the ribbing and mild sexual innuendo that most others engaged in. He was always respectful of Brooke, almost to a fault. As she eventually found out, the reason was that he was infatuated with her. To his credit, he'd been honest with her and announced his intention: he would divorce his wife and marry her.

For Brooke, it was a thunderbolt out of the blue. Her first instinct had been to assume that he was kidding. They hadn't as much as shared a friendly hug. No physical contact of any kind had occurred between them, yet he was seemingly ready to commit without "test driving," as the one dear friend she'd shared the story with called it. However, his serious brow and actual nervousness over her possible reaction had told her he wasn't joking. As vulnerable as she'd been at that moment to having a little romance in her life, it had taken her all of ten seconds to decide.

Shocked at her response, he'd asked her why.

She could see still the expression on his face, a handsome face. Lyle was smart, good looking, fit, and had the kind of bearing that would take him places . . . and she was proved right, in that today he was the assistant director of the FBI in Washington and candidate for director someday. At that moment, though, she hadn't been able to go along with his plan no matter how flattering it was.

Later she would find out that he'd idolized her; he had no doubts of his love; he knew he'd met the person that he was meant for; even without sex as the usual convincer, he knew. Almost like a throwback to the days when there was no premarital sex. Except he was already married, so she knew he wasn't a eunuch.

Even to this very day, her only partial regret over her declining his offer was that for some reason she'd lied in answer to his question. She'd told him it was because they worked together and that if they married it wouldn't affect his career but it would ruin hers. Such was the way of things, unfortunately. Even though she was right about that stigma, her real reasons, the ones she chose not to share with him, were much deeper.

To Brooke's way of thinking, she couldn't start off a life-long relationship on the tears of another woman. It went against everything she held dear as a female. But deep down inside, it was also because he'd been using Brooke as a parachute out of his marriage. Lyle should have divorced the woman first, making a clean break and then taken the chance that Brooke might or might not have been available when the dust settled. Instead, he would've had his wife doing the free fall, taking all the risk of finding another life partner, while he held onto Brooke for the ride. At her most basic level, it just hadn't been fair, not fair at all, and she couldn't have been part of . . .

Her thoughts were interrupted by a knock at the door.

"We're ready to go."

"I'll be right there." Brooke got up and checked herself in the mirror. The shocking news had momentarily caused her to forget what she was about to do. The outrageous allegation having totally obliterated the gravity of her next appointment, she touched up her lipstick, grabbed her bag, and left. Again, not bothering to check her office voicemail.

.G.

Security was tight at Saint Patrick's Cathedral. Due to the imminent threat and her team's total focus, there wasn't time to go to each individual funeral of the nineteen people killed in the rocket attack. So this one memorial service was organized for the workmates and families to grieve collectively. In the following days, each victim would be buried separately in his or her hometowns and with their families in attendance. But for now, this ceremony was the only way for the unit to grieve and to keep the investigation on pace in a race against time.

"Ronald Bixby . . ." the monsignor read out loud, "son, brother, nephew. We pray for you and your family."

As the names were read aloud the family members sobbed and cried. Each name brought new gasps and wails as the oppressive reality of the finality of it all collectively resonated across the cathedral.

For the family members it was a bad nightmare from which there was no waking up, no escape. As for Brooke, she hadn't had a minute to grieve properly. But now in this hallowed gothic basilica her emotions became a torrent of cringing, reverberating images. The echoing off the stone and marble of each name as it was read aloud brought shimmering images of the agents and coworkers fading into her field of view. Her hands shook. Tears welled up and her chest heaved with shortened breaths, as all the trauma and danger of the last few days finally found a weak spot in the mental steel that was the armor plating surrounding her sanity.

As she turned her head away from the altar, her eyes fell upon a little girl of three or four. She was in a little jumper dress with white shoes dangling down from the pew that she and her family were sitting in. The man next to her had his arm around her, holding the innocent child close as she played with a little doll in her hands.

"Charlene Logan . . ." the priest read out loud, "daughter, sister, niece, mother . . . we pray for you and your family."

"That's mommy," the little girl said innocently.

The man sitting next to her tried to hold back, but lost his stoic battle as his quivering lower jaw opened and an "Oh my God" escaped. He then pulled the little girl in tighter and kissed the top of her head and rested his cheek on her hair and the pink barrette in it.

As roiling heaves erupted from within her, Brooke abandoned trying to hold back her emotions and she broke out in deep sobs. So unprepared was she, that she had no hankie, no tissue. *Why don't I have a tissue?* the outwardly stalwart director and former agent-in-charge of just a few seconds ago asked the woman inside her. It was the first time she'd needed one since her brother, Harley, died.

Peter Remo, sitting next to her, handed over his hankie. She accepted it with a nod, and dabbed her eyes.

She sensed she was attracting attention. She had to get out of there.

She rose and headed to the side aisle. She walked over to the father and child. She smoothed the little girl's hair. When the father looked up at Brooke with teary eyes, she extended her hand to him. He went to shake it but instead she placed Charlene's broach in his and folded his fingers around it.

When he opened his hand and saw the cracked and singed broach he had gotten her on their first Christmas together, he breathed in rapid breaths, attempting to stave off full-fledged wailing.

Brooke put her hand on his shoulder and gave him a squeeze for strength and walked away.

She made her way past the little gift shop and went out a side door. The NYPD patrolman on post on the other side of the door was there to stop people from entering, so he just nodded as she flashed her creds and hit the street.

Thirty seconds later, George Stover exited the same door. "Did a woman come out of here?"

"Yeah, she flashed federal tin."

"Which way did she go?"

He pointed east. "That way, I think."

George was off down Forty-Ninth Street, with a still-noticeable limp.

.G.

Brooke had walked south a few hundred feet and hailed a cab on Fifth Avenue and told the driver to head to South Ferry.

After a few minutes snaking through the midday traffic to get to the FDR South, the driver looked in the rearview mirror and said to the woman who was crying in the backseat. "You okay, lady?"

Brooke nodded through her tears and closed her eyes.

.G.

"No, I don't know. She disappeared and she is not answering her phone. I dunno. I guess it hit her pretty hard. I mean, how could it not? I don't even know how I'm keeping it together," George said into his cell phone from the corner of Fiftieth and Madison. Still scanning in all directions for a glimpse of the head of his unit.

.G.

In the backseat of the cab, Brooke kept seeing that little girl, Charlene's daughter, who would never know her mommy. Then she thought of Charlene who would never see her daughter ride her first bike, the dress she'd wear to the prom, beam as she graduated, cry as she got married; Charlene would never hold her grandchildren. Brooke laid out on the backseat and cried into her folded arm.

The driver was concerned. "Lady, please don't throw up in the back of my cab, please."

.𝔊.

Being hopped up on heroin, the drug of choice for suicide bombers, Rashad saw the red lights as pomegranates dancing in his windshield. His cell leader, having heard the funeral was over on his phone, said to the young Saudi, "Go now, and soon Allah will greet you. Remember, release the button as you pass the middle of the church. Drive straight and fast. Let nothing get in your way. The suit will protect you all the way in, as will God." He tapped the bundle of erratic teenage energy that was his human-guided bomb on the shoulder.

"*Allahu akbar . . .*" the youth said, invoking the old Libyan national anthem as he shut the door on the huge Ryder truck.

.𝔊.

"Event ended, attendees exiting at this time," NYPD Patrolwoman Kylee Boyce's portable radio crackled as she shielded her eyes from the sun glaring right down Fifth Avenue at Fifty-Fifth. She was one of six cops assigned to the intersection, which was as far south on Fifth as any vehicle could get until the ceremony at the church was over. In all, one hundred and eighty cops were stationed at roadblocks from Fifty-Fifth to Forty-Fifth from Madison Ave to Sixth, creating a thirty-square block frozen security zone. The measure was not announced. It was sprung on the drivers of New York thirty minutes before the service and now that the service had ended, for probably a half hour more. All she knew from her 104th precinct muster in Queens this morning was that it was a memorial service for the people who'd died in that building explosion and fire down on Park Avenue South. That, and her standing orders: nothing but a boss or brass gets through . . . nothing.

Two consecutive car horns in rapid succession turned her head north, looking up Fifth. She saw some schmuck in a truck run a light at Fifty-Ninth. Then the truck plowed through Fifty-Eighth and sent two cars spinning out of the way.

"Damn . . ." was all she said.

From the corner of her eye she saw a big cement mixer truck, one with the polka dots, trying to cross her intersection here at Fifty-Fifth.

She waved him on into the middle of the street, yelling, "Everybody get out of the way! Everybody get out of here."

The cement truck driver was startled when she jumped on the passenger running board and screamed, "Stop the truck. Stop the truck. Get out! Run!"

Instinctively, the driver put the parking brake on before he bailed. Kylee un-holstered her Glock and aimed at the driver of the oncoming truck. Still standing on the running board, she was shaking and she said under her breath, "Shoot straight, girl."

.G.

Rashad was screaming . . . His adrenaline surged with the drugs and had him balls-to-the-wall, all out. He was grinding the transmission because he had the truck in second gear. That way there would be more torque to move vehicles, people, and barriers out of the way. When he saw the big blue, red, green, and yellow polka dots he laughed. They too danced in his way. "Woooo," he said as he realized without a hint of self-preserving fear that there was a cop pointing her gun at him from the side of the polka dots.

.G.

Kylee wasn't aware of the fourteen shots she emptied into the front of the oncoming truck and its windshield.

The Ryder truck smashed into the side of the huge cement hauler right at its heaviest point; the spinning drum full of stone and mix. The yellow truck's back wheels rose up as the chassis rotated then came crashing down onto the street again. The engine was driven into the driver's cab of the rental truck as it crushed up against the seventy-thousand-pound stationary object in its path.

The mirror of the rental truck snapped off at impact and hit Kylee in her chest, right under where her hands were raised in front of her face as she prepared for the collision. It knocked her to the ground and forced the breath out of her. She slowly got up. Smoke and gritty dirt hung in the air. Other cops were now running to the wreck. She peered into the crushed, bloody cab. He was dead, all right. But . . .

"Get the bomb squad, NOW!" Kylee yelled. Other cops finally got to her.

"What is it?" one of them said.

With her arm reaching into the crushed cab, she turned only her head. "I got my hand on a plunger that got pressed by the accident. I ain't letting go. Get the bomb squad here." She then breathed in and out in fast shallow breaths as she was finally aware of the pain in her chest—her ribs were broken.

.𝔊.

Four blocks away, Paul shook his head. "Should have used a radio detonator." Then he walked away.

Later he was with Dequa. "It would have been the coup de grâce but Hamzah's man failed."

"Yes, it would have been a blessing to rid ourselves of the entire unit, as you failed to do . . ."

Paul felt the sting of criticism but knew better than to respond.

"I understand the hostages were freed. Another request you failed to accomplish."

"The army was there when I arrived. There was nothing I could do against a platoon of soldiers with nothing more than a knife."

"The guards you employed, if they are alive, will they be a problem?"

"All they know is I was a representative of the New York mob and we wanted the family under control because Prescott owed big gambling debts. It was all cash and I only met with them in the countryside."

"Very well. By the way, Prescott was released."

"What?"

"I am told it was Chechen rebels. Our friend in Russia was convinced of it."

"Chechen? Of what possible . . ."

"It is not our concern any longer. Our focus is now the mission. The north team is ready. The south team nears their ready point. It won't be long. Maybe the misfortune that has befallen us today will be of no consequence in the end if the police are slow to trace the truck and the contents, praise be to God," Dequa said, using the English word for *Allah*, as he walked off.

"The truck . . . the truck!" he said out loud then ran to catch up to Dequa. "I think I have a solution!"

Dequa was near the point where he wanted to put a bullet in Paul's head. His failures were beginning to add up. But Paul was his number-one muscle and as an American could penetrate and operate with greater impunity than any of his men. So he sighed and said, "Yes?"

"The north team, they have finished the fabrication and have left the house for the time being, haven't they?"

.G.

"Somebody wanna tell me how the hell this happened? How did a jihadi in full battle armor get a truck loaded with ammonia bombs into the city, much less Fifth Avenue?" Bridge was fuming.

"It's the fact that he was targeting the rest of your team that's troubling," the police commissioner said.

"It's still Director Burrell's team. I am just standing in . . ." Bridgestone said as he realized that was a dumb thing to say. He was, in fact, in charge now. George, the highest-ranking member of Brooke's team, didn't have the tactical and strategic experience to take over the show.

"Director Burrell has been missing for six hours now. She may be dead. Like it or not, you are it, my friend," the commissioner said.

"Yeah, I know." Bridge threw down his pen.

George came in at that moment. "She still isn't picking up her cell."

"Can't we track it?" the commissioner said. Holding out his phone.

"We tried but Director Burrell turned off anything that would give away her location. All we know is Lower Manhattan by the cell tower's track."

"I saw her leave the pew, but I just figured she needed a moment; I've lost men in battle, but she lost 'em in Midtown Manhattan," Bridge said.

"Is there a difference?"

"George, in theater you don't have time to grieve. Here in the city, the worst thing to have is the time to ponder the loss; question if you did everything you could to keep your people safe. That really plays with your head after the bullets stop flying."

"So she could just be in self-imposed isolation . . ."

"Not answering her phone when she sees it's us," the commissioner said.

"Maybe try another phone, one whose number she won't recognize," the commissioner said as he handed George his phone. "Here, it's a Long Island number she doesn't know."

"Or maybe she needs to see a number she knows?"

.𝔊.

The president was refereeing a wrestling match in the situation room of the White House. His top advisors were going at it. The issue started out as a contingency plan for succession if Brooke's absence was due to assassination. The cell, presumably SOM37, had tried twice, and the fear was that they might have gotten lucky the third time. The Director of Homeland Security, Davis, was engaged in an argument with the temporary Secretary of the Treasury, Tolland.

"What the hell were we thinking, putting a women in charge of this?" DHS said.

"Warren Cass personally selected her. She has handled this from the beginning," Tolland said.

"Yes and we have nineteen dead, scores injured, and have been so ineffective against the terrorists that they nearly succeeded in blowing up the signature Catholic Church in America. I'd say she isn't batting a thousand here."

"She's still the best we have situationally . . ."

"If she's still alive!"

"We don't know that she isn't," Tolland said, his voice starting to rise.

"Then she is AWOL?" DHS said.

"No . . . I mean, I don't know," Tolland said.

"Face it, she's either dead or cowering somewhere."

The president had had enough. "Alright. Hold it. First, neither of you are cleared to know what I know about Brooke. She isn't anywhere cowering. She's the best we have, man or woman, and I have personally witnessed her valor and commitment to this country many times over. However, if she has met with an untimely death, then your only task is to appoint a replacement so that her team, which has the lead on this, continues without interruption. In her last . . . latest communication with me she indicated that the attack was imminent. We can't afford to disrupt the chain of command by putting the wrong person on top."

"Sir, not a person. Make the FBI lead agency on this. Burrell already had them in the mix. They have the oversight capability to take over and get results," DHS said.

"There is another option, sir." Bill Hiccock spoke up for the first time.

The president turned to him. "Go on . . ."

"Bridgestone is there and he's stepped in till Brooke returns."

The president raised his eyebrows. He mulled it over and made his policy decision. "Bridgestone it is."

Tolland was neutral, but Davis allowed his disappointment to show on his face. Not that it mattered. The boss had decided.

"Bill, you know the man. Call him, tell him he's got the ball."

"Yes, sir, Mr. President."

The president went to get up and everyone in the room stood. "Oh and Bill, only while Brooke is MIA!"

"Got it, sir." Bill trotted out of the room to make his call.

"We'll at least it's a man . . ." DHS muttered under his breath.

The president heard him, stopped dead in his tracks, turned and said, "Fer Christ's sake, Davis, stop being a fucking misogynist . . . It's the twenty-first century, man."

"Yes, sir."

.𝔊.

Brooke sat on the seawall at the tip of Lower Manhattan, looking out across the water. The Statue of Liberty stood as silent sentinel over the harbor. Various ships, boats, and ferries crisscrossed the harbor as she sat. Her phone vibrated. She glanced down at the 631, Long Island area code, but didn't move an inch to get it.

Her mind was a debating society. The two parts of who she was were warring and going at it. The Warrior in Brooke was screaming to stop this nonsense and get back to work. The Woman in Brooke argued that she had failed to live up to her number-one rule: "Everybody gets to go home . . ."

"No, I ain't saying nothing like that, Ramón. All I is saying is that you didn't have to lie to me . . ."

"But I didn't . . . You going to believe Darnell or me?"

Brooke looked over to the young couple arguing as they passed her bench and their words faded. Right now she would settle for arguing with Mush. Just to hear his voice. She needed him. He would see her point. *No, he'd side with me,* the Warrior Brooke in her brain countered.

She pulled her feet up under her, onto the bench, and wrapped her arms around her legs and rested her chin on her knee. Her phone buzzed again. This time she didn't look. It eventually stopped as she focused on a spot in the middle of the bay. The undulating water hypnotizing her, she imagined it was the Arctic or the Pacific, wherever Mush was right now. How she needed him; how much she needed to be held in his arms and for him to tell her that everything was gonna be all right. She unconsciously tightened her arms tighter to her body as if he indeed had his arms around her. It made her sigh. The phone buzzed again. This time she looked and was shocked. The caller ID read out as USS NEBRASKA.

"Hello . . . Hello . . ."

"Brooke?"

"Mush . . . Oh my God! How did you . . . How can you . . . ?

"Brooke, are you okay?"

"Yes . . . no. I'm good but not . . . I mean, it's been a hard forty-eight hours, Mush. Oh, how I miss you . . ."

"I miss you too, babe. Look, you got a lot of people very worried about you."

Her head was clearing . . . "Wait a minute, Mush, how can you be calling me right now?"

"Somebody named Bridgestone tapped a favor with CINCPACFLEET and then the president approved the order. So I got an Emergency Action Message to surface and call my wife. What's going on, Brooke?"

"Oh Mush . . ." was as far as she got before she started crying.

A half hour later she was standing by the railing at the seawall, her eye makeup a mess, as she said into the phone, "I am looking at the water right now. Thinking of you."

"Brooke, I'll be home soon. I am going to make this my last tour. I've earned the points to call my own shots. You won't need to do this anymore. I'm sorry my absence led you to this."

"Mush, this was just a routine white collar crime, until it turned into a national security threat. Otherwise, I'd be home right now, coaching soccer and watching submarine movies."

"I love you so much, Brooke."

"I love you too, Bret," Brooke said, using his first name, which was how she always addressed anything serious to him.

"I gotta go, babe," he said.

"I know. Can't wait to see you."

"Me neither."

The call ended. Brooke looked out at the water. It was then she realized she hadn't told him about the foolishness with the president and the supposed affair. Now she felt bad. She didn't ever want Mush to hear it from someone else. She wanted to tell him first so she could let him know that hurting him was the last thing in the world she would ever want. As she turned to walk to the street and get a cab, she saw Ramón and his girl sitting on the steps kissing. *That's better,* she thought as she picked up her pace towards State Street.

She hailed a cab, got in and, after telling the driver where to go, got out her cell phone and called Morgan Prescott. It was not an official call but something that came out of her conversation with Mush.

.𝔊.

"Brooke's in the building," George said as he popped into Bridgestone's office, which was about to become Brooke's again . . . Bridge hoped.

"No, Brooke is here," she said as she entered and put her bag down on the table.

"Brooke, I can't tell you how glad I am to see you. Some lamebrain thought it would be a good idea for me to step in until you came back . . ."

"Thanks . . ."

"You okay?"

"I am now, because of you." Brooke gave him a peck on the cheek.

Bridge had had many commanding officers but that was the first time any of them had ever kissed him. "I didn't do anything."

"That call was the most important call of my life."

"Oh, that?"

"Yeah, that! How did you ever pull that off?"

"The commander in chief pacific fleet, who is your husband's commander, and me went through SEAL training together, so I tapped an old poker debt."

"And how much did the president owe you?"

"There, I kinda owe him, ya see. They don't blow a nuclear missile submarine's location, ever. That little phone call cost the government a few million dollars in scrambling TACAMO aircraft and diverting active units to cover her while she was afloat and vulnerable, emanating open frequencies."

"Yeah, they don't like their very expensive boats exposed like that. I learned that when they pulled me from the Indian Ocean. Which of course is classified so we will speak of it no more."

"You know, the president said a very logical thing. He said, 'the *Nebraska* is out there to protect America from a far off threat. Whereas Brooke is dealing with an immediate threat to the nation right inside our borders.' He made the choice to sacrifice the operational details of a deep deterrent fleet missile boat to get you back on the team."

"How did he know that phone call would do the trick?"

"He was in command of a fighter squadron in the first Gulf War. He knows what it is like to lose people. And so do I. So we figured it was the best medicine to get you up on your feet and back in the game."

"I don't know, Bridge, sounds a little too touchy-feely for macho guys like you and the boss."

"Let's just keep that little chestnut between us, okay Brooke?"

"Got it."

Bridge got out from behind the desk and waved his hand for Brooke to take her chair. "Please . . . I'd rather face a platoon of bad guys than try to tackle one more FEID stroke 1213-s form."

"Yeah, the paperwork kinda takes all the fun out of it," Brooke said as she took the seat. She opened the briefing folder on her desk and scanned it.

Her eyes widened as she read the preliminary report of the attempted suicide bombing. "When did this . . . ? Oh, thank God!" She scanned the contents. "This woman cop, Kylee, I'd like to meet her. She saved the day!"

"Yes, it could have been really bad. Twenty-five hundred pounds of nasty would have left a deep crater on Fifth. And they'd be killing two birds with one stone."

"How do you figure that?"

"It's obvious they were targeting the team and they would have certainly destroyed St. Pats."

"I guess the crusades are still with us," Brooke said.

"No, hate, ignorance and the trumping of ideology over the value of human life is still with us."

"You are just knocking down every myth I ever had about you, Sergeant."

"I'm just glad you're back, Brooke. Now let's get these sons of bitches before they hit us." Bridge left her office.

Brooke opened her desk draw. She found the gold-leafed card and dialed the number. "Brooke Burrell-Morton for Mr. Valente . . . Yes, I'll hold.

Valente picked up the phone on his end. "Director Burrell, it's good to hear from you. I was relieved when Warren told me that you survived that horrible attack."

"Pure luck, but it was awful. A lot of good people died."

"Well, I'm glad you are safe. So how can I help with your investigation?"

"Mr. Valente, I am not calling you about the inquiry. I have a request."

"Call me Julie. What can I do for you?"

"I have convinced Morgan Prescott to create a trust fund for the children of my staff that got killed in the attack."

"He agreed to put that kind of money up?"

"I kinda asked him to . . . because we saved his family and he kept saying he could never repay us . . . and I was just talking to my husband and suddenly it all clicked."

"I see."

"But the fund needs a trustee, someone to administer it and make sure the intention to pay for the children's education is executed.

Based on your history and public service, I have a feeling you are that man."

"Well, I'm honored. How much did Prescott commit to?"

"Ten million, and he will manage the portfolio so it's bound to grow."

"Well, of course I'll do it. I think it's a great idea. And thank you for asking me."

"Thank you, Julie. I needed to do something. The thought of all these kids losing a parent and what they are going to have to go through . . ."

"What do you want to name the fund?"

"The Nigel Otterson fund."

"Who is that?"

"A wise man who never got to be a father."

"It's a very nice thing you've done here."

"Well, maybe I'll sleep better."

Chapter 35

Good Neighbors

"So, Steve, the bomb squad came out because of the cargo in the back of the truck, which police officials are categorizing as industrial chemicals that were being transported illegally by the driver and could, I emphasize, *could* have interacted during the cleanup from the accident and exploded like a bomb. Reporting live from Fifth Avenue in Midtown, I'm Reggie Lang, News 12 . . . back to you, Steve . . ."

"Reggie, what have we learned about the driver?" the news anchor asked.

"All the medical examiner's office is saying at this time, Steve, is that the body is being put through a battery of tests to determine if the driver was either ill or under the influence at the time of the accident. Their findings, as usual in these kinds of cases, will be . . ."

"They are lying to their public," Dequa said as he muted the sound on the news.

"Should we call the papers and claim responsibility?" Amid said.

Dequa consider it for a moment then decided against it. "Why have some of the population leave the city, which would surely happen? It would just lower the casualties. Maybe we let them have their perceived success in containing the truth of the attack."

"It is amazing how they have managed to make our actions seem like accidents. The rocket attack, this truck . . . it is almost as if Allah . . ."

"No, Amid, it does not matter what they think today. Soon they will bury their dead in numbers that will cripple this city and bring this nation to its knees. Then they will know forever that they have been lied to."

"You have great faith, Dequa."

"You don't?"

Amid froze as the question sliced through his soul like a saber. Fear tingled all over his skin as he was searching for the words when Dequa smiled. Amid felt light headed and just smiled in return.

"The northern team will be diverting them tonight," Dequa said referring to Paul's plan.

.𝔊.

Jim Aponte was getting that look from his wife. They were at it again, at almost nine o'clock. Reluctantly, he got up from the couch and looked out his living room window. He took out his cell phone to call the cops on Wally and his brothers who just kept banging and making a racket on whatever it was they were customizing. He looked at the phone and decided maybe not to get them in trouble for doing the same thing he loved, working on his car. So he went out the front door to try to reason with them one more time.

.𝔊.

"He is coming now," one of the two who stayed behind said. "Let's get out the back."

Jim walked right up to the garage door and rapped on it. "Wally? Wally? It's Jim. We got to talk, buddy." Jim listened . . . The hammering had stopped. "Wally?"

He went to the front door. The house lights were now off. He hadn't noticed that before. He knocked on the door . . . tried the bell . . . looked through the living room window . . . even tapped on the glass. No one was home. He stepped back to look upstairs when he noticed the light coming from the garage door, which wasn't all the way down. "Well, at least I can see what you guys are working on," he said to the empty house as a form of permission to assuage his curiosity.

Jim lifted the middle door of the three and was taken aback. No car! In fact, no tools, just a beat up metal garbage can all dented with hammer blows. Not even any hammers. "What the hell?"

He entered the garage. There were eight huge blue plastic barrels and the place smelled like shit. Literally. He was confused then he saw something on the bench. It was a stick of dynamite. There were a few wires and a battery on the surface as well. He stepped backwards, almost tripping over one of the plastic barrels. It was heavy and didn't move.

Jim had always considered himself a fair-minded man. Being a dark-skinned Puerto Rican, he knew of prejudice and the way people jump to conclusions about you by the way you look. He hated that. Fought it all his life. Now he was in a beautiful, quiet, mostly white neighborhood. Most of the folks were kind enough. There were a few knuckleheads who gave him sneers and cold looks but, on the whole, he got along fine with his neighbors and was even on the community advisory panel. So when the four Middle Eastern boys moved into the old Hornsby place, even though his wife had a mild concern, he put his best spin on it—this is America, they have just as much right to be here as we do.

Now he was looking at his worst nightmare. But even at that moment, he tried to give them the benefit of the doubt. He went around their house looking for tree stumps—something that might explain TNT, although it was still stupid to have it lying around. Then he closed the garage door and stepped lively to his house.

"You did good; they stopped," his wife said.

"Wake up the kids. Call your mother. We are sleeping over there tonight," he said as he picked up the phone and dialed 9-1-1.

"What? What are you talking about?"

"It isn't safe here. There is something going on over there and I want you and the kids as far from it as possible. Now go get the kids and call your mom."

He pointed to the upstairs as the police answered the phone. "Hello, this is Jim Aponte. I live at twenty-one . . ."

.G.

As Brooke and George were walking out of the meeting room, Bridge walked up to them pointing back to the room so they about-faced and went back in.

Detective Harris followed them in.

"Whatcha got, Harris?" Brooke said as she sat back down.

"Yonkers PD just found a bomb factory, fertilizer, ammonia nitrate, fuel..."

"Just like the truck..." George said.

"I'm heading up there now. There's a stick of TNT that matches the batch number assigned to Empire Construction."

"Your floater?" Brooke said.

"Exactly," Harris said as he turned to leave.

"I'm going to scramble the New York FBI crime scene unit."

"Whoa... who's in charge?" Harris stopped in his tracks.

"You are, and I'll put it in writing."

"You got that kind of juice?"

"I made them an offer I was willing to refuse," Brooke said referring to her demanding of a director's grade pay and power, hoping they'd turn her down and she could stay in Hawaii.

Later, Brooke was all alone in her office, writing a letter to Mush. In the moments in between the demands of the job and on those rare nights when she got home before midnight, she'd just write to him. In her way it was like talking over the day's events and being close to him. She never thought about sending them; it was just a way for her to stem the loneliness of his long deployments in command of the USS *Nebraska*.

She toyed with the idea that on some distant anniversary she'd ask him to get over here and sit by his old lady... that she had something to read to him from that young woman he married. She had seen pictures of the Morton men and they aged very well. She smiled as she thought of Mush with grey hair and a little paunch saying, "*Why don't you bring that young girl over here to sit on my lap.*"

She was writing about the incredible shock she felt at the accusation that she'd had an affair with Jim Mitchell, essentially Mush's and her boss.

Then she remembered. She picked up the phone and dialed. "Hello, the first lady's office, please." She had the insider's number to the White House switchboard.

"Hello, this Brooke Burrell-Morton I was..."

"Oh good, we've been trying to reach you. Thank you for calling back. Just a moment please." Brooke wasn't sure what she was talking about, then it dawned on her to check her phone. *FLOTUS. FLOTUS.*

FLOTUS, were the last three caller ids. She held the line, and somewhat braced herself for the First Lady of the United States.

"Brooke . . ." a familiar voice soon came over the receiver.

"Mrs. Mitchell . . . er. Hi. How's everythi . . . Are you okay, Delores?" She just couldn't play cute like everything was fine and dandy while not acknowledging the awkwardness of the situation.

"I was wondering the same about you," FLOTUS said.

"I am flabbergasted that anyone could think . . ."

"Brooke, I know. It was cruel and unfair."

"Delores, I heard that you interceded on my behalf . . ."

"Not just yours, mine, my family's, our presidency and our legacy. You know, Brooke, something like this, if you don't nip it in the bud, it lingers, festers, and becomes the fodder for mudslinging, dirty tricks, and sometimes even impeachment."

"Still, just the same, you stood up for me and for that I will always be in your debt."

"Listen, Brooke, I don't know about you, but I've had enough, enough of these 'gotcha' media ambushes. It's patently unfair that a woman can't spend time with a man and not be accused of bedding him down. It's infuriating, this double-standard bull . . . crap. I almost wish I had not interceded; that I'd let it play out, then lowered the boom and shame all of them back to 'J' school. You know, I used to work at the *Denver Post* before I met Jim. Some reporters are okay, professional and responsible members of the fourth estate, and I guess I should say, a mainstay of our freedoms. But let me tell you, there are a few scum-sucking bottom feeders out there who deserve to get their just desserts in Macy's window. Scratch that . . . have their fannies whipped in Bloomingdale's window."

"Well, Delores, at least you're not bitter!"

They both laughed and that released much of the tension and bile that this whole sickly affair had dredged up.

"Oh, Brooke. We must have a few whisky sours over this one."

"Delores, I'm there. You just say when."

"After the mid-terms, then if I get a little soused it won't matter. I'll be the wife of a lame duck."

"You sure you haven't started early there with a little nip of cooking sherry?"

That started another round of laughter.

Twenty minutes later, with heartfelt goodbyes, they hung up. Brooke had a warm feeling that the woman on the other end, who belonged to the world, to history, had a place in her heart for Brooke, and that just made her feel ten feet tall.

She grabbed the pen, and returned to her writing, "*Well, you'll never guess who was just on the phone . . .*"

Chapter 36

Home Stretch

Dequa had placed a two-dollar bet on the number eight horse, Hanny's Hanover the Third, for a win in the sixth harness race. It was a long shot at thirteen to one. He had the racing form under his arm and pencil behind his ear, blending in with all the other race goers on this unusually warm night at the trotters. From the grand stand, Dequa focused his binoculars on the number eight horse as the driver in the sulky behind it guided him around the track and into position behind the outstretched gates attached to the pace car. The starter sat backwards in the car. When all the horses were at the moving gate he would call the start of race and the 350-horsepower modified Lincoln Continental he was in, that served as the rolling starting gate, would accelerate as the horses did the same but with only one horsepower each.

Dequa panned the overly powerful binoculars to the right, at the guardhouse to the Yonkers reservoir just beyond the track's ground. Its darkened glass, closed-circuit cameras and other sensors were well known to him, but what he didn't know was why the two county sheriff's Ford Broncos, both with heavily weaponed tactical patrol force members at the ready, were now also parked there. He immediately had two nerve-rattling thoughts: one, that they had uncovered his plot; or two, the Fifth Avenue bomb attempt just had every agency a little on edge. *What did the Americans call it? Oh, yes, an abundance of caution.*

As the field of horses rounded the far turn, the crowd yelled and coaxed on their horses. Each hoping theirs, and theirs alone, was heading to an easy payday. Dequa also started saying, "Go, number eight! Go number eight," to join in. Anyone looking at him could see he wasn't looking to his left at the far turn but to the far right. No one looked at him, though, because in the middle of a race every one of the twenty-five thousand fans were looking at only one thing, their horse.

He passed the binoculars to Paul. "We have a new wrinkle."

.G.

Paul at first looked at the horses coming down the stretch then slowly panned over to the right side of the track and the high-fenced entrance gate to the vital New York City facility. "Hmmm. The good news is if they stay in the vehicles we can take them out in the first seconds with the two shoulder-fireds we have left. Then take out the guardhouse with the SAW."

"You think the glass not to be bulletproof?"

"Highly unlikely. Bullet resistant maybe, but under a full concentration of three hundred 5.56 mm rounds, the booth and everything in it will be shredded in three seconds."

"Good then. I do not have to concern myself with this end?"

"No, I will give the proper directives to the northern team. They will be ready and effective," Paul said.

"I hope you'll make the same report on our men in Michigan. They too need to be ready and effective," Dequa said dryly as he rose from his seat and walked up the aisle to the exit.

Paul followed as the track announcer broadcast, "Hanny's Hanover coming up the inside rail, Mama's Boy closing, they are neck and neck . . . and at the wire, its Hanny's Hanover by a nose! Mama's Boy second and Sweet Night to show."

On the seats they just left was the winning ticket, which paid twenty-eight dollars.

.G.

Sharon Cass waited in the private office of the administrator of Walter-Reade medical center. Owing to her status as the wife of a cabinet member, albeit recently resigned, she was afforded every comfort.

The hospital administrator entered with the head of his psychiatric unit, Dr. Mark Haden.

"Mrs. Cass, the good news is that your husband is not suffering from a mental disorder."

The woman breathed a big sigh of relief. "Then what made him act that way, Doctor?"

"Were you aware your husband was taking pills for his duodenal ulcer?"

"Why yes. It was very uncomfortable for him at times, almost debilitating."

"Yes, he told us, and he also mentioned he sought and obtained experimental drugs from Europe, not approved by the FDA."

"I do remember that at first the medicine his doctor prescribed was not helping much. He complained about that all the time."

"Well, Mrs. Cass, the intense medication he obtained is also indicated to manifest bouts of paranoia in a large percentage of patients. Now in Europe they monitor for exactly that condition, but your husband being under no such care, and the drug not available here in the US, meant he was being affected by the high dosage he was self-administering. H2 blockers, even FDA approved ones, are regularly monitored for paranoia symptoms."

"Will he recover?"

"Yes, over time the effects will dissipate and we'll get him on a diet, and a lower dose protocol. But you can help by monitoring what medicines he is taking. If you have any questions, please don't hesitate to call me."

"Yes, thank you, Doctor. I will." She didn't mention that she had been the one to bring him a refill of pills whenever she traveled with her girlfriend to Europe.

.G.

"We're about to move the barrels, sir," an ATF&E bomb tech said to him. The dynamite had been removed first. They had already taken samples from the barrels to check for taggants, the chemical markers that they could take back to Washington and use to trace most explosive compounds back to their source.

"Okay, proceed."

Harris was surprised. The feds were actually complying with his directives. It was a totally new experience for him. *Looks like Burrell had juice after all,* he thought.

Harris watched as two big guys using a barrel hand truck, tilted the barrel while the other slid the lip of the hand truck under. They were moving the third one when Harris spotted something. "Hold the work." He walked over to the spot that had been covered by the barrel. "Get a set of photos of these. Somebody see if they can lift a transfer of this. Look for more . . ." Because this one was narrower than those he had seen before, Harris had hope.

"Detective?"

Harris turned as another fed approached, female this time.

"Crime scene still got a lot of lab work to do, but on the surface, these occupants ate a lot of Middle Eastern food, no liquor, no computers, not even cable. Only clothes we found were in the laundry basket. We'll try to recover DNA on whatever soiled undies we can, but there isn't too much here."

"Thanks, Agent, let me know what they find."

A Yonkers PD patrol officer approached. "Detective Harris, this is Mr. Aponte . . . He lives across the street."

"On the corner . . ." Aponte pointed out with his thumb over his right shoulder.

"The house with the great lawn?"

"Yup."

"So you called this in?"

"Yeah, I had asked them to turn down the racket a few days ago. The wife was all over me . . . You know, kids and all."

"Go on."

"Well, then last night they started up again. So she says, call the police. Hey, they seemed like okay guys, so I really didn't want to start a block war, so I figured let me try one more time."

"Block war? Is that a thing up here in the suburbs?"

"Try having the nicest lawn or prettiest house. People are just jealous sometimes . . . Anyway, I get here and the noise stopped, then I see the garage open . . ."

"All the way?"

"No, just a crack at the bottom. I called out, looked around, but no one was here. But the light was coming through the bottom of the door. So I opened it. Saw all the barrels, then I saw the dynamite and that's when I called the cops. We got families and kids on this block . . ."

Harris looks around the garage, "What do you mean by racket? Loud music?"

"No, hammering, banging, even power hammer."

"What were they banging on?" Harris said, looking around the garage for something obvious.

"I dunno."

"Well, what kind of thing were they working on?"

"A car, I thought, but I guess I was wrong."

"Why a car?"

"Heard a lot of metal work, pounding mostly, like banging out an old fender . . . Although, they were either really bad at it or they had a lot of fenders because it was constant over a few days and nights."

Harris directed one of the feds whose name he luckily remembered. "Agent Bowers, can your team look for hammers and anything that might have been struck by hammers . . . Especially something metal-like."

"There was a garbage can beat to shit here in the middle. We tagged and recorded it, then moved it."

Harris looked to Aponte.

"Maybe this time, but the sound from before was bigger."

He turned back to Bowers. "Keep looking . . ."

Then he turned to Aponte. "Tell me about them."

"I really only ever talked to one of them, Wally, the friendlier one."

"Friendlier?"

"Yeah, I had seen the others occasionally but they really kept to themselves; you know, no eye contact, never a smile. Almost like they wanted to be invisible."

"But not Wally?"

"No, he was nice enough. Next to the others he was like, what do they call it?"

"Call what?"

"You know in the beauty pageant, the one that everybody gets along with . . . Miss Congeniality. Next to those stone-faced others, he was Miss Congeniality."

.G.

"I hated that movie . . ." Brooke said.

Harris, who was now back in the office, smiled. "I dunno, kind of made you feds look almost human."

"For a whole year, whenever I said, I work for the FBI, I'd always get . . . Oh, like in *Miss Congeniality*?" Brooke looked down at the glossy print on her desk of the mark on the garage floor that Harris had snapped. "I liked Sandra Bullock in it, though."

"So we may have the tire track there that could be like the one she figured out in *My Cousin Vinny*."

"That wasn't Bullock . . . it was . . . what's her name . . . 'You blend . . .' Marisa Tomei!"

"Right, but what we got here struck me as narrower than a car width."

"So tell me."

"The lab boys."

"Which lab would that be?" Brooke said with a slight smirk.

"The FBI lab, thank you very much. They say this tread is from the smaller wheel tire of a U-Haul type five-by-eight-foot trailer."

"The truck on Fifth Avenue was a two-and-a-half-ton Ryder. Could it have fit in the garage?"

"No, the truck would have been too tall. But, your FBI lab rats are good. They used some kind of infrared laser thing to see roughly three sets of these on the garage floor."

"So the U-Haul was what they were banging on?"

"Could be."

"How much does one of those carry?"

"Eighteen hundred pounds max is what the company said."

"They mention if they rented three out?"

"They got twenty-four thousand of these things in the Tri-State area alone."

"You know the drill," Brooke said as she put the picture down.

"Got a team working with their computer guys on all five-by-eight rentals that cover the period of the banging."

"Here's the big question, did anyone in the neighborhood see a big Ryder truck on the driveway?" Brooke said.

"No. And that's maybe where the U-Hauls come in. Maybe they used them to bring the barrels to wherever they loaded the truck."

"All three?"

"Two would have done the job, but maybe they weren't good at packing."

"And it doesn't explain the banging."

"Yeah, that's nagging at me, too."

"Good work, Harris. I wanna know if you find out anything that makes the nagging stop."

"Will do." Harris got up and left.

Brooke hit the intercom button on the phone. "Ask Remo and Kronos to come in to my office, please." She looked down at the photo of the tire tread. "Twenty-four thousand . . ."

"Yes, boss," Kronos said as he flopped down sideways on the chair in front of her with his legs over the arm. Peter Remo followed but sat like a grown up.

"Guys, I got another puzzle to add to your pile. What part of—or should I say—is there a part of bomb making that requires hammering or pounding for a long period of time?"

"You mean like tenderizing the components?" Kronos said.

"Is that a real thing or are you just being a wise ass."

"Ass option," Kronos said.

"We'll look into it. Is this about the Yonkers' bomb factory?" Remo said.

"Yes. We can't directly tie it to the Fifth Avenue truck."

"That's scary. You thinking there could be another one or more trucks out there?"

"Now you know why sleep is so hard to come by."

Remo slapped Kronos on the back. "Come on, K, let's get on this."

"Thanks guys."

.G.

3 DAYS UNTIL THE ATTACK

It took a day, but by eight in the morning the New York State Police, Troop E, Zone Two, had traced the plate to a U-Haul trailer rented out of Columbus, Ohio six weeks earlier. Paid for two months, one-way drop off service to Florida, in cash. The rental company was currently trying to track down any surveillance footage of who may have rented the five-by-eight-foot unit.

At the quarry site, three New York State highway maintenance vehicles had offloaded two bucket loaders and a bulldozer.

The owner of Seneca Excavation was on hand as well as the teacher, Mr. Herns. They both agreed that the soil in the middle of the bowl was depressed and curved in, as if a deeper excavation had suffered a collapse. The loader had hit a wheel lodged in between two boulders. The loose consistency of the dirt they were dredging out confirmed it had recently been turned, filling in the crater-like void.

They were thirty feet down when the bucket hit something. The work stopped.

A team from the army's corps of engineers moved in with ground-penetrating radar. Their scan showed something fifteen feet further down. "Well, there's something down there," the army engineer said.

.G.

"Detective Harris, NYPD, for Mr. Butz." He tapped his pencil on the desk as he waited to be connected.

The woman with an Arizona accent got back on the phone. "Well, I am real sorry, but Mr. Butz is out of the office for a brief spell. Can someone else help you?"

"I'm waiting for his call back on a very urgent matter."

"What is this in regard to?"

"Security."

"Hold on, maybe Mr. Wells can be of assistance . . ."

"No, I don't . . ." Too late. She already had him on hold.

"Security. Wells . . ."

"Wells, this is Harris in New York."

"I got it. Was just going to fax it."

Harris took the phone from his ear and looked at it with a crazy look. "Got what?"

"The rental contract and a still from the security camera."

"Great but don't fax it; email it if you can."

"Then why did you give me your fax number?"

"I didn't."

"Wait, who is this again?"

"Harris, NYPD."

"Isn't Waterloo far from New York City?"

"Are you asking in just general geographic terms or am I missing something?"

"You are not New York State Police from Waterloo?"

"No, I am working with the federal government on a threat assessment of a possible terror plot that may involve one of your trailers, with Mr. Butz."

"Sorry, I thought you were guy from Troop E."

"Slow down. Why don't you start from the beginning."

.ɞ.

Harris burst into the conference room interrupting Brooke, Remo, Kronos, and Bridge. "We got something."

"Good 'cause we are just retracing our steps," Brooke said.

"Get this, some high school teacher upstate takes his class on a field trip and comes across the site of a huge explosion. They find an Ohio plate . . . a trailer plate. They dig and find a mangled five-by-eight U-Haul blown to bits."

"This is good, Harris. Bridge you are a former UDT guy."

"I am not that old, Brooke. We've called ourselves SEALS since the 60s, you know. Underwater Demolition Team was just too limiting."

"SEALS? That's navy. I thought you was army?" Kronos said.

"Was that too, after I got swimmer's ear."

"Really? That can . . ."

Brooke laughed. "No, Kronos, he was a senior chief in the navy, but then the army needed his exceptional skill set."

"Wait, so you went from senior chief to sergeant major; isn't that the same pay grade? What kind of sucker move . . .?"

"Kronos," Brooke said, holding her hand up like it was Mrs. William's kindergarten class. "Bridge, you and Harris get up there, fast."

"How fast?" Harris said.

"Get over to the heliport. Chop out to LaGuardia. I'll have a G5 waiting."

"Yeah, that's fast."

.ɞ.

As they trotted from the New York State Police helicopter that they'd caught on the west side of Manhattan to the gleaming FBI G5 on the tarmac at Butler Aviation, its turbo-fan engines were already turning. Harris whistled. "That Brooke certainly makes shit happen."

"That's because she has grit my friend. They wouldn't dare say, 'no,' to her."

As they boarded the jet, the copilot greeted them. "Look, guys, we got the call the last minute. We got no cabin attendant. So I get to do this. In the event of an emergency your masks . . ."

"Forget it. We've all been on a plane. Just get us in the air. How long?"

"First, I got to tell you that you must wear seatbelts . . ."

"Look, we know . . ."

"No, you don't know . . . We are landing at Airtrek Airport."

"Never heard of it."

"Me neither, but it's a dirt field. We could come down and get stuck in the dirt. That's one hundred forty miles an hour to a squashed gnat on the windshield in point zero seconds."

"Got it! Seatbelts, thanks."

"We've got priority clearance for takeoff. You guys must be on something really hot." He turned to enter the cockpit as the stairs automatically folded into the fuselage as the main cabin door automatically closed. The copilot made sure it was locked and sealed then armed the door's emergency chute/life raft then took his seat in the cockpit. Their preflight checklist already having been done, the small corporate bird rolled to its number one for takeoff position.

Bridge yelled out through the opened cockpit door, "Hey, can this thing land on dirt?"

"We'll find out in twenty-six minutes," the other pilot said.

Both men looked at each other and simultaneously said, "Fast."

.𝔊.

Shipsen-Deloitte had spared no expense in appointing their opulent Cayman Island offices. Their clientele ranged from the curious tourist to the serious art investor/collector who took maximum advantage of the island's notorious financial privacy laws. The London-based provenance company wrote hundreds of millions of dollars, euros and yen from that location every year.

Through special arrangement with the Cayman Island's Government, FinCEN agents were through the ten-foot crystal clear doors at 9:01 a.m. local time. The manager of the art house hurried to greet the ten men and two Cayman officials as they entered. He spoke to the local men first. "What is the meaning of this?"

"These men are here as part of an international investigation. I'll let them explain," he said as he nodded to the American.

.𝔊.

The BBC news van had just set up when the reporter rolled her hand in a gesture that the studio was switching live to them immediately.

The cameraman called out, "In three . . . two," then he silently threw one finger at her, which was her cue.

"At one minute past two this afternoon, British authorities entered and suspended all business activities here at the world headquarters of Shipsen-Deloitte. We are told by a top Scotland Yard source that similar raids are being held at this exact moment at offices from Prague to the Cayman Islands. All we know so far is that the cessation of business stems from an investigation by the US and Interpol into money laundering schemes to finance terror groups. We have footage of just a few minutes ago when the afternoon calm of this quiet little section of Savile Row, in Westminster, was visited upon by scores of police vehicles . . ." She stood looking at the camera until the cameraman said "Clear." Then she looked down at a monitor on the sidewalk and watched the video that was being broadcast as she pressed an earbud into her ear so she could better talk to the director back at the studio. "I'll do the wrap up then we'll wait and see if I can get a quote or bite when they come out."

.𝔊.

Bridge and Harris emerged from the State Trooper car that had met them at the dirt-runway airport for the quick drive with sirens all the way to the quarry. Trooper Selma Gains, information officer for Troop E, met them as they got out. "Gains, State. I assume you want to contain this?"

"Definitely, until we know what we are dealing with here."

"Got more and more press finding their way up here every hour. What do I tell them?"

"Is 'no comment' still fashionable?" Bridge said.

"Short lived. Then they start looking for leaks and speculating."

"Look, Gains, if this is what we think it is, the bad guys can't know we are even here. If you can't black it out, then use a cold case cover story."

"Got any ideas?"

"Jocko Pizzarelli," Harris said.

"Okay, I'll bite," she said.

"Mob lieutenant who went missing five years ago. I was on the case but it went cold. I'm thinking they dumped Jocko up here," Harris said with a knowing look to Gains.

"Works for me," Bridge said.

"Works for me too. Joint operation then, NYPD NYS?" Gains said.

"Again, if we can't black it out, then yes," Bridge said as he and Harris walked off.

.G,

Work had proceeded to the point where they had the whole carcass of the trailer unearthed and had a spiral path of sorts leading down the fifty or so feet that Bridge estimated it was. As they approached, Harris saw the flattened wheel with the narrow tire.

There was a forensic explosives expert from Rochester PD at the bottom. The first thing Bridge noticed was that the roof of the trailer and the sides were relatively intact. The bottom, the chassis, was blown deeper into the dirt.

.G.

Meanwhile, Selma Gain's mother, having raised no foolish children, would have been proud of what her daughter came up with for the non-denial denial. Right before she met the press that was being kept on the other side of the notch behind police tape, she took out her cell phone and wandered close to Officer Gabriel Rice. He was a townie and worked for the sheriff. She also knew he was a sieve. Real gossip hound as she had found out the few times their paths crossed out here in Midwestern New York State.

"Got it, Jocko Pizzarelli. New York mob. Went missing five years ago. Send us the dentals . . . I will. They think they're close to the body but they're still digging. Yes, I will . . ."

She closed the phone and purposely didn't look at Rice as she walked off towards where the reporters were corralled. They all quieted down when she arrived at the tapeline. "I have a quick statement and I will not take questions. You boys covering this live, consider this your one-minute warning. Then she saw a female reporter from channel nine and nodded to her in deference to the "boys" line.

A minute later she introduced herself, her rank, and spelled both her first and last names for proper attribution and delivered a very short statement.

"We have no comment at this time." Then she walked away after an eruption of questions.

Five minutes later, she smiled as she saw a group of reporters around Rice as he was sucking up all the fame of being an unnamed source. *The legend of Jocko Pizzerelli lives.*

.G.

Bridge asked them to rig the back loader with a chain and they flipped over the intact top of the trailer; then they saw it. Welded to the top was what looked like a metal umbrella. Bridge examined it and made it out to be one-inch thick steel plating five foot or so around. The peen marks on the scorched metal showed the forming of the concave shape.

"That would make a hell of a racket to form," Bridge said to Harris.

"It must weigh half a ton," Harris said.

Bridge turned to the forensic expert. "Have you done a test?"

"Yes, this is Semtex, definitely RDX and PETN scoring and pitting along the dish here."

"Any guess as to how much would make a crater this deep?"

"Oh, I'd say five hundred to eight hundred pounds, easy."

"Plus a thousand pounds of steel plate. We're there at the maximum load on the trailer: eighteen hundred!"

.G.

Brooke had an ATF&E bomb tech in her office in thirty minutes. "Harris and Bridge are due back in twenty minutes. Peter, Kronos, listen to what Nick here from ATF&E thinks of the dish the boys found."

"Well, as I was explaining to Director Burrell, from the pictures it looks like the shape is actually parabolic. Like a satellite dish."

"And it was welded to the top of the trailer?" Peter said.

"That's what they said."

"So then you think the parabolic shape is a force director?" Brooke said.

"Brooke, a what?" Remo said.

"It's like a magnifying glass, focusing the full power of the explosion to the center of the dish." The bomb tech arced his hands in the rough shape of dome.

"And since it was pointing down this explains why they found it fifty feet down?" Kronos said.

"Exactly!"

"And our best guess is that there were three of these things," Brooke said.

"Scratch one. That must have been their test bomb," Remo said.

"Okay, so they want this thing to shoot downward. What does that tell us?" Brooke said.

"Subway. Drive it down Broadway and if you time it right you'll kill thousands at Times Square."

"The downward force rules out using it inside a car tunnel. Although I would order an immediate ban on all such rental trailers on bridges and tunnels to err on the side of caution," the bomb tech said.

Brooke took it all in. Peter Remo noticed her expression. "What is it, Brooke? You don't look convinced."

"I think this is bigger than the subway. London proved you could get the same result with backpacks."

"With all respect, that wasn't thousands," Kronos said.

"They've already hit us for thousands . . . And I know they have tried bigger things. And this current cell seems more . . . desperate . . . more organized than any of those."

"So you are thinking bigger than 9/11?"

"I hope to God I am wrong, but remember this started out with put and calls in advance of a terror plot. There are no stocks for the subway. And if there are only two bombs, they are localized. That wouldn't dent the stock market enough to make a hedge play worthwhile."

"So, then the bombs might be initiators?" Kronos said.

"How so?" Brooke asked.

"They may start a more devastating catastrophe."

"I'm seeing your point, Kronos, but that still leaves the question of why they shaped the charge downward."

"Gas mains?"

"Again, devastating but still localized. I think they are going for bigger. Kronos, Peter, call in anyone you have to. Ask Bill Hiccock to run it by his people and his network. We are not seeing the same opportunity that they are."

Remo shook his head. "I don't get it."

"What?" Brooke said.

"Parabolic focused explosions? These are terrorists. That seems like real egg-head nasty shit."

"Parabolics?" Kronos said. "Parabolic curves are tenth grade high school crap, Peter . . . and remember algebra was invented in their part of the world."

.G.

Dequa was at the whiteboard filled with formulas and diagrams. "The synchronous relays will not be a problem in that they are triggered by deviation from the grid frequency. In our scenario, it all reduces together, simultaneously across the entire infrastructure. Therefore we are never outside the deviant range."

"I don't know, .0167 cps is a very tight margin," Yusuf said.

"But here the system helps us defeat it."

"Yes. Yes, you may be right . . . Still, I'd like to run a few more simulations to make sure we are factoring in rotator torque under load conditions."

"That is a valid point. Run the simulations. We might have to adjust the delta factor here," Dequa said.

Paul was standing behind them and had listened to everything but still didn't have a clue as to what the hell they were talking about. Although he got that Dequa hadn't figured on something that could screw up the whole thing. When they finished, they erased the board.

Dequa was brushing the marker dust off his hands when he turned to Paul. "Paul, the north team has had a very successful test. They are ready and will be in position at the appointed hour. Your job will be to ensure perimeter security of the central station. We need at least five minutes, maybe ten if the rotator torque is indeed a factor," Dequa said, nodding to the erased board.

"The first response will be plant security. That won't be a challenge because they won't be expecting anything on the scale I have prepared. For the next wave of responders, I am going to need at least all ten of my first team in position in order to give you your ten minutes. It would take that long for them to assess the situation and decide on a strategy. By then, if you guys got it right, the city will already be a living hell," Paul said.

.𝔊.

As soon as Bridge returned, he and Brooke sequestered themselves in her office as she downloaded what the brain boys had come up with and their speculation as to the probable timings and nature of the attack.

"Brooke, the more I hear, the more convinced I am that we need a rapid way to respond to whatever and wherever they are going to strike."

"Your RDF idea?"

"I was toying with the idea of multiple assets strategically placed and ready to go at a moment's notice. And now, with what Remo and Kronos are saying, I think it's time for me to draw it up and send my rapid deployment force up the chain of command."

"In this case, it won't be a long trip; I am the last link to the top of the chain, Bridge. But do you really think you can get all the equipment and personnel we need turned around in twelve hours? Assuming we have that long?"

"Well, we've got at least a division of men and two hundred fixed wing and rotary aircraft that are normally stationed within a three-hundred-mile radius of the city. And thanks to your chat with the president, he put all forces on PTDO elevated alert, so all it would take is an order from the commander in chief and they'd go from the Prepare to Deploy Order to REDCON1 to immediate deploy. Once we are at Ready Condition One and we get that deployment order, we'll be cocked and ready to kick butt."

"How long from the DEPORD before we are capable?"

"Well, for example, the pods on the Apache attack helos would have to be loaded with Hellfire missiles and other ordnance packages. Figure three hours. Flight time to New York City from, let's say Fort Drum—three hundred plus miles upstate, where these birds nest—is about two hours at cruising speed. Supplemental parts, equipment trucks and support personnel can convoy down the Thruway in five hours thirty-five minutes to Times Square. So I'd say total time from alert to locked and loaded . . . nine hours."

"Sounds miraculous."

"Our boys train that hard to pull off miracles every day."

"You sold me. What are you going to call this plan?"

"I was thinking, *Archangel*."

"I like it. Someone to watch over me, us, the city . . ."

"Something like that."

"Start writing. I got a meeting with Barnes. I'll get him on board."

.G.

"A high school science teacher?" Harold Barnes, director of FinCEN, said for the second time to Brooke as she briefed them on where they were.

"When you stop to think about it, sir, this whole operation is being run by a high school soccer coach, you know."

Barnes squinched his face, then remembered that's what Brooke had been doing when they recruited her. "What have we got from Prescott?"

"Kitman."

"Barry Kitman?"

"He was pulling Morgan Prescott's strings on the financial side."

"So how did the Russians wind up with him?"

"Not so much the Russians but the oligarchs. There are only two options. The oligarch was working for Kitman or the other way around."

"And we don't know which one of them is behind the terror attack?"

"Or if they are at all. Could be they just caught wind of it and are trying to cash in," Brooke said.

"It would make sense. If America is weakened then the oligarch's share of the world's economy increases tenfold instantly."

"That's a pretty big profit motive for just lending logistical support. Also they side with the very group who otherwise might attack them next."

"Smart play all around in their book," Barnes said.

"And if Kitman is behind it then he just scores big hedging on the knowledge of the attack," Brooke said.

"So then that brings us to the only possible third financial player . . ."

"You mean the terrorists themselves?"

"Why not? For all we know ISIS is deep in the stock market through third parties and foreign investments. Look at what they're doing with just the oil money they take from the captured wells. What's Prescott say?"

"Swears it was all put and calls for Kitman while they held his family. He wasn't in it for any piece of the profit," Brooke said as she waved her hands in a flat gesture.

"You believe him?"

"Yeah, I do. George didn't find anything in three months at Prescott Capital Management. We thought he was hiding it, but it wasn't even in PCM; it was across town at Kitman."

"So it was funded by artwork?"

"Yes. The pieces are coming in now. Working with Interpol and SWIFT, we just raided Shipsen-Deloitte's offices in five countries."

"So SOM37 sold junk art for millions and was funded by ISIS right under our noses as a simple art sale."

"Yes, thousands of overvalued works yielding hundreds of millions of dollars. The sales were made through the cells needing the money to certain Middle East benefactors that are probably fronts for ISIS."

"Anything from the captors down in Grenada?"

"Unfortunately, all local hires who believe they were working for the mob."

"Russian mob? Prescott was held at Borishenko's compound."

"I've got the bureau's organized crime division on it, but they only ever spoke to the one man who paid them. And I have a feeling, an instinct actually, that it's one of our prime suspects in all this: we are calling him Paul. He may have contracted with the locals."

"So who's Paul?"

"We don't know, but he may be connected to a few deaths that happened on the periphery of all this. We have established a bloody trail of victims who were either complicit or used unknowingly. Most of the bodies that sprang up in Prague and Sweden, and a few we suspect that will never surface down in the Caymans, were in position to take worthless pieces of art and establish them as major works with a reflectively high price tag. Or cover the transfer of those funds. Then Paul eliminated them."

"Wait a minute, the priest, the one that tried to kill you?"

"The imposter priest. Yes, that was him and he also may be responsible for the rocket attack on our satellite office."

"To finish the job . . ."

"Not a comforting thought but definitely in the stack," Brooke paused.

Barnes instinctively paused as well and held back his next question for a few seconds. "How are you holding up under all this?"

"Fine, sir."

"I was in law enforcement for twenty-seven years before I went to the Treasury. I have a masters in criminology and a minor in psychology, but everything I need to know to sense that you are not fine. I learned from my three daughters."

He could see her stoic mask break apart as she looked at him.

She softened. "I let them down. I couldn't protect my team. I should have anticipated their play. Should have moved to more secure offices." She pounded her desk with her fist with each of the next four syllables. "Nine-teen-peo-ple would be alive and twenty-three others wouldn't be maimed and wounded. I got too focused, got too into tactical and not enough into strategic."

"You were attacked by an enemy who stops at nothing . . . Hell, they even tried to blow up Saint Pats."

"I exposed our flank. I didn't assess the threat properly."

"You're right. You fouled up on this one, Burrell."

"I know."

"I want a full report of this debacle, pending disciplinary action."

It was a bitter pill, but Brooke totally understood the need to write this up, even against her own best interests. "Will do, sir. I'll start on it right away."

"No you won't. You'll start on it the day after you thwart this attack."

A small grin started to escape from her mouth but the nineteen dead pulled it back. "Thank you for the show of confidence in me, sir."

"Hell, you've earned it." He stood up to leave. "Let me know whatever you need."

"Sir, I need you to support my recommendation to the president that he initiate *Archangel*."

"I never heard of this."

"It's being drawn up now. You'll have a copy as soon as I do. It will give us a fighting chance to stop or at least limit whatever is coming our way."

"Do you like this plan?"

"Yes, sir. And more importantly my chief of military operations is drawing it up."

"Send it to me. I am already predisposed to like it."

"Will do. And again, thank you for the confidence, sir."

"I'll get out of your hair. Good luck and carry on." He smiled a reassuring smile and left.

Brooke sat in the empty office and looked down at the folder on her desk. It was the death benefits forms for each of the agents and staff that had been killed. As director of the group, she had to sign the forms so that the families could get burial and life insurance payouts. With a deep breath she opened it. The government bureaucrats that would process the forms would have to deal with occasional tear-smudged ink on a few of the pages.

Chapter 37

Yogi Moose

Wallace Beesly was an analyst working for Graystone Equities. He was a frequent guest on the various business shows that populated the cable networks. He had predicted many stock market trends in the past, and with each successful prediction gained more and more stature as a go-to analyst on the street.

Beesly, who had originally trained as a mainframe programmer back in the 80s, used his ability to write routines and algorithms to do predictive analysis that was rich in data points and therefore very accurate. Still, the markets responded to random elements such as the human psyche versus groupthink or, more specifically, human greed against fiscal conservatism. So logical trajectories or trends only got you so far. It was human panic or euphoria that had the last say in the direction and outcome of any given event, day, or era of the markets.

He had just finished his next big research paper entitled "Trends Out of Municipal Bonds and Infrastructure Stocks." Before him on the screen was three weeks of analysis, now in the form of a chart. The curve was unmistakable. Someone, some huge institutional investor had, over the years, taken major positions in all these sectors and now, quietly, over time, placed put and call contracts on the very same portfolios.

He decided to see if this was unprecedented or cyclical in some nature so he wrote a program in C, his favorite code, to interrogate the vast database of every move in stock market history and find any similar dumping or pumping in the past.

It was about one hundred and twenty lines of code. When he hit "compile," the progress line was quickly calculating hours and hours for the program to complete, so he got up and went downstairs to Dunkin Donuts for a double turbo-shot cup of brew.

.G.

2 DAYS UNTIL THE ATTACK

Paul arrived in Dearborn, Michigan, at 1:00 a.m. He flew commuter from Westchester County Airport in New York. He was met by a man who drove him an hour into the woods, where his ten-man "First Team" facility defense unit was armed and ready to show him what they had trained for.

Each night-vision-capable man had a MP5 machine gun and seven hundred rounds of ammo. They each carried four grenades and two smoke canisters on their webbing. They had all seen action in Afghanistan; the older ones had battled against both the Russians and Americans. Two of them were released detainees, having been inmates at Guantanamo Bay eighteen months before; they had eluded their trackers and slipped over the Mexican border into Texas. They relished the opportunity to become martyrs in this grand act of God that would bring the Great Satan to its knees.

Paul watched as they exhibited excellent shooting and counter-insurgency skills. He turned to their leader and said, "Your men are ready. Move your operation to New York. Soon the great victory will be upon us."

For his part, the team leader thought Paul an infidel. Although he had converted to the faith, he was too . . . too . . . "white bread," as he understood the American term. But Dequa had made this American the man in charge, and the team leader was duty bound by oath to obey Dequa's man rather than slit his throat.

.G.

At 5:30 a.m., Remo and Kronos were running simulations across Bill Hiccock's SciAD network. Bill, the science advisor to the president, had established the network as a top-secret cluster of the nation's leading scientists and technological innovators who'd taken an oath of secrecy to defend America. The name SciAd itself stood for Scientists in America's Defense.

Using what they knew about the skill sets of the missing "student" visa violators, they played out multiple war games with the brightest minds in America and extracted probables from each run.

So far they had the following odds, denial of service: electrical, thirty-three percent; denial of service: Internet; thirty percent, biological, twelve percent; chemical, twelve percent; nuclear event, three percent; and the ever popular 'unknown-unknown' at ten percent. They had until 7:00 a.m., at which time Brooke was expecting to order a heightened alert at whatever entity they felt was vulnerable.

They ran a second set of scenarios, this time tempered by the assumptions that somehow Prescott, and possibly Kitman, had some sort of role as well.

One of the ninety-two element members of the SciAd network wrote back at that point. "If you are considering a financial impact component, one of the best guys I know is Beesly at Graystone. He was one of us before he went over to Wall Street. He's got a good track record in predicting market events. I'd give him a call and read him in or swear him in or whatever you need to do to get him to cooperate."

.𝔊.

Yogi Moose's ears perked up at the low buzzing noise. Yogi Moose was a weird name for a dog, but somehow it's what the little girl in the shelter had called him. When her mother told her she couldn't have another dog, the little girl had said goodbye in a way that broke Wallace's heart. So he'd switched from getting a cat to giving Yogi Moose a good home and rescued the older, dopey-looking dog from the gas chamber.

There was the buzzing sound again. The dog lifted his head. On the third ring he put his paw on his master's sleeping shoulder. Wallace awoke and squinted at the clock. A fuzzy 6:00 a.m. caused him to sink deeper into the pillow and say in a muffled voice, "Come on, Yogi, I'll walk you in thirty minutes."

Then he heard the vibrating phone. Wallace turned over to licks all across his face as he fumbled for the phone. He put his arm around

Yogi in that definite way that said, "Calm down. I love you, but daddy's on the phone right now." Yogi kept his eyes on Wallace as he panted.

"Hello?"

"Wallace Beesly?'

"Who is this? How did you get my private number?"

"This is Peter Remo with FinCEN. We need you to help us defuse a very dangerous situation."

"Is this a joke?"

"I assure you this is deadly serious."

Yogi's head spun around towards the direction of the front door. He yelped and backed out from underneath Wallace's arm and hit the floor running, barking all the way. The doorbell rang followed by very loud knocks, followed by, "Federal Agents, Mr. Beesly, please open the door." Followed by more knocking.

"You sent agents to my house?"

"Time is critical, sir. Would you let the agents in? I can't go into this over an unsecured line."

"Let them in?"

"Yes and please bring photo ID to the door."

"Photo ID?"

"Please hurry."

Wallace swung his feet out of the bed and picked up the bottom part of his sweats from the floor.

He opened the door. Yogi was still barking.

"Sir, please secure your dog."

"Don't worry, he'll just lick you to death."

"Just the same, I don't want to have to shoot him if he attacks us."

"Hold on." He closed the door. "Come on, Yogi, in the bathroom, come on . . . That's a good boy."

He reopened the door.

"Good morning, sir," the agent said as if they hadn't just spoken.

"Now you want to be nice to me, after you threatened to shoot my dog?"

"No, I want to see your ID."

"Shit." He closed the door again, then went to the dresser and retrieved his wallet.

He opened the door, dangling his driver's license.

The agent took it, looked at the photo and back at Wallace's groggy face. "Are you a natural born citizen of the United States?"

"Wha . . . er . . . yeah, Beaumont, Montana. What's this all . . . ?" He yawned.

"Are you now or have you ever been an agent or representative of a foreign government?"

"No, no, why?"

"Do you affirm or swear that the information you just imparted is the truth?"

"Yeah . . . sure. What's this all—"

"Hold on, sir." The agent handed him a phone.

"Hello?" It was the same guy. "Didn't I just talk to you?"

"This is a secure line. Will you agree to help us?"

"I don't know what 'it' is, but this big guy is ready to shoot my dog, so my immediate answer is 'go jump in a lake.'"

"Mr. Beesly, this is a national crisis. We need your expertise to avoid what could be a calamity."

"Something with the stock market?"

"No, bigger. But before I can divulge any further information, you need to tell me that you are willing to help."

"Two agents with guns and secure phones? And *now* you're asking if I am willing . . . You mean I have a choice?"

"Yes sir, this is just a crisis. Had it been deemed a national emergency, you'd be here by now."

"Where's here?"

"FBI New York headquarters."

"You say this is serious?"

"Look at the agents, sir. We went to a lot of trouble to get to you. If you agree, they will drive you back here immediately."

Wallace pulled the phone away from his ear. He looked down at the floor. Yogi barked from the bathroom. "Hush boy, I'll let you out in a minute." He looked down at the phone; he rubbed his eyes and brought it back up to his ear. "Do I have time to feed and walk my dog?"

.𝔊.

"Dequa, all cells and units are ready."

"Anything on the authorities?"

"As far as we can tell they took the bait on the Yonkers' house and are looking for leads to Rashad's truck."

"Good. We'll start the countdown at midnight."

.G.

1 DAY UNTIL THE ATTACK

Brooke was startled when the elevator door opened and she came face to face with a mangy mutt. His expressive eyes melted her heart in an instant. She then snapped out of it as George walked by. "George, why is there a dog in the office?"

"Remo and Kronos. Do I have to say more?"

Brooke looked down at the little soul then looked both ways and, seeing the coast was clear, bent down and gave him a pat on the scruff, then tickled him behind his ear. "Thanks for saying, 'hi,' to me this morning . . ."

She got up and headed to her office but made a right turn into Kronos and Remo's. "Fellas, why is there a dog . . . ?"

"Sorry, that's Yogi, Yogi Moose," Beesly said.

"You named a dog Yogi Moose?"

"I didn't, a little girl did."

"And what did they name you?"

"I'm Wallace Beesly. I just came on this morning . . . very early this morning," he said with a turn to Remo.

"He didn't have time to feed him so . . ." Kronos said.

Brooke turned to Remo. "I'm listening."

"Wallace is an ace at predicting market trends. We got him from a member of Bill's network."

"Okay, Wallace, what can you tell us?"

"Not much, but in a few seconds the routine I started yesterday will finish its final nested sort and then I might have something." He walked over to one of the two-screen computers on the table that flanked the other side of the room Remo and Kronos had taken over. "I was able to log on to my main frame at work. And . . . here it is. Just finished."

Brooke looked on as Wallace entered keystrokes in a flurry.

Kronos walked over and read the screen. "Sweet. Why'dja write it in C?"

"C language, best there ever was . . ."

"Hey, I like this guy," Kronos said turning to Brooke and jacking his thumb in Wallace's direction.

Brooke saw his face change as he leaned in closer and hit more keys. "Oh, God."

"What?" everyone else said at once.

"I entered parameters yesterday for a finding I was doing on put and calls."

"Why?" Brooke said.

"I had a working theory that someone or some entity was quietly buying up sector stocks; I thought it might be a prelude to a corporate takeover, which is always big news. So I wrote some code to interrogate the data base and see if a similar pattern of moves had happened before any major takeovers or mergers in the past."

"And?" Brooke said to the guy who was once again glued to the screen. ". . . And?"

"And now, what with the phone call this morning and this . . ." He stopped again.

Brooke realized he was talking about what had popped up on the screen so she got closer to it. "What's this?"

"My graph showing peak times when major moves happened correlated to big takeovers and mergers."

"Yeah, I got that, what was the 'Oh God' for . . ."

"Oh, God. There were ten times when the peak happened, but this one here is third-quarter fiscal year 2001."

"Third . . . that would be September."

"2001!" Kronos said.

"Holy shit," Remo said.

The moment hung.

"Can you give us a time frame, between the activity and the event?" Kronos asked.

"Working on it," Wallace said as he hammered more keys. "Oh, my God."

"Wallace . . ." Brooke said impatiently.

"Sorry, today, tomorrow, maybe the day after, but the indexes are converging in the next twelve to twenty-four hours. Like they did here on 9/10," he said pointing to a place where four colored lines converged on his chart.

"How accurate is this?"

"The data is perfect. Whether my extrapolation has flaws, well, that I'd have to recheck."

"Kronos, this is your wheelhouse; help him. Let me know if this is real, ASAP.

"Peter, what did you guys come up with overnight?"

"Got it all printed up, right here."

"Grab a cup of coffee and be in my office in two minutes. Oh, and get yourself one too."

Remo smiled. "Good morning to you, too."

.𝔊.

When Brooke got to her office, there was a legal document on her desk. It was a notice to appear. She read it and decided to give it to George. Then she picked up the phone. "Secure line, POTUS, emergency interrupt, director level, Transistor."

She unconsciously smoothed her blouse and ran her fingers through her hair. She looked at her watch. At this time of the morning her interruption would be right in the middle of the presidential daily briefing given to him by the Director of National Intelligence. *Appropriate*, she thought.

After a few clicks and beeps the connection was made.

"Brooke, you caught me in the middle of the PDB. What's up?"

"Sir, we have reason to believe we are on a twelve- to twenty-four-hour clock relative to the attack."

"What is the basis of your assessment, Brooke?"

"Financial chatter, sir. We believe that the financial market's play is coordinated to cash in on the attack. And sir, we believe it all ties in to Morgan Prescott, Barry Kitman, and probably Warren Cass."

"Believe?"

"I trust my people, sir. Many of the indices are tracking exactly like Sept 10, 2001."

"So you are sure?"

"I wouldn't risk getting on the bad side of the DNI for busting up his briefing if I weren't, sir."

"Okay, Brooke, what do you want?"

"Sir, in two minutes your military aide will receive a briefing package on a contingency plan I ordered drawn up. Its code name is *Archangel*, and it calls for three joint military rapid reaction forces to be deployed at three strategic points in and around the city. Since we still don't know the nature and scope of the attack, they will be within two-minutes flight time to any part of the five boroughs."

"US Troops? In New York City? Brooke, I'd have to invoke some serious statutes."

"I know, sir, but it's the fastest, best chance we have to respond, if not disrupt the terrorist's plans."

"How long did you say before you are expecting an attack?"

"Imminent, sir. Hours . . . Days."

"I can't unleash that much firepower over that period of time, Brooke."

"Sir, twenty-four hours then."

"You're that sure?"

"Sir, just give us this day."

"Quoting scripture won't help your cause, Brooke."

"It's part of a prayer, sir. And I am praying we are still in time . . ." Brooke listened but all she heard was the president's breathing. She closed her eyes, trying to will him to say yes over the phone. She decided to break the silence and protocol. "Jim, please . . . give us this day!"

"Director Burrell . . ."

Brooke immediately wished she hadn't gotten that familiar with the commander in chief. She tensed for what was coming next.

"Burrell, are you still there?"

"Yes, sir. Sorry, sir."

"The package just walked in. I'll get back to you."

Brooke let out a deep breath as she hung up the phone with great care. She shouldn't have called him by his first name, not now, not under these circumstances.

Remo came in with the coffee.

Brooke nodded in appreciation and watched as he ripped open three packets of sugar and dumped them into his small coffee. She took that first sip then, switching gears, said, "So brief me on what you fellas came up with last night."

"Brooke, the highest probabilities are one, electrical service disruption and two, Internet."

"How far down was nukes?"

"Less than five percent."

"Thank God. I never want to go through that again." Brooke actually shook with the memory of the Hammer of God affair, a foiled suitcase nuke attack that fizzled on Thirtieth Street where the giant lead-lined egg now sat. "Points of attack?"

"The power grid. There are thousands of spots where you can wreak havoc, mostly localized; but there are also safety measures in place all along the wires, so it would be a quick hit but probably not too sustaining." Kronos shrugged his shoulders.

"So why plan a power grid attack if it's not going to give you a big yield?" Brooke asked.

"Good question. That may throw all the cards to Internet disruption," Remo said.

"Same issue. It's just a little bigger, that's all," Kronos said.

"So it doesn't seem like you would fire a missile into an office building just to take us off the trail of a hack."

"Brooke, what you are saying is that they must have a bigger plan. Something that has wide-spread devastation, something out of the box."

"Look, so far they've been anything but stupid, so I am going to go with the big bang theory. But it makes sense to shore up the usual security on the grid and whatever is vulnerable on the Internet. So do it."

"Brooke, I can't do that," Remo said.

"What do you mean? Why can't you?"

"I mean, I don't really work here. Who in the government is going to take my orders?"

"Sorry, I forgot. I'll have Director Barnes sound the alarms. Write up what we want."

Just then George came in. "You wanted to see me?"

She handed George the folded blue-jacketed subpoena. "Go see what this is all about. It's our case against the professors who are charging profiling. If you have to, just take the tongue lashing and leave. The judge has been fair till now, but he probably can't stem the tide."

Chapter 38

Kevlar

"Why isn't Miss Burrell here herself?" Judge Kelley said with just a hint of annoyance.

"Sir, Director Burrell is deeply involved in critical government business at this juncture."

"Why is it that people in government always think the law doesn't apply to them? Well, Mr."—he looked down at his card—"Stover, I am not accepting this . . . In fact, my chambers, now!"

Plaintiff's attorney, Brenda Nussbaum and government lawyer, Jules Fienberg walked towards the chambers.

"Just Agent Stover, counselors."

Once inside the chambers, Judge Kelley motioned to a chair across from his desk. He took off his robe and hung it on a standing coat rack as he passed it. He sat down, folded his hands, and looked at Stover like a father who was about to administer corporal punishment to his seven-year-old son. "Agent Stover, I should hold Burrell in contempt, but I am not. Instead I am going to ask that you sit in this office and just think about what considering yourself above the law means to a free and open democracy. Do you have a smart phone?"

George was thrown by the question. "Er . . . yes, yes I do."

"Good. While you sit, you might consider calling her and telling her to get down here."

Stover was mildly shocked. *This guy is really a hard ass.*

"Or don't call her. Just sit here and ponder the big picture." Then he slid a folder in front of George. "Sit here and when you are ready, come out and tell me how she is *not* coming. I'll rule from the bench."

He got up, put back on his robe, and headed for the door. "Oh, and take all the time you want. It's going to take me twenty minutes to award the case to the professors."

George sat, a bit confused, then he looked down at the folder; it contained all the information on the lapsed visa "students" that Brooke was trying to find out about in the first place. "Son of a bitch," George said as he took out his iPhone and snapped a shot of every sheet.

Out in the court room, Nussbaum was concerned. "Your Honor, what's the federal agent doing in your chambers?"

"If he listened, he may be trying to get his superior down here."

"Can we proceed without her?"

"Certainly. I am going to ask the clerk to read your complaint into the record."

"Is that necessary, Judge? My clients would certainly wave the right to have it re-entered," Nussbaum said.

"Owing to the nature of this case and the possibility of reversal, I feel it's prudent at this juncture to err on the side of caution and ensure it's all in the record."

Nussbaum turned from the bench and rolled her eyes as the clerk read the four-page document aloud. Two minutes in, George emerged from the chambers. The judge held up his hand to stop the clerk. "Well, Agent Stover?"

"I'm sorry. Director Burrell-Morton is completely unavailable for this proceeding."

"After rendering this verdict I will rule on her disposition. You are free to go."

Fienberg spoke up. "Your Honor, may I have a word with my client's representative?"

"Yes, but not in here." The judge waggled his fingers towards the doors at the rear of the courtroom.

Outside, Fienberg waited for the door to close. "What happened in there?"

George was about to tell him but then thought twice. Even though Fienberg was a government attorney, he was still an officer of the court. If George told him that the judge had given the government everything they wanted to catch these bastards right before reprimanding the government for attempting to do the very same thing, he might feel duty bound to report the judge. George also understood it was he who'd opened the folder; the judge might deny giving his permission.

George would be liable. "I thought better of calling Brooke so I sat there and passed the time."

"I think Nussbaum has won this one, so her appearance here wouldn't have changed a thing. Tell her I'll appeal any contempt rulings he makes. Not to worry."

"I assure you, this is the last thing on her worry list."

.G.

"Pay dirt!" George said as he unceremoniously burst into Brooke's office.

"What happened in court?"

"You lost. We won," George said.

"Sounds good . . . I think?"

"The judge chewed me a new one about you not showing, then ordered me into his chambers."

"He was that upset?"

"Yes, but upset with his having to rule against you, probably . . . because he left me in there with one of the evidence folders. I just printed out these pics I took." He handed Brooke the folder.

"Wow. All fifty-seven are here?"

"Sixty-two!"

She handed them back to him. "Okay, George, I want these destroyed."

"Huh?"

"Still have the pictures of the dossiers on your phone?"

"Yeah . . . but . . ."

"Erase those too, but first scan the contents into text. I don't want any court documents surviving to hang our friend the judge. He risked his career and possibly jail time to help protect this city. He deserves our protection. Keep the mug shots, but erase the forms. Only the text survives."

"Got it. Twenty minutes tops."

"I'll have the team waiting to go through them," Brooke said.

.G.

In two hours, the team was finishing up in the large conference room. Everyone had taken three dossiers and got right to searching and tapping INS databases and other TSA files.

George took the lead in presenting their findings to Brooke. "We got four likelies that fit in with the probable target percentages. First is Yusuf Boutros, studied electrical engineering in Egypt, got his masters in France. For a short time he worked at Électricité de France then in 2006 he was transferred as chief engineer of high voltage operations to their then new British subsidiary, EDF Energy. He entered Atlanta's Hartsfield-Jackson on a student visa seven months ago; Georgia Tech has no record of him ever attending. Checking employment database at Con Ed, a similar-looking man, Yusuf Botros, spelled differently, works as a control operator at the Ravenswood number three plant in Long Island City. We have the head of Con Ed security on the way over."

"Wow, now here's a guy who can play a terrorist right out of central casting . . . Get a load a that mug," Harris said, looking at the pockmarked, straggly bearded face with cold, dead eyes.

"Make sure we don't rattle Yusuf too early or we may lose the trail."

"Gotcha. Next is Dequa Quraisha. He's a real cutie. Former member of the mujahedeen, they say he was the equivalent of a general. Also holds a master's in electrical engineering. His name rang a bell at the CIA. They suspect him of all kinds of nasty stuff against the Russians in Afghanistan during the 80s. He is a person of interest in two Al-Qaeda-claimed bombings in Amsterdam and Lagos, Nigeria."

"Sounds smart and deadly," Brooke said.

Harris just couldn't help himself. "Hey, I know I'm a guest and all here, but you feds really screwed the pooch on these guys. How the hell could you let them into our country? Is anybody awake down there in Washington? . . . Hello!"

"The hand we've been dealt, Rolland."

"Great. Just great. Our own government is stacking the deck against us."

Kronos took the next one. "This guy is interesting, Waleed Maghadam. Chemical engineer but here again never reported to Rochester Institute of Technology after entering seven months ago. He could be the same man CIA has a rough sketch of as being the bomb maker for Al Han Nasuri. A high-value bull's-eye for the US."

"The Fifth Avenue truck and the upstate quarry?" Brooke asked.

"Highly possible. He's got the chemical chops to make the brew that goes boom," Kronos said.

Remo pointed to the next picture. "And now the best for last and this pays for the whole endeavor if everything else is wrong. Number four is your old friend, and guy you shot on the ricochet, Shamal. That was a hundred-to-one shot, by the way. He also came in seven months ago, but all we have on him is that he played soccer and minored in geological surveying; he was probably aiming for surveyor work at an oil company or something. We figure he was muscle."

"That son of a bitch killed Nigel just to lure me out. If we connect him to any of these men, I want to personally nail their butts to the wall."

"I'd have liked to put a few rounds into his cranium for Joe," George said.

Brooke had to think for a second. Joe . . . Joe Garrison; the decapitated man on the subway that was supposed to have escaped all this with a schoolbook. "So this Shamal was also the one who pushed or forced Garrison to leave the train between the cars?"

"That's the guy whose picture the subway eye-witnesses picked out of a stack," George reminded the group.

"How's Beesly doing?" Brooke said.

"Let's go find out," Remo said.

.𝔊.

Remo and Brooke entered the office where they had set up Wallace Beesly with a fast computer.

"Wallace, what do you have for us on Kitman?" Brooke said.

"Oh God . . . wait till you hear."

"No, I can't wait . . . There's a whole tick-tock thing going on here, Wallace."

"Okay . . . so first Kitman Global is clean as a whistle."

"Where's the 'Oh God' part?" Brooke said.

"When I started digging into Kitman's personal history I found something funny."

"Wallace, what did you find?" Brooke's impatience was starting to show.

"He's like two different people. His high school yearbook picture has him heavier. But in recent photos he's a string bean. Also, there must have been a typo. They have his name under his picture as Barry Kidman."

"So lots of guys change after high school," Remo said.

"I dunno, he seems to have gone from being large-framed to medium-framed; that's skeletal . . . But even if I buy that, he grows up a kid in an orphanage, does his senior year of high school on a catholic scholarship, then joins the Peace Corps and winds up in Afghanistan in the 80s helping refugees. Ten years later, he comes back and suddenly he's a financial wizard," Beesly said.

"Is there an Afghanistan MBA program?" Remo said.

"I've heard enough. I'm kicking this over to FBI for a full background check. Nice work Wallace. Now, can we attach his finances so we can track them?"

"That's the bad news."

"Didn't know there was bad news," Remo said.

"The majority of his wealth is in Kevlar."

"Wait, Kevlar, as in a bulletproof vest?" Brooke said.

"More like bomb proof. We may never get to his money."

"How do you figure that? We are the feds, you know."

"Kevin 'Kev-Lar' Lawrence. He's a top financial transaction lawyer. Best in the biz. Makes bulletproof financial entities. Credited with inventing the Paper Safe.

"The what now?" Remo said.

"Most transaction attorneys attempt to protect assets, which have been negotiated as collateral, in big multi-billion dollar bank loans. Kevlar makes a stack of documents that lock the money up, away from judges and creditors—like it was in a safe, a safe made out of papers, a Paper Safe."

"The courts and attorneys can't crack paper?" George said.

"Prescott mentioned a Paper Safe, but I thought it was a generic term," Brooke said.

"Then he started to say 'Kev' when I interrupted. Sorry Brooke," George said.

"The average transaction attorney's fee for big deals runs around two hundred k; Kevlar's minimum fee is five hundred thousand dollars."

Kronos whistled. "Why does he get so much 'scarole?"

"What?" Brooke's aide, Betty, who was acting as recording secretary, writing everything down in shorthand in a steno book, asked, raising her hand.

"It's neighborhood for money, Betty, green like escarole . . . the Italian vegetable. Fuggedaboutit." Kronos waved his hand. It was futile.

Beesly picked up. "Why is his fee that high? Because all his deals held during 9/11 and again through the 2008 financial crisis when the biggest players were going belly up and the courts were attaching everything to get liquidity; all his deals were untouchable. All the islands he created to hold money were impenetrable and immune to judicial invasion."

"Yo, I just got it. Double meaning. His papers keep the money safe; he makes safes out of paper," Kronos said.

"Don't mind our friend here with the 168 IQ. He's a little slow if he doesn't get a Ring Ding and chocolate milk every few hours." Remo gave Kronos a slight burn.

.𝔊.

"I sink this putt and you owe me a Delmonico steak, in Monaco," Kevin said.

"It'll have to wait until my G5 is out of the shop," Jonas said as he winked and hitched his elbow at one of the other's in the foursome. It was a joke of sorts because he actually owned a G6 private jet.

"A likely excuse . . ." Kevin waggled, then checked the distance for the tenth time. He exhaled and brought back the putter head. Suddenly, a heavy thumpeting noise rose up. Everyone on the eighteenth hole looked east as the huge helicopter flared and landed in the fairway just beyond the green. The large letters FBI on the side swung into view as the pilot rotated the craft.

"Uh, oh. Charlie, quick, use the golf cart to get away. They're onto you," one of his foursome laughed.

The prop wash blew Kevin's ball further away from the cup and it rolled down the side of the elevated green. "Oh c'mon, it was a gimme," Kevin complained as he threw down his putter.

The men watched as a woman exited the copter followed by two men. The first thing she did was remove her heels and throw them back in the bird, then she strode up the side of the green to the foursome. "Which one of you is Kevin Lawrence?"

"The green shirt," Beesly said, pointing.

"Hey, it's Wallace Beesly," Charlie said to the others, and then turned to Beesly. "I lost a lot of money because of you."

.G.

Brooke walked right up to Kevin. "Mr. Lawrence, I am Director Brooke Burrell-Morton attached to FinCEN. Sir, I need you to come with us."

"Am I under arrest?"

"No, sir. This is a case of national security. Your country needs you."

"I already served my country, Director."

"Yes, I know. Four years air force, two commendations and two promotions, but I need you now."

"For what?"

"We'll talk on the chopper, sir. We have to get back to our headquarters."

"I'm not going anywhere with you. I don't have to recognize your authority. Besides, I am winning the round, a very rare occurrence."

"Sir, can we step away from these gentlemen?" Brooke extended her arm over to the far edge of the green.

"You better go, Kevin, she looks serious," Charlie said.

When they were out of earshot, Brooke looked him in the eye. "Okay, I am going to wave security clearance and tell you up front what this is all about. In the next twelve to eighteen hours there may be a vicious and devastating terrorist attack on New York. Somehow the funding, and maybe the way to stop these guys, lies with Kitman. You worked for him and . . ."

"Hold on. I was hired as a freelance consultant, short period, then it was over."

"Noted, but still, while in his employ you hid assets. We believe those assets are now fueling the attack."

"Do I need a lawyer? Because you just accused me of being a co-conspirator in all this."

"Exactly. And we still have rendition, Mr. Lawrence."

"So you're saying either I play along or tomorrow I wake up in a Saudi prison and you forget I am there?"

"I'm saying your country needs you right this minute, and I can arrange for immunity if you should happen to be unintentionally involved."

"Arrange for immunity, or guarantee?"

"Sir, I answer directly to the President of the United States. I can guarantee immunity on the matters I just discussed with you."

Kevin looked at Brooke. She was as serious as a heart attack. Then he looked at the chopper. The large turbo fan engines still running meant this wasn't a fishing expedition and that she had clout to violate a dozen FAA rules just to interrupt his putt.

"Director Burrell-Morton, I accede to your wishes."

She extended her arm towards the idling whirlybird. "Mind your head getting in."

.6.

As the bird lifted off, his golf mates were partially stunned. "Well, looks like Kevin is in deep shit," Charles said.

"No, I think they made a deal. Her body language wasn't aggressive and Kevin was more passive."

"Kevin passive? That'll be the day."

Chapter 39

Hunting Deer in Dearborn?

By the time they got back to Midtown headquarters, Kevin Lawrence had been read in on the financial forensics and some of the threat matrix that Brooke and her team were trying to fend off.

Brooke gathered George, Remo, Kronos, and Betty, the recording secretary, into the secure conference room. Once the door was closed and the "Remo Switch" safe light was on, she knew the room was off the grid and secure. "Here's what we suspect, and there is almost no time to act if we are right. Kitman, through the Iranian Sataad, the underground network of banking, is funding an ISIS cell or cells which may go active in the next"—she looked at the big clock on the wall—"ten to fourteen hours. It's too late to stop the funds and it would be meaningless since, as we know, they are already armed and manned. But if we can get a lead on where the monies are placed, we might be able to figure out what their target is . . ."

"Or targets," Remo said.

"Yes, targets. Then maybe we can interrupt their plans. Mr. Lawrence, you hid billions for Kitman . . ."

"Hold it right there . . . Do you know what I do?" Lawrence interrupted.

"You hide assets," Remo said.

"Wrong on two counts. One, these are not assets; they are hard-fought, hard-negotiated secured collateral. That money is all but spent . . . gone. It is already accounted for both legally and as part of a structured instrument or loan. Technically, it doesn't exist as liquid. And the second part of your two-word accusation is also wrong because these funds are not hidden. They are right out there in the open. In fact, court rulings, findings, and court orders initiate my work."

Brooke was starting to get the idea that this guy had his shit wired tighter than the feds who hired her. She was about to ask a question, but he wasn't finished.

"In fact, transparency is necessary for my clients. They need to see the money at all times."

Aha! Brooke thought, *now I have him.* "Who are your clients exactly, Mr. Lawrence?"

"Kevin, please. Oh, you know, the scum of the earth types. Little companies like Credit Suisse, Chase, First Boston, the Department of Treasury, and Veteran's Affairs. Oh, and the FBI and CIA agent's union's pension funds."

"What?" Brooke said.

"You got a federal health plan? A pension coming from the FBI? It's actually money that needs to be protected against things like government shutdown or overthrow."

Brooke was speechless.

Remo jumped in. "Okay, but why all this precaution if there's nothing dirty or barely legal going on?"

"Bankruptcy judges are the most powerful entities in the legal system. Extreme latitude. They can go anywhere, attach any asset, pierce any corporate shell and, in general, maraud deep into a company's financial landscape, raping and pillaging. They make Sadam Hussein and Attila the Hun look like Mother Teresa. Hitler was once quoted as saying, "I want to come back as a bankruptcy judge. That's where the real power lies."

"And what you get paid for thwarts these bankruptcy courts?" Brooke said.

"Paid very well, because they do."

"Well, Mr. Lawrence, I need you to crack into Kitman. I believe some of the funds you locked up are fueling the terrorists."

"Do you have a conviction?"

"No."

"Well, then what you are looking to do is exactly what my clients pay me to stop from happening. Fishing expeditions have killed as many businesses as actual crime. If you can't pierce Kitman Global

Investments' securitizations, it's because you are trying to do something extra-legal."

"I can compel you," she said.

"No, you can't."

"Yes, I can."

"No, I mean, I have no operational authority once I deliver. I just build the fortress. I don't live in it or run it. Once I set them up they are self-running self-securitizations."

"But you know the way in?"

"There is no way in. That's what I do. I build it with no doors, no windows. No light gets in and so no judgment can attach it to a failed financial institution."

"Do you realize that you might be helping ISIS get funding?" Remo said.

"That's your speculation . . ."

"Maybe, but we are in the eleventh hour and you need to remember I work for the department of the Treasury. I am sure that if you were seen to be uncooperative, the Secretary of the Treasury and a few other ancillary powerbrokers could put a dent in your half-a-mil for a Paper Safe business," Brooke said.

"Why do you continue to threaten me? I am here, aren't I?"

"Yes, but I need action. Trace Kitman's funds and tell me what the cells are doing with it, what they are buying and where they bought it. Before this city explodes."

She stood up. "George, Kronos, you give him everything he needs. If you need more bodies, just ask. Peter, come with me. Bridge has something."

.G.

"Gee, I've never been down here."

"Very few have," Brooke said.

"What is this, NORAD?" Remo said as they entered the round room with big screens on the wall and a number of desks with technicians busily typing, turning knobs and throwing switches.

Bridge was in the middle of it all, and turned when he heard them. "Good, you're here."

"This is where you've been, Bridge? I was wondering," Remo said.

"Put up satellite feed 2021, Chuck," Bridge said to the tech sitting next to him.

On the big screen in the center of the forward wall a greenish-hued night vison image appeared of an area of terrain that had many men moving in a specific, military way.

"Small arms training?" Brooke said as she watched the figures on the screen run then crouch, then rock with what looked like the recoil of their weapons, then up and running again.

"Chuck, increase the resolution."

The picture zoomed in.

"From the kick and barrel flame, I am calling that a SAW."

"Okay, so not-so-small arms training."

"Where is this, some Al-Qaeda camp in Afghanistan?" Remo said.

"No, Michigan. And if I had to guess, these two guys watching are rating the maneuvers and tactics."

"What do you think they're training for?"

"You see the way they are advancing—each one covering the next? That's a siege move," Bridge pointed out.

"This exercise is simulating the taking of a heavily armed facility under fire," Brooke said.

"We've increased security at all power, water, and subway systems as well as roads and bridges with teams that are armed to the teeth," Remo said.

"We're going to need 'em. These boys are hard trained, and not the usual fumbling idiots we see in their training videos in the desert."

"Mujahedeen?" Brooke said.

"Most likely, somehow in this country and operational."

"Okay, when was this feed?" Brooke said to Chuck.

"Yesterday morning, 3:18 a.m. local time, from three hundred miles up."

"And . . . ?" Brooke said to Bridge.

"Michigan National Guard and State Troopers were dispatched to the coordinates, but that was six hours after this video. They've found nothing but shell casings."

"That's how you called the SAW from the video?" Brooke said.

"Let's say the ejected 5.6 mm cartridges confirmed it." Bridge half smiled.

"So where did they go?" Remo said.

Chuck, the tech, spoke up. "Checking now. We make four vehicles at the training camp. We are doing a pattern-recognition search now and cross checking with all highway, street, and tollbooth cameras. It's slim, since we don't have a plate number, but we are looking for these four types of cars grouped within a minute or so time window from one another, and figuring they are headed east; but we're not ruling out an attack anywhere else in America."

Brooke picked up the phone. "Get me Barnes." She put her hand over the mouthpiece. "If they are headed here, we better beef up the security. I think we should have armor at vital points."

Peter Remo whistled. "Brooke, tanks in the street? I dunno. That's not going to look too good in the news."

"A crumbled, stricken city with maybe thousands, hell, millions dead, will look better?" She removed her hand, "Director, sir. I think we need to raise the threat level. I want all-out force protection to essential high-level targets and assets in the next twenty-four hours. Yes, sir, we have them dead to rights training for a full-on military assault somewhere—we're betting New York, sir. Thank you.

"He's calling the White House."

"It'll stop there," Remo said.

"Nah, Mitchell is a warrior. I think he'll understand a prevent defense," Bridge said.

"I hope so, Bridge, I hope so," Brooke said.

.G.

Kevin Lawrence, Kronos, and George were each banging away at a multi-screen terminal in the FBI's IT department, which Brook had commandeered for them. Lawrence was able to pierce three levels of his own Kevlar and was trying to crack the last code when Kronos came over dangling a memory stick on a lanyard.

"Okay, once you're in, I wrote this code that will interrogate the system and get velocity, source, and destination on all transactions. From there we can do a standard metadata dump and try to get down to the item SKU, the store, and maybe even the salesclerk's ID . . . If we're lucky," Kronos said.

Lawrence just grunted.

"Stuck?"

"This last level, I keep falling for my own trap. Damn it. I should be able to outsmart myself."

"Let me try."

"You? What do you know about deep-level securitization-layered protocols?"

"Not a friggin' thing. But I know the shit out of computers . . ."

Since he hadn't gotten anywhere for ten minutes, Lawrence shrugged his shoulders and said, "What the hell . . ." He got up and Kronos sat down, typing before his butt hit the chair.

"I see you got multiple comparator strings with a variable polynomial supplicant."

"Hey, watch it, you just cracked half my intellectual property."

"No big whoop, Kev."

Kevin Lawrence's eyes widened as Kronos was having intimate, digital programming code sex with his creation. As his fingers flew over the keyboard, Lawrence caught enough to yell, "Okay stop! I'll take it from here."

Kronos turned and smiled. "You really are paranoid."

"Look, really, get up, go over there. I'll finish it up now."

"Suit yerself . . ." Kronos got up and saw Remo coming towards them.

"How you guys doing?"

"We're in," Lawrence said.

"Nice work," Remo said.

"Not just me. Kronos busted through the last layer for us," Lawrence said.

"Kron-os."

"Yeah, whatever."

.G.

George and Remo entered Brooke's office where Bridge and she were pouring over a map of NYC on the wall. Red circles indicated every vital, high-value target that could be on a terrorist's Christmas list, if these guys were the type to celebrate the Yule.

Bridge recapped their last half hour's work. "So aside from expanding the security at the airports and increasing the perimeter out another mile in the two bodies of water that lead to the runways, everything else is fortified."

Remo looked at the map. "You've missed one. Two actually."

Brooke looked at Bridge then back to Remo. "Okay smart guy, where?"

Remo put his finger on Forty-Second Street and Park Ave. or where Park would be between Madison and Lex if Grand Central wasn't there. And with his other hand he spread his thumb and middle finger so it spanned the East River. "M42 and the rupture doors."

"Oh wait. Yes I remember reading about M42 in Linda Fairstein's *Terminal City*."

"I've been wanting to read it, me being a train buff and all," Remo said.

"Wanna clue me in," Bridge said.

"M42 is the area deep down below Grand Central Terminal. It's the Dynamo room where . . ."

"Right, yes. Okay, now I remember. The power for the entire Metro North. During World War II, a sergeant with a Thompson submachine gun guarded it. He had one order: 'Anybody comes down the stairs, shoot to kill.'" Bridge held his hands like the Tommy gun was in them and he was pulling the trigger.

"Hitler wanted to destroy that room throughout the war. They even caught four saboteurs who were dropped off on the shores of Long Island by U-Boat to blow it up among other things," Brooke said as she picked up the red sharpie and made a circle around Grand Central. "Good point, Peter, but what's the East River about?"

"At each end of the Long Island Railroad tunnel, here and here, that goes under the river, there are gigantic hundred-ton doors on cantilevers designed to slam shut if those same German U-Boats got into New York Harbor and shot a torpedo into the tunnel, which is actually a concrete tube sitting on the river bottom. Those doors would seal the tunnel, because if it flooded there would be no stopping the East River from flooding the entire underground subway, train, and utility networks. That much pressure would also weaken many of the heaviest skyscrapers at their foundation. Not to mention low-level flooding as water sought its own level across the city."

Brooke turned to one of the agents who were standing behind them. "Ralph, get on this right away. Talk to the city and railroad engineers and report back ASAP."

Ralph left the room.

Remo looked at the map. "What are these big boxes here, here, and here?" he said, pointing to the red boxes drawn in sharpie and filled with slashes in the middle of Central Park, Citi Field in Queens, and over in Liberty State Park on the Jersey side of the Hudson River.

"Forward Operating Bases for *Archangel*," Bridge said.

"The what bases for the who?" Kronos said.

"*Archangel*, Bridge's plan to rapidly respond to whatever it is we're facing," Brooke said. "So what have you guys got for me?"

"Pay dirt!" Remo said.

"Yeah, it took Lawrence forever to almost crack his own code, but then he let a real pro sit down and bada-zing . . . done."

"Zing? Anyway, Mr. Humility aside, Kronos's second program got us down to some purchases actually made from a credit card account, if you can believe it." Remo unfolded the printout.

"I can believe it," Brooke said. "First, the World Trade bombers back in '93 used credit cards to rent the truck they detonated in the garage. We caught 'em when the 'rocket scientists' went back for the deposit."

"Eerily coincidental," Remo said.

"Second, they are forced to use credit cards in many cases, because nowadays cash sets off red flags."

"We got a rental charge for two of the three U-Hauls."

"Hold it. How do you know it was three? The tire tracks from the floor of the garage in Yonkers were positive for two different trailers but inconclusive on there being a third." Brooke said.

"We got two rentals and neither match the serial number of the one they found in the crater at the quarry."

"That's a little thin for the existence of number three, but I am feeling generous today so I'll give it to you. What else?"

"A charge for one-inch steel plate from Blackman Steel out on the Island, three plates five-by-eight foot."

"Okay, so we got one mangled steel plate back from the test explosion at the upstate quarry, so two more supports your three U-Haul theory."

"Here's the best part. Boat rentals in the Cayman Islands; a payment to Ultra-Class Jets for ten-hour charter service to the Czech Republic; that has to be for the first leg of Prescott's flight. And a US Air round-trip ticket LaGuardia to Wayne County Airport, or otherwise known as the gateway to Dearborn, Michigan, yesterday!"

Brooke pumped her fist. "We got names yet?"

"No, but we got enough to bring in Kitman," George said.

"And close him down," Remo said.

"But none of that stops the attack," Bridge said.

"George, call Barnes. Tell him I am requesting every computer tech we have on this—it's a drop-everything priority. I want them to take over what Kronos and Remo dug up. I want names and what they ate for breakfast. Then I want to brief you on your next mission."

.𝔊.

When George got back to Brooke's office, Detective Rolland Harris was there. "Hey, Rolland, when did you get in?"

"Brooke called me in. I just got here. I was on my way to Blackman Steel when she called and said we already knew about it."

"Rolland, it took two of the most geekiest computer guys on the planet to dig that up, how did you . . . ?"

"I detect . . . remember?"

Brooke walked in at that second. "You can explain it in the car, Detective Harris. George, you are going to be lead on the takedown of Kitman. I got a seven-vehicle caravan downstairs, just like two weeks ago, only today you are in charge, the lead agent. Harris here is your local to give you NYC authority for anyone outside the federal writ; that document will meet you on Central Park South by the time you roll up to Kitman's office."

"Thanks, Brooke, for your confidence in me."

"You've earned it, George."

Chapter 40

Catching a Plane

One of Kitman's three Maybachs, the sapphire blue one, was parked in front of his Central Park South office building. The driver, Kadeem, Kitman's personal bodyguard and an ex-Pakistani Intelligence Service agent, was licensed to carry a Sig Sauer P226 under his jacket but not the two AK-47s and two grenade launchers in the trunk of the half-a-million-dollar luxury tank with its bulletproof "protectee cage" that was the rear passenger area.

Kitman exited from the building and walked lively to the car as the former ISIS operative held the door open. He got in without saying a word. Once inside, he pulled down the back of the front seat that opened to a laptop computer of sorts with the keyboard on the tray part and the screen set into the seat back. He glanced at his itinerary. He was wheels up at Teterboro in thirty-nine minutes, then nonstop on his personal Gulfstream G650 to United Arab Emirates. The reason was the Arab League Summit symposium, at which he was giving the opening speech as, amusingly enough, an American capitalist investor. But it was a perfectly timed event to get him out of the city and the country when Dequa's men pulled off their attack tomorrow. At 3:00 p.m. today, the two hundred employees of Kitman Global Investments would, on a pre-programmed basis, start dumping and buying stock in the "put and call" play that would eventually net him and his "masters" one trillion dollars and fuel the caliphate for the next one hundred years.

The Maybach had to wait for a Central Park horse and carriage to clip-clop by before the driver made an illegal U-turn to head west on

Fifty-Ninth Street then onto the West Side Highway. As they passed Columbus Circle, seven Federal Chevy Yukons, lights flashing but no sirens, shot across Seventh Avenue and onto Fifty-Ninth Street, east bound.

The seven vehicles pulled up and the Treasury, FBI, and SEC investigators they carried emerged. An NYPD police car, also on silent approach, pulled up and a sergeant got out and handed George the federal warrant, signature ink still wet. It gave him the right to shut everything down and collect evidence.

George, Harris, and the cop were first through the door and immediately requested that the security guards step away from their phones and consoles. The NYPD sergeant was all they needed to see to comply. The cop then went to the head of security's office to isolate him and his staff from any early warning. George wanted to make sure that the loss of data files was not suffered this time like when they'd hit Prescott Capital Management.

The agents, aided by NYPD detectives who arrived minutes later, fanned out on all floors of the top ten that Kitman Global Investments occupied. George and Harris met Kitman's private security man at the elevator to the top floor, his office.

"We are here to arrest Kitman. Stand aside," George said.

The guard hit a big button on his desk and there was a loud click from the door. "May I see your identification please."

Harris flashed his gold shield and ID and George flashed his fed creds.

The guard reached for the phone. "I'll check with building security."

Harris slammed the phone back down and drew his Glock. "Enough bullshit. Open the fucking door or I'll open your fucking head."

George reached into the man's jacket and pulled his gun out and pocketed it. "Now press some more buttons and unseal that room."

The guard acceded to the request that came from the gun in his face. He punched seven digits into a keypad and the door clicked again. George rushed into the office, gun first, as Harris zip-tied the guard's hand around the back of his chair.

"He's not here," George said as he emerged from the office.

"The guard was stalling to give him time to get away."

"Yeah, I got that, but to where?"

He took out his phone as he walked to a picture on the credenza behind Kitman's desk. He picked up a photo in a frame. "Kronos, George here. Take down this tail number for a private jet, N2562."

"You think he flew the coup?"

"We can track him to home or wherever he's lunching in the next twenty minutes, but if he's jumping the country we don't have a second to spare." He put the phone closer. "Yes, go ahead . . . When was it filed? . . . Thanks, Kronos. Call me if you can find anything else." He closed the phone. "Let's go. That's his plane and it filed a flight plan to the UAE out of Teterboro." They ran out of the office as the detectives escorted the guard away and started gathering evidence.

George tried his phone in the elevator but the signal was weak. As soon as they got to the lobby he hit redial. Harris was already on his phone calling for a DMV registration search for any car belonging to Kitman or any of his subsidiaries, which his contact could get from Kronos. As George was giving him Kronos's number, George's phone connected. "Brooke. We may have a flight risk with Kitman. Can you get that fancy chopper wet and wild at Westside Heliport? Teterboro. He may be jumping. Good."

They loaded into the lead SUV and told the driver, "Westside Heliport, lights and sirens all the way."

.G.

After the doorman of the next building over confirmed that Mr. Kitman's blue Maybach was parked there ten minutes earlier, the call went out as an all-points bulletin. The NYPD, Port Authority, Jersey State Police, and every municipality on route to Teterboro Airport was put on alert to set up roadblocks and intercept any blue Maybach.

.G.

The Port Authority Tunnel Lieutenant was getting coffee when the alert came in. He put the second half of his ham and cheese sandwich in his mouth and with his free hand tore the alert off the old-style printer. He read it immediately and went to his dispatcher. "Bob, put this out. Have all units be on the lookout for this car. Then he walked to the office next door. It was the monitor room, filled with a wall of TVs that were fed from cameras inside, outside, and at all the tunnel approaches, including the surveillance at the two big ventilators that exchanged the poisonous carbon-monoxide-laden air with the relatively fresher New York City air.

The officer on watch turned as he entered. "What's up, Lou?"

"Keep a sharp eye out for a blue Maybach. Go to Tact 1. Report if you see it."

"We got a tag?"

"Not yet."

His next stop was the muster room. "Okay, everyone, let's get down to the plaza. We are looking for a blue Maybach. No tags, but there ain't gonna be too many of those."

"What are we dealing with, Lou. A&D?"

"No, this ain't an armed and dangerous alert. It's a person of interest, detain till arrival."

"Crap, feds!"

"Don't matter. We got a job to do."

The eight cops quickly got up and checked their leather as they headed out the door.

.G.

Kitman's driver squinted as the setting sun's glare nearly blinded him when they emerged on the Jersey side of the Lincoln Tunnel. The helix up ahead that corkscrewed up to Route 3 was clear. He'd make Teterboro in plenty of time.

.G.

The PA cops fanned out onto the toll plaza of the tunnel with their backs to the setting sun, looking eastbound for cars coming west through the tunnel.

.G.

The Maybach was in the middle of climbing the helix on the far side of the tunnel as Kitman reviewed some financial numbers on the screen of his built-in terminal and was taking a sip of coffee when the large luxury sedan suddenly swerved right, causing a little of the coffee to slosh over the edge of the cup. "What the . . . ?"

"Sorry, sir. There was a blown-out truck tire in the road," Kadeem said.

Kitman grunted with mild annoyance and dabbed his hand with a fine cloth napkin from the center console's amenities insert.

.𝔊.

"You got an overturned tractor trailer on the approach ramp to one and nine and residual delays all the way up to the traffic circle . . . More *Eye In The Sky* traffic coming up on the eights. This is Tom Colletti, traffic, NewsChopper 880. Now here's Susan Combs with the News 88 weather watch." Tom switched off his on-air mic, and immediately hit his radio transmit button. "Newark Tower, this is N880, repeat message . . . over"

"N880, be advised police are requesting additional eyes, New Jersey area, looking for a sapphire blue Maybach heading west. Possible destination Teterboro . . . over"

"N880 to Newark Tower, copy that . . . over"

Tom looked out over the landscape from fifteen hundred feet above the Meadowlands and angled his machine to the left to check out Route 3 and Route 46. He switched his gimbaled-mount high-definition TV camera out of standby mode and moved the joystick as he zoomed in on the cars below. With the gyro-stabilized mount and the 600 mm, pure optical glass lens, he could read a license plate from three thousand feet above. He had nine minutes before his next report.

.𝔊.

Two Hackensack motorcycle cops got on to NJ 120 and took positions on both sides of the roadway, one on the median and one on the side. A mile ahead of them four NJ State trooper cruisers lined up, two on the right, two on the left. If the motorcycle cops reported the Maybach passing their location, the four state cars would execute a rolling roadblock, eventually slowing the fifty-five mph traffic to a standstill. Then they'd have the Maybach in a box. The cycle cops would approach from the rear while the state cars siphoned off all the traffic in between.

.𝕲.

In his rearview mirror, Kitman's driver's eyes were momentarily diverted by the flashing lights of one of the two State Trooper cars that pulled off to the side of the road, but thought nothing more of it than they must have pulled over a speeder.

.𝕲.

"Newark Tower to N880, Newark Tower to N880 come in . . . over."

Tom took his hand off the camera control joystick and hit his transmission switch.

"N880 to Newark Tower . . . over"

"N880 immediately execute a 'descend and maintain' to eight hundred feet. Incoming direct vector emergency aircraft to Teterboro, coming in hot to your left."

Tom hit the collective and dropped the Sikorsky copter like the first drop on a rollercoaster. He looked up and to his left and saw the big, white helicopter overtaking him with its turbo fan engines full out. As it passed overhead, he saw the large letters FBI on the side of the cabin. He pushed forward on the collective and took off after them.

.𝕲.

In the speeding chopper, George looked over to the seat next to his and noticed Harris was a little green around the gills. "Don't like flying?"

"I hate helicopters . . . If God had wanted them to fly he would have given them wings." He pointed up and added, "That motor stops and this thing has the aerodynamics of a wall safe. Give me a quiet cabin thirty thousand feet up with a good-looking, long-legged stewardess with a great rack getting me drinks."

.𝕲.

Andrea Crain, the FBI pilot sitting right in front of him, instinctively dropped the craft one hundred feet in an instant, making the NYPD Neanderthal in the back groan loudly . . . and bringing a small smirk of satisfaction to her face. She then turned halfway and announced. "One minute out."

For the first time, Harris realized the pilot sitting right in front of him was a female. He looked quizzically at the back of the chair as he pushed his stomach back down his throat.

.G.

The Maybach pulled off Washington Avenue and up to the Teterboro VIP area. Kadeem popped the trunk and got out. He was retrieving Kitman's bag when a helicopter zoomed low overhead. He looked up and saw the FBI letters on the side as it touched down about twenty-five yards from him. He went to the side rear window. Kitman opened it.

"What do you want to do?" Kadeem asked.

"Let's go get coffee and come back later."

He went around to the back of the limo to put the bag back when two men emerged from the copter coming right to him. A noise from behind him turned him around as five cop cars entered the airport. He looked back down at the trunk. The AK-47 machine guns were locked and loaded. The bullet resistant back of the car would give him enough cover. He was reaching for the grenade launcher when Kitman appeared.

He took the AK-47 and said, "The struggle goes on. We have done our part. They cannot stop what God has helped us . . ."

He was interrupted by George's voice. "Federal Agents. Step away from the vehicle, now."

He looked in his bodyguard's eyes. "Our grandchildren will revere our names." Then he hitched his head towards the police cars as Kitman swung to the side of the trunk lid and took a bead on the two agents approaching . . .

Kadeem grabbed the other AK and turned and sprayed the black-and-white units that had just arrived.

"GUN," George yelled, as he and Harris immediately split up and hit the deck and rolled. The bullets whizzing over their heads slammed into the body of the copter. They had their guns out and were returning fire.

Andrea immediately felt the searing pain in her thigh as the hot lead, slowed by the acrylic lower side window of the helicopter's cockpit, burrowed into her femur.

.𝕲.

At five hundred feet, Tom aimed the HD camera of NewsChopper 880 at the gun battle that came startlingly fast. He watched as cops scurried out from three of five cop cars firing their weapons. Two other police cruisers had no movement as they were pretty shot up in the first seconds of this firefight. "Master control, I got a gun battle at Teterboro. Feed is up. Start recording. Repeat, unfolding gun battle . . . Get me live!" Tom narrated what he was seeing, hoping they were getting all this. "Tom Colletti, NewsChopper 880 coming to you live over Teterboro airport where a fierce gun battle suddenly erupted . . ."

He continued reporting while he watched as two cops grabbed shotguns and blasted away at a man behind an open trunk lid. In a plume of pink, the machine gun shooter spun around and collapsed in the trunk.

The other man was still shooting at the helicopter and the two feds, now prone on the ground, returned fire. He saw the shooter's shoulder recoil. He registered that as a hit. But the man kept firing with the other hand.

One of the cops with a shotgun charged at the man, whose back was to him. His first shot on the run missed. The man turned and hit the cop dead center and he went down, but the move uncovered him and one of the shooters on the ground hit him twice. The man also fell halfway into the open trunk.

.𝕲.

The cops ran to the car as George and Harris ran to the copter to check on the pilot. Kitman was bleeding badly as he reached into the trunk with his blood-soaked hands. With his remaining strength, he pulled a pin on a grenade.

As they opened the door of the cabin to help Andrea, from over by the car they heard, "Oh Shit! Move! Move! Move!"

.𝕲.

The blast wave from the explosion hit Tom's copter in an instant and caused it to wobble. He had enough pilot skills to regain control even at two hundred eighty feet above death. The Gyrocam mounted under his front skid stayed on target as the smoke cleared and revealed the mangled back of the limo and body parts spread out in a spray from the rear. Two cops a little further out were staggering. One was on the ground writhing in pain. "It . . . It . . . there was an explosion! The car exploded! Right here, as police approached, it just . . . just exploded. I see many casualties and, be warned control room, it is a gruesome picture. Once again, reporting live over a violent . . ."

.G.

Both George and Harris were deafened by the ringing in their ears. The trunk lid had blocked the force of the detonation from reaching them and the FBI copter, but not the ear-piercing percussive wallop. The prop wash from a hovering news helicopter blew away the smoke of the explosion and Harris saw the carnage. "Stay with her, I'll go . . ."

Harris was off. More police cruisers arrived. Harris found a wounded cop on the ground. His torso was ripped open. Harris knew enough to know he was in bad shape so he took off his belt and wrapped it around the bloody uniform. Then he looked up and waved at the helicopter overhead.

.G.

Tom saw one of the men on the ground waving him down and pointing to the downed officer. "Control, I am being waved down by a man, probably an FBI agent. I think I know what he is asking . . . I am going to train the camera on us as I land. I'll continue from my cell phone." Tom landed the copter, dialed the station, and popped in his earbuds. "Do you read me, Control? Good. I am leaving the chopper."

.G.

"He's not going to make it . . . Can you get him to a hospital right away?" Harris said, pointing down at the injured man.

Tom looked down; there was so much blood. His first instinct was to decline, saying he was press and his job was to cover the story . . . but Tom had been a medevac pilot in the Iraq War. Only one ambulance had gotten to the area. The street outside, and for as far as he could see, was jammed with arriving and abandoned police vehicles. The ambulance was blocked from leaving. He looked down at this fallen public servant who got up every day and tried to help people, who now lay dying . . . The old call to duty kicked in. "Control, I am going to medevac this officer to the nearest hospital. Hackensack University Medical Center is thirty seconds away and has a heliport. Please alert them on Med Emergency Frequency one. I am two minutes out. I'll try to keep reporting but I am going to be a bit busy for a few minutes."

.G.

Harris helped him carry the man towards the copter. Two of his fellow officers quickly joined them. "We'll take him." They gingerly loaded him into the seat of the news helicopter. One of the EMTs from the only ambulance jumped into the bird with his bag and applyed a gauze patch and rolled up the officer's sleeve to administer a shot. The helicopter was up and away in thirty seconds, heading towards the medical center's landing pad on the edge of the airport.

Harris went back to Andrea as she was waving off the other arriving EMTs. "Go help them. I can wait." Harris grabbed a medical bag from the back of an ambulance and helped her out of the cabin and onto the tarmac. "The good news is I seen this done a dozen times . . ."

Through deep breaths, Andrea asked, "What's the . . . the bad news?"

"I've never done this before . . ." he said as he found the scissors and cut away her pants around her upper thigh. He took some iodine solution and swabbed the wound. She recoiled at the sting. "Sorry."

"S'okay . . . thank you for doing this."

Harris looked up at her and smiled. "No problem . . . At least you won't think I'm a complete asshole."

Chapter 41

The Evil Portfolio

"Kitman's dead," Bridge said as he came into Brooke's office grabbing the remote and turning on channel two.

"What? What happened?

"He decided to meet his maker rather than surrender. And he tried to take George and Harris and a few local cops with him." He turned towards the TV.

". . . boro airport. Our own NewsChopper 880 was on the scene. We've edited out some of the more disturbing footage but police are now calling the gun battle that broke out at this normally quiet airport that serves the wealthy and business communities 'as fierce as they come' in the words of one police spokesman who wished to remain anonymous. In an unusual turn of events, our own reporter, Tom Colletti, went into action and airlifted a critically wounded Moonachie township police officer to a nearby hospital. He is in stable condition but his prognosis is guarded. We'll have that report a little later in the program. Now we are going live to our street team at Teterboro where they've got the latest . . ."

Bridge muted the TV.

"How are George and Harris?"

"Fine. The FBI pilot took a round in her leg, but she'll be okay."

"She? Andrea?"

"I don't know her name."

"What's your gut telling you, Bridge?"

"Well, they found an AK-47 in the trunk, which had a small armory in it. The wooden stock had notches in it. I've seen that before. The mujahedeen sometimes would notch their guns for every one hundred

Russian invaders they killed. One of the two dead guys was probably one. And I could kick myself, Brooke."

"Why, what did you do?"

"It's what I didn't do. He was flaunting it in all our faces, in the world's face. I never connected that the word 'kitman' is synonymous with 'taqiyya.'"

"Holy shit!" Brooke blurted out, snapping her fingers. "'War is deceit.' It's part of the Hadith."

"Exactly. Taqiyya, or the pass you get from God to lie to infidels."

"It was that obvious and we all missed it."

"Yeah, makes you feel pretty dumb doesn't it. He was telling us all along that he was lying to us about his true intentions and true beliefs. What balls. So for that reason, my money's on Kitman being the bankroll if not the brains behind the attack, or he would have just surrendered instead of pulling the pin on the Paradise Express."

"How bad?"

"We lost five cops; four more in the hospital; five with your wounded pilot friend."

"Dear God, we've got to stop these men. We can't keep losing good people."

"Brooke, in war, you lose people."

"War?"

"ISIS has declared war on us. We better gear up or we'll have a hell of a time catching up."

"Okay, what's in your playbook?"

"Squeeze the contacts the FBI and local authorities have in the suspect communities; come down hard, trace all leads of stolen weapons, police and military equipment, or missing ambulances, fire trucks; they'll use whatever they can to cover their movements until they strike. We now have this much confirmed. We are no longer in lone-wolf territory. Flash-to-bang is now zero. We are up against an organized attack."

"Do you agree with the brain boys, that their play is imminent?"

"Yes, and I think Kitman trying to get out of the country is an indicator. Speaking of the brainiacs, have they got any financial forensics yet that can give us a lead?"

.𝔊.

Wallace Beesly, Kronos, and Remo were finishing their report to Brooke.

"So you all agree that there were large put and call orders in place awaiting triggers?"

"And it was all pre-distributed. If Kitman died, it was still all safe and secured," Wallace said.

Peter added, "Had we not pierced the Kevlar wall, those transactions would have netted trillions after an attack," Peter said.

"You kind of buried the lead there again, Pete. You broke through the wall? Good work, guys."

"Yeah, so at least they won't be able to party for the next one hundred years on the trillions they was gonna make," Kronos said.

"Okay, I want specifics. Maybe finding out where they held positions will tell us what their plan is."

"Disaster supply replenishment is one group, or at least the best name we came up with for some of the industries that are awaiting the trigger," Remo said.

"What are those?" Bridge asked.

"Everything from medical supplies, stretchers, hospital beds, linens, ambulance services, building materials, cleanup services, rehabilitation, coffins, crematoriums, and cemeteries."

"The smart thing about this strategy is that it comes in waves. The windfall isn't right after the attack, but days, even months after, when the supply has to be restocked; that's when holding the kinds of positions Kitman intended would turn into platinum. No one would even notice."

"Okay, that's one group. What's another?"

"Heavy construction, but with an edge towards municipal works," Remo said.

"How so?" Brooke said, sitting down.

"Looking into the kinds of suppliers and contracting and engineering firms, this all points to public works projects."

"Highways?" Bridge said.

"Possibly, but the trajectory of all the companies on this list points to things like water, sewage, drainage. Big concrete cast pipes, sewer vaults and the like."

"Next?" Brooke said.

"Electrical resupply, the big players: GE, Allison Charmers, copper wire and transmission line manufacturers, transformer companies;

all the power grid construction companies outside of government authorities."

"I think I know where this is going but I don't want to believe I'm right. What's your consensus, guys?"

"Brooke, these guys were planning to cash in, not so much on the attack but on the aftermath, and from the scope of what he was setting up, the attack was going to be one mother of an event. Something that would devastate infrastructure for years to come," Kronos said, amazingly without any colorful lingo.

"Bridge, what kind of attack could create that sort of wholesale damage to a city?"

"We can rule out nuclear."

"Why?"

"Because none of these things, these rebuilding projects, could be done for decades after a radiological device was detonated over a wide area."

"Plus, I didn't find any industries usually tied to Rad suits or potassium iodide, which would be needed by the freight train full, every day," Kronos said.

"Okay, here's what we'll do: In a half hour I'll have the FBI, NYPD, and every head of every city authority and their security people, and hell, even the Boy Scouts if I need them, in the big conference room. We don't let them out until you guys have three attack scenarios of something this large and this devastating. Then we take those and put our additional resources there and hope we are right. If not, we'll still have the current level of elevated protection in place. God willing, that will be enough."

A quiet fell on the room. Nobody spoke. All eyes were on Brooke. Her eyes darted then stopped; she tapped her pencil on the pad. Her head moved from side to side as she weighed two opposing thoughts, then she spoke. "Okay, big question. Bridge and I are pretty sure Kitman is the top of the pyramid here. He's probably ex-mujahedeen, if there is such a thing. The attack would be the victory. Why the aftermath cashing in on something materialistic?"

George had entered the room with Harris during the interlude. George jumped in, "Iranian Sataad."

"George, Harris! Glad you're okay. Right after this I want you both to fill me in. What about the Sataad?"

"It's clear to me now. Kitman was a true believer, probably a deep mole," George said.

"He came back from Afghanistan a different guy, literally!" Beesly said.

"He was ISIS's guy on Wall Street. Maybe even before we knew there was an ISIS. He was propped up with oil money from certain sympathetic parties around the world. With a bankroll like that, he couldn't miss becoming one the wizards of the street. It was just a matter of time," George said.

"With the trillion in windfall from the attack, ISIS could fund the caliphate for the next one hundred years. Regain control of all of Europe and Northern Africa, then set their sights on the Great Satan in the year twenty one hundred," Remo said.

"Kitman's dead. And thanks to you guys, the long and shorting is neutralized. Now, do we have anything on timing of the attack?" Brooke asked as she scribbled a note on the pad in front of her.

"Wallace has the best-probable window," Remo said, giving him the floor.

"Again, based on what I believe the triggers to be against optimum time to snatch the market away from imitators and profit seekers who will descend once there is an event, I'd say . . . now. They are going to strike now!"

Chapter 42

Ratcheting Up

Dequa sat in stunned silence as the news that Kitman had been killed sank in. Before him on the TV was the constant replaying of the gunfight filmed from the air above. To him, it was as if God himself shot the video. He hesitated. His thoughts became knotted. *Was this a sign to abort, or a divine inspiration to proceed.* Kitman was strategically crucial but not a tactical element in the plan; he had done his part by funding and protecting the means of arming, training, and support. However, Dequa regarded the brilliant mujahedeen warrior, who'd so skillfully infiltrated the capitalists of the West and become a trusted insider of those infidel dogs, as his leader in more ways than financial.

Dequa now regretted having once raised doubts as to Kitman's willingness to give it all up for the great struggle. He chided himself for ever doubting this man, Kitman or El-had Berani as he knew him, who'd taken on the Russians and the early American invaders so brilliantly and had been so tactically astute as to make them curse the day they'd set foot on Afghan soil. As the TV told of his rise on Wall Street and his many associations with captains of industry and politicians, Dequa realized how great this man's deception had been. So skillful was his ability to fool the West that he, Dequa himself, had been taken in and believed that Berani had turned infidel. Dequa vowed that if he lived through this day, he would atone for this blasphemy of such a true hero and devout man. Then Dequa prayed.

.₲.

Brooke was in the conference room with the heads of all New York City's major infrastructure agencies. An assistant popped her head in and quietly walked over to Brooke. She bent down and whispered, "White House on line two, Director."

"Thank you," she said quietly, then addressed the room. "Gentlemen, ladies, if you'll excuse me for a second, something needs my attention. Mr. Bridgestone, would you come with me. This concerns your plan."

Brooke shut the door of her office and hit the speakerphone. "Burrell-Morton here."

"Hold for POTUS."

Bridge reflexively stood taller.

"Brooke?"

"Mr. President, thank you for getting back to me so quickly."

"Your *Archangel* RDF plan is approved. I've instructed the Pentagon, the National Guard and the governors of New York, New Jersey, and Connecticut to comply with your proposal and it is now an official war plan of the United States of America."

"Thank you, sir."

"Brooke, you're under a lot of stress there. Is there anything I can do from my end to assist?"

"Sir, that was the big one, and your personally smoothing over any intramural squabbles makes it all an easier road."

"It ruffled a lot of feathers from the Central Command, the joint chiefs, and right up to my own steaming mad Sec Def, but in my executive order, I specifically note that anyone not adhering to your orders will answer directly to me, whether they're a general, private, or county commissioner."

"That should certainly do the trick, sir."

"Almost as big a stink was made over your Internet part of the plan, *Suppressor*. White House council is still going at it with the FCC and two congressional oversight committees, but I wrote a finding that should ultimately quash any injunctions."

"We need to blind the millions of eyes who will tell the bad guys what we are up to, sir."

"Brooke, do you still think this could be as bad as your report indicated?"

"Sir, I got the best minds here, and any way they slice it, the enemy is planning something of titanic proportions and, it seems, with a plan that can reach out for one hundred years."

"Good God . . ." There was silence.

"But, Mr. President, my guys have cracked their most secure lists. We now know where the money was going to go to fund the caliphate. Kitman died believing it was set in stone and nothing could stop it. He didn't count on Kronos, Wallace Beesly, and Peter Remo, sir. They are, right this minute, sending those targets to the CIA. Sir, it's like a contact list, a who's who of every terror group and their supporting allies all over the world. We are going to be able to put a giant dent in the balance sheets of ISIS, Al-Qaeda, and every other enemy of the free world."

"That's amazing, Brooke. Well done. Please let your team know that they have done this country, its people, and much of the population on earth a great service and I am personally indebted to them."

"Thank you, sir, I know that will mean a lot to them."

"Nothing more left to do than to wish you good luck, Brooke. I'll be praying for you and your team."

"Thank you, sir . . . Oh, sir?"

"Yes, Brooke?"

"Sergeant Major Richard Bridgestone drafted the proposal you approved, sir. So I am very confident in its ability to interdict or eliminate the threat."

Bridge silently waved her off. He didn't like being credited.

"Is he there now?" the president asked over the secure circuit.

Bridge gave her a "See! Now look what you did!" gesture then relented. "Yes, sir. I'm here."

"Time we had a beer, son. I still owe you for saving New York City a while back among a few other things."

"You owe me nothing, sir. It's my duty. But I will take you up on the beer."

"Good, looking forward to it. Brooke, Sergeant Major, be careful. Keep me apprised of events. God speed."

The line clicked. Brooke looked at Bridge as a smile appeared on her face. She stood up and held up her hand. Bridge slapped hers as she said, "Yes. We are approved. Get out there and make your prep. You are running the show, Bridge."

"This is all going to kill my undercover profile, you know."

"Look at the bright side; you can finally have a library card under your real name."

Bridge gave her a quizzical look and bolted out of her office.

She opened Bridge's briefing book for *Archangel* and smiled. There she saw her code word for this op was, "Stiletto."

.G.

ATTACK IMMINENT

Paul had assembled the North and South teams at an abandoned warehouse in nearby New Jersey that was their staging area. The overall general depression of this part of town almost ensured that no one, except for the occasional vagrant or drug dealer, would even notice any activity in the old Eastern Mills textile factory. The dilapidated building had once been the lifeblood of the "Embroidery Capital of the World," as the locals had boasted fifty years earlier.

While Dequa was up in an office preparing to come down and address the "troops," Paul walked the line of twenty-four men and inspected their weapons, making sure they each knew their place in the two pre-attack scenarios that he had drawn up to buy the ten minutes of precious time that it would take to execute the main attack. After he finished addressing the men, Dequa would lead them in their final prayers, because even though Paul had planned and readied many means of escape for them, and especially himself, he knew, and he believed they knew, that none of them would likely live longer than ten minutes after the attack started. As for his own survival, he would use his "strategic command post" away from the battles to ensure his unmolested escape to his South Sea safe house.

Dequa emerged from the office and climbed up the rickety staircase overlooking the floor of men, weapons, and vehicles. He stood for a moment on the second landing. Emotions overwhelmed him. He raised his hands. Before he knew it he was speaking.

"We have been blessed that the power of change, for the next thousand years, has been placed in our hands. Today we will begin the end of the great struggle. You will all have a place in paradise as heroes, martyrs, and the great liberators of a religion and people too long oppressed. You will become the champions of countless generations that have been left to die in poverty and ruin. Today you will strike a blow against the greatest of Satan's disciples. In one hundred, two hundred . . . a thousand years, the events we are about to embark on today will be taught to every new generation. For them the world will be at peace. There will be no war, no poverty, no famine. The one true religion, and our faith in the supreme entity, will guide all men of faith to prosperity, goodness, and fruitful lives in service to Allah and our fellow man. Whoever among us that shall perish today, will live forever in the glory of Allah. We will now pray for our victory in his name."

All the men in the room, including Paul, acceded.

.₲.

All told, *Archangel* was the most ambitious and complex domestic mobilization since the Civil War. The three large assembly areas called for in Bridge's plan had been filling up all day, pursuant to the president's orders. The largest base, designated RDF 1, on the green grass of Liberty State Park right outside Jersey City, New Jersey, had a closed-circuit TV camera system that connected it to the two other Rapid Deployment Forces bases: RDF 2 in the Great Lawn in Central Park, and RDF 3 located in the large parking lot at CitiField in Queens.

Nine hours to the minute after the word went out from the Pentagon, each *Archangel* Forward Operating Base, or FOB, had its compliment of Apache AH64, OH58D and AH-1 Super Cobra attack helicopters, refueled and at the ready. In all, six platoons of Marines, Special Forces, and SEALS were amassed and ready to go. Added in the mix were ever-increasing amounts of specialized weapons and tactics men, including members of the Army EOD bomb disposal units, Navy Dive Teams and NBC specialists who could neutralize or at least contain any nuclear, biological, or chemical threat.

There were twenty light-utility UH72 Lakota helicopters assigned to the National Medical System for fast battle medevac service.

From the three RDF FOBs, any point in the metropolitan area was two minutes flight time, at balls to the wall. The choppers wouldn't even have to land; the Rangers and other A-team troops could rappel from hovering copters in seconds.

NEADS was up and they had two E8-JSTARS, tactical command post airplanes in the air over New York as command control and communications relays to the troops on the ground. But also to support the North East Air Defenses System and their two F-22 Raptors, which were circling the sky above Manhattan in case all this was just a ploy or diversion and ISIS's ultimate plan was a redo of 9/11.

.𝕲.

Three hours before, in a joint press conference, the governors of New York, New Jersey, and Connecticut, along with the chairman of the joint chiefs and the heads of Homeland Security, FBI, Port Authority Police, and NYPD announced a "Readiness Emergency Test." It was introduced as an unprecedented coordination between federal, state, and local authorities. They alerted the public of this snap drill designed to test the viability of pre-positioned resources in the extremely unlikely event of a natural or manmade catastrophe.

At every point, the leaders stressed in calm, clear voices, that this was *not* in response to any specific threat but done out of an abundance of caution in light of recent events like Hurricane Sandy and the now-public aborted Fifth Avenue truck bomb.

The governors and their staff also asked that the press "please refrain from reporting on any specifics of deployment, equipment, or even location of these 'practice' areas to maintain the operational integrity and the safety of our men and women who are drilling to protect all of us." In return, the press was promised unprecedented embedded access to the next drill and hourly reports from the governors' podium on the progress of these drills.

It was messy, what with the onslaught of questions, but essentially the cover story held and a voluntary virtual news blackout of sorts was initiated. That bought the RDF forces at least eight hours of relative mobility without any news cameras revealing their methods, tactics, or location to the enemy.

.𝕲.

In rapidly erected DRASH tents, part of the expeditionary logistics packages located at the three bases, all the members of the RDFs were assembled. In Queens and Central Park, they gathered in front of large-screen TV monitors.

Bridge spoke live from the Liberty State Park location. "Today, you are part of the largest Rapid Deployment Force ever assembled in this nation's history. You all come from different branches of the military and government agencies. Separately, you have all trained for this; today we combine all that we have learned, all that we have trained for, and all that we have accomplished into one critical mission in which failure is not an option. I am here to announce, as many of you have suspected, that this is no drill. Repeat: this is no drill. An organized group or groups, which we believe to be ISIS-based, are planning a devastating attack on this city. Intelligence indicates the attackers are planning for death tolls in the hundreds of thousands to millions. At this time, we don't know the means of the attack or their intended targets for that matter. That's why we have received the Prepare To Deploy Order from the commander in chief. From this point forward, we are at Red Con One."

The men reacted and murmured because up till this point they hoped it really was a drill. But a PTDO and "Ready Condition One" were no bullshit; it meant full engagement was imminent.

Bridge paused and let his announcement sink in for a moment. "At any second, including this one, the alarm may sound and you will be our nation's first and probably only line of defense. I know I don't have to remind you that you'll be going in weapons hot, but we are still on American soil. I want accuracy, clean kill shots, no spray-and-pray and no rock-and-roll. We are all professionals and I know each and every one of us will follow the rules of engagement, acting as our training dictates and our sacred oath to this country demands.

"The people of this city, the people of America, and our commander in chief are counting on us not to fail, not to waver . . . to terminate with extreme prejudice anyone who is intending harm to our fellow Americans and our way of life. The political leadership has paved the way for us to operate within our borders. May you all be safe, may you all be accurate in your shooting, and may you all save us from the terror about to be unleashed. Now, I'd like to ask the Navy chaplain to lead us in prayer."

Bridge looked to his right, then his left, and caught a glimpse of the man approaching the podium. Bridge was slightly taken aback. He stepped up to the man of God. He wore the insignia of a chaplain and captain's bars but the man was an Imam. Bridge asked, "Are you up for this, Chaplain?"

"Of course, Sergeant Major. I got this . . ."

Bridge saluted him.

"Oh, and Sergeant Major . . ."

"Yes, sir."

"God bless you and your mission."

"And God bless you, Chaplain."

There was a slight stirring among the troops as the Imam took the stage. But not a single disrespectful word was uttered. The room quickly quieted down.

"In the chaplain's service, we come from all denominations, and we are instructed in the tenets and traditions of over seventeen world religions. Our job is to help our warrior men and women connect to their God, spirituality, or whatever they hold dear within their personal belief system. Our motto back at the home office is the old saw: 'There are no atheists in foxholes.'"

The soldiers laughed.

"Today you may be called upon to go into battle. May God protect you and keep you safe. May your actions be guided by him to be just and righteous and may you be judged not harshly in the afterlife for the act of taking of any life you may be forced to commit as you faithfully execute your sworn duties, before God, to protect this nation and the people we all so dearly love. And by that I mean all the people—of all races, of all creeds, and of all places in society—for we are all God's children, even the atheists . . . And you are now his instrument for protecting his greatest gift to all of them, that of their own lives."

The man of God then clasped his hands together, looked up for a moment, then right, left, and finally into the camera at the other troops who were watching in the two remote base camps. "In a minute, I will ask you all to pray according to the traditions of your chosen religion or for those of you not of faith, to just quietly reflect. But first I need to acknowledge the obvious: As you can see, I am an Imam by religious standards, but as you can also see I am a captain. The bars represent the commission by the President of the United States as an officer and gentlemen of the armed forces. The chaplain insignia designates me the Priest, Rabbi, Reverend, Minister, Imam, Llama, and all-around utility infielder for the many denominations that serve this great nation. Those who you may do battle against today have a distorted view of God's way. They bend and twist the meaning and spirit of a great religion to meet their own political and militaristic ends. Millions of Muslims around the world are disgusted with these acts that have no place in the world today, but these godless individuals, they are using horrific exaggerations to create force multipliers and bring on confrontation. No matter what the enemy does today, their first act of aggression was against the Quran, a book and a way of life that I love and believe in. As I look out at all of you, Christians, Jews, Baptists, Episcopalians, Muslims, Buddhists, and those in the back and the other camps that I can't see, I will pray to Allah for your success in eradicating this blasphemy of Islam. Amen and Ameen. Now please take a moment to pray as you desire or silently reflect . . ."

To his surprise, Bridge was emotionally moved by the words of the Imam. His eyes were actually misting up. Although he had seen and known acts of courage, including those he himself had been credited with, he now saw it in a whole new light, a holy light. Softly, under his breath, he uttered, "Bless you, Imam."

Chapter 43

Locked and Loaded

The rusting garage door of the old abandoned textile factory in Jersey City opened and a stream of vehicles rolled out. A large red Con Edison gas truck was followed by two large black tour busses, each towing a five-by-eight-foot trailer painted a matching black behind them. Then a yellow Yeshiva school bus, loaded with what at first looked like bearded seminary students. Last were two ordinary sedans; Paul was driving one and Dequa was in the passenger seat of the other.

.Ԍ.

Bridge had taken off in the command copter and the pilot was doing a racetrack pattern across the city. The thought being that if anything popped, being airborne would give him that many more seconds of edge. Of course, if something happened at the other end of the pattern they were orbiting, then the edge would be nullified.

.Ԍ.

In more than a few newsrooms across the city, emails claiming to have attached photos and videos from citizens who had taken candid images of troops on the highways and the streets were pouring in. Supposedly these shots were from rooftops showing concentrations of soldiers and equipment in Central Park. But for some reason, the downloads of these items was excruciatingly slow. Amazingly, the deal struck with the media held. The editors and reporters respected the "quarantine" for the time being. But competitive pressures were building. And the various news outlets monitored each other to see who would bust the dam first so that they could all flood the airways, reporting on this with abandon.

.⊕.

When *Archangel* was approved, along with it was Kronos's crazy idea to plant a virus on the World Wide Web. He called it *Suppressor* and had written it up in a matter of hours. *Suppressor* effectively scrubbed metadata from every image file posted on the Internet. If the GPS coordinates in the data file of a photo were within a three-mile radius of one the RDF staging areas, then the file was rerouted to a buffer that would eventually deliver that file in two days' time. This throttling was totally legal, since the speed of delivery was not guaranteed by the Constitution, and was especially open to manipulation under a liberal interpretation of the Net Neutrality protocols which, as an unintended consequence, actually opened the door for bandwidth manipulation either way. The techno-sapien genius was confident that a digital veil of secrecy was in place around *Archangel*'s Forward Operating Bases.

.⊕.

At headquarters, Brooke and her brainy guys were still trying to crack the nut of where the attack or attacks would come from. So far the emergency drill cover story was holding . . . but reporters were starting to get curious and were getting closer to the RDF bases.

She had Remo, Kronos, and Wallace broken into three teams with various agency personnel. In big generic terms, they were Water, Power, Subway. Individual targets like bridges, tunnels, and airports wouldn't have the impact that could trigger the kinds of windfalls that Wallace claimed could make up Kitman's post-catastrophe payday. No localized attack could generate the kind of rebuilding, and thus the profits, the terrorists were expecting.

Wallace's own group, Subways, had developed only one specific threat. The system was too spread out and the kind of devastation that could be induced didn't seem to meet the level of the put and calls. There was one chilling thought: tunnel breach. Although the large flood doors that Remo had spoken of had been un-welded after 9/11, they were again welded back into the safe, open position after New York had experienced a tremor of the Pennsylvania earthquake in 2012. The rumbles had renewed the fears of them slamming down and cutting a train full of commuters in half. Out of their group came warnings to the Coast Guard and NYPD harbor unit to be on the lookout for explosive charges placed on the seawall near the old World Trade Center "bath tub." The path trains ran on the other side of that wall. And although they were a smaller transit system in the city's web of underground tunnels, a breach in that wall would flood every underground subway system in Manhattan, Brooklyn, the Bronx, and Queens, which were all connected. A civil engineer stated that such a rush of sea water into the system could weaken the foundations of nearby buildings and super-compressed air trapped below the street by onrushing waters could cause explosive ruptures of water, gas, and electric lines. That made it a major event worthy of the profile they were looking for.

Kronos's group, Power, had a few nasty things to look into but all of them concerned points in the grid, like substations and power plants. But the electrical grid was loaded with redundancies and trip breakers designed to isolate any sudden change in the load or generating capacity. Again, with these safeguards in place, nothing could be amassed to create a catastrophe the likes of which would create the need for the materials and services the bad guys hoped to profit from.

Peter Remo's working group, Water, was also a little bogged down by the imagined enormity of the terrorists' goals. Number one was a biological or chemical additive to the reservoirs, but this would be a short-lived, defensible attack. The entire water system had thousands of monitors and incredibly sensitive ways to detect foreign substances. Even too much bird droppings in the water system rang bells. Therefore, any biological or chemical additive would set off alarms from every precinct up and down the water supply system. Plus there were many reservoirs, so that even if they managed to deposit the hundreds of tons of any substance that it would take to raise the particulate of the city's tap water even one percent, it would still take a day or two for the water to reach New Yorkers. Even longer for those in buildings with water tanks, which was every building over five stories in Manhattan alone. That would yield plenty of time to take corrective measures and alert the public and isolate the contaminated reservoir. Although minor riots and civil unrest might occur if water was rationed, that still didn't rise to the level of casualties in the five or six figure range.

Brooke called in the three men to confer about where their groups were at, as time was ticking away.

"Okay, the two biggest threats so far seem to be contamination of the water supply and flooding of the subways?"

"Seems so," Remo said, looking to the others for concurrence.

"Fellas, what are we not seeing? What are we not considering? These ISIS guys so far have been smart. They are striking a blow for something they believe in. They want it big, bigger, I believe, than anything we've come up with so far."

Remo spoke for them. "Brooke, in this post-9/11 city, there isn't much room for them to operate on such a grand scale; again, if you exclude nukes."

"Okay, how about outside the city? How about a multi-pronged attack? Where the actions combine into the kind of devastation we think is at hand." Brooke leaned in. "Guys, the president only gave us a twenty-four-hour window on Posse Comitatus, but I figure the press is about three hours away from blowing this whole op wide open. Let's try putting your groups together. Let's see if there's any combination of things that can add up to the big event the bad guys are planning on. Think fast and think correctly!"

Chapter 44

One. If By Land

4 HOURS UNTIL THE ATTACK

The Rip Van Winkle Bridge, 122 miles up the Hudson, was the perfect spot for Dequa and his men to cross the Hudson. True to its fairy tale name, it was a sleepy little bridge where there was very little in the way of vehicle inspections. So both tour busses rolled right through the tollbooths just like many bands that played the casinos in western New York State and Canada. The glossy black trailers hitched to the backs of the busses didn't raise so much as an eyebrow since they weren't the orange and silver of a rented U-Haul. The Yeshiva bus was a regular site at this bridge to the Hasidic communities nestled in Liberty and Fleishman's New York. And although the red Con Ed gas repair trucks were a little out of their natural environs, the two hard-hat-clad workers in the front of each truck had valid Con Ed IDs, so the trucks were given a pass. The two private cars just passed through normally. The entire assault team had just crossed their most critical hurdle, traversing the Hudson without exposure by police who were vehicle checking each truck and large vehicle that tried to cross the George Washington or Tappan Zee Bridges, or the Lincoln or Holland Tunnels. They were now on New York State terra firma with no interstate checkpoints that could foil their mission.

They stuck to the truck routes that had no tolls or police scrutiny. They drove exceedingly safely at just under every speed limit, lest they attract any attention. In three hours and thirty-five minutes, they would be at their appointed positions to initiate the attack.

.6.

The large conference room was packed as all three groups now worked on combinations of scary scenarios that might cripple a city. Advocates and naysayers quickly formed within the group, as the room polarized over intramural agency turf. Many times the suggestions were taken as some sort of slight against the other agencies' perceived deficiencies in their defensive posture. A couple of times Remo had to place his thumb and middle finger in his mouth and let out an ear-piercing, Bronx schoolyard whistle, which quieted the warring parties down.

Kronos then asked a simple question. "Okay, what's outside the city that can hurt us, besides the reservoir contamination?"

"There really isn't anything," the head of DPW said.

"How about denial of service?" Kronos said.

"Denial of water service?" the head of the department of Water and Power said with a scrunch of his brow. "Isn't that a computer thing?"

"Well, is your supply chain run by computers?"

That perked Remo up. "Yes, like a few years back, manipulating computers can cause all kinds of havoc," he said, referring to the Eighth Day affair, which he had not been a part of but had had heard a lot about—mostly from Kronos, one of the heroes who'd thwarted that cyber-attack.

"No, no, no. Every important step in the system is manual. Computers are only used for monitoring and analysis. At the end of the control chain, a man turns a wheel or throws a switch."

Kronos picked up on the word *switch*. "Bingo, could those switches be overridden in any scenario?"

The man from DPW was stymied. "I . . . I . . . don't think so. I mean that's possible, but there are, to the best of my knowledge, no computer-controlled switches, relays, or water gates anywhere in the system; I'll run it by my engineering department right now."

Kronos turned to one of the agents manning the computer. "Gus, can you put the water system up on the big screen." Kronos got up and walked over to the map on the monitor. He crossed his arms as everyone in the room waited for him to say something. He got real close, then walked back to the other side of the big table as far as he could get from the screen. Then walked up again real close.

Some of the men in the room exchanged looks and even rolled their eyes.

They all turned with a snap when Kronos blurted out, "What's this?!" He had his finger on a point where water tunnels number one and two seemed to almost come together.

The man from the DPW had to move over in his seat to see around Kronos to what he was pointing at. "Why, that's the Yonkers' reservoir."

"Got it, but what's these two lines mean?"

"That's just where water tunnels one and two are near to one another?"

"How near?"

"I dunno, twenty, thirty feet. Why?"

Kronos turned to Remo. "Fucking Yonkers, man!"

Remo turned to the man. "Is there a water tunnel number three yet?"

"No. Still under construction."

"So those two tunnels are the only way the entire city of New York gets its water?"

"Yes . . . it's . . ." The man's face suddenly drained of all color.

.G.

In Somers, New York, fifteen miles north of the reservoir, the two buses passed a diner. Coming out of the diner, Somers Patrolman Eugene Bristol had just gotten his coffee and was getting in his cruiser when he noticed a tow chain dragging along the ground and sparking behind the big black bus that was towing a small trailer behind it. Although it wasn't any kind of moving violation, it could get snagged on something and ruin the under carriage of the bus or cause the trailer to come loose. So he figured he'd alert the driver.

.G.

Dequa saw the cop car pull behind the first bus then turn on its lights. He spoke into his phone.

The bus pulled over. The older cop got out of his car and walked over to the driver's side. The window slid open. "What is the problem, Officer?"

"You got a loose chain back there; it could be a real problem."

"Thank you. Can you show me?"

"Sure." As the town policeman walked to the back of the bus, the second bus pulled up right alongside but behind the stopped one.

Eugene waved his hand as he spoke. "You can't block the road. Pull up ahead if you guys are traveling together. This will only take a minute, you can't block the . . ."

Four bullets from an MP5 in short burst perforated his windpipe, carotid artery, and lungs; the cop was dead before he hit the floor. With the second bus giving cover, two men came out of it and dragged the body into the bus. Then one of them took the officer's hat off the ground and got in the patrol car. He fumbled with switches until he killed the flashing lights and then pulled out with the busses. Twenty miles outside of town, they left the car and Eugene's body down a small dirt country road, out of the main road's line of sight.

.G.

Harris ran into Brooke's office after she called out to him.

"Harris, the quarry explosion upstate, how big?" Brooke said standing next to Kronos, who had the reservoir maps spread out on the table in the corner.

"We found the wreckage fifty-five feet down. They said it was like an ice cream scoop of earth fifty-five feet around."

Kronos had the detailed layout of the water tunnels under the Yonkers reservoir. "I make the pipes to be forty-five feet apart."

The DPW man was there with his engineer, Reilly, on the phone. "Yes, 46.4 at the nearest."

"And from this plot it looks like they cross this access road, at the north end of the reservoir, at a thirty degree angle." Kronos traced the path with his finger.

"That's right," Reilly said over the phone.

"How deep are the pipes, er . . . tunnels at that point, Reilly?" Remo asked.

"At that point it's a twelve-foot circumference with the bottom at around fifty-five feet under the grade of the roadway."

"And we have three students who have previous water authority experience in foreign countries," Brooke added.

"Don't forget the dead guy. He was a surveyor."

"And the clincher is that the bomb factory house was right across the thruway and, as I remember, with a clear view of the race track and of that northern gate of the reservoir," Harris said.

"Okay, I am going to call it for the reservoir. But here's my question: we think they have two U-Hauls, right? Where's the second one going?" Brooke asked.

"That's easy. Given the spacing, they need two bombs to knock out both tunnels. Based on the way the pipes are positioned at an angle under the access road, you'll need both; one about . . . seventy feet behind the other," Kronos said, checking the distance on the ruler that helped him with the two-hundred-feet-per-inch scale of the plan's inset of the roadway.

"Get me Bridge on the command chopper on the double," Brooke said to the military aide now assigned to her by the Pentagon.

.G.

Dequa was annoyed as the first bus raced up to his car and flagged him down. Stopping the convoy was not wise. Amad ran from the bus to Dequa's car's window.

"Dequa, there is news of troops on the way to the city. It's all over my Twitter, and I checked Facebook."

Dequa was about to pull out his gun and shoot this young idiot who intentionally risked operational security to do his BookFacing and twittering. His face grew angry and red.

"I am sorry. I know you forbade this, but it is a valuable source of information."

Dequa softened. "Are there any units in the city?"

"Not that I have seen pictures of, although there are tweets. But here is an image of a convoy."

He reached out his hand and looked at Amad's iPad. The picture was of army trucks on the New York State Thruway crossing the Tappan Zee Bridge. The old mujahedeen warrior was relieved to see that there were no tanks and no personnel carriers in the picture. They would have been a problem.

He handed back the device. "It makes no difference. That bridge is almost an hour away from the city. We are committed. And, if they are just mobilizing now, it's too late for them. Get back to your bus." He closed the window and waved his hand for the driver to go.

His driver turned and said, "You believed the press when they said they are only practicing preparedness?"

"It is better for us. They will not be armed during a practice session on American soil. They have laws against it. But we are well prepared for any token resistance or police actions they can marshal."

.G.

On the quiet residential street in Yonkers, a local police cruiser was stationed outside the "Bomb Factory" house. Although the authorities tried not to cause panic, the story of the discovery of the house and its volatile contents had leaked out to the press, eventually forcing the revelation that the alleged Fifth Avenue accident, with the truck full of fertilizer from the chicken farm, was in fact an attempted suicide bombing. Not that anyone in Yonkers government expected the bomb makers of the Fifth Avenue truck bomb to come back, but the cop car was there so the neighbors, like Jim Aponte, slept better knowing that they were being watched over.

Patrolman Bob Krantz had been parked here since eight in the morning and was trying to avoid sleeping altogether. Sitting outside an empty house that had been scrubbed clean by the feds and sealed with police tape was the most boring duty any human could pull. But that was the lot in life of probationary policemen just out of the academy; they were the kind of dead-brain jobs rookies like him got assigned to. He depended on coffee and Red Bull to keep him awake in broad daylight!

He couldn't imagine what Gene, his academy mate and the cop on the shift before him did in the middle of the night to not go stark raving mad with boredom.

Bob was just crushing his second Red Bull can when a blue and white Con Ed van pulled up behind him. Since the house was the last on the dead-end block before the Thruway, the Con Ed van couldn't be there for any other reason.

.G.

The man in the Con Ed van watched the cop get out of his cruiser and walk to his driver's side window.

"Morning. What's up?" the young cop said.

"I have a job order here to disconnect this house from the mains," he said as he held up the clipboard with the work order on it.

"Let me see that," the cop said as he reached in for the paperwork. "Yeah, this is the right address, but this place is a crime scene."

"I'm very sorry, Officer. But I have my dispatcher . . . He says the power's to be cut. There is no one paying the bill . . ." Then he added, "You know." And gave the common shrug of a worker following the orders of a superior.

"What do you have to do? Can you do it from outside the house?"

"I can disable the meter from outside, but I need to throw the main breaker in the basement first, so I don't get electrocuted. Safety first."

"Nobody told me anything about this."

The Con Ed guy just shrugged.

"Krantz portable to Central," he said into the mic clipped to his shirt.

"Central to Krantz portable, come in."

"Central, be advised I have a guy from the electric company here. Says he's got to disconnect the house I have under surveillance from the main power. Got a job order and everything."

"Krantz portable, stand by."

"How long will it take?" Krantz said as he waited for his orders from his superiors.

"Two seconds, once I open the box in the basement. Just flip the main breaker to off."

The radio crackled. "Central to Krantz portable, escort the electric company guy into the house then reseal and secure the premises once he's done."

"Krantz portable to Central, ten-four."

"Okay, let's go," Officer Krantz said to the Con Ed guy.

The guy opened the side door of the van and took out a big tool bag.

"I thought you said you just had to throw a breaker?"

"Could be an interlock box. Besides, all my screwdrivers are in here too . . . you know." Fareed had forgotten to say "you know" as often as he had been trained in language lessons to make him sound like a New Yorker. His pulse rose because he promised himself he would not fail . . . *er, screw up.*

The cop mumbled as he led the way, "Interlock . . ."

The policeman broke the yellow police tape across the front door as Fareed carried in his equipment.

"That's probably the basement door," Krantz pointed.

They found the light switch and headed down the stairs. Fareed walked up to the power box in the corner and squatted down to open his tool kit.

Krantz looked around. "You know there's enough room down here to build a great train layout, you know, one of those . . ." The cop's eyes went wide as the knife went right through his back and into his heart. He fell over dead. Fareed left the knife in him and lugged the tool bag upstairs to the corner bedroom. Using a utility knife, he tore up the corner of a wall-to-wall rug by the window and there, on the floor, were many three-eighth-inch holes drilled onto the wood, which made no pattern and, more importantly, made no sense to any nosy investigators. He took out a folded piece of paper from the bag and laid it out with the marks on two of the edges against the corner molding of the walls. On the paper there were only three holes, which lined up with the most important ones in the floor, the ones he was here to use.

He placed one pointed peg of each leg of a surveyor's tripod in each hole. He used a steel rod bent into an "L" shape and brought the tripod to the exact height under the rod's extension. Then he locked it down tight. Next, he opened the case and brought out the Topcon DS 203AC Motorized Total Station. The computer-controlled laser transit system had been pre-programmed a month before when they'd occupied the house. He had learned this skill from Shamal, who'd been killed by the woman agent. But now the machine did all the work. Its five-hundred-megabyte memory was more than enough to align itself and find the exact same spot that he and Shamal had triangulated using the other two remote heads. Today they'd only need this one. It would lend an accuracy of plus or minus two inches, and that was well within the "circular error probable" as Waleed the bomb maker had calculated. He looked at his watch: five minutes.

.𝔊.

Kronos was in the IT department calculating the impact of losing the water supply system to a city of eight million people with the engineers and planners at the DPW over the GoToMeeting multi-screen conference.

His smart phone beeped and he looked down. It was an email from Remo with the subject line, "Hey, Brain Boy, why wasn't this suppressed?" Kronos opened it and saw the attached picture that had been posted on Twitter of an Army truck convoy rolling though the Tappan Zee Bridge tollbooths. He typed out his response with blazing thumb speed, "The Tap bridge is like 60 miles away from New York, well outside the 3 mile radius of each RDF staging area here in the city. What did you want me to do, shut down the entire friggin' Internet?"

He tossed the phone down on the table and rejoined the conversation with the city officials. "Okay, so let me recap: 1.2 billion gallons of fresh water a day is consumed by the city. But between the miles of pipe from Yonkers and the water towers atop most buildings in the city, there is a window of four days before . . ."

"Er . . . eight days with strict conservation and a public information blitz," the city engineer said.

"Correction, four to eight days of potable water before the taps run dry. If they detonate, it would take two weeks to repair the tunnels?"

"Yes, with round-the-clock construction."

"Hey, what if we just fix one? Then how long?" Kronos could see the engineer's eyebrows rise. He doodled some figures on the pad in front of him.

"Good idea. With one tunnel repaired we could get fifty percent of the water supply back to the five boroughs in five days."

"We can survive that. We're friggin' New Yorkers here," Kronos said as he left to tell Brooke the good news.

.G.

"I don't buy it," Brooke said.

"Brooke, these guys know their shit and they say five days . . ."

"No, I don't mean your conclusion. I mean I don't buy that they are going through all this for something that won't amount to little more than inconvenience for not even a week."

"A moment ago I was happy; what a buzz kill," Kronos said.

"Peter, what else do you do with water?"

"Bathe, shower . . . holy shit! Fight fires!"

"That's it, interrupting the supply isn't about drinking water." Brooke ran out of the room.

They followed her back into the IT room.

"Gentlemen, are the fire hydrants of New York on your water system?"

"Yes!"

"Certainly."

"From 1917 when they laid the pipes."

"Okay, listen carefully. We are now back to the one-two punch scenario. They are shutting off the firefighting capability of this city, which means they expect to start a fire, a big one. And we have ruled out nuclear, so I want all of you to come up with scenarios for how to burn down this city. Kronos, get me estimates on how long before the water in the system runs out. That should tell us how big the fire they are contemplating will be."

"I can answer that," one of the engineers on the videoconference said. "I ran these numbers a few years back after the San Francisco FD ran out of water fighting a five-beller at Mission Bay—ninety pumper trucks ran the system dry. They had to use the backup reservoir."

"Then we're toast, mister, because they aren't doing this for just one five-alarm fire," Brooke said.

"San Francisco is a totally different supply matrix than us. We've got a thousand times the capacity under normal conditions."

"But if they detonate?" Brooke pressed.

"The residual water in the pipes will be 300 million gallons. If you are fighting one five-alarm fire you are going to go through ten million gallons on average."

"So we can fight thirty five-alarm fires?" Kronos said.

"No, because at some point the pressure drops. So I would say twenty—twenty-five tops. And then it depends on where they are; more pressure for a longer time as you go south, less pressure, sooner to the north."

"Okay, water aside, now I need to know how you make a fire or fires all over the city."

"Back on Christmas Eve, 1994, they planned on hijacking and crashing Air France 8969 into the Eifel Tower to shower flaming jet fuel all over downtown Paris," Remo said.

"Wait, seven years *before* 9-11 they tried to use a plane as a weapon?" the engineer asked from the videoconference screen.

"Don't dwell on it. It *is* infuriating," Brooke said as she got up to leave then stopped and addressed the man on the screen. "By the way, what caused the fire in SF?"

"Welding torch."

"Who's here from FDNY?"

A man in a blue suit with crossed trumpets on his lapel spoke up. "O'Malley, Chief's office."

"What's the biggest cause of major fires in this city, sir?"

"That would be electrical, ma'am."

"Crap, six of our students have electrical distribution backgrounds," Kronos said.

"Kronos, hit it and tell me how I short circuit the city into a blazing inferno, and I need to know that five minutes ago." Brooke left and realized she'd just used one of her husband's favorite command toppers, *and I need it five minutes ago . . . Mush.* She hadn't had the time to think of him since this morning. When he got back to Pearl from patrol, she'd need a month just to fill him in on all that had gone down in the last week. She hoped she'd be there, and not dead, when he piloted the USS *Nebraska* into Pearl.

.G.

Jim Aponte was just coming home for lunch, a definite perk of being the head of technology at the casino attached to Yonkers' Raceway, right across the Thruway from his house. He noticed the Con Ed van at the Bomb House down the street.

.G.

Bridge was screaming into the headset. "Target one, the Hillview reservoir. Due south of the Racetrack in Yonkers. Possible bombs in trailers. Interdict and eliminate, weapons free; repeat, weapons free on my authority. Shoot straight, minimize collateral damage. RDF 3, you're the closest. Go. Go. Go."

He then switched the interphone to crew. "Billy, get me there as fast as you can."

The pilot of the helicopter executed an immediate one-hundred-eighty-degree turn as they were currently over Brooklyn's Coney Island on the southern tip of the racetrack pattern.

"Nine minutes out," the pilot said in return.

Bridge switched to Tac 2. "Bird Dog to RDF 3 leader. What's your ETA on site . . . over."

"RDF 3 leader to Bird Dog, six minutes out . . . over."

"Shit," Bridge said after he switched off his mic.

.G.

The combined security team at Hillview was in a jurisdictional dispute over who was in charge. The newly appointed military liaison officer, a lieutenant from the New York National Guard, wanted all the security personnel out on the roadway armed and ready to interdict whoever tried to get to the water tunnels beneath. But the captain of the security guards had his orders, which were to protect the reservoir at all costs. He had no guidance as to the access roadway and was waiting for a decision from his superiors.

The military man had had enough and ran to get two DPW dump trucks to block the drive at the Central Avenue northern end.

.G.

The two black busses made a hairpin turn off the Central Avenue service road and started up the access way to the main gate of the Hillview reservoir. The guardhouse was on the other side of high, brown security fences, with dark windows. As they approached, the lead bus's front windshield exploded from inside out as a SAW automatic weapon opened up on the small guardhouse. In ten seconds its barrel was red hot and hundreds of rounds had imploded the bullet-resistant glass. Everyone and everything inside was torn to shreds.

Four security guards who were outside the small structure returned fire. Two men from inside the bus put a steel plate in front of the driver. Bullets pinged off it as he slowly moved the bus forward. He opened the door to the bus and looked to his right where a piece of frosted glass was held in place by an aluminum arm coming off the dashboard. He slowed the bus to a crawl until a small red dot from Fareed's laser at the house appeared at the edge of the four inch square glass. With gunfire all around and bullets pounding into his shield, he gingerly moved the bus into position so that the dot was dead center of the glass, just as he had trained to do a hundred times over the past two weeks, in the early morning hours in the deserted parking fields of New Jersey shopping malls. He stopped the bus with a hiss of the airbrakes and applied the parking brake. Having completed the task he had specially trained for, he was now expendable, so he grabbed a machine gun, stood, and returned fire while using the plate for cover.

.𝔊.

The second bus had an ultrasonic measuring tape, the kind you get from Home Depot for forty-eight bucks, on the dash. The driver of that bus pointed it at the back of the trailer attached to the bus in front of him and watched it, as he inched his bus forward. He was trying to get to nineteen feet, four inches. At that distance, the trailer behind his forty-five-foot bus would be dead center on top of the second water tunnel forty-three feet below. As the readout displayed twenty-two feet, an explosion rocked his bus.

.𝔊.

A Cobra gunship had fired two rockets at the second bus. The hits were low and rocked the bus, kicking up asphalt and dirt. Then the copilot, using his heads-up display, zeroed in on the trailer behind, which they were told was the business end of the attack. He purposefully aimed just under the small trailer. "Foxtrot One!" he said as he flicked the safety cap off the red button on his collective and pressed it. The missile hit just under the trailer and the eight-pound Semtex warhead exploded with enough force to flip the thing up in the air and back twenty feet from the bus. The pilot then heard the sound of large caliber bullets ricocheting off the Plexiglas windshield of the Cobra. He turned his head as the gimbal-mounted Gatling gun right under the cockpit moved, as if part of his central nervous system, towards the door of the bus where the shooter was working an AK-47 and firing away. The pilot walked the line of fire right through the door of the bus, almost cutting the front end off. As it sagged away from the rest of the vehicle's body from being perforated by thousands of .50 calber slugs, the shooting stopped.

.𝔊.

In the first bus, Amad ran to the red button. He hit it just as his world went bright orange for a nanosecond before going black as the fireball from the missile of the second Cobra gunship to arrive on station made a direct hit on the lead bus. The explosion was simultaneous with the detonation of the trailer, although the jolting of the bus angled the trailer so its fearsome destructive power, which was originally focused down, was now askew and the crater it made was more elliptical and shallower than the deep, perfectly round "ice cream scoop" they'd intended to make in the roadway. The exploding trailer took out the whole body of the already burning bus.

.𝔊.

The National Guard lieutenant pulled up in one of the two dump trucks that he'd gone to get and immediately jumped down from the driver's side with his sidearm cocked, taking out a terrorist who was aiming a rocket-propelled grenade at one of the choppers as it was landing. Before it touched down, a squad of marines emptied out and started securing the area. Sporadic gunshots were heard as they tracked down a few of the terrorists who'd decided to choose death over life.

The gunfire had subsided when suddenly the ground rumbled. An extremely loud hissing sound built up to ear-shatteringly shrill as the ground under the carcass of the first bus exploded. A gush of water rose fifty feet in the air! The mangled bus was thrown thirty feet by the surging pressure. The roadway around the geyser began to crumble as huge chunks of asphalt went airborne and pelted the ground and the troops. One chunk hit the rotors of the just-landed copter, and the broken-off rotor spun and ripped up two hundred feet of grass to the right, slicing a running terrorist in half along the way, before coming to a rest, jutting out of the ground like a javelin. The pilot did a superior job of wrestling the now-unbalanced damaged bird to safety as it wobbled all over the ground like a bucking bronco at a rodeo.

Then another spout of water as big around as a storage tank rose up sixty feet or more from the ruptured water tunnel. Everyone and everything was deluged. Men found it hard to stand under the relentless downward force of thousands of gallons per second.

.𝔊.

As his helicopter arrived, Bridge saw the huge geyser almost as high as he was flying. He hit the transmit switch. "Bird Dog to Home Plate, Bird dog to Home Plate . . . come in . . . over"

In the conference room, Brooke heard the call sign; she turned to the officer on her right and nodded. "Bird Dog this is Home Plate . . . over," he said.

"We had one breach. It looks like one of the bombs went off. I see one geyser in the south position. The northern tunnel isn't affected yet. But someone should shut it down. It's only a matter of time."

"On it," the DPW guy said as he barked orders into his cell phone.

Brooke leaned into the mic in front of the comm officer. "Bridge, this may not be over . . . er . . . over."

"What happened? . . . over."

Annoyed, Brooke blurted out, "Can you just call in from your cell? . . . over."

In ten seconds, the phone rang. Brooke hit the speaker button.

"Bridge. Okay, we think there is a second prong. In all likelihood it's going to be some kind of attack on the electrical power system."

"I thought we ruled that out?"

"It's back on the threat board because we believe they were looking to stop our ability to fight fires with the bombing of the water tunnels. The thinking is they are going to start a huge fire by some electrical means. Kronos and Remo are working on that angle now in the conference room. Bridge, can you dispatch all your teams to hover near major electrical installations? We'll send coordinates up as soon as we have them."

"Are you sure you want to pre-commit to this," Bridge asked over the speaker.

"What's your option?" Brooke said.

"Let me keep RDF 2 in Queens. I'll reroute RDF3 and put RDF 1 in the air. That way we'll have one group ready if something else comes at us that we're not expecting."

"Okay, good plan. Approved. Execute. We'll get back to you when we know more." Brooke turned to the communications officer. "Patch me into the FBI."

"New York Bureau dispatch, Agent Sanders," came over the speaker in the room.

"Sanders, this is Director Burrell-Morton. I have director one status and my authorization code is Transistor. I want a team of agents to interrogate survivors and prisoners at the Hillview reservoir in Yonkers. I want the team airborne in three minutes. We need to know if they can tell us where the rest of the attack will fall."

Brooke left the room.

.ϐ.

The Yeshiva bus crossed the Fifty-Ninth Street Bridge behind the red Con Ed gas service truck. The two sedans were right behind. Dequa's phone rang.

.ϐ.

"Dequa, it is Fareed. The Americans have attacked the northern team but the bombs have miraculously done their job. There is a very large amount of water coming out of the ground way up into the air. May I leave this place now and join you?"

.ϐ.

"Yes, Fareed, we will need everyone." Dequa hung up. He had no way of knowing that Fareed couldn't see that only one tunnel had been breached so he reported to his team over their walkie-talkies, "The northern team has had a great success. It is up to us now to make sure their sacrifice was not in vain. Be alert and don't let the godless bastards gain an inch of ground."

.ϐ.

Fareed exited the front door and, after taking two steps, he fell forward from the impact of the aluminum softball bat to the back of his head.

Jim Aponte stood over him. "So you guys thought you could blow up the reservoir and get away with it . . . bullshit!" Jim then went inside to find the cop from the cruiser parked outside.

.𝔊.

Brooke entered the conference room as they were in the middle of a common debate. "Power distribution computers can't be hacked to make fires. They can be hacked for denial of service at some level. But the entire system is designed to disconnect, like a fuse or circuit breaker in your house."

"Okay, but that would be because of over-draw of power like in a short?"

"Essentially yes, although in high tensions lines it could be due to inductive losses from the counter EMF. That kind of induction surge could trigger a circuit breaker as well."

"That's it," Remo said.

"What's it?" the Con Ed chief engineer said.

"Induction! What if they are planning something that won't trip the breakers?"

"What are we talking about? Like the breakers in my house?" Brooke said.

"Yes, but these main power breakers would be as big as your house."

"Yes. Brooke, they look like giant mouse traps, only they slam 'open' if there is an instantaneous power drain caused by a short circuit," Remo said.

"So then, Peter, what did you mean they could do something that won't trip the breakers?"

"It's in the back of my head. Geez, what was it?"

"You have to defeat the device mechanically. That's the only way I can imagine it being bypassed," the engineer said.

"No, that's not it . . . What was it?" Peter said, tapping his finger on the table.

Kronos was enjoying this.

Brooke noticed. "What could possibly be so funny that you are smiling at a time like this, Kronos?"

"Are you friggin' kidding me? Look at this. Finally he can't think of something. Brain boy here is having a brain fart. It's friggin' hysterical."

"You are such an odd duck, Kro . . ." Brooke was interrupted.

"That's it! Hysterical!"

"Huh?" Brooke said.

"Um, Hysteresis . . . Hysteresis losses," Peter corrected himself.

"Okay, but those are already accounted for in the inductive load calculations of the grid. So I don't think that's it," the Con Ed Engineer said.

"Wait. What are we talking about?" Brooke demanded, not to be left out of the conversation.

"In anything with a coil of wire, the presence of electricity produces an opposing force that reacts against the initial voltage. In fact, it's called inductive reactance."

"So that's a bad thing?"

"Not good or bad, it just is. We build the coils and transformers, motors and what have you, to keep the reactance where we need it to be."

"But reactance is not only a function of the coil, it's also the applied frequency!"

"Okay, now you are getting way out there," Brooke said raising her hands.

"It's easy, Brooke. Reactance of a coil is dependent on the frequency of the current put into it," Kronos explained like he was detailing how to make a two-scoop ice cream cone.

"You think that helped me?" Brooke said with a half-chuckle.

"The frequency of the grid across America is a constant sixty hertz," Kronos tried again.

"Not exactly," the other engineer from Con Ed said. "We do allow for a deviation of .0167 cycles per second."

"True, but for the purposes of his theory it's negligible." Remo then stood up. "Gentlemen, what if they intend to alter the frequency of the power transmission?"

"Can't happen. There are synchronous breakers as well. If a turbine or rotator were to go out of sync it would be cut from the grid."

"Why?"

"Why? Because the resulting counter EMF would cause the other turbines to . . . to . . . to overheat . . ." the chief engineer said, slowly seeing some merit in Remo's point.

"Okay, so let's say they somehow reduce the frequency of the output to . . . let's say fifty-four cycles or ten percent."

"Again, can't happen."

"Humor him, please," Brooke said.

"Well, let's see." Both engineers grabbed their pencils and started scratching out formula's and filling them in and talking amongst themselves. They finished and the chief engineer spoke. "The hysteresis-synchronous curve for a ten-kilowatt transformer tells us that at a ten percent reduction in power line frequency, the inductive reactance of the coils would increase eight hundred percent. But again can't . . ."

"Yeah I got that. What is the average transformer rated for in terms of maximum operating temperature?" Peter said.

"Off the top of my head I'd say . . . I would say a fifty percent margin for heat dissipation before the coils breakdown."

"Or in other words, if veering off the designed resonant frequency of the device is sufficient enough, it will cause a rise in core temperature to the point of melting the device?"

"Wait. Core temperature? Isn't that a nuclear reactor thing?" Brooke was confused.

"Sorry, Brooke, I should explain. All transformers have iron cores that focus and transfer the induced electricity efficiently."

"So, if I am following you, the transistor . . ."

"Transformer."

"Sorry. This transformer would heat up if someone changed what you called the constant hertz? How much hotter would it get if, say, they can do the ten percent Peter was proposing?"

"At eight hundred percent more reactance, the heat would be sixteen times normal."

"What's normal?"

"Core temperatures are usually between 120 and 150 degrees Fahrenheit, depending on load."

"So the fifty percent margin gets us to 225. But sixteen times 225 is . . . is . . ."

"Is 3,600 degrees!" Kronos said.

"Iron melts at 2,700 degrees," Remo said

"One more thing, Peter. At these power levels, the rapid rise in temperature would be almost instantaneous," Kronos added.

"Meaning what?" Brooke asked.

"Meaning a transformer suddenly under these conditions would explode like a bomb."

"Okay, so how many transformers are in the system?" Brooke said.

"Around 28,000 and change," the Con Ed man said, then realized the sudden danger in that number.

"What? Where are these?" Brooke said.

"On every pole, under every street," Peter said.

"Plus, everything in every house that has a motor or transformer or ballast is also tuned for sixty cycles per second," Kronos said.

"Oh my God. You're saying people's washing machines, TVs, and refrigerators will explode?"

"Theoretically, yes."

"Please, please. We must stop this speculation," the man from Con Ed urged. "Synchronous deviation is impossible. There are safeguards at every place along the distribution line."

"What are they?" Brooke asked.

"You know those breakers that are as big as a house? Well, a smaller device called a synchronous breaker will trip the large breaker if the frequency went beyond twice the allowed delta or .0304 percent. So you see this whole line of speculation is implausible." The chief engineer of Con Ed read the faces in the room. They were very skeptical. He relented and said, "Look, I'll show you." He turned to the computer operator. "Can I access my computer from here?"

.𝔊.

There was a truck yard alongside the Ravenswood generating station so the red Con Ed gas repair truck was as conspicuous as a piece of straw in a haystack. They rolled right up to the gate, waved to the security guard, and he let them pass. He didn't notice the Yeshiva school bus turning into the driveway until it was almost up to his little guard booth. He stepped out and a hand came out of the driver's side with a gun in it and he felt his chest explode as he fell to the floor. The door of the bus opened and sixteen men wearing bulletproof vests piled out with weapons and grenades. Two army humvees with mounted

.50 caliber machine guns reacted to the sight of the fallen guard and came towards the front gate. The back doors of the red Con Ed truck that had passed them opened up and six men got out with squad automatic weapons and shot the humvees from behind. The six soldiers in the two vehicles were killed instantly. The men fanned out quickly and approached the massive generating station known as "Big Allis," the largest generator in New York's power grid. Eighty percent of the electricity used in the five boroughs came from her.

Inside the distribution shed located out in the transformer farm on the river side of the power station, Yusuf heard the shots and went into his lunch pail. He pulled out a 9 mm Glock-26 and calmly, without a scintilla of regret, put a bullet in the head of Frank his co-worker and "friend" for the last three months. Frank's head hit the control panel, leaving it bloody as it slammed down when he collapsed, dead.

"Now you see, I am the terrorist," he spit on Frank's crumpled form. Yusuf then went outside and there were two linemen pulling a new feeder cable from a towed spool of heavy wire. He walked up to them.

"Hey, Yusuf. How's it going . . ."

Ron's words were cut off as a bullet entered his forehead. Ted jumped back. "What the fuck, Yus . . ."

The side of his temple exploded as Yusuf extended his gun hand almost to Ted's face and pulled the trigger.

Yusuf then went to the large forklift over by the building.

.G.

"Here we go. Here's my screen at work. Now let me get the transformer camera up and I can show you the transfer relay, which acts as a breaker," the chief engineer said as the picture came up on the big screen in the conference room.

This time Remo got up and walked close to the screen.

The chief engineer joined him. "You see this large device here?" He outlined it with his finger on the large screen. "That's the relay or breaker."

"It does look like a large mouse trap," Brooke said.

"So you see . . . if anything happens, sudden load or synchronous fault, this unit kicks in and breaks the circuit and then the whole station is off line and off the grid."

"Has that ever happened?"

"Once since it was installed. You remember the blackout of 2003?"

"Hey, what's he doing?" Remo asked.

"Who?"

"That guy with the forklift."

"I don't know. He's right by the mousetrap, er . . . relay," Brooke said.

"What's he doing?"

"I'll tell you what he's doing. He just shunted the relay with that huge girder. And now he's going back to get the other one," Kronos said.

"Why didn't it spark?" Brooke said. "Is it off?"

"Nah, it's not off. It's carrying current. What he's doing is shorting out the contacts so when it trips and breaks the circuit, the circuit will go through the girders instead." Kronos used his hand across his two spread fingertips as he explained.

"It will be like the relay never tripped," the engineer said.

"Is this the safeguard you said would stop every transformer and refrigerator in the city from becoming a fire bomb?" Brooke asked as she turned to the comm officer. "Get me Bird Dog now!" Then she turned to her agent. "Get me a chopper fast! I want to be there."

"Bird Dog is on the radio, Director Burrell," Comms said.

"Bridge. Target is Ravenswood generating station on the Queens side of the East River north of the tram and the Fifty-Ninth Street Bridge. Four big red-and-white smoke stacks. You can't miss it. I am going to join you. Direct everything you got there. We're calling in NYPD, ESU, and Hercules teams for additional support."

She bolted out of the room. The comm officer grabbed the mic and said, "Over."

Chapter 45

Grounded

Yusuf had the next twenty-by-two-foot steel girder on the forks of the heavy lift. He misjudged the distance and the end of the girder hit a terminal on the top of one of the step-up transformers in the farm. He froze. His machine had rubber tires, but he was now ungrounded and forty thousand volts were flowing through him and his machine; but without a ground there was zero current to kill him. At this point the voltage was like the barrel of a gun but it needed amperage as the bullet. Slowly, he started backing the lift away. At first the massive girder was adhering to the magnetism that was focused on the top of the terminal. The enormous one-ton piece of metal was now acting like a giant bar magnet. The metal slid off the forks as the machine moved under it. If the metal beam hit the ground while still attached to the terminal, the whole plant would short out and the relay would activate and break the main distribution circuit even though he had already shunted half of it. Big Allis would be off-line and their whole mission would fail. Every time he rocked the handles that operated the lift in an attempt to wiggle the girder loose, it just got closer to toppling off the raised forks. Worse, he couldn't get off the lift without jumping clean away, because if his foot found the ground so would the path of electricity, and at that high-voltage level the amperage that would go through him would cook him in an instant.

.G.

"Is he stuck?" Brooke asked.

"God dammit, somebody answer the phone," the chief engineer said as he frantically tried to reach his people at the generating station.

Remo got his attention. "Do you have any other video feeds?"

The chief engineer tapped an agent next to him on the shoulder and motioned for him to take over working the computer. "Show him the other feeds there from the thumbnails on the side of the monitor. I'm trying to get some fucking idiot to answer the phone."

"Got any of the front gate?" Brooke said.

The agent scanned the list of cameras on the right side of the screen and found "Main Gate." He clicked on it. Someone in the room muttered, "Good, God."

On the screen was a scene of carnage: dead soldiers draped across two humvees near the camera, and farther off by the guard shack a blue uniformed body lay in a pool of blood.

.𝔊.

Out back in the transformer farm, Yusuf was still trying to free the girder. One of the south's team members made it to the back area of the building and saw Yusuf struggling. He ran as he called out, "I'll help you."

Yusuf barely had a second to scream, "Nooooo!"

The young man went to step up onto the forklift. As soon as his foot touched the metal cowling over the engine, he completed the circuit to the natural ground. His body began to smoke and cardiac arrest was instantaneous so he didn't scream; Yusuf, holding the wheel of the now-electrified machine, burst into flames as his body shook from the forty-thousand-volt surge of now-deadly current. A split second later, the spasming body of the young man who tried to get on the machine exploded.

.𝔊.

Dequa entered the generating facility. His men had killed the entire shift of workers. He stepped over bloody bodies on his way to the master control panel. His chief engineer was busily setting the gauges and flow valves.

"Any difficulties?"

"Not here, but Yusuf has yet to report the shunting of the master breaker."

"I'll go check on him. Expect the counter attack any second now."

"We'll be ready as soon as the shunt is in place."

Dequa trotted out to see why Yusuf hadn't completed his task in the appointed time frame. As he turned the corner of the building, he was momentarily stunned by the horror. Dequa, who was trained as an electrical engineer at the University of Tripoli before the Russians had invaded his beloved Afghanistan, quickly surmised the chain of events. The girder leaning on the step-up transformer's exposed terminal told him all he needed to know about the delay. The ash and boiled body fluids and two burnt leather shoes told him someone had attempted to get onto the lift. What he didn't know was who it had been and if they were doing it to stop Yusuf, or help him. The still smoldering body in the seat of the machine was unrecognizable, but he assumed it was Yusuf. He scanned around and saw what he was looking for. He ran over to the side of the building and found a stack of skids that the forklift used to move freight around. He grabbed one and ran back to the lift.

He placed the wooden skid on the ground and stood on it. He thought about it for an instant and rechecked his logic. He took a deep breath and stepped onto the machine, half expecting to die in a blaze of plasma, but the wood was dry and it provided lifesaving insulation from the ground.

He got up on the machine and placed his foot on Yusuf's immolated body and shoved him off the seat. Part of his rear end stayed stuck to the melted rubber seat. The mission first in his mind, he sat down on the boiling, fatty remains. It burned his own rear end. But he endured because everything they had planned for, trained for, and sacrificed for, as well as the next thousand years of Utopia, were at stake. He gently pushed the lever that lifted the forks forward. He eyeballed the girder to be level, at which point he drove forward with the wheel and turned slightly to the right. He slowly crept forward as the sound of helicopters faded up at a distance. A main feeder cable was now up against one end of the metal beam. Very carefully, he pushed forward as the beam pivoted against the feeder cable. The fork bucked a little but eventually the magnetic attraction was defeated and the heavy girder fell to the ground harmlessly, although with a resounding clang that sounded like an echo under water. He backed up, lowered the fork to the ground, and gunned the machine forward. The forks slipped under the beam at the middle and he raised it up. He spun the wheel a few times as the forklift pivoted. Now the girder was poised to span the blades of the relay. Once it was in place, the electricity, which would have been stopped by the disconnection of the relay contacts, would have another way to complete the circuit through the massive steel beam. The shunt had been made. Now when the change in the line frequency triggered the master kill switch, the arms of the relay would drop away, but instead of the electric circuit being broken, the beam would effectively take over, offering a very stable path for the electricity to feed the city—very deadly, decreasing frequency electricity.

He jumped down from the large yellow Hyster forklift and ran, as best he could with a blistered butt, back to the main building.

.G.

RDF 1 and 3 were twenty seconds out. Two Black Hawk units would hover over the roof and ten operators would rappel down on ropes. The Cobra gunships would hover and take up defensive positions to cover the platoon of men who were landing in two Chinooks in the front equipment yard.

Bridge didn't like the tactical scenario. The fact that they had met no resistance yet meant one of two things: there was no resistance or, worse, they were dug in with fortified positions and holding their fire until his troops were in a crossfire kill zone.

A single Ranger scrambled to the abandoned Yeshiva school bus and tossed in a flash bang grenade. He then went in through the front door and scanned for any children or enemies. When he got to the back of the bus he opened the emergency door and yelled, "Clear!"

The first squad of troops off the Chinook advanced relay fashion around the bus. Then it exploded! Sharp shrapnel that was the body of the bus and shards of glass went in every direction. Seven soldiers died instantly, four were sliced up and seriously injured.

.G.

Dequa rejoined his engineer at the master control panel as his job of slowing the rotator was underway. He heard the explosion outside. "They've reached the bus. We only have a few minutes."

"When the speed dropped below fifty-eight cycles per second, the entire New York power zone was dropped from the northeast grid," the engineer said. He didn't have to add that this was automatic due to the national electric grid system's own protection mechanisms. Relays like the one Dequa shunted in the state's pathway to the national grid.

At that point there was no longer any interfering voltage to electromotively speed up the rotator, thus inadvertently turning the giant generator into a motor. A motor that would have been taking electricity from the national grid, rather than feeding it. Now free of the state and national grid's counter EMF, the approximate rate of slowing they could achieve meant the rotator would reach thirty cycles per second in four minutes. Prior to that, at fifty cycles per second, most coils would start overheating; at forty cycles per second, smaller devices would start melting; and at thirty cycles per second, also called thirty hertz, everything that had a coil, every transformer on every pole, or under every street, as well as every motor in every home, from air conditioners to refrigerators, would explode. With the two steel beams shorting out the master disconnect, there was no way to stop the reduction in frequency's devastating effects.

.G.

Brooke was in a helicopter that had landed atop the FBI building and scooted her off for the three-minute flight to the eastern shore of the East River. As they approached, she saw the gun battle and the burning bus in front of the building. She was listening to the Tac 1 channels and catching bits and pieces of the battle in one ear and a link to the conference room in the other. In the chopper, she slid on her Kevlar vest and put on a helmet. She strapped on the webbing that held twenty magazines for her MP5. She checked her sidearm and looked forward, waiting for the door to open as the FBI chopper slowed for a touchdown.

She hit the street out in front of the facility and took cover behind a car parked at the curb. She chanced a look above the fender and saw some troops engaged in firefights with unseen men in well-guarded positions in the various recesses and windows of the building. She raised her weapon and took aim at one window where every few seconds a figure would appear and let go a short burst then roll back behind the wall. She switched the selector switch on her automatic weapon to the three-burst position, and when he appeared again, she pulled the trigger three times with a slight sweeping motion. She thought she saw him go down. She watched with her sights trained on the window for at least ten seconds but he never showed again. She panned her gun looking for the next target when Bridge came up behind her.

"What the hell are you doing here? If you get clipped who's going to run this outfit?"

"George's got it. Besides . . ." She paused and pulled off another three-round burst, looked, but knew she'd missed her target. "He's due for a promotion. What's the situation here?"

"At least ten shooters well positioned and well armed with heavy squad weapons. We lost twelve or fourteen, I think. I'm still holding RDF 1 in case there's another prong attacking another power station. Do you have any idea what they're doing here?"

"They are trying to slow down the generator and start a million fires across the entire city."

"Later, you'll explain how that works, but for now, I am going to order in the Cobras and take that building down brick by brick."

"Approved. But have them hit the fuel tanks first. That will kill the generator. As I understand it, if it stops so does their plan."

Bridge gave orders to the gunships. In twenty seconds, ten rockets hit the front of the building in close, thunderous grouping. The façade started to crumble. When the smoke cleared, much of the opposing fire went silent. Bridge signaled for the second platoon to approach.

The second platoon got halfway to the building when the back doors of the red Con Ed truck swung open and a .50 caliber machine gun opened up on the unit. Two troopers went down immediately as the rest scrambled for cover.

"Cobras, red truck, hit it."

From two different directions, two missiles hit the truck at almost the same instant. The fireball emerged from the truck for a split second then the whole truck exploded.

"Medics!" Bridge yelled as he ran forward. He skidded to a stop when a grenade bounced off the concrete just past him. He dove down and hugged the ground. The blast went off and he felt the searing sting of fragments in his thigh and calf. He winced and looked at his leg. There was some blood, but the frags must have ricocheted off the ground first so they weren't deep. He heard a machine gun burst behind him and then someone landed next to him.

"You hit?" Brooke said.

"Not too bad. I'm good. What part of 'you shouldn't be here' isn't getting into your head?"

"Don't be a chauvinist, Bridge."

"That's not . . ." He was cut short by a line of bullets that crashed into the ground right before them.

"Son of a bitch," Brooke said as she pulled on her eyelid trying to loosen some concrete bits that had bounced up into her eye.

"How much time do we have?" Bridge spit out some gravel.

"My brain trust says they can do what they're here to do in five minutes or less."

"We got to move. We got to get in there and stop 'em."

There was a huge flash and then a large explosion rocked the ground; they both covered their heads. After a few seconds they looked up and saw the Cobras had hit the three fuel tanks outside the building as Bridge had ordered, in an attempt to cut off the fuel to the generator. The heat was intense and caused them to move. They ran to the front door and spread out to each side.

Bridge pulled a grenade from his webbing, pulled the pin, and rocked his arm back to toss it into the lobby. Suddenly, a man appeared in the doorway. He was unarmed. He was walking in shock. He had two bullet wounds, one in each of his shoulders.

Bridge quickly pitched the grenade over to the exploded Con Ed truck then pulled the man down and shielded him from the blast. Brooke took cover on the other side of the door.

.G.

"I've switched to the emergency fuel reserve. It's inside the building and should be good for twenty minutes. We are at fifty-six cycles. At this rate we will only need three more minutes," Dequa's engineer said.

The grenade that Bridge aborted blew up outside, causing Dequa to say, "The Americans are getting close."

.G.

In Sunnyside Queens, Martha Klein was walking her dog, Chili, who liked to christen the wooden pole that was there to hold up power lines, although most New Yorker's wrongly referred to it as a telephone pole. As Chili lifted his leg, Martha's attention was drawn to a buzzing sound coming from over her head. She looked up and saw nothing but the garbage-can-sized thing atop the pole. It was just like the ones on a few of the other poles on the block. The sound got louder, but still she saw nothing that could be buzzing that loudly.

.G.

In a gas station on Eleventh Avenue in Manhattan, owner Julio Ramirez was wondering if his tanks were low, because his pumps started slowing down the flow of gas. He also smelled something like fried grease pinching at his nostrils.

.G.

At an older Park Avenue skyscraper, all the elevators slowed down. The building superintendent tried to restart the system's motor-generator in the elevator room, but it started smoking.

.G.

Many TV and radio stations around the city, those with the older-style wall clocks, started running over the hourly network newscasts as they were telling the time to the split second from clocks that were running three seconds slower, for the first time ever.

.G.

Dequa looked at his watch. The synchronous meter on the control panel was now reading minus fifteen percent, or nine cycles less than the sixty-cycle norm. The process was slowing now because the generator was still attached to the city's local grid due to the shunt. As a result, the conflicting current it was receiving at sixty cycles from the local grid eroded the rate that the giant armature was slowing. For its part, the armature was having an identity crisis of sorts. It was starting to act like a motor being turned by electricity from outside—from the local grid—rather than acting like a device being turned to make electricity. His engineer was busily turning dials in an effort to overcome the electromotive effect.

Dequa was suddenly aware that the gunfire had lessened. He called over his radio. "Paul, Paul, what is the situation? Have they breached?"

"The first line has been broken. I can see the Americans have breached the main door. The secondary teams will be engaging."

.G.

Brooke spun around as she held the radio that she had taken off of one of the dead terrorists to her ear. "Paul!" she said out loud and immediately looked for an observer's position from where he would be directing the battle. Suddenly, the attack was secondary to her. Even amid the gunfire and carnage all around her and with the adrenaline coursing through her veins, her anger rose.

.G.

"Activate the ADS," Dequa said into the radio and grabbed his gun as he turned to the engineer. "I must go. Do not leave this panel, no matter what."

.G.

"Bridge," Brooke called out to him as he was taking cover twenty feet into the building ahead of her, "what is an ADS?"

Bridge was temporarily stumped and shrugged his shoulders.

"They are about to use something called an ADS. Be careful! I've got something to do." She scurried off in the direction of the street. There were fifty cop cars and more arriving every second, along with ambulances and fire trucks. The MPs were supposed to hold a perimeter, but something must have gotten fouled up. She found the Queens Borough Commander. She had not put her ID around her neck and had a bit of a time wrangling it out of her back pocket with the body armor and webbing she was wearing. "Commander, I'm the agent in charge. Damn, here it is." She held up her ID.

"I know you. You used to be FBI New York. I have ESU thirty seconds out."

"Good, we need the firepower. But right now, I need you to lock down every street, every building that has a direct line of sight to this plant. They've got an observer somewhere out here who is tipping them off to our every move. I also have reason to believe he is a mass murderer and extremely dangerous. Tell your men to approach with caution."

"With all this lead flying, I won't have to tell them to be cautious."

Brooke never heard what he said as she was off running towards the first place she would have picked to command the battle from.

.𝔊.

Bridge had twenty troopers in position in the main lobby of the giant facility. A Con Ed man arrived wearing borrowed body armor too big and bulky for his slight frame with a helmet that he kept having to balance on his head. He had the layout to the building. "There is a huge movable wall here for turbine replacements and the like but it is welded shut and only used for major repairs. The only way into the main control room from inside is through this corridor."

Bridge spoke to the men. "That's the way in. We go in pairs, cover to cover. You two, you've got our six. You and you, keep back and watch the upper floors." He waved his arm and the first pair advanced ten feet and took cover behind a guard's desk.

The advance went well and soon the doorway was clear. Fifteen troops hustled through when suddenly they all started screaming in agony. Bridge felt a sensation of heat and recoiled to the side. Most of the men scrambled sideways; two went down screaming. Bridge could see their faces were burnt and blistered. He screamed, "Microwaves! Everyone take cover." Then he ran outside the building.

Out in the equipment yard he found what he remembered seeing on the way in. He marshaled some ESU cops. " Guy's, each of you grab a sheet of this corrugated metal and follow me. Keep it in front of you, like a shield, at all times. We got an Active Denial System in there and it's stopping us."

"What's that?" a heavily geared-up cop asked.

"A microwave beam weapon that cooks you alive."

.𝔊.

Originally designed as a crowd control device, Dequa's engineering "students" had copied the American design but increased the frequency and power so instead of sending heat a fraction of an inch under the skin, which made any human flee the beam, the beam went right through as it would through roast beef in a microwave oven. Dequa was applying bursts to the device and the Americans were retreating. Because they knew the power in the building would also be affected by the frequency slowing, just like the rest of New York City, they ran the ADS off a portable generator; its exhaust was starting to make Dequa choke in the confined space at the end of the long hallway. He saw a soldier at the end appear and he hit the button. The man immediately recoiled and threw something in his hand. A few seconds later, the grenade went off with a concussive thud. Then two soldiers appeared simultaneously and tried again, tossing two more. The beam rendered them unable to get out of the way and Dequa could hear one scream as the grenades went off halfway between he and them.

The fluorescent lights at the facility flashed erratically, a sign that the power frequency had dropped below twenty percent. Soon fluorescent lights would have their ballasts, the coils that energized the gas in their tubes, ignite from the tremendously inefficient off-frequency power and every office building, factory, and neon sign on Broadway would burn. He was deciding on whether to just leave the ADS on and let it burn out in sixty to ninety seconds of continuous use while he'd try to escape, when something down the hall caught his eye. Five men were approaching, carrying sheets of corrugated metal. He hit the switch and immediately the sparks flew from the makeshift shields like aluminum foil in a microwave.

Bridge had the men tie rope around the shields so that they held them up from behind without exposing their fingers at the edges. Some of the shields were slipping as the metal bent and folded so they had to stop to keep re-hitching them, holding them tighter.

Dequa saw the men approaching and left the machine running and swung around his machine gun and opened fire. Bullets pinged off the metal. One soldier went down as a bullet hit the flat hollow between the waves of the shaped metal. He started burning and writhing on the floor. Another soldier got in front of him with his shield blocking the ray, but that was two men out of action. Bullets were bouncing off Bridge's metal, but it was working. They were approaching the satellite dish-looking element of the ADS. Because it was a wide beam, but still a beam, as he neared, Bridge veered right of the ray and the sparking stopped. He dropped his shield and fired. The man at the device got off a burst as he was hit. One bullet hit the wall right by Bridge's face and concrete chewed into his cheek. But the guy was down. Bridge then rocked a full magazine into the dish and guts of the machine and it went dead. He dabbed at his face with his glove as he neared the downed man and kicked away his weapon.

.𝔊.

Dequa looked up, the gaping wounds in his chest making a sucking sound as his lungs tried to capture air. The overhead lights blinked off; he looked up at Bridge and smiled at the sure sign that soon the lower power frequency would ignite the ballasts coils in every fluorescent light fixture in the city into an incendiary bomblet. Then he said something in Arabic as his life slipped away.

.𝔊.

Bridge ran into the main room. Bullets immediately crashed all around him. He took cover behind a desk. More soldiers were coming in. There were at least five men firing down on him and his men. At the far end of the large room, a man stood at a console. Two men at his side were firing back at the invaders.

The marines, SEALS, and other special ops guys who'd been thrown together on this impromptu mission went to work and did what they do best. In fifteen seconds, all the threats were neutralized. Bridge ran to the control panel. He pulled the body of the engineer, who'd been feverishly working the controls until a bullet entered his skull, off the large control panel. The dials and gauges were dancing and he didn't have a clue what was going on. "Kronos, Pete! I am here at the controls. What do I do?"

.𝕲.

"You're on. Don't fuck up!" Kronos said to the Con Ed chief engineer in the conference room.

"Look to your right as you stand at the console. On the flat panel just above the controls there is a clear plastic box . . ."

A claxon horn was heard over the speaker in the control room.

"Oh, you found it."

.𝕲.

Bridge pulled his hand away from the big red button that was marked EMERGENCY FUEL CUT OFF SWITCH. "Yeah. Anything else?"

.𝕲.

"No, that should do it." There was a collective cheer that went up in the conference room. Kronos slapped the chief engineer on the back. "Way to go, man!"

Over the cheers no one heard Bridge say, "Oh shit!" over the radio link.

.𝕲.

Bridge stood still as the room vibrated and the giant Allison-Chalmers generator picked up speed. "Hey, I thought I killed this thing. Come on, somebody, what's going on here? This thing isn't dead, yet." He turned and yelled, "Get me some explosives on the double!"

Kronos came over the radio. "Yo, hold your horses there, Bridge. Hey, hey, Con Ed guy, tell him what's going on."

The voice of the engineer came back on. "My friend, without its fuel supply turning the rotator, and since it's still hooked up to the smaller local New York City grid, which it was overpowering before you cut the fuel, the generator is reversing into a motor. It's actually speeding up back to its natural resonant frequency. There is no need for concern. It will happen till we break the shunt they put across the master disconnect relay."

For the first time today, Bridge let out a sigh, and dropped his shoulders. He hit his Tac radio mic. "Brooke, it's Bridge. It's over! Facility secure, threat neutralized." Then he turned to help the wounded.

.𝔊.

"Thank God, Bridge. Have George alert the president."

"Where are you?" Bridge asked.

"I'm after the son of a bitch who killed Nigel and half my team and nearly you and me."

"Good hunting. Say hello for me."

"Will do . . . Oh, by the way, well done, Bridge."

"It was a team effort—your team, Brooke."

"Duly noted." She clipped the mic back on her vest and turned the corner. There, in a Ford sedan, was a man using binoculars. There were two other men in the car with him. She quickly hid behind the edge of the building, but it was too late; they'd seen her. She heard the doors close and saw the car pull away. She darted back behind a parked car and hit her radio. "Bridge, get your choppers to follow a black Ford Taurus that's going south on Vernon Boulevard. Our guy's in it. Also send backup to the corner of Forty-First and Vernon." As she finished, the car she was behind shook as a fusillade of bullets slammed into the rear corner panel. Brooke squatted down and swept her MP5 under the car while holding the trigger, the tires exploded as the spray of bullets fanned out wide. They caught the two men attacking her in their lower legs and feet and they went down. She then rolled to the side of the car and scurried across the street, putting more distance between her and the men who, although down, could still shoot if they could control their pain. Shots rang out and she heard yelling; she looked over the edge of the Caddy she was using as cover and saw four Hercules Unit cops kicking away the guns from the two guys they'd made dead on the ground. Brooke got up and waved to one of them and ran off to get to a car. She found a detective's car running with its dash light going.

Two blocks away, she rolled up to the roadblocks she had ordered. She got out, flashing her ID. "Burrell. I am the agent in charge. Did a Ford Taurus come this way?"

"Someone started to come down this street but when they saw us they made a left. We called it in, but there's a lot of commotion right now . . ."

Brooke ran back to the detective's car she'd "borrowed" and jammed it into reverse and did a spinning U-turn, like in the movies.

"Shit, that girl can drive . . ." the roadblock cop said to his partner.

Chapter 46

Needle in the Haystack

Brooke drove the entire four square block area within the lock down zone. There were hundreds of police holding the perimeter. They had one order: no one gets in or out. With a cop every ten feet, Paul couldn't have slipped through the net. Her office was distributing the airport picture of Paul to every cop's PDA and cell phone.

She returned to the Ravenswood and saw Bridge helping with the litters and walking wounded. The scene was crawling with cops, FBI, Homeland Security, and soldiers. There were body parts and blood everywhere. She approached Bridge. "Anybody look at that face? Have you looked at your face?" she asked as she brushed away a small chunk of concrete that was embedded in his cheek.

"Haven't looked in a mirror all day. We lost a lot of good people today."

"But we didn't lose a city. Bridge, if these bastards had succeeded the death toll would have been in the millions. Every home, apartment, office, business, and utility pole would have been an incendiary bomb. And had they knocked out both water tunnels instead of one, there would have been twenty minutes worth of water to fight a million fires with, and that's only if all the fire houses didn't burn down before they got the rigs out."

"Was there any damage?"

"I'm hearing dribs and drabs but a few older buildings and the like did catch fire. There's no death toll yet. Something about a transformer on Thirty-Fourth Street, but no one's talking any big numbers so far."

"Did you get the scumbag?"

"No, he's in this lock-down zone somewhere. I got an APB out. I just know he's too smart to get caught; he's got to have a plan."

"Maybe he's in the pile of dead terrorists over there," Bridge said, hitching his thumb over his shoulder.

"No, I saw him pull away in the Ford I called in."

"Well, he can't be far."

Brooke was distracted.

Bridge looked over at what she was looking at. "What?"

"Hold on." She called Kronos. "Kronos, can you send me a surveillance camera feed that shows the Vernon Boulevard entrance to the plant right before the attack? Well, convert it then. I need to see it on my phone ASAP!"

A major walked up. "Director Burrell-Morton?"

"Yes, Major."

"Ma'am, I have orders to get you to Washington for a debriefing."

"Who cut those orders, Major?"

"Ma'am, this is a direct order from the commander in chief."

"I am too busy to leave."

"I am not supposed to take no for an answer."

Brooke let out an exasperated groan. "Can't you un-find me for a while?"

"'Scuse me?"

"Hold on." She redialed her cell phone. "Jim, Brooke. Look, I got a major here trying to take me to see you. I'm still really busy here. There's a giant loose end I need to tie up. I'm fine. We got a lot of dead people, but the city is safe . . . for today. Thanks for trusting us and giving us this day."

The major's eyes were wider than saucers as he looked at Bridge. "She called the pres—"

"They're having an affair," Bridge cut him off.

That earned Bridge a sharp elbow jab in the side from Brooke.

"Yes, a full report. I . . . yes, but . . . I had to be here. It's my job and my duty. Besides, I've never been so much the office type when this kind of action is going down, Jim, but thanks for your concern. Okay. Will do." She handed the phone to the major. "Here, he wants to speak to you."

The major froze. He gingerly grabbed the phone and hesitantly spoke into it. "Hel . . . Hello?"

Bridge was enjoying this.

"Sir, yes sir. Of course, sir. Not a problem. Yes, sir. I will. Goodbye Mr. President, sir."

"By the way, Bridge, the boss wanted me to tell you, 'Good work.'"

"That was the president!" the major said.

"Yeah, I know," Brooke said. She took back her phone as it beeped; Kronos's download was coming in as an attachment to email.

"Major, since you're here for a while, can you help me with my after-action inspection?" Bridge asked.

The major followed Bridge into the facility.

Brooke watched the short video clip on her phone of the moments before the assault began. It showed the street right outside the plant. She looked at the screen, then the street. As she was flying in to the fight by chopper, she'd noticed an ambulance right outside and to the left of the gate. She hadn't thought about it until she saw it a few minutes ago and it was still there. Yet, it had been there well before any municipal units could've responded or arrived.

Brooke heard the report on the radio that the Taurus had been found a block away from where she was standing. No sign of the driver. She checked her sidearm and walked towards the blue-and-white Hatzolah ambulance. There was one EMT tending to a wounded Con Ed employee on a gurney inside.

Brooke stood at the open back doors. "How you doing?"

"My leg, it is killing me," the man said with a groan.

"I need to ask you a few questions. Are you up for it?"

"I need to move him to the ER," the med-tech said.

"You working alone?"

"My partner helped get two others out and jumped in the other company ambulance. He'll be at the ER."

Brooke turned her attention back to the man on the stretcher. "Where were you when all this started?"

"I was in the pump room, just coming out for some coffee, when all the shooting started. I didn't get two feet and I was on the ground. I didn't know I was hit. It hurts like a bitch."

"I know, been there myself." Brooke turned to the EMT. "Can't you give him something?"

"Better to do that at the ER. We really have to go."

"You always wear a mask?" Brooke asked.

"Nowadays, you can catch anything from blood, sweat, or other bodily fluids," the EMT said as he threw a sheet over the man to keep him warm.

"Why haven't you elevated the leg?"

"I was going to do that . . ."

"But you were leaving."

"Look, lady, it's been a tough day. Don't come over here and tell me how to do my job."

"Okay . . . sorry, Paul."

The EMT was startled. He grabbed for a pair of scissors and lunged out the back of the ambulance at Brooke. She turned into him and caught his arm as he went to plunge the scissor into her chest. She threw him over her hip and onto the ground with a Judo throw. She had her gun out in a flash. "Freeze!"

Paul looked up at her, then right and left. With all the commotion, everyone was looking at the still-smoldering façade of the building and all the activity with the wounded. Paul put his right hand up in front of him as he turned his head away. "Look, I got ten million coming to me. We can split it. You let me go and five million is yours."

"Where you getting this money from, Paul?"

"It's my fee for helping them."

"Helping them?"

"Yeah, the money is already in my account."

"Okay, stand up."

Paul stood up.

"Turn around."

"What?"

"Turn around and put your hands behind your back."

"But we had a deal."

"No, you just told me what I needed to know, that's all. Now we have a professional relationship. I'm a cop and you are a murderer. And you are going to burn for Nigel, the nineteen people on my staff, Cynthia, and however many more you killed just to help these guys."

Brooke reached around back for one of the zip tie hand restraints coiled off the back of her vest when suddenly she was knocked to the ground. The man on the gurney fired his gun right through the sheet, hitting her center mass.

Paul sprang up and slammed the backdoors closed then jumped in the driver's side. He hit the lights and siren and pulled away.

Brooke couldn't catch her breath for a few seconds. By the time she was able to breathe someone noticed her on the ground.

"Lady, you okay?"

"I'm okay." She touched the middle of her bulletproof vest, where the slug had embedded in the Kevlar webbing. "Maybe a busted rib . . ." she said exhaling from the sharp pain when she probed the area. Get me my radio over there." She pointed to the radio that had flown off her vest as she'd spun down to the ground.

"This is Stiletto. All units, stop and detain a blue-and-white Hatzolah ambulance. Driver and patient armed and extremely dangerous. Repeat, approach with caution . . . Stiletto . . . over and out."

She put her head back down as EMTs rushed over. She took a deep breath and began to sit up, but she got a radiating pain from her rib cage. She rolled on to her side and picked herself up with somewhat less discomfort.

"Whoa, not so fast lady," the arriving medic said.

"I'm okay, just a little bruised . . . I think."

"Let me be the judge of that."

"Sorry, no time. Gotta go."

"Lady . . ."

Brooke was back in the detective's car and speeding off. She blew through the roadblock as the cops just managed to get the two police cars out of her way. She grabbed the radio mic. Stiletto to central, K."

"What's Stiletto . . . identify yourself, K."

"Director in charge of all RDFs today, Burrell-Morton. Get me a patch to commander RDF forces, code sign Bird Dog, and also patch me into aviation, on the double. K."

"Central to Stiletto, hold for liaison officer. K."

Brooke drove south towards the Midtown tunnel. She was blowing through lights as the siren and dash light helped clear the way.

The radio finally came back on with a different voice. "Central to Stiletto, Gladiator."

Brooke hesitated. If she broadcasted the answer to her challenge code, it would be public. "Stiletto to Central, this is the last authorized use of this challenge code, Transistor. K."

"Roger that. What else do you need, Director Burrell?"

"I am in pursuit of a blue-and-white Hatzolah ambulance last seen heading south on Vernon Blvd. Occupants armed and extremely dangerous . . ."

Brooke had to swerve away from a garbage truck that entered the intersection ahead of her. She noticed the driver had earphones on and was jerking his head up and down to music. He slammed on the brakes when he saw her dash light in the corner of his eye. "Asshole . . ." she yelled as she passed.

"Repeat that?"

"No, not you. Report location of ambulance immediately. Set up rendezvous with my FBI chopper somewhere along the route."

Brooke put down the mic then remembered. She picked it up again. "K." The car hit a bump and she caught her breath as she felt a sting on her right side.

.𝔊.

Practically every first responder in the five boroughs was either at the Ravenswood generating station or at the various fires that had started around the city. One of the worst was a transformer in an under the street vault right outside Macy's, which went up in flames that reached through the metal grating on the sidewalk and immolated three Thirty-Fourth Street shoppers alive. There weren't too many assets available to help Brooke interdict Paul, if he hadn't ditched the ambulance by now.

.𝔊.

NewsChopper 880 had just gotten clearance to fly again from New York Air Traffic Control after they had ordered a ground stop during the operation. Tom took off from the Wall Street helipad where he had put down when the order from ATC came through. On the ground, he had been listening to the police scanners, which normally advised him of traffic accidents, and heard the all-points bulletin on the Hatzolah ambulance. *They're using a Jewish ambulance?* He thought as the irony struck him.

He swung his bird north and over the BQE. Just above Humboldt Street he saw the blue-and-white box shape with all lights going, as traffic moved out of the way. Tom's immediate thought was that there had to be at least twenty of these rigs working out of their Brooklyn base. Still, he called it in on his NYPD emergency frequency. "This is N880 to Central, K."

"Central to N880, comeback, K."

"Possible suspect ambulance heading south BQE just above Cadman Plaza."

.𝕲.

"Central to Stiletto, be advised ambulance matching description seen on BQE, Cadman Plaza. K."

"Patch me through to whoever has eyes on it. K."

"Ten-four. K."

Brooke was ripping down Flushing Avenue a half-mile above the Plaza when Tom came over the radio. "This is N880 to Stiletto? K."

"Tell me you've got eyes on the ambulance? . . . K"

"Yes. He's turning off the BQE. Looks like he's headed for the Manhattan Bridge. K."

"Stay on him. Heading there now. K."

Brooke hung a hard, fishtailing right off of Nassau Street onto the Flatbush Avenue approach of the Manhattan Bridge.

The ambulance had come down the ramp off the Brooklyn-Queens Expressway only thirty seconds before. Due to the traffic volume it had had to wade through, it was only one hundred yards ahead of her.

Up ahead, mid-span of the bridge, Brooke saw the lights of the ambulance as it was trying to nudge through traffic. She was stuck in the same slowly moving bridge traffic as well. Then she had an idea. "Stiletto to N880, K."

Chapter 47

Catching a Train

The fact that most traffic copter pilots, in fact most chopper pilots period, were hotdogs was in little dispute. The boredom of sitting high up in their perches every day, reporting the same traffic snarls and routine fender-benders eventually got to these guys, most of whom had seen action in the military. So Tom eagerly took the challenge from whoever this woman was on the radio that seemed to be in charge. He knew the company would probably fire him, and the FAA might revoke his license, but the whole city was in a panic and under attack so he figured it was a good reason to get written up.

.G.

Drivers on the Manhattan side of the bridge watched in amazement as the news helicopter hovered right above the traffic at the Manhattan end of the bridge at Canal Street. Slowly, as the chopper descended, the traffic came to a halt. Traffic cops on Canal Street ran towards the odd spectacle. Tom got out and was trying to stop some of the intrepid New York drivers who were actually trying to get around his machine. "Whoa, hold it, buddy. Where do you think you're going?"

The cops arrived. "What the hell is this?"

"I got orders from the feds to block this bridge. Help me. They got some ambulance stuck up there and they don't want it to move."

"Hold, wait, they are trying to stop an ambulance from getting to the hospital?"

"I think it's stolen; got some really bad honchos in it . . ." He was distracted from the cops. "Hey, cowboy, where you going . . . ?" Tom yelled to a guy in a van that almost took out his tail rotor.

"We'll take it from here," the cop said as his partner got the confirmation of Tom's story over the radio and nodded.

"Great. Hey, do me a favor, get everybody away from my aircraft. I'm going back up.

.G.

Brooke was out of the car and running through the now-stuck vehicles, although very painfully as her bruised ribs complained with almost every foot fall. She saw the ambulance about two hundred feet ahead in the left lane. She crouched low and approached from the rightmost lane.

.G.

Paul was frustrated with the traffic. But then he heard something that made him rethink his plan to get to his second exit point, the Wall Street heliport. There, he had a helicopter waiting to take him to Teterboro and his chartered jet to Turks and Cacaos. From that "not too finicky about passports and papers" island nation, he would go on to the South Seas and the ten million. But what he heard on the ambulance's police scanner froze him.

"All units, the federal authorities have closed the Manhattan Bridge in pursuit of an ambulance believed to have suspects fleeing the attack on Big Allis. All non-assigned units converge on the bridge."

Paul looked around. So far no cops were charging the ambulance but he knew that wouldn't last long. He looked in the back at Girbram, a member of his cell that had also gotten a job at Ravenswood with Yusuf. He had taken a slug in the leg. He would only slow Paul down.

"What are we going to do?" Girbram asked.

"We?" Paul said as he put the barrel of his gun on the sheet over Girbram's heart and fired.

Paul went out the driver's side of the rig and looked for a way off the bridge.

.𝔊.

Brooke saw him get out. She was hidden from his view by the back of the ambulance. She stepped lightly with her gun pointed straight up. People in the cars around her ducked and some were mesmerized. Some idiot beeped his horn.

.𝔊.

Paul instinctively turned in the direction of the beep and caught a glimpse of someone moving between the cars to his rear. He ran towards the middle of the span.

.𝔊.

Brooke followed from the far side of the cars. Then Paul disappeared. Brooke lost him the next time she popped up between the cars. She stood and scanned the area but saw no sign of him among the people who got out of their cars to see why the traffic was at a standstill. She ran over the edge of the roadway and up ahead saw Paul climbing down the slanted girders of the bridge. Smaller lattice-like straps of steel across the girders made for a simple ladder of sorts.

Brooke closed her eyes. She considered just calling it in and letting the cops handle this, but she knew Paul would not give up, and he'd use the people in the cars as hostages at some point, and maybe get away. Then she remembered all the death and pain this son of a bitch had caused and before she had a chance to stop herself, she holstered her gun and was over the side fitting her foot into the lattice work while holding onto the grimy girders.

.𝔊.

Paul jumped the last few feet from the girder down onto the pedestrian walkway. The M train rumbled right down the middle of the bridge that carried cars and subway traffic between Brooklyn and Manhattan.

Paul looked back and, seeing the woman's arms and hands holding onto the steel cross-girders as she descended, took a shot at her.

.𝔊.

The bullet hit the beam and shattered in front of Brooke. It caused her to slip and fall the last five feet to the ground. Her vest took the brunt of it but a fragment pierced the fleshy part of her left arm. Her sleeve became wet with blood but it wasn't too deep.

She groaned as she shook away the pain and unsteadily got herself up. A runner who was jogging by stopped to help her.

"Thank you. But take cover. Get everybody down. I'm a cop and there's a guy with a gun up ahead. Get everyone down."

Another shot rang out and skidded across the concrete of the walkway. There were only a few pedestrians on the walkway. And the jogger crouched low and yelled at those who were walking.

The walkway provided no cover for her. The cyclone fence that separated the walkway from the train tracks had a service gate a few feet from her. She took out her gun and fired three times at the lock. She swung the gate opened and got out of the line of fire as a bullet whipped by where she had been standing a split second before. The long fence between her and Paul offered a small amount of cover, in that he couldn't get off a clean shot through the chain link from an angle.

.𝔊.

From his cockpit, Tom called out over the NYPD radio frequency. "The woman, Stiletto, is pinned down in a gun fight in the middle of the Manhattan Bridge. She needs help." He didn't notice the red indicator light flashing above the "recording" button of the copter's high-resolution camera.

.𝔊.

Paul aimed but couldn't get a clear shot through the wire of the fencing, so he found the next gate and also shot the lock off. Once inside the subway's right-of-way he advanced along the tracks towards Brooke's position.

Brooke was taking cover behind a tool shed on the trackside of the bridge. As she peeked around the corner, a shot ricocheted off the edge of the structure. Instinctively, she let out a groan and flailed her body against the shed as if she were hit.

.𝕲.

Paul saw her get hit and he stepped up his pace. With his gun stretched out in both of his hands, he carefully approached the shed that Brooke had used for cover. He was four feet from the side of it when she suddenly rolled out on the floor and fired as soon as she cleared the shed. Paul couldn't drop his weapon fast enough and his bullet angled over Brooke's head. But Brooke's shot was also a little off the mark. Instead of being dead with a solid hit center mass, Paul grabbed his side.

"Drop the gun!" Brooke commanded. "Drop the gun or I will drop you where you stand," she said, getting to her feet in three separate painful moves, while keeping the gun trained on his heart.

"Okay . . . Okay." He dropped the gun. "You know we can still make a deal."

Brooke's blood began to boil. "How much? A million?" She fired into his leg and he fell back onto the tracks. "A million for Nigel? Or two million for Charlene Logan?" She fired into his other leg. "Make it three million for Cynthia." She fired again in his thigh. "Or make it five"—she fired again into his other thigh—"for my staff—nineteen people that will never go home again."

Paul was in agony. But he managed to pull a small .32 caliber pistol from his waist. He cocked it and aimed it at Brooke.

Neither heard it, but she saw it out of the corner of her eye. It was a blur for a split second, then the speeding front of the M train slammed into Paul just as he got a shot off. Brooke averted her eyes to the moment of impact. When she opened them a second later she said, ". . . and that was for Joe Garrison."

Then, as though she had just seen something she couldn't make out, she tilted her head sideways. The look on her face was one of someone trying to remember what she had just been thinking. Then she coughed. Blood trickled down from her lips and she collapsed.

Chapter 48

The Departed Shall Return

ATTACK PLUS 3 DAYS

The steps of City Hall were outlined in black bunting as tribute to the ten citizens who'd perished and the many other deaths suffered by those thwarting the attack. That number of citizens, although too high even at ten, was far less, by a factor of a million, than if the evil scheme had succeeded. A somber mayor sat next to the President of the United States while the Cardinal of New York delivered the invocation from the podium. The families of the fallen wept as they sat in chairs lined up at the foot of the steps.

Although officially a day of national mourning, it was also a day of recognition. The opportunity, as the mayor put it, "to hail the bravery of a few, who gave so much, to protect so many."

Also on the steps that clear blue morning, consoling each other, were the survivors of Brooke's decimated team. Peter Remo and, Vincent "Kronos" DeMayo (as the president would call his name), stood with Detective Rolland Harris. NYPD Police Officer Kylee Boyce, who'd stopped the Fifth Avenue truck bomb, stood at attention. Next to her was James Aponte, and a few other folks who'd helped authorities uncover the various threats. The directorate of MI6 was in from London to honor the memory of Nigel Otterson. Tom Colletti, the news chopper pilot, was also on the steps while in the gallery below, the wife and kids of the Moonachie Township police officer he'd saved smiled at him in deep appreciation.

There were easels spaced between American flags on poles with the pictures of the forty-two who died defending the city. They were the faces of the federal agents from Brooke's unit that had died in the line of duty in the rocket attack. As well as the soldiers and police officers, including eight from New Jersey and one from the Yonkers PD. On the other side of the steps, the seventeen Con Ed workers who'd died in the assault on Big Allis were also honored in black-draped, framed photos.

Considering it his solemn duty, Sergeant Major Richard Bridgestone, who normally would not expose himself at such a public gathering, compromised his operational security and attended the ceremony, standing in the place where Brooke would have stood.

The mayor finished his remarks. The wailing of bagpipes started up as the NYPD Emerald Society paid its tribute.

The president looked down at the box of medals for posthumous bravery he held in his lap. *Too many*, he thought. Then he thought of Brooke.

The television networks had made the decision to carry this somber event without comment. Just letting the ceremony unfold before the cameras. The bagpipes' eerily mournful tones dissolved into revered silence. The only sounds being heard were wafting in on the morning breeze; the far-off beat of security helicopters standing guard at high altitude and the light murmur of traffic off in the distance.

In this silent moment, the church bells of New York City pealed as a coordinated farewell to her dead.

As the sound of the last bell rang out and then faded back into the ambient rumble of lower Manhattan, the president got up and walked to the microphones. He bowed his head for a second. His emotions evident as he took a deep breath before unfolding from his suit pocket his prepared remarks. "Our freedoms and our liberty are the most precious of American ideals. They endure today because of the price the good men and women, who we gather here to commemorate this day, have paid. This city, this nation, has suffered a blow, but not a knockout. Our way of life will never be extinguished, never be abridged and never be placed asunder, not as long as heroes like the ones we honor today live among us . . ."

.G.

Nurse Phyllis Pasquarella was holding up her iPhone and showing her day-shift replacement the most impressive selfie she'd ever taken.

It was of her and the President of the United States! Standing right next to her at her station on the fifteenth floor. Both women's eyes were wide in excitement as the very man she had stood next to in the picture, was now on the TV addressing the nation.

The tall navy officer interrupted, "Excuse me . . ."

One look and Phyllis said, "Room 1501, first room on your right."

.G.

She was sleeping. There were IVs in her arm and a soft plastic oxygen cannula under her nose. The navy man looked down to see the Medal of Freedom pinned to her blanket. It had been awarded to her personally by his and her "boss," who'd been there an hour earlier. He was sorry he'd missed the moment but his thirteen-hour flight from Diego Garcia had fought head winds over the Pacific. He had heard how the president insisted that the hospital be his unannounced first stop. The rerouting of the motorcade for the impromptu visit and little ceremony had driven his secret service detail crazy.

Now with just the two of them in the room, he approached her and kissed her forehead, smoothing back her hair gently with the trembling tips of his fingers, trying not to disturb her. He didn't expect his reaction to be the one of trepidation and fear that hit him the moment he saw her, in this room, in the bed, hooked up to all manner of machines.

The doctors had told him over the phone that she wasn't even aware of the bullet that severed her femoral artery in the gunfight on the bridge. *Adrenaline*, he thought.

The beeping of the respiratory monitors punctuated the low sound of the TV as the president continued to speak about courage . . . about her.

He put his hand on hers. He felt the surgical tape on the IV needle in her arm under his fingers. The president finished his remarks and a lone bugle played "Taps." Even on the TV behind him you could hear it echoing off the buildings across the way from City Hall.

Her lips were dry and parched. He poured some water into a cup and, with his finger, lightly moistened her lips. She stirred. Her eyebrows raised then her eyes half opened.

He smiled and said softly, "Hi, babe. You had us all worried here."

It took a second for her eyes to focus but then she closed them again as a broad grin escaped from her sleepy face. "Mush, you're home!"

"For good. I am going to take care of you. Be there for you. Be there for our family."

She nodded her head in a gesture for him to come closer.

He leaned in, kissing her on her cheek as he did.

She swallowed a dry swallow then said, "We'll have . . . have to work on that . . ."

.Give Us This Day.

A Letter from the Author

So you can sleep tonight...

Thank you reading *Give Us This Day*. Rest assured, not one thing in this book will lend a credible idea to any persons wishing to do harm to America or any country. In every case where technology is defeated to create calamity within this book, I have exaggerated the effect, impact, and ease of manipulation. No scenario in this book is possible, due to safeguards and redundancy throughout our infrastructure. If I write that a shift in frequency raises the temperature of a transformer core, it does, but only by mere degrees, well within design specs. I simply, for dramatic purposes, grossly exaggerate the heat produced and consequences thereof. In fact, anyone trying to replicate any of the scenarios in the book, would immediately be frustrated, identified, and stopped. Hey, maybe that would be a good thing? Okay, any knuckleheads reading this: try it!

Acknowledgments

Writing is a very solitary experience. Yet, luckily for me, it has also been a very collaborative medium. I am blessed to have some incredible people who lend their expertise, experiences, knowledge, and smarts to my writing, thus helping me write about lives I have never lived. In no particular order they are:

Col. Mike Miklos, US Army Ret.—for the warrior code, spirit, and details that guide my depicting of all things military and homeland- defense-centric.

Len Watson—A polymath whose grasp of applied technology along with his own authoring chops greatly enhance my journey through the technosphere.

Anthony Lombardo, Retired First Grade Detective NYPD—An amazing weapons, police procedure, and law enforcement culture human database with a great smile and warm and friendly way about him that makes some of the more gory things in life more accessible.

Marie McGovern—A genius who can spot a dissonant note in 130,000 words with laser-like accuracy and mete out a hammer-like critique that helps me bang out all the dents and rough spots in the forming story.

George Cannistraro—A brilliant author in his own right, his sense of story dynamics informs every plot point and pivot I write. He has a very acute sense of balance between plot and character.

Gary Stanco—The financial wiz who turned my meatball knowledge of financial markets into a palatable offering of fine prime rib. Any "financial irregularities" you may have encountered are purely the results of my ignoring his excellent advice for the sake of the story.

Grant Blackwood—The author who is entrusted with carrying on the spirit and the letter of one of my literary heroes, Tom Clancy. Grant was there at the beginning of this novel, and his message of "irrational optimism" has guided not only this book but many other parts of my life as well.

Kurt Skonberg—A partner in a leading New York law firm who guided me through the fun, exciting, and breathless world of securities collateralization (or is it collateral securitization?) and still manages to be one of the funniest and coolest guys I know.

David Ivester—An acquaintance who became a fan, a fan that became a beta reader, a beta reader that became an editor, and they all, I'm delighted to say, became my friend.

Chris Zizzo—An analytical engine disguised as a really great guy. His objective, no-holds-barred review of my work deftly challenges me to be better in my construct, logic, and application of technology.

Lou Aronica—My publisher and muse. He never tells me what to write but rather compels me to write better. Also, I am deeply grateful to Lou for slotting this book in for production, sight unseen and manuscript unwritten. That kind of faith in my work is as good as it gets.

Ellen Russell – Who kept me on the politically correct straight-and-narrow with amazing insights into women-in-the-workplace etiquette. No sooner had she pointed out a faux pas in my dialog than no less than the President of the United States fell prey to the same oversight and was publically excoriated by feminist groups for it. If only he had Ellen Russell to advise him as well.

Nora Tamada—A new member of the team who took a decent manuscript and shaped it into a readable book. Her exemplary work is everywhere your eyes fell as you read this novel.

And Monta who sets the tone for my desire to write a female character that approaches her level of beauty, kindness, and intelligence.

Lastly, as I am always aware, I thank you, the reader, for without you I am writing to myself. Thank you for coming along on this trip. I hope you had a good read. Let me know about it: Tom@TomAvitabile.com.